TIMBER BEASTS

TIMBER BEASTS

A Sage Adair Historical Mystery
of the Pacific Northwest

S. L. Stoner

Yamhill Press
P.O. Box 42348
Portland, OR 97242

Timber Beasts

A Yamhill Press Book

Copyright © 2010 by S. L. Stoner

Cover Design by Alec Icky Dunn/Blackoutprint.com
Interior Design by Josh MacPhee/Justseeds.org

Printed in the United States. This book may not be reproduced in whole or in part, by any means, without permission. For information: Yamhill Press at yamhillpress@gmail.com

Edition ISBNs
Softcover   978-0-9823184-0-9
E-book   978-0-9823184-1-6
Audio Book   978-0-9823184-2-3
Large Book   978-0-9823184-3-0

Publisher's Cataloging in Publication

Stoner, S.L., 1949 –

Timber Beasts: A Sage Adair Historical Mystery of the Pacific NW/S.L. Stoner.
p.cm. – (A Sage Adair historical mystery)

1. Northwest, Pacific–History–20th century–Fiction. 2. Labor unions–Fiction. 3. Logging–Fiction. 4. Martial arts–Fiction. 5. Forest reserves–Law and legislation–Fiction. 6. Detective and mystery stories. 7. Historical fiction. 8. Adventure stories. I. Title. II. Series: Sage Adair historical mystery.

PS3619.T6857T56 2010   813'.6   QBI09-700003

For George R. Slanina, Jr.
who never gives up on the struggle

ONE

June 1902, Roseburg, Oregon

THE BURLY MAN lurched out of billowing steam and smoke to grab at the ladder that was bolted to the locomotive's side.

"Howdy, Clancy," the locomotive fireman above him called without pausing in his swivel between wood pile and fire box. "Thought we'd have to pull out without you!"

"Nah, no way I'd miss this trip," the railroad security bull called back, each word spoken with the careful annunciation of an experienced imbiber. He started pulling himself aboard, his heavy boots with their loosely tied red and black leather laces, clanging as he stumbled up the worn steel rungs of the narrow ladder. Once aboard, Clancy busied himself retrieving a steel coupler pin from a storage compartment. With a grunt he stood erect, bracing himself on widespread legs, his big hands caressing the fourteen-inch-long metal bolt which was tied to a coiled hemp rope. Lifting the rope closer to his squinting eyes, he used a dirty fingernail to scrape at brown bits flecking the hemp strands before giving it a yank to make sure it was securely tied through the bolt's eye. Satisfied, he stepped to the locomotive's window and hawked phlegm into the sunlight before leaning back against the cab's vibrating wall and closing his eyes. Next to his boot, the coupler pin jittered atop the steel plate like a young retriever on a tight leash.

The fireman paused, his eyes on the ten-pound hunk of metal. His shoulders twitched and he looked toward the locomotive engineer who sent him a cautionary head shake. The fireman shrugged and returned to stoking the fire box. "She's at full burn," he shouted seconds later. "Let 'er rip." As the locomotive began rolling forward, the fireman slammed the iron door shut and rested his rump on the sand box. Lips compressed into a thin line, he turned his face away from Clancy and the railroad bull's leashed companion.

Eighty miles to the north, the iron wheels of another train clickety-clacked into the distance. Two brothers remained behind, hunkered down in long summer grass south of a wooden water tower.

The dark-haired younger boy threw a handful of torn stems toward the metal tracks. "Darn! That was the third train we couldn't ride 'cause there weren't no open doors. Matthew, I'm so hungry every time I swallow, my stomach says, 'Thanks.'"

Red-haired Matthew made no answer. His clear blue eyes were surveying the jumble of a nearby collapsed shack. Getting up, he pulled two eight-foot planks loose and swept off the pill bugs clinging to the damp undersides. Planks in hand, Matthew waded back though the tall grass to where the dark-haired boy now lay motionless on his back, his eyes watching the maple's leafy hands flutter against the intense blue sky.

As Matthew dropped the planks, Billy stirred and raised up on one elbow. Matthew gestured toward the boards, saying, "I have us a back-up plan. I talked to some of the hobos back home and these here planks are just the trick. You still got that rope stuffed inside your bindle?"

Billy sat up, a dubious scowl lowering his eyebrows. "What you got swimming about in your head now, Matthew? What can we do with them planks?"

Matthew tugged two lengths of twisted hemp loose from inside a rolled-up blanket. "A rope is a mighty fine tool. In fact, this here rope is going to solve our problem. When the next train stops to pick up water, if there's no open boxcar, we'll crawl underneath and tie the planks to the cross pieces that run between the side rods. Then we'll lay down and ride our planks all the way to Portland.

Billy's eyes widened. "Underneath the train! You're crazy. I'm not riding underneath any train." Alarm cracked his fourteen-year-old voice.

Matthew tossed the rope onto the planks. "All right, Billy, we won't ride underneath the train, but there won't be any open boxcars. The railroad bulls in Eugene lock 'em before they ever reach us. You ain't gonna try the planks, okay. Then, I guess we'll be staying here in this grass until it grows right over us." He dropped down beside his brother.

Billy rolled onto his hip. "Well, how about we walk to Portland?"

Matthew sat up. "Just how can we walk almost a hundred miles on empty stomachs and no money? The way I see it, we either ride the rods or turn around and try to catch a train back to Marshfield and the cannery."

"The cannery? We can't go back there. Folks'd laugh at us after all our talk. Besides, if I see one more dead fish, I'll puke."

Matthew nodded vigorously and said, "That's right, we can't go back. Besides, you don't belong in the cannery. You belong in a good school. The teacher says you got a 'fine mathematical mind.' When we get to Portland, I'm getting me a job so you can go to school."

"Aw Matthew, I'm not sure I want more schooling. I'm thinking it might be fun to be a printer's devil. Help make books and magazines. Besides, you like schooling and reading lots more than I do."

"Don't you try to back out now, Billy. You agreed that you'd be the one to go to school. You go back on that promise and I'm heading back to Marshfield."

Billy flopped down onto his back. "Well," he began with a sigh, "I guess I don't mind going back to school." He voice took on an edge of excitement, "It's going to be fun living in a big city. Aunt Ida living right downtown – can you imagine everything new we're gonna see?"

The two boys lay in silent contemplation until a whistle wailed from the south. It was the train coming up from Roseburg. Billy jumped up to scan the tracks. "Should be here in about five minutes," he said.

Matthew scrambled to his feet. "So what's it to be, Billy? The rods or back home?"

Billy sighed. "I guess the rods. Are you real sure it's safe?"

Matthew gathered up their bindles and the ropes. "Sure enough. The hobo said folks ride the rods all the time. After we wedge the planks atop the cross pieces, we tie the rope around to make sure the planks don't move sideways. Then we lay down and hold on tight. In no time at all we'll be at Aunt Ida's kitchen door."

The train chugged around the far curve, white smoke streaming down its back. The boys crouched behind the maple as the engine rolled past in its long screeching stop. There were no open doors in the line of boxcars.

Matthew dashed toward a wooden-sided boxcar that rode higher above the rail bed than the other cars in the line. Matthew shouted over the screech of the braking train. "Hurry! The train'll be pulling out in five minutes. We'll tie your's first."

They worked quickly, tying Billy's plank forward on the rods, about four feet ahead of his older brother's because Matthew wanted to keep an eye on him. When the locomotive jerked forward, its thirst slaked, their stomachs were pressed into the planks, bindles tied so that the blanket rolls lay snug against their backs. Each brother held tight to the rod at the head of his plank. As the train picked up speed, fright closed their eyes and white-knuckled their fingers.

Within a mile, terror gave way to the realization the planks were secure, swaying rhythmically as the train rolled along the rail bed. They grinned at each other across the four-foot space. Once the flash of railroad ties turned commonplace, the boys looked toward the summer fields rolling past, framed by wooden boxcar, flashing metal wheels and glinting steel track.

Two hours later, the train began jerking to a halt. Green pastures stretched out on either side of the track. Likely another water stop at one of the big wooden water tanks the railroad planted at intervals alongside the track. They stayed put. No sense running the risk of being spotted by a railroad bull.

Above the tick of cooling steel, they heard the crunch of approaching footsteps on the gravel roadbed. The footsteps stopped and started, moving ever closer as a railroad bull rattled boxcar doors, checking for hobos.

When the footsteps stopped at their car, Matthew twisted to look past his own feet at a pair of black boots standing on the roadbed gravel. Red and black braided laces crosshatched their way up the boot tongues. The bull grunted as he tugged at the locked door. Yet the boots didn't step off toward the rear of the train. Matthew's heartbeat began thudding in his ears. He stared at the boots, waiting for a sneering ugly face to appear beneath the car. As his terror intensified, Matthew closed his eyes and pressed his nose into the plank. He willed the boots to crunch away. A few seconds later, they did.

Matthew opened his eyes and he exchanged a relieved look with Billy as the boots moved toward the locomotive. They paused for a few seconds near the front coupling of their boxcar. At the train whistle's toot, the boots hurried away. Seconds later the steel wheels began turning and Matthew whooped with relief.

They'd made it! He'd missed them. The train wouldn't be stopping before it reached the Portland railyard. Soon they'd be surprising Aunt Ida on her doorstep. Matthew could almost taste her cherry pie.

The train jerked forward. As it picked up speed, a shriek rose above the rail clack. Matthew looked toward Billy and saw a heavy metal bolt bounce up from the roadbed and slam into Billy's back. The boy was writhing on his plank but couldn't escape the reach of the bouncing hunk of metal. How come it didn't drop away? Then Matthew saw. The bolt was tied to the end of a rope stretching from the front of the boxcar. That's what that son-of-a-bitch bull had been doing up there at the coupling.

Something wet hit Matthew's face. He loosened his hand to feel the wet, crying out as he recognized bright red blood. "Billy . . . Billy!" Matthew shouted louder than the rattling train and the rushing wind. "Billy, get your knife. Cut it loose! Billy, Billy!"

His brother twisted his head toward Matthew, his mouth open, his eyes wide and rolling, frantically searching for escape, terror deafening his ears. As Matthew screamed instructions at his brother, he saw the demon bolt leap up from behind to slam into Billy's head. Billy's eyes closed. His fingers released their grip on the rod.

"Noooo . . . ," Matthew screamed, panic sending his hands scrabbling along the rod toward his brother's plank until his body stretched across the open space between them. One hand clutching the rod, his other hand grabbed at his unconscious brother. The train banked into a curve. He snatched his hand back, nearly falling as the plank under his knees tilted. Billy's body slid down the plank until his feet hit the rod and he rolled off.

Matthew screamed again. "Billy . . . noooo . . . Billy!" For an instant, Billy's body lay across the track. The boxcar bumped. Rushing air shoved streamers of bright red across the underside of the car. Matthew hung transfixed, stretched across the open space between the planks. Then his arm muscles quivered in fatigue and began to give way. Even as his mind went numb, the instinct for survival took over. Inch by painful inch, Matthew moved his hands back down the rod until his body was squarely atop his plank. Gasping, he lay there, a mewing whimper coming from his throat. Four feet away his brother's empty plank jostled whenever the killer bolt slammed into it. At last, the plank fractured and fell, leaving the bolt bouncing up from the railroad ties to gash the boxcar's wooden bottom. Then its tether snapped and it, too, was gone. Matthew ground his face into the rough wood plank and sobbed, his heart torn open, his mind flailing.

TWO

Same day, Portland, Oregon

SAGE ADAIR'S ANKLE twisted, sending his foot in a different direction than the rest of him. Sage lurched, cursed but kept running. Only two blocks covered and he was already slowing down, sucking air, getting clumsy. "'Panic overthrows mind and kills body.' Now who'd said that?" he wondered. "Fong, had to be Fong."

"Faster, pick up your feet." Sage huffed the words. Wasted breath. Should have kept my trap shut, he thought. Sweat streaked the face of the fellow running alongside, his shorter legs moving him as fast as they could pump. Still, his speed was no match for Sage's six-footer stride. Sage slowed. Can't leave the stranger, "Bob" he'd called himself, in this kind of fix.

The field ahead, lying between the cobbled street and train tracks, was their only hope. Its leggy grass concealed a clutter of rusted metal, broken glass, wood scraps and the sucking bogs of early summer potholes. Maybe those men chasing them wouldn't realize the danger. Could slow them down.

"Careful . . . now, lots of . . . crap lying up ahead in them weeds," Sage managed to squeeze out as he sucked in more air. "Watch where you go." His companion merely grunted.

Sage gauged the distance to the south end of the railway yard. That hobo camp was over a block away. If they could get into those scrubby alder woods, they could lose the men who were chasing them. The trails there were as familiar as the back of his hand. And, he might find comrades—enough to outnumber their would-be attackers.

The shriek of steel wheels killed that hopeful thought. A freight train was rolling in from the south, its brakes grabbing hold as it slowed rounding the curve. Its length cut off access to the hobo camp. Ditch that plan. Sage tamped down a surge of panic. Find another option.

A locomotive's whistle hooted. Sage's eyes landed on a second train that was readying to roll north out of the yard, its exhaust chuffs starting up. Risking a misstep, he looked over his shoulder. All five of the heavy-footed louts were matching Sage and his running partner, stride for stride. Strangers, every one of them. But their intent was clear. Mean and mad they were. Angry pursuit equaled a bad outcome—no doubt about that.

"Who are those guys anyway?" Sage huffed, his head still swivelled to look behind. Three of them six feet tall, the trailing two, inches shorter. All in good wind. Not a one slowing. All five thudding down the boardwalk like a herd of crazed buffalo.

"God awful . . . bad . . . men," his companion wheezed out.

Sage's work boot snagged on a rusty tin strap, snapping his attention forward. Balance recovered, he considered the two trains. In seconds the incoming train would block their path, trapping them. That departing freight train would be pulling out about the same time since smoke was billowing out its stack as if it were about to explode.

So, if they could cross the tracks in front of the incoming train, they could hop the departing train. The incoming train should block their pursuers. That's the plan then. He heard his mother's voice in his head, "It's a case of chicken or feathers, my boy, chicken or feathers." "Damn bloody feathers at that," Sage muttered.

If we don't beat that incoming train, we'll have to fight. No other place to run. Sage grabbed hold of the other man's arm and increased their speed, nearly jerking the smaller man off his feet.

"We got . . . only one chance," Sage said through teeth gritted with effort. "They're too close on our tails . . . for us to angle off."

Sage's chest ached for lack of air. His throat was burning. They might not make it. What chance did they have if they turned and fought? He glanced at the Bob fella. About twenty-five years old. No brawn to him. Wiry, though. Ropey muscles. Two to five odds. Not for-certain sure they'd get trounced but certain sure they'd get hurt.

A gunshot cracked, sending dust spurting skyward a mere two feet to their left. That sight poured strength into their legs. Both picked up their pace. Fisticuffs maybe, but not fists against bullets. Any fool knew better. Even one stumbling through a railyard, a stranger at his side, with no idea why five men seemed intent on thumping the two of them.

"What's got 'em so riled?" Sage asked.

"You . . . don't . . . want to know," the other gasped, ". . . can't let 'em catch us."

At their rear, the thundering ceased as the five pair of boots left the wooden boardwalk and hit packed dirt. The three tall, two small, were in the railyard.

"We need to get you on that northbound train there. The one about to pull out . . ." Sage sucked in air, then continued. "Drop off before it reaches Seattle. Telegrams outrun trains. Pick a small town. Disappear."

"Right," the fella responded.

The oncoming train was close. If neither of them tripped, they just might make it. As if Sage's thought had physical power, the other man stumbled and fell to one knee. Sage tightened his grip, dragging the man forward even as Bob scrambled to get his feet back under him. Excited yips sounded close behind. That stumble had cut their lead.

The incoming train's whistle loosed a deafening blast that drowned out all other sounds. The engineer must have spotted them. Too late, Mister Engineer, Sage answered. We're not stopping now. Nothing to do at this point but keep our hindquarters moving.

Their running feet reached the railroad bed's slight incline. Sage's legs wobbled as they staggered up the slope and let momentum hurtle them across the tracks. For a brief instant, their pale straining faces moved across the headlamp's chrome medallion. Then the train was rushing past at their backs. They'd made it.

"You ever ridden the rails?" Sage asked. Both men were bent over, hands on knees to catch their breath, the whoosh of air off the moving train cooling their sweaty backs. Bob's response was a reproachful look.

"You got money?" Sage asked next, after they'd settled into a slow trot alongside the train that was about to depart. Ahead, its locomotive's rods began pushing forward, forcing its heavy drive wheels into motion. All along the train's length, the boxcar couplers clanked as they settled into traveling alignment.

"Not much," the other man responded. "Gave up nearly every cent for the privilege of riding under a load of hay. Got so darn hot I thought I was going to ignite the pile my own self."

Sage grinned. So Ole Bob here can string more than ten words together. Not that they'd had time enough to do more than meet, greet and take to their heels. Sage pulled a wad of bills from his pocket. He stripped off a single bill and handed the remainder to the other man.

Bob grabbed the roll and stashed it in his jacket. "Well, gee. Many thanks," he said.

"Better move it into a safer place. There'll be others riding with you," Sage said.

Bob flashed Sage a rueful grin, nodded and transferred the bills to a location inside his pants. The other man said something but Sage didn't catch the words because he'd seen a boxcar with wide-open doors rolling toward them.

"Hurry," Sage urged. A few more steps and Sage was grabbing Bob's arm once again. Lowering his shoulders and relaxing his waist, Sage planted his feet and twisted, just as he'd been taught. Bob sailed straight into the boxcar like a sack of flour.

"Wait," Bob called as he scrambled to the door, "You've got to come too! They'll kill you!"

Jogging to keep up with the rapidly accelerating train, Sage shouted back, "Don't worry about me, my legs are longer."

Pure chest-thumping, no doubt about it. There was no more running left in him, not even one block. Besides, he couldn't spare the time to wait for a train to ride back from across the river. He had an appointment he couldn't miss. He needed another plan.

As he veered away from the departing train, Sage shouted. "Keep your eyes peeled for railroad bulls. Especially just over the river at the Vancouver railyards! Some real bastards work security on this line!"

The man's yelled response was lost to distance and the metallic squeals of the nearby braking train. As his train began a slow sweep toward the river bridge, Bob waved an arm and ducked out of sight. He, at least, was safe. No one would be catching that train now. Bob's only worries for the next few hours would be railroad bulls and any hobo jackrollers he might encounter inside the boxcar. These days, an open boxcar rarely left a train yard empty of 'bos. Unemployed migrant workers, some good, some bad, were traveling everywhere across the West, searching for steady work and a piece of land to call home.

Without breaking stride, Sage turned toward the arriving train. It had slowed to such a crawl that a young man was able to roll out from under a boxcar and stumble off in the direction of the hobo camp. Tricky maneuver. Not one most men would try. Sage considered the distance to the train's end. Despite the train's slowing, that caboose would soon clear the track in front of their pursuers.

Sage caught hold of a ladder welded onto a yellow boxcar and started upward. "Damn legs," he thought, as his boots clumsily scrabbled on the rungs. Age was slowing him down, robbing him of stamina. His muscles were complaining. There is a big difference between being twenty-two and thirty-two. In days long past, he could have run twice as far and climbed atop this boxcar with wind to spare. No more. Age and maybe too much comfort, were slowing him down. Reaching the roof, Sage threw himself onto his stomach, feathering himself flat just as the train jerked to a halt.

Directly below, scuffles sounded in the roadbed gravel. The pack had rounded the end of the train. Curses and shouts wafted upward when the men couldn't spot their quarry. Sage lay still, his breathing shallow. It would be a simple matter for them to check the train's roof. Everything depended on them believing that both men had hopped that northbound freight. It was a gamble.

He allowed himself a grim smile. Such was the life of a derring-do labor movement spy. Still, it'd sure be a helluva an outcome—getting beat up or killed over something he knew nothing about. Ole Bob. Now, there was a name as fake as the "John Miner" moniker Sage had offered up during their exchange of names. Anyway, whoever that Bob fella was, he surely had aggravated someone.

Well, Sage'd never know. That's how they were waging this never-ending battle. No help for it, Sage told himself–not for the first time. The cryptic telegram from his Denver-based labor leader, St. Alban, sent Sage out into the summer's evening with a mission to accomplish and no way to ask questions. Anyway, Bob was right. Sage was very likely better off not knowing, just in case they caught him. Ignorance rang truer than a lie every time. Leastways, that had been his experience.

Sage's cheek pressed against the cool metal roof. He slowed his breath, closed his eyes and tried to loosen his muscles so he'd be ready to bolt. He worked out his avenues of escape. Up or down the train? To caboose or locomotive? Surely they wouldn't attack him in front of the conductor or the engineer. Or, he could drop down off the other side. But that would mean another run through the rubble. A stray mustache hair pressed crosswise against his cheek, poked into his nose making him stifle a sneeze. He felt a sudden urge to turn reckless. To take to his heels and flee the boxcar, the railyard, the men below. Sage banished that thought by looking down the length of the train. Come to think of it, he'd never much liked trains. Trouble seemed to always roll right along with them. Sure enough here he was, splayed out, on a perfectly fine evening, with a splat of dried bird shit two inches from his nose. Tangible proof that his prejudice against trains was dead on.

Sage strained to hear the men. All was quiet. His earlier offhand assurances to his mother echoed in his head, jeering as a raven's currr-ruk.

"Not a thing to worry about," he'd told her. "Simple mission. Meet the guy in a saloon, escort him to the train station, send him off on the first passenger train. An hour at most. Be back long before soirée starts. Stop with your worrying. It'll give you wrinkles."

"Better wrinkles then those kicks in the noggin you seem to like getting. I'm not the one running off to meet who knows who.

I'd think you'd have learned by now that things don't always turn out like you plan," she said.

"You're right. As usual. Don't know why I even bother poking you. It's always me that ends up getting the biggest poke."

She'd given his shoulder a consoling pat and said, "As Mr. Fong would say, 'young eggs shouldn't quarrel with old stones.'"

"Young eggs." He'd chuckled over the truth of another one of Fong's sayings as he'd descended their secret staircase.

Now here he was, hiding on a boxcar roof, and nothing had gone at all like he'd planned. A lone seagull was circling low overhead. He idly watched its maneuvering until he realized that the thugs crunching back and forth below on the roadbed might decide to investigate what had the bird so all-fired curious about the top of this particular boxcar.

Sage carefully eased himself onto his back and bared his teeth at the seagull until it flew off and he was left staring upward into an empty, darkening blue sky. If I get off this damn roof without getting trounced, I won't mess with trains again. And, I will no longer make predictions about how St. Alban's missions are going to work out. The gods apparently frown on such hubris.

Dusk had pooled beneath the alders when Matthew staggered into the hobo camp, tears streaking his grimy face. At the sight, gathered wood was dropped to the ground, tin plates were released to drift down to the wash tin's bottom, partially furled bed rolls fell from hands, and whalebone combs were shoved back into the ragged pockets of men whose hair remained untidy. All the settling in activities beneath the spindly tree limbs were abandoned as the 'bos gathered around the sobbing boy. Within minutes, kindly hands had wrapped him in a blanket, thrust a tin can of warm coffee into his trembling hands and led him to the fire. After a few false starts he told them, through chattering teeth, about his trip to see his aunt starting from north of Eugene. About his brother Billy.

When Matthew reached the point in his story where he described the red and black boot laces, a man the others called

"Meachum" threw his empty tin coffee cup at the ground so hard it bounced. "I know those boot laces. Every man of us does," he said.

Heads nodded around the campfire, the men's weathered and careworn faces solemn. Meachum continued. "He orders them 'specially braided by a cowboy eastside of the mountains. Clancy Steele murdered your brother. Had to be him. That Clancy's meaner than a stuck snake. There's others he's killed with that rope and demon coupler pin," he said, voice bitter.

Matthew jumped up, throwing off the blanket. "Where is he?" he demanded. "Where's Steele?"

Another man spoke up from where he hunkered close by the fire, his stick jabbing into its embers with enough force to send sparks spurting upward, "Clancy likes to drink over to the Slap Jack Saloon after a run. That's right over there where you see that chimney smoke." The man pointed the charred stick toward the uneven row of dilapidated brick and clapboard buildings ranged along one side of the railyard. At the nearest end of the row, a thin trickle of smoke curled skyward from a blackened metal stovepipe.

Matthew dropped his own tin can, and took off toward the saloon. Meachum, the man who'd named Steele, glowered down at the man who'd pointed, "You knucklehead!" he growled, before trotting after Matthew, his voice raised, calling, "Hey, boy, now you can't be going after Clancy. He's sure to kill you!"

Matthew's stride only lengthened. Soon he was leaping over the tangle of railroad tracks, Meachum's shouts growing fainter as the older man dropped behind.

Only one of Matthew's feet hit the wooden sidewalk before his body burst through the swinging doors and into the saloon. Though it was still early, the air stank of sweat, stale beer and bad cigars. Few patrons sat at the tables. Near the door, a man hacked into a handkerchief. At the far end of the bar, laughter brayed out from a burly man. He had one meaty fist wrapped around a mug of beer while his other was grabbing a woman's waist, jerking her toward him. Her short skirt revealed white-stockinged legs nearly to her knees but her shriek was coy, not fearful. Matthew's eyes flicked from the sight of her exposed legs to her companion's black boot, where it rested on the wooden foot rail. The red and black boot laces were unmistakable in the pale light of the incandescent bulb dangling above the big man's head.

With a shout, Matthew launched himself, his hands reaching for the man's thick throat.

The big man moved fast. He shoved the woman away so hard she staggered into a table. His arm came up and swept Matthew in the same direction. The boy hit both the woman and the table on his way to the floor. In an instant, the big man was over him, a heavy boot swinging back to kick at Matthew's head. Then he was staggering to the side, fighting for balance even as a strong hand grabbed Matthew's arm, jerked him to his feet and propelled him out the saloon door in one smooth move.

Matthew was shouting, "I'll kill you! I'll kill you!" over his shoulder as the hobo Meachum yanked him away down the sidewalk. In that instant between the saloon door's opening and closing, the big man's jeering laughter followed them down the boardwalk.

Matthew tried to jerk his arm away from his rescuer but Meachum held on. "Now, boy, you can't take on Clancy," he said, "You'll be hurt bad or maybe killed. Let me take you to your aunt's house."

"I'm going to kill him, I will kill that bastard even if I die trying!" Matthew shouted but he stopped resisting and allowed Meachum to wrap an arm around his shoulders and lead him away.

THREE

Sage climbed the narrow wooden staircase to the third floor, a kerosene lamp creating a dimly lit path before him. He'd lain atop the rail car for a good half hour after the curses and gravel scrunch below had ceased. That delay made him late for what was supposed to have been his riskiest and real mission of the day. Risky in the sense that failure could doom St. Alban's careful planning where Sage was concerned. The thought clenched his muscles until he willed them to relax. Anticipating failure was the way to attract it, he told himself.

He'd done everything he could to prevent failure. He'd been careful. Almost obsessively careful. Like tacking down this carpet strip to deaden the sound of footfalls on the staircase. And there was the servant's staircase itself. Its doors into the first and second floor hallways were hidden behind floral wallpaper he'd pasted up himself. No hired workman involved. No danger of barroom gab about the stranger from back East who'd created secret staircases and false cellar walls in his newly-purchased building.

At the last turning, a gas jet left burning at the top of the stairs flickered. Beyond it lay order, comfort, safety. Sage doused the lantern. Reaching the top landing, he snuffed out the gas jet with a twist. Carefully, he pulled the door open to cautiously crane his head round the heavy tapestry they'd hung across the opening. The third floor hallway was empty and silent. Both his mother's and Fong's doors were closed. Only his own door stood open.

Once inside his room, Sage tossed off his workingman's garb while he surveyed the room as he always did. First to make sure no intruder had penetrated. Then looking for some small betrayal that said he was something other than what he pretended to be. Everything appeared normal. A red brocade coverlet held down the four-poster bed. Gold-backed hairbrushes sat aligned atop the highly polished surface of the walnut bureau. On the west wall, twilight's final glow glimmered through the lacy curtains. They hung across the four double-hung windows that formed the bay nook jutting out from the building's front. In that nook were three ladder-backed chairs surrounding a small table on which stood a whiskey decanter and a single shot glass. It was a stage set, lit by softly sputtering gas jets mounted on green, velvet-flocked walls. It was a setting created to reflect the life of the wealthy and wholly predictable, John S. Adair. Just one of the components of their carefully crafted lie.

Dropping his dirty outfit onto the floor, Sage headed for the bathing tub down the hall. Once bathed, he stood before the basin mirror, mechanically stropping his straight razor, planning yet another transformation from the workingman, John Miner, into the gentleman who belonged to the room down the hall. That man was the debonair restauranteur. Someone welcomed by the very people his mother and his special friend Lucinda frequently derided as 'money royalty' and 'useless nobs.'"

Sage tested the blade with his thumb. Interesting, he mused. The two otherwise completely different women in his life shared a similar contempt toward their so-called social "betters." Too bad they didn't know each other. And never would, he assured himself.

Vigorously frothing up the soap, he slathered it over his stubbled jaw and thought about the hours that lay ahead. Tonight, he was launching St. Alban's bold plan. Just one hour from now, he'd be flashing his pearly whites at those "useless royals," in a fawning show intended to retain and strengthen their approval of Mozart's convivial host.

He frowned at himself in the mirror, face half shaved. Better not to get cocky, the ruse wasn't going to be all that easy. Success meant having to hide his real feelings as thoroughly as he sometimes hid the shock of white hair sprouting above his temple. All the artifice was about as comfortable as new boots.

Sage searched his reflection for stray whiskers. Only when shaving in this uncertain light, did Sage seriously consider giving in to his mother's desire for an electrified building. He'd noticed that most people turned conservative as they aged and resisted new technology. Not so Mae Clemens. Years of coalfield shack living had made her a fierce proponent of indoor plumbing, steam heat, and electric lighting. Well, she was living with two out of the three so-called "modern conveniences." Up to now though, he'd resisted electrical circuitry, except in the kitchen downstairs.

Five minutes later, his sprucing up was done. He was once again, John Adair, the prosperous, attractively shallow proprietor of Mozart's Table. His mustache was waxed into just-so curlicues and the white blaze above his right temple shone dashingly once again.

Sage returned to his room and pried open a tin of shoe polish. He carefully spread the thick shoe black onto the leather of his dress shoes.

Funny how his shoes had mirrored the changes in his own life. He'd started out with the hand-me-down heavy leather high top boots he'd worn to protect his feet from the hard anthracite coal. They'd been so oversized he'd worn two pairs of his uncle's socks just to keep them on. Next, came the sturdy school oxfords he'd worn when he'd been the fostered child of the rich mine owner. Years later, he'd begun his days by pulling on knee-high Indian moccasins. They'd been soft, pliable and perfect for picking his way across the arctic tundra. And now, tonight, he'd lace on these thin-soled dandy's shoes which were good for nothing but show.

His musing stopped at the sound of cutlery pinging against china. Supper sounds were beginning to drift up the stairwell from three floors below. Mozart's was yet another component in their careful plan. The restaurant was no financial necessity. Interest off his Klondike gold strike and subsequent investments far exceeded their needs. No, Mozart's Table existed for an altogether different purpose. It offered the stage on which he performed his social chameleon role. More importantly, Mozart's gave him entree into Portland's elite upper class. Like tonight's soirée.

He didn't hide all of his past. Mozart's upper class patrons knew he was raised in the East. They also knew that he owned the building that housed Portland's second most exclusive restaurant – the Portland Hotel being the first. They saw that he dressed expensively and he made no secret of the fact he'd graduated from Princeton University. Or, that he had money to burn. His entire life was constructed so that minor truths hid fundamental ones. No hint that John Adair was both a coal miner's son and a spy for the expanding labor movement. And there was his crucial connection to Vincent St. Alban. The man miners affectionately called "the Saint." St. Alban remained Sage's most closely guarded secret.

An anguished wail sounded in the street below. Sage pushed aside the curtain just in time to see a sobbing youth, accompanied by an older man, turn the corner into the side street that ran alongside the restaurant. Their departure left the street below empty except for a pair of waiting horses hitched to a sidewalk ring, sleeping heads drooping between buggy shafts, and a solitary man who seemed to slink the length of the restaurant's front wall before he, too, disappeared around the corner.

Sage let his forehead rest against the glass, its chill sending him back to another time. Once he'd wailed like that. The memory still stabbed, painful and sharp.

Sage straightened and reached to twitch the lace curtain back into place. This was not the time to dwell on the past nor on the troubles of that wailing kid in the street below. The job ahead needed his full attention. He'd have to pick another time to muck around in memories.

Still his fingers paused, he remained staring down into the street until his focus shifted to the oval of his own reflection in the window glass. His face, with its blaze of white on his temple, appeared to be floating just below the surface of murky water. Then a shadow blocked the room's light, snuffing the eerie vision. Fong had entered the room behind him and was picking the discarded clothes from the floor.

"Stop that! You are not my personal servant." Startlement caused Sage's voice to sound more imperious than he'd intended.

Fong paused, his raised eyebrow the only change in the angular planes of his otherwise impassive face. It was an unlined face, despite the Chinese man being beyond the age that began wrinkling most Occidentals' faces.

"To them," Fong's slight smile was indulgent, "I am Fong Kam Tong, your obedient houseman." He gestured toward the world beyond the windows.

Heat rushed up Sage's neck into his face. "It's like this. When you wait on me, I feel like a spoiled rich man who occupies a much smaller place in the universe than he imagines." Sage spread his hands apart in supplication. "Mr. Fong, you're my equal. Hell, you're more than my equal. You're my teacher. I should be waiting on you."

Fong's smile was mildly sardonic. "Ah, you can if you choose to. I give you permission." His face instantly sobered. "You accomplish job for Mister Saint?" he asked.

"I did, but not as planned. Found the guy in Dilly's Saloon, drinking milk right alongside men drinking redeye. He's either a fool or stronger than he looks. We set off toward the train depot. All of a sudden, five men were shouting and running at us. So, our plans got revised and he hopped a freight. Never learned who he really was or why he was running."

"You have to fight?"

Sage smiled, "Nope. But I did toss him aboard the boxcar using that pivot move you just taught me."

Fong returned the smile. "Good to keep up practice," he said.

Sage snorted and turned to paw through the bureau drawers. "It's worked, Mr. Fong. The restaurant's drawn them in, like hungry trout after bugs. As of tonight, after all our posing and posturing, John Sagacity Adair has obtained entree into Portland's most elite circle."

"Yes," Fong said, "so it seems."

Sage stopped searching the drawer and turned to look at Fong. "I would think that you could show a little more enthusiasm over this soirée tonight. Nearly half a year, we've been angling for this invitation." Sage snatched a white handkerchief and crossed to the wardrobe where he pulled both a bow tie and a long tie from an inside rail.

Fong shook his head. "No, I think tonight good. I am happy about invitation. You obtain it much quicker than hoped." But his face remained solemn, his lips slightly pursed.

"When you look like that, I know there's more you want to say. What?" Sage demanded.

"You too tensed up. Last few days, I am thinking you need a personal pursuit."

"Personal pursuit? What do you mean?" Sage kept the neck ties in hand but crossed his arms and waited.

"Like bamboo flute or maybe painting." Forehead slightly furrowed, Fong looked at him directly.

"Oh, you mean a hobby." Sage relaxed and studied the two ties as he said, "That suggestion is not what I would call particularly helpful at this point in time."

"A person too tense, he make mistakes," Fong said, as he began folding the clothes. It was their practice to keep John Miner's tattered outfits somewhat soiled.

Sage dropped onto the ladderback chair. Besides teaching Sage a Chinese fighting style that Fong called "the snake and crane"—an offering Sage appreciated—Fong also liked to intone impenetrable Oriental sayings.

"You're itching to give me one of those 'Confusion' lessons, right?" Sage asked.

"No, not Confucius. More like Lau-tse."

"And this wise Chinese sage said what?"

"No, he not say it. Likely he would say it if he thought of it."

"Oh. So, it is you, Mister Fong Kam Tong, who is saying it right this minute?"

"Yes."

Sage suppressed his impatience. This conversation topic would end faster if he just stayed out of the way. "Okay, so what does the most venerable Mr. Fong have to say?" he prompted.

"He say that a 'soul needs unbreakedness.'"

That was it? "Mr. Fong, you are both my friend and teacher, and the last thing I would ever want to do is to offend you, but why the heck do I need to hear about unbreakable souls? Tonight of all nights?"

Fong made no reply. Instead, he nodded toward the ties in Sage's hands. "Best you wear long tie. Now the fashion," he advised.

Sage tossed the bow tie into the bureau drawer, and pulled out two white shirts, showing them to Fong.

"For people to notice you, wear pleated shirt, it looks more fancy," Fong said.

Sage laughed, and hung the pleated shirt back inside the wardrobe before shrugging into the flat-fronted muslin. "No, Mr. Fong, tonight I want most to be the unnoticed observer."

"Unbreakedness? That's not even a word," Sage muttered into his chest as he buttoned the shirt, smoothed it into his trousers, and fastened up. Chinese religion made no sense half the time. At least when Jesus told a parable, he provided enough information for a guy to figure out its meaning.

"Likely not word in English," Fong responded, demonstrating yet again his acute hearing and his opinion of the English language's linguistic limitations.

"Oh. So, this 'unbreakedness,' that's a Chinese word?"

"More like idea that is shown."

"How nice," Sage said. He slipped on his coat and spread his arms wide like a circus ringmaster. "Je suis finis! My ensemble is complete. Let the game begin!"

"Think I go on roof. Practice bamboo flute," Fong said.

Downstairs, Sage's mother, Mae Clemens, stood at the entrance podium, welcoming and seating the restaurant customers. The dining room decor was expensively simple. Mahogany wainscoting and cream-colored plaster offered an elegant backdrop for the ornately framed copies of European paintings they'd hung between paired gas sconces. Spotless white linen covered the fourteen tables. Two tall black walnut sideboards, cutlery, glassware and china arrayed on their open shelves, flanked the swinging doors into the kitchen. Overhead, from the wall adjacent to the restaurant foyer, a tiny mezzanine balcony curved into the room. There three musicians bowed their stringed instruments, sending Amadeus

Mozart's lyrical compositions wafting into the room. The diners, some of them obviously wearing their Sunday-best, chatted quietly. Gas-fed crystal chandeliers, dangling from the tin plate ceiling, bathed everything in a warm flickering light.

Sage's mother led a rotund couple to their table, the man trailing her sweeping skirts like a self-important goose. You couldn't tell from her placid expression that Mae Clemens much preferred working in the kitchen alongside the "real folks." Like him, she did whatever was necessary to maintain the pretense and never complained. And, like him, she hoped to see the greedy brought down, their haughty power taken away. Mae Clemens carried her own painful memories. Sage didn't know all of them. Some came from betrayals she wouldn't share. The ones he knew about, were more embittering than his own.

Sage watched as she handed out the menus and summoned a waiter. She was a striking woman even at fifty-five, although neither pretty nor beautiful. Half Irish, half French, bold angles sculpted her face, the strength of her features emphasized by silvered black hair tightly knotted at her nape. She never tried to soften her looks, curling a few strands as other women did. Instead, she told him, "Each day, I see more of my mother's face coming out in the mirror. My grandmother's too. I like it for the memory. I like to think what they'd say about this easy life of mine."

Now there was a thought to smile over. Mae Clemens wouldn't recognize "easy" if it were a thirty-pound lap cat. She labored endlessly at one thing or another.

The music overhead hushed. His mother was standing before him, a quizzical look on her face.

"Good evening, Mrs. Clemens," he said, suppressing that smile-provoking tweak of absurdity he always felt whenever he called her by her maiden name. That particular subterfuge had been Vincent St. Alban's parting command. "For safety's sake" they were to keep their relationship secret. Somewhat grudgingly, they'd both complied. Grudging, because they'd only just bridged years of separation.

Mae spoke softly, "You'll be on your way now?" Her eyes, the same changeable dark blue color as his, gleamed with excitement. He smiled. At least she, unlike Fong, knew and appreciated what this evening's soirée meant to all their hard work.

Briefly her hand touched his, her body shielding the action from sight.

"Yes," he told her. "Tonight going well so far?" Sage kept his voice low.

"It was, until some boy asking for Ida showed up at the back door. Pretty soon they were both bawling. Then they tore out of the kitchen, Ida still in her apron. We were so busy with customers I can't begin to say what upset them. I expect we'll be learning about it soon enough.

So that boy wailing in the street must have been on his way to see Ida. For just a brief instant Sage hesitated. Should he leave? Ida might need him. Then he shook the hesitation off. There was nothing he could do for Ida right now. Besides, his mother could handle it, whatever it was. Ida was a practical, level-headed woman. And, Mae Clemens had more sense and determination than most men. He'd bet on them both handling whatever had come up.

Where's Mr. Fong?" she asked.

"Fong's up on the roof torturing the pigeons with his bamboo flute. The day he learns how to play a real melody, my ears will sing 'Hallelujah,'" Sage answered.

She chuckled. "I'm thinking your ears will grow long as a donkey's before that happens. His kind of music isn't meant to be melodious like we're used to. Anyways, the pigeons seem to like it. They keep coming back."

"Hah. They're carrier pigeons. They're supposed to come back. That's why he feeds them and keeps their coop stuffed with clean straw." Sage leaned toward the hall mirror, straightening his hat and pressing the curl more firmly into the tips of his moustache. "Fong tells me I should take up a hobby," he said to her reflection.

"Hmm . . . now there's an idea. You do seem wound fairly tight."

"You, too?" What was going on? These were the only two people who knew the importance of tonight's soirée and both of them seemed fixed on the idea of him finding a hobby.

And, she didn't let it go. "Can't say I've thought that much about a hobby, but it makes sense," she said as her fingers reached out to refresh the crease in the lace curtain covering the door window. "What else did Mr. Fong say?"

Fong's sayings seemed to intrigue her. Times like this, he felt like one of Fong's pigeons, flying coded messages back and forth between the two of them.

"You'll like this. He told me that the soul needs 'unbreakedness.'"

Her fingers paused in their curtain pressing. "Hmm."

"You know what that means?"

"Maybe." Her fingers began creasing the lace again. "It's a bit like the smell of summer berries in the woods. There's a whiff of knowing what he means and then it's gone. I'll need to think on it a bit. He said 'soul?'"

"Yes, he said 'soul.'" Sage rolled his eyes heavenward, not caring if she saw. Why was it that she, the ever practical one, never seemed to find Fong's sayings beyond strange?

"I didn't know Mr. Fong believed in souls," she mused.

"You must forgive me," Sage said. "Somehow, hobbies, souls and this entire discussion of 'unbreakedness' are not my uppermost concern tonight. I face a tiresome evening with a roomful of idlers who need to believe that my only concern is the thriving of my business and the continued garnering of their precious favor." His lips twisted in a parody of his restaurant host smile, "When," he continued, leaning forward and speaking in a whisper, "in fact, I am busily ferreting out their secrets so we can toss rocks into their well-oiled gears."

She'd been nodding along as he spoke. "Yes, son. I expect your mind is pretty well fixed on what will happen at this soirée." She dropped her fingers from the curtain and turned to him, showing him a bleak face. "You stay alert, Sage. Your Black Irish good looks might bedazzle the ladies but their husbands are something different altogether. If they're up to no good, they'll be on their guard. Don't make the mistake of thinking that folks like them are soft-headed just because they laze about in luxury. They'll fight hard and nasty to keep what they've got. Just like rats cornered in a dust bin."

Sage nodded soberly. She was right. Men who exploited others to get more than they needed had stone hearts and a vicious streak, they managed to keep hidden beneath fancy duds and lipless smiles. He flashed her a bedazzling Black Irish smile, donned his hat and left.

As he stepped onto the sidewalk, Sage nearly collided with a man hurrying past. The man had his face buried in a white hand-kerchief, a coughing fit convulsing his body. He looked like the same man Sage had seen earlier skulking along the front of the res-taurant. Sage idly watched the man cough his way up the street and disappear.

A hansom cab rattled round the corner, its driver erect on his perch behind the compartment, his high-stepping horse in the lead. Sage hailed the cab. Taking his seat on the tufted cushions, Sage spoke the address to the cabby through the hole in the cab's roof and settled back. At last he could give full concentration to the challenge ahead. The time had finally come to "do or die."

FOUR

THE HANSOM WHEELED to a gentle stop under the mansion's portico. Sage handed coins up to the cabbie, pushed back the apron and stepped down. With a touch to his top hat, the driver clucked his horse into action. Soon the hansom's rear lantern was a bobbing red pinprick.

Sage sucked in a deep breath, searching for that "center" place Fong was always talking about. Of course, whatever center existed had decided to take a hike. His innards felt more bumptious than a rock rolling downhill. Failure, that's what he was facing. These people would see right through him. He was a fool to think they'd be so indiscrete as to let a stranger overhear their secrets. The idea was absurd. A fantasy.

The breeze touching his face seemed to carry St. Alban's voice, "Their arrogance is their greatest vulnerably, Sage. Never forget that. Use it." Easy to say, but St. Alban wasn't the guy about to enter a room full of arrogant strangers. Part of Sage's problem was exactly that. Their complacent arrogance. He flat didn't like these people. As the itinerant John Miner, his surroundings felt comfortable as a worn work glove. Traveling the rails in his shabby clothes, squatting around hobo fires, sweating next to other field hands–he felt as if he were home. They were his kind of people–hardworking, genuine. His biggest fear was not measuring up in their eyes. And, their opinion was important. It was the only way he knew to honor the sacrifices some of them made to keep up standards that would be easier for them to abandon.

Tonight's soirée offered up a different kettle of fish. It wasn't as if he didn't know people like them. He did. He'd spent nearly a decade fraternizing with his foster father's rich friends–but he had never fit in. Always the interloper. An uncomfortable nobody hovering on the fringe. That familiar awkwardness had a way of seizing hold in situations like this. His pricey suit felt as if it had been bought for someone else. His handmade shoes squeezed his toes in ways his heavy workboots never did.

Sage turned away from the imposing house with its two-story high portico and sauntered to the end of the circular driveway. He stopped, inhaled deeply and sought distraction in the vista. The hills to the east stood as black humps against the cloudy night sky. Scattered lights glimmered in the dark fields encircling their bases. At his feet, beyond a closely packed spread of tin-roofed warehouses, the bare spars and rigging of anchored ships formed a small, swaying forest. Bright lanterns in its midst bobbed like summer fireflies. Men were loading the ships, hurrying so they could catch the seagoing tide. Sage's lower back twanged with remembered pain. Stevedoring strained muscles until they shredded.

Gazing down on the westside's miniature buildings and the eastside's sparsely settled farmland he realized why, in every city, rich people seized the hilltops. From this far above, Portland appeared an Eden. Neither squaller's specter nor the cries of hungry bellies broke the hilltop peace.

No, in fact, this birds' eye view would enable some to pat themselves on the back and then think of something else. The scene was an illusion. Portland was merely a shrunken version of east coast cities. The suffering in these cruder sweatshops and tenements stung just as sharp. The remembered stench of the dingy rooms where pale gaunt-faced men and women worked and lived seemed stronger in his nose than the scent of the rose blooms at his side. No one would invite those men and women to dine in that mansion at his back.

Sage's thoughts braked. Maybe that was the answer. He might have trouble locating his energy "center" but he did possess a "center" of sorts. Sage turned toward the mansion, anxiety gone. Not only could he do this tonight. He damn well wanted to.

The Dunlop's butler was on top of his job. The black-lacquered door swung open and he peered out with a look of polite inquiry. His face held none of the contempt it might have shown had it been "John Miner" presenting himself for this exclusive soirée. First test passed, then. The hired help wasn't going to slam the door in his face.

Sage mounted the granite steps. Fong's parting advice had been what? Ah, yes. He'd told Sage to be "the crane's beak." Whatever that meant. Fong was always telling him to act like that bird. What was there to know about cranes anyway? They dipped in swamps for insects and fish and, like race horses, they flew with their necks stretched out.

The butler greeted Sage with a "Good evening, sir," as he gestured toward an archway. That threshold opened into a hazy mix of cigar smoke, perfumes, and pomades. The scene carried him back into the pretentious mansions of his foster father's social set. Expensive walnut sofas, tables and chairs shone beneath the crystal chandelier. Velvet wine-colored drapes, Albusson floral carpets and the requisite curio cabinet displaying French figurines all competed for admiration.

As did the people. Self-conscious laughter, flitting sidewise glances and fingers twitching at ties, curls, and moustaches. Rubies, emeralds, a few of the more expensive diamonds, dangled from female ears and necks. The dresses were also standard fare. Satin, lace and beads atop whalebone corsets that were squeezing bodies into the distorted S-curve of uplifted bosom and jutting fanny. The men sported tailor-made suits, much like his own. Shirt fronts, a few ruffled but most flat and gleaming snowy white. None projected either ease or comfort. Funny how such rooms always seemed to underscore human imperfection. Except for his hostess, no one quite measured up to the surroundings.

All but five of the sixteen people present were clustered together near where he was pausing to take measure of the situation. This larger group occupied a loose circle of those heavy, fussily-carved Victorian chairs popular with the newly rich.

The remaining five, all men, sat clustered together in the drawing room's far corner. Sage recognized four of them. The fifth man, however, was a stranger. His face was an inverted triangle, a long nose, and eyes canted upward at their corners, much like the wolves Sage had watched slink among the Yukon's sparse trees near winter's lean end.

Sage stared at the man until he realized the stranger was staring back. Behind a wavering plume of cigar smoke the stranger's eyes narrowed, whether due to the smoke or suspicion, Sage couldn't tell. For the second time that night, a chill scrabbled up Sage's spine. He tried to relax his face into bland indifference and continue his casual survey of the room. When he saw the man finally look away, it felt as if the air instantly lightened.

"Mr. Adair, I am so delighted you came to my little soirée." The intrusion of Arista Dunlop's voice disoriented him momentarily. Turning, Sage summoned a smile and bent toward his diminutive hostess. With her large brown eyes, swirl of golden hair and heart-shaped face she was easily the prettiest woman in the room. "Ah, Madam Arista, I am most honored by your invitation," he said. "It is a lovely room you have created here. I've not seen its equal elsewhere."

She laughed and gave his arm a gentle pinch. "I don't believe you. I know you've visited the great houses of Europe, you scoundrel." She caught up his hand, leading him toward the larger grouping of guests. "Everyone," she called to get their attention. "Everyone, I am sure you know Mr. John Adair. He owns that delightful restaurant we all love to frequent, Mozart's Table. I told him it was high time he got to know us as people rather than just as customers."

And Sage had, in fact, already made the acquaintance of most of those present when they'd dined at Mozart's. All returned his bow with friendly greetings. Arista waved a languid hand toward the group in the corner but made no move in that direction. "I'd reintroduce you to my husband and his friends, but they've got their heads into business and would only bore you terribly." Dang. He was left with no polite way to insert himself into that smaller group's discussion.

Sage accepted a whiskey from Arista's butler. He chatted to one person then another until he reached the empty chair situated nearest the corner group. There Sage took a seat, careful not to look in their direction.

Sage exchanged greetings and made small talk with the people sitting on either side even as his ears strained to hear the other group's conversation. For some minutes only indecipherable mutters and solitary words reached him. Then the words began coming more distinctly.

"Now that I'm on the commission, there's no worry about that streetcar franchise. What I'm worried about is our other matter." That was Dunlop, his host and the town's wealthiest merchant.

"Mr. Adair," came a woman's voice at his side, nudging Sage's attention back toward the circle of guests in which he sat. "I do so love the adorable name of your dining establishment. However did you come to call it that?" She was the wattle-necked elderly matron sitting on his left, her chirpy voice overriding the voices Sage was straining to hear.

He smiled directly at her, saying, "Well, Mrs. Winch, fortunately my patrons are generally of the social class that enjoys classical music–discerning people like yourself. And since I am an admirer of that great composer, Mozart, it seemed a happy choice." She tittered in response until momentarily diverted by a maid offering a tray of cheese and flat biscuits. Sage shifted in his chair to aim one ear more directly at the corner group.

". . . whether Gilcrease is on board . . . that's where our money is. If he doesn't cooperate, we're . . . no way we can pull it off. Will . . . knuckle under or not?" The question came from Cyrus Gardiner, the local point man for the railroad.

Dunlop's voice was confident *"Don't worry about Gilcrease,"* he said distinctly, *"He will do exactly what we tell him to do."*

Evidently Dunlop's words failed to reassure the railroad manager, because Gardiner again spoke in the same querulous tone. *"Gilcrease better cooperate and soon . . . only a few weeks left. And what about our other problem? The deal . . . smoothly until . . . Perry here couldn't hold his bourbon . . . ."*

"So, Mr. Adair, I notice that Mozart's serves fresh produce even in the very depths of winter. Where do you obtain those snap beans at a time when the rest of us must settle for root vegetables?" This demand for attention came from the Presbyterian minister,

Reverend Williams, seated on Sage's right. The man's cultured tones and well-cut black suit left no doubt that his ministry catered to the wealthy elite. The cost of the man's suit could fill a soup kitchen's pot for a month.

"*I've told you it's handled!*" came an angry outburst from behind. Sage tried to listen closer even as he scrambled for a response to give the minister who was balancing a cup and saucer on his knee, the look on his face a mixture of inquiry and puzzlement.

Still Sage paused, straining to determine who was speaking now. "*I'm tired of hearing about it . . . you're the one that brought him into it. It was your job to take care of him.*" Ah. That was the slurred, peevish voice of Louis Perry, well-known financier and somewhat lesser-known drunk.

It was time to switch full attention to the minister. "You are right, Reverend, the local selection is meager given our short growing season," Sage responded. "During the winter, I normally purchase produce from a greenhouse south of the city or sometimes I buy it off a refrigerator ship that's in port from South America . . . although that is fairly expensive."

"*What do you mean, 'it's handled'?*" This time, it was Senator Hipple's voice and so loud that those in the larger circle paused conversations and glanced toward the corner.

Hipple continued, lowering his voice in response to audible shushing but his anger was unabated as he hissed, "*Perry, if you've done something else stupid . . . I swear I'll . . . *"

"*Now, don't lose your temper, Senator.*" Perry's words, although slurred, were easily overheard by Sage, "*I put us in this spot, so I was honor bound to get us out of it. That's what I've done. As a matter of fact . . .*" Perry's voice pinched off as if he'd received some nonverbal admonishment. Fiercely spoken *sotto voce* murmuring came from the corner and Sage's ear flushed hot. Fearful that they were already staring in his direction, he resisted the urge to peek at the small group

"I must admit, Mr. Adair, I cannot abide cabbage at any time," the minister began, intent on keeping his social discourse firmly with the vegetables.

Sage laughed aloud and slapped his knee. "Oh, Reverend, truer words were never spoken."

The minister blinked. His smile turned hesitant.

The butler sliding open the mahogany pocket doors rescued Sage from prolonged social awkwardness. Behind the doors stood a table glinting with silver and china. Everyone got to their feet, Sage offering his crooked arm to the chirping Mrs. Winch. As they moved toward the table, Sage realized that the stranger's voice had been the only one he'd never overheard coming from the corner. Still, what he'd overheard was more than intriguing. So much so that Sage fought an urge to click his heels like a wee old country leprechaun. St. Alban's information was right on the money. Those men were involved in some scheme. One that had recently turned risky. Gardiner's comment about there being only a few weeks remaining meant Sage had limited time to uncover the secret and figure out how to disrupt their plans. Excitement twitched his arm beneath Mrs. Winch's fingers. Good thing the old dear was prattling too much to notice.

The dirt street fronting the railway yard was empty until a saloon door thwapped shut, muffling the rumble of male voices and women's shrieks as if they'd been doused in a water bucket. The big man reached the wooden sidewalk, planted his legs wide and swayed, muttering, "Too tired anyway. To hell with her!" A loud belch helped relieve the pressure in his gut. He set off southward, his boots splashing through the puddles left by a recent shower.

A block from the saloon, just outside a gaslit circle, someone stepped from an alley entrance. The big man halted, immediately wary. He squinted but couldn't see the other person's features. The big man signaled he was ready to fight by pulling his ham-sized fists from his coat pockets. Then he relaxed, letting fly another loud belch before saying, "Ha! So it's you. I knew they'd send you back to meet my terms. Those high and mighties know better than to mess with me, now don't they?"

The big man stepped forward to poke his meaty forefinger into the smaller guy's chest, giving a snort of derision when the other flinched away from the blast of his boozy breath.

Still, the smaller person's face remained bland as he lifted a hand to gently catch and still the poking finger. The big man didn't pull it away. Instead, his face turned puzzled, then stretched into an exaggerated leer. "Hey, whatcha wanna do, hold hands? Hah! You're not my type. Whaaa . . . ," he began but someone else's arm quickly snaked over his shoulder, choking off further words and jerking his head back. A blade slashed into his neck and blood geysered toward the guy who now grasped the big man's wrist tightly. The big man's knees buckled, dropping him to the ground. The guy holding the wrist simply let go so that the dying man's arm flopped to the pavement.

Seconds later, two pairs of boots thudded away down the alley leaving the body twitching at lamplight's edge. One black boot nudged a puddle, the trailing end of a red and black shoelace floating atop the puddle's surface.

Arista Dunlop set a fine table. The prime rib roast was succulent, the baby green peas tender as if picked within the hour, the whipped potatoes well-seasoned, if a bit rooty tasting– likely last fall's crop. Sage forced himself to chew and swallow. Nerves had a grip on his gullet. Across the dining table from him sat the sharp-nosed stranger who'd been introduced to him as 'Otis Welker.' Sage watched Welker surreptitiously, wondering why those pale blue eyes were so disconcerting. Welker's easy smile as he talked with his dinner companions gave his sharp features a genial cast. The women's trills of laughter and the way both kept spontaneously touching Welker's forearms, left no doubt that the man possessed charm. Still, there was an undercurrent to Welker that made Sage uneasy.

After the uniformed maids cleared the dinner table, Arista Dunlop sang out above the chatter, "Oh, Mr. Welker," she called, "Do show us those magic tricks of yours."

After a slight hesitation, Welker transformed into a facile parlor magician. With swift showy moves he caused a large dried pea to appear on the white tablecloth followed by three shellacked walnut half-shells. Everyone craned forward to see.

Welker's sinewy fingers placed the pea under one of the shells, which he then began sliding about the table. The parlor magician ceased moving the shells and looked up.

"The left-hand one!" a man guessed. Welker lifted that shell, revealing the empty space beneath it.

He began moving the shells again. Sage forced his eyes away to study Welker's face. The man was surveying his table partners, one by one, even as his fingers flew and patter flowed from his lips. Welker intercepted Sage's look and his penetrating eyes seemed to counter it for an instant before turning flat and looking away.

He's trying to spook me, Sage realized. When Welker looked at him again, Sage deliberately flashed what he hoped was a con-spiratorial grin. Confusion flitted across the other man's face and his hands fumbled. He glanced down to recapture his rhythm. Sage allowed himself a small smile of satisfaction.

When the shells stopped circling, a woman pointed and squealed, "That one!" And, indeed, the pea lay beneath the walnut.

"Ah there, dear lady. You have bested me at my own game." To everyone's laughter, Welker presented her with the pea, flourishing it, as if it were a jewel. He didn't look in Sage's direction.

Sage walked toward home after refusing many offers of shared carriages. Mozart's was only two miles or so and downhill. It had rained while he'd been inside. He hoped the rinsed air and scent of early roses might flush a persistent ache from his forehead.

Through casual questioning of the dinner guests, he'd learned that Welker worked for the Baumhauer Company, a big Minnesota timber trust. Nobody, however, seemed to know Welker's precise function within that operation. Still, it had to be something im-portant given the deference shown Welker by the other men. Even the bombastic Senator Hipple seemed to go out of his way to be ingratiating. Did Welker's participation in the scheme mean that the Baumhauer Company itself was also involved? Not necessar-ily, Sage told himself. Wolves like Welker were always hunting for a chance to make a killing.

Sage mulled over the snatches of talk he'd overheard. Some-thing about a man named "Gilcrease." Who was he? Why was this Gilcrease's reliability so important to the success of their scheme? And what mistake had that drunk Perry made? Obviously, he'd done something to put their machinations at risk. Might as well sniff down that trail too. And, find out about Gilcrease until something more definite turned up. The trick was to keep gathering facts until those facts coalesced into an answer. A successful approach in the past. Besides, what was the alternative?

A soft noise, like the scuff of a misplaced foot, stopped Sage's musing. Experience sent him ambling toward the curb, away from the dark shop doorways. He lifted his arms a few inches away from his body, quieting his own rustle so he could focus on what his ears were telling him. His whole being strained to hear that next footfall behind him.

When it came, definite and unmistakable, his legs wanted to run. Fong was forever preaching that the best response to a physical threat was "first to run, second to fight." Sage looked around him. Late yes, but the mild weather meant other people were strolling the street. Not too many, but surely enough to deter a mugger.

Crossing into the blackness beyond a pool of gaslight, Sage pivoted toward the sound. A figure hesitated then stepped into the light. It was Welker.

"Mr. Adair, I seemed to have alarmed you. I thought perhaps that it was you who walked in front of me but I wasn't sure, so I hurried to catch up." He offered his long thin hand for a shake. His fingers felt like icy bones.

"It seems we missed the opportunity to become acquainted this evening," he said, "Although we were introduced briefly, we never had the opportunity to converse."

"Good evening, Mr. Welker," Sage responded, relieved that his own voice sounded as oily as the other man's. "Are you walking far this evening?"

"For a few more blocks only. I'm staying over at the Portland Hotel."

"Well, I am passing by the hotel myself. I'll happily accompany you," Sage said, matching his steps with Welker's. "So, how do you find your stay at the hotel?" he asked. To his ears, his words sounded incredibly stilted but then, as far as Welker knew, they were just two strangers trying to make conversation.

"It's very comfortable. I always enjoy staying there." Welker's tone equaled Sage's in banal formality.

A few strides later Sage said, "Your parlor magic was very much the high point of the evening."

Welker gave him an easy, sardonic smile. "I find that the deceptive arts fascinate people. Most think that everyone but themselves can be deceived. Have you not found that to be true?"

Sage's mind flailed. How was he supposed to answer that? Was Welker making an insinuation or has he got me spooked as a colt caught out in a lightening storm? He settled for an "Mmmm" of agreement.

When they arrived at the hotel's driveway, Welker spoke again, "Ah and here we are already. I'll bid you goodnight, Mr. Adair. I look forward to seeing more of you. I understand you are relatively new in town. I'd like to hear more of your history." Welker shook Sage's hand again. The glint in his eyes could be either amusement or polite friendliness. No way to tell. But, as he turned away, Sage had to stop himself from reaching up to rub the stiffness from his own face.

Thoughts about the curious exchange with Welker preoccupied Sage as he strolled toward home. Was Welker insinuating that he's seen through Sage's own deception? Sage thought back to that first time their eyes had locked across the room. In that instant, Welker's defenses had been down. Sage'd seen through Welker to his cold, grasping heart. Had Welker seen through him? And what did that poke about Sage's history mean? Had a management spy already told Welker of Sage's presence in Portland? No way to know. But every tired sinew in Sage's body shouted that Welker was a threat. Sage just wasn't sure about the nature of that threat.

Still uneasy, Sage rounded the corner of Third Street where Mozart's occupied the bottom floor of the three-story building. Eleven months prior, Sage had used some of his Yukon wealth to purchase the narrow cast-iron fronted structure. This late at night he'd need to enter quietly. By now, Ida Knuteson, the cook, and her husband, Knute, would be asleep in their second-floor apartment. His mother would be abed but awake on the top floor, listening for the sound of his return. And Fong, well, Fong could be anywhere.

Sage's step faltered as his senses sprang alert. Mozart's windows blazed with light when they should have been dark. And, seconds later, the front door knob turned easily instead of being locked. Entering, Sage was immediately halted by the tableau inside the dining room. Fong stood motionless, brows furrowed, arms crossed over his chest, his attention on the normally cheerful Ida. She sat hunched over a dining table, her face covered by her work-reddened hands and sobbing as if her heart were shattered.

FIVE

FONG SWITCHED HIS gaze from Ida to Sage, his black eyes piercing. Sage started to speak only to stop at the sound of a muffled whoosh. Mae Clemens strode through the kitchen's swinging doors. The tray she held carried the strange combination of a china pot and teacup, water glass and whiskey bottle. Fong stepped forward, taking the tray and sliding it onto Ida's table. With nimble precision he yanked the stopper and splashed a couple fingers of whiskey into the glass before pushing it toward Ida. Hand trembling, Mozart's cook tilted the glass to her lips and swallowed, her eyes staring at them all with a kind of witless desperation.

The floor seemed to shift beneath Sage's feet. An awful explanation plummeted through his mind, straight into his stomach like a rock through water. Someone was hurt or dead. Had to be Ida's husband, Knute. She had no other family here.

Knute being dead or maimed wouldn't surprise him. Two months ago, Sage had watched Knute simultaneously feed wood chunks into two screaming industrial saw blades. A conveyor belt kept his hands moving at a near blur, inches from the insatiable whirling disks. Had those shingle blades extracted a toll for one moment of distraction? A horrific vision of bloody stumps flared bright.

Sage's mother knelt beside Ida to wrap an arm around the sobbing woman's shoulder. "Knute?" Sage mouthed.

She shook her head. Not Knute. Relieved, Sage strode to the sideboard, snatched a glass and returned to pour himself a shot from Ida's bottle. Her reassurance and the whiskey's burn tamped down his jitters and surging panic. Except for Knute, and maybe St. Alban, everyone Sage cared the most about was in this room. But, who was in trouble, if it wasn't Knute?

The answer came in a remembered sound. The wails of the boy as he rounded the corner. His mother's words, ". . . some boy asking for Ida showed up at the back door. Pretty soon they were both bawling." That must be it. The boy.

Catching sight of Sage, the cook's sobs choked off. She snatched up an apron corner to dab at a face puffy and moist from tears. "Oh, Mr. Adair," she wailed, "it's a blessing that you finally got here. An awful thing happened. What in the world am I to do?" Shock had bleached her complexion and widened the pupils in her normally mild blue eyes. Sage touched her shoulder but snatched it back when Ida's double chin started wobbling. She ducked her head back into her apron.

This wasn't a scorched pie or charred roast. It must be that boy. Sage snagged a nearby chair, swung it to the table and sat down. He put his hand atop hers and said firmly, "You need to tell me what happened."

In response she straightened in her chair, making an obvious effort to pull herself together before quavering, "Oh Mr. Adair, it is too terrible beyond all belief. I never thought I'd live to see such an awful day." She choked and couldn't continue.

Sage's mother stepped into the breach. "I'm thinking it'd be easier if I tell Mr. Adair, Ida," she said, rising from the floor, grimacing as her knees cracked. As she sat down, she gestured Fong into the remaining seat at the table.

Mae cleared her throat before saying, "Ida's had more shocks tonight than a body can bear." She related the gruesome details of Billy's death. Her spare recitation did not diminish the horror of that boy's terrified final moments beneath that rattling, rocking boxcar. Sage shook his head but said nothing. It was a memory that would torture Billie's older brother, "Matthew" his name seemed to be, for the rest of his life. What did he do wrong? What could he have done different? Why hadn't he been smart, strong or brave enough to save his younger brother? The litanies of a childhood horror latched on and never let go. This Sage knew all too well.

What happened to young Billy stirred a vague memory. There'd been a story about railroad bulls using a roped-up coupler pin to kill hobos riding the rods east of the Rockies. But that was hundreds of miles away, out on the prairies where it was near impossible for a man to jump a freight without being seen. He'd never heard of a coupler pin being used like that in the Pacific Northwest. Of course, it'd been a few weeks since he'd made the rounds of the hobo camps, as he'd been too busy courting Mozart's wealthy patrons, angling for that invite into their inner circle.

Sage felt a cramp and looked down. His hand was white-knuckling the whiskey glass. He relaxed his fingers. Damn the greedy hearts of the railway millionaires and their hired thugs. The Railroad Trust's exorbitant freight charges were forcing thousands of small farmers off their land and into the migrant life. And, then they compounded that evil by hiring thugs who attacked the very same people. Every train rolling into the yard carried yet another tale of railway bulls maiming or murdering a migrant worker.

Damn every single one of the Trusts. Collections of greedy predators, they infested every corner of the economy—steel, oil, banks, insurance, beef, timber—Carnegie, Rockefeller, Armour. Utterly ruthless, every man jack of them. They steamrolled anyone who got in their way.

Consequences be damned. He, St. Alban, and others had seen enough. It was time to push back. Do whatever they could to stop the Trusts. Might be a fool's mission writ large but no matter. He wouldn't abandon it. He couldn't. No more than he could have abandoned that stranger, Bob, in the railway yard today.

His mother's voice intruded. He realized she'd kept on talking. The story wasn't done. Apparently, it hadn't ended with Billy's murder.

"Anyways, Ida and Matthew rushed off to the police station,' she was saying, "where our fine men in blue promised they'd telegraph down the line to start a search for the body. But, they also made it clear that they weren't going to get up off their lazy backsides and arrest Billy's killer." She reached over, lifted Sage's glass, sipped, shuddered and raised her voice, "Even though they knew that demon's name! Matthew told them!" Before Sage could ask, she spat the name, "Clancy Steele!"

Sage started. Clancy Steele? A familiar name but why? A vague, hulking figure lumbered across his mind's eye but as he tried to conjure it clear, it receded. Later. He'd remember later why the name was familiar. He always did.

Sage looked toward Ida who remained hunched over, her head in her hands. He patted her shoulder. The story all told, he could comfort her. His gesture triggered a torrent of words that included the words "police, arrest" and "Matthew and Knute."

Ida must have realized she wasn't coherent because she straightened, wiped her eyes yet again, sucked in a deep breath and said clearly, "And now those stupid police are out to arrest Matthew."

Mae Clemens nodded and picked up the story, "After they returned from the police station, Ida sent Matthew up to stay with Knute while she finished cleaning down here. When she went to their apartment, they'd run off."

Sage struggled to connect the absence of Knute and his nephew with the idea that the police were hunting the kid. Did they think Matthew killed his own brother? That made no sense. What a harebrained idea.

Mae paused. She filled the teacup and pushed it toward Ida. During the lull, Sage looked around the restaurant. A few short hours ago, this room had known only conviviality. Now it was witness to tragedy and woe.

His mother continued. "So we were sitting here talking about where the two of them might have gone when the police came pounding on the door. Two big lugs pushed their way in the instant Mr. Fong unlocked it. They demanded we produce Matthew."

Sage envisioned the scene. Likely those two policeman thought the two women and small Chinese man would be easy to intimidate. Maybe they'd be right about Ida, she was no fighter. But those officers were dead wrong about the other two. Luckily it hadn't come to that.

Mae Clemens leaned forward. "They told us that Clancy Steele was dead, down near the railroad yards. Someone slit that cuss's throat ear to ear." She looked him in the eye, her lips compressed into a grim little smile. "I was glad to hear it and made no bones about saying that. 'More power to whoever did it,' I told those half-wits, 'I hope whoever done us the favor don't get themselves caught.'"

"Gave them an unfettered dose of your feelings, did you, Mrs. Clemens?" Sage asked and got a glower in response. Sometimes he worried that Mae Clemens' forthright speech might pose a risk to their undercover operation. But, she'd proved unstoppable on that point.

"'I certainly did," she said with lifted chin. "Sure as frogs bump their hind ends when they jump. And I'd do it again." She sent him another sharp look to let him know she hadn't appreciated his sideways rebuke. "Anyways, they said that when Matthew was at the police station he kept hollering that Steele deserved to die. That's how come they came busting in here. They figured the boy had hitched his words to action. But, like I told you, Knute and Matthew had already gone. When you came in, we were discussing whether Matthew might just be the one who killed Clancy Steele. Ida says not." Ida shook her head vigorously in denial. "And," Mae continued, "to add to the tangle, we can't figure out where the heck Knute went or if he's with Matthew or not."

Sage sat back. This was bad. If the boy murdered Steele, he'd hang or rot in prison until he was an old man. Even if he hadn't, once the police decided differently, they'd look no further. The coppers weren't going to search for another culprit when they already had one near to hand. They'd rather make their rounds, stopping off to guzzle beer, play cards or flirt with women. They preferred to patrol the comfortable realm of inept thieves, domestic spats and wandering cows.

Leaning forward, Sage asked Ida, "Tell me about your nephew Matthew. Does he know how to use a knife?"

Ida sniffed. "He's been working in the cannery gutting fish since he turned fourteen. He's fifteen now. I'd guess he's good with a knife." She reached past the tea to gulp another swig of whiskey which set her coughing. Ida normally shunned "spirits" as she called them. In fact, Sage suspected that his cook was a secret temperance woman, though her job at the alcohol-serving Mozart's presumably kept her mum on the subject.

Catching her breath Ida continued, "Matthew's plan was to get Billy away from that cannery. Bring him here. Get him in school. Matthew was going to find a job to pay for Billy's tuition." Her face crumpled. "Ohhh," she wailed, "what am I going to do? My poor sister. She loves those boys more than the air itself."

Sage thought the answer inescapable as far as he was concerned. Of course, they'd help Ida straighten this mess out. He looked at Fong and saw calm acceptance in the other man's expression. Otis Welker's mocking face flashed momentarily into and out of Sage's mind. Waiting wasn't going to fix Ida's problem. It was here, now, and desperate. Welker and his ilk would have to come later.

As if sensing Sage's thoughts, Ida raised her head and looked at him, appeal and hope in her red-rimmed cornflower blue eyes.

He patted her hand yet again. She was a good woman, Ida was. Hard-working, quick with kindness. Seized every opportunity to lighten a person's day with a cheery word or little joke. She and Knute were family of a sort. And now her nephew Matthew needed help. But what could they do? Where should they start? A vague plan sprang to mind. First, they should search for Matthew and Knute, assuming the police hadn't already found them. The other bear of a question was "who killed Clancy Steele?" That question needed a quick answer, before Ida's surviving nephew got offered up to the hangman. While the city's new courthouse might be an artful pile of chiseled stone and mahogany interior, the wood scaffold in its courtyard was as crudely timeless as hanging itself.

He looked toward Mae Clemens. His mother's eyes contained the same resolution and acceptance as Fong's. All three were unanimous then. Ida's predicament took precedence over their mission for St. Alban. Sage switched his gaze back to Fong. The other man quirked his eyebrows and snicked a glance toward the restaurant's windows. Yes, they'd better get a move on.

"Ida," Sage said softly, waiting until he had her full attention, "Fong and I will do everything we can to find Matthew and Knute before the police do." Fong nodded vigorously. "We're going to go out right now to look for them. I want to stay with you but we need to start looking. Do you understand? Can you stay with Mo . . . Mrs. Clemens here? Will you be okay?"

Ida nodded, her face lightening slightly as faint color returned to her cheeks.

Sage gave her hand a firm squeeze and stood. His mother smiled at him, approval warm in her face.

Upstairs in his room, Sage stripped off his finery while Fong pulled the wrinkled, dirty work clothes from the canvas suitcase stowed beneath Sage's bed. Their earlier clash over Fong's acts of servitude completely forgotten.

"I'm thinking I should go to the rail yards and try to find out what happened to Steele before the facts get too gin-soaked. Now is when I'm most likely to get the truth. I don't know about you but I don't believe a fifteen-year-old country kid could murder an experienced railroad bull," Sage said.

"Yes, I agree," Fong said, "I think that plan is best. Me, I will search for the boy and Mr. Knute. If the police have not found them, they will come back this direction sometime soon. I will hide them away."

"Alright then, we both know our jobs," Sage said. "Damn. This trouble of Ida's couldn't have happened at a worse time."

"Any time worse," Fong responded gently.

A flush swarmed up from beneath Sage's collar. "I didn't mean that like it sounded. Nothing's worse than the death of a child." He was silent, thoughts snagged once again on the image of that horrific death beneath the boxcar. Poor innocents. So many poor innocents these days getting maimed, killed and worse. He cleared his throat to dislodge the knot that had grasped his windpipe.

"You know what I mean though, Mr. Fong," he said. "It doesn't seem so important now, in light of what happened to those boys, but our plan did work. The soirée, I mean. I overheard enough to learn that they're definitely up to something. Betcha the scheme is exactly the one that St. Alban wanted us to find out about. I even have a few names for us to start looking into."

Fong smiled widely. "Ah. That is good. So, tonight successful?"

Sage returned the smile. "My gut tells me 'yes.' Maybe extremely successful." Sage carelessly tossed his long tie in the direction of the dresser. It landed in a dangle from atop the mirror. He left it there. The aroma of stale work clothes wafted up, a pungent recall to the task that lay ahead. Bad luck that he had to shove aside the information he'd gathered at Arista's soirée. Their months of conniving would come to naught if he couldn't get to work on what he'd overheard. Oh well, at least it wasn't raining.

Fong's thoughts had stayed with the soirée. "Ah. Like crane in water, you pluck up small bites of information. That is good." Satisfaction tweaked his cheeks into a tiny smile.

"Oh, so that's what you meant when you talked about that bird's 'bill.'" Sage had seen slow-moving cranes standing in the shallows, their infinite patience a deadly threat to the water creatures swimming between their stick-like legs. "You meant I was to pick up information like a crane picks up bugs and minnows." Under his breath Sage muttered, "That darn bird, again." He pulled on a denim jacket, patted its pockets and opened his dresser drawer to grab folding money and a few coins, then turned to find Fong smiling at him from behind hands formed into a bird's beak.

Sage ignored the gesture. "I know I've heard of Clancy Steele, but it seems to me I've seen him also," he said.

"Your memory is bad for such a young person," Fong said as he shut the half empty suitcase and slid it back under the bed. "Steele visited restaurant. You pointed him out to me."

At that nudge, Sage remembered. Steele was a big man wearing a suit so small that his flesh rolled over the collar while his trousers squeezed his legs like sausage skins. In contrast, Steele's dining companion had been urbane, impeccably dressed. The odd pairing had drawn Sage's attention to them. With a start, Sage realized Steel's urbane companion had been Cyrus Gardiner, the very same railroad manager Sage had overheard conspiring at the soirée. Now there was an odd coincidence.

Sage's disguise was nearly complete. It was the same one he'd worn earlier in the day. He called it "John Miner" because that was the alias he used whenever he wore it. John Miner came out whenever Sage's mission for St. Alban needed a man who could pass, like a fish in the sea, among the city's unemployed. So his overalls were frayed, his denim jacket patched, and his work boots scuffed. A glob of lamp black smeared into Sage's white patch blended it into his black hair good enough pass in the dim light of the places he'd visit that night. Besides, John Miner always wore a stained, flop-brimmed hat. Sage quickly stripped the wax from his moustache so that it drooped over his upper lip and covered most of his mouth. The mirror confirmed the Miner persona was complete. Looking back at him was the face of a tired man who'd spent a fruitless day searching for work. Someone more than ready to hunker down behind a glass of stale beer and drown the cold stone of failure in his belly.

"How do I look?" Sage asked.

"Face too clean. Whiskers all gone." Fong said, patting the smooth sides of his own face.

Sage opened the window, swiping up sill grime to smear on his face and hands. That done, he clapped a soiled hat onto his head and turned toward the door. There he paused, feeling for the first time, an ache in his shoulders and the anxiety circling inside him like an old dog who'd lost his place to lay. "I have trouble finding that center you talk about when I'm into one of my roles. Why is that? I don't seem to be so jittery when we practice the snake and crane. It's not excitement. I can use that to advantage. Keeps me sharp. It's more like I'm fighting against something," he said.

Fong tilted his head to the side, studying Sage. "Jitters cause distraction, not so good. Easy for you to make mistake when there is no center, a breakedness."

That "unbreakedness" thing again. He should have known. Fong was going to be absolutely no help whatsoever. Sage pulled his hat far down over his forehead, "Oh well," he said. "Right now, Mr. John Miner has to hit the streets, broken or not." Sage's voice sounded more confident to his ears than he felt. "So, forget the jitters," he told himself. "Concentrate on the real dangers. Like the muggers, shanghaiers, and drunks looking to beat their frustration into someone else's head." He'd focus on dodging them and getting answers about Steele's murder. Otherwise, there'd be no helping Ida.

"Remember, you are not John Miner." Fong called after him.

"I am when I'm wearing this getup."

"Maybe that is the problem," Fong replied. Sage didn't bother to respond. It had been a long day and the night promised to be longer still. He was too tired to figure out what the other man meant. Right now his task was Ida and Knute and that boy who was somewhere out there, the day's awful memories vivid in his head.

Sage pushed aside the tapestry hiding the back staircase into the building's cellar, then paused to call back, "Mr. Fong, what's this Matthew boy look like? Can you describe him?"

Fong came out into the hallway to say, "He a bit shorter than you, Mr. Sage. Two inches maybe. Hair is the color of the cinnamon spice. His nose sharp. He has spots . . . ah . . . freckles on face. He is wearing shirt of big green squares."

The boy in the street had been wearing that shirt–the boy who'd been crying just before Sage had left for the soirée. No surprise. The timing was too coincidental for it to have been anyone else. "Yup. I saw him earlier out the window. Well, good luck finding him and Knute, Mr. Fong."

Fong bowed slightly, his palms pressed lightly together. Sage dropped the tapestry into place, his mind already mapping out the saloons he'd be visiting in his search for Clancy Steele's murderer. He'd have to watch his step. Whoever had killed the railroad bull wouldn't take kindly to the idea that some stranger was nosing around.

SIX

THE STAIRS ENDED in a space concealed behind a huge provision shelf. From there, Sage traveled thirty feet to the end of a dank tunnel. There a short wooden ladder led up to a trap door. Neck bowed against the underside of the door, Sage snuffed the lantern and hung it on a hook he'd attached to the ladder's side. Musty blackness pressed in and he fought the twinge of irrational fear that inevitably sprang into being at this point in his exit.

Crouched atop the ladder, he ignored that rustle of involuntary panic as he strained to hone in on the sounds of the world outside. No voices, no scrape of a boot, no hacking cough. It was an inhospitable alley for the homeless. The police patrol, their palms receiving regular contributions from Mozart's owner, made certain of that.

Sage's fingers scrabbled for the bolt until he found it and silently slid it open. An inch-wide wedge of dim light and the musty smell of earth slipped through the opening. Still he waited, listening again. All he heard was the scuffle of wharf rats and the distant rumble of wagons rolling over paving blocks.

In one fluid move Sage clambered onto the alley dirt pack and quietly lowered the trap door back into place. He searched the murky shadows. No one in sight. Just the alley's sooty brick walls and the dust bin bulwark they'd fashioned to shield the trap door's entrance from the sight of passersby. From outside the alley's mouth came the raucous ditties of the drunken sailors clomping down the plank sidewalk. Muzzy with drink, tales all told, the sea cowboys were stumbling home to narrow ship bunks that would rock them to sleep in the rhythm of the river's flow.

Sage leaned against the brick wall, head hanging down, until they passed. Some nights, the idea of endless waves, forced inactivity and limited happenstance exerted an almost irresistible allure. Not tonight. Once silence fell, he stepped into the street.

Slap Jacks was the third saloon he'd entered that night. Small groups of men and women slumped around scattered round tables. The bare electric bulbs dangling overhead gave their faces a sickly cast of black and grey. They didn't stop talking or swigging down their poison when he stepped inside, letting the door thwap shut behind him. Only a couple of men bothered to squint disinterestedly in his direction. John Minor was neither enemy nor friend to them. Just another barroom Joe, his history of spotty employment and uncertain abode settled into his features like the dust in his clothes. This newcomer was no harbinger of problems, though he'd maybe spring for a drink if he was flush.

Slap Jacks remained a typical smoke-filled dingy joint, no better and no worse than any other saloon in the North End section of town. The saloon was flush enough to sport a long bar of varnished fir and a gilt-edged, cracked mirror reflecting an array of whiskey bottles. The sawdust beneath Sage's boots clumped with spittle and spilled beer. Slap Jack's philosophy of cleanliness ran along the lines of, "whatever hits the floor, stays on the floor." In the farthest corner, three men tortured fiddle, harmonica, and tinny piano. Once their musical effort sputtered into silence, people's conversations became intelligible. As in the previous saloons he'd toured, most folks were jawing up a storm over Clancy Steele's sudden and bloody demise. Sage drifted toward the largest group, slapping a nickle down on the nearby bar. Smeary glass of weak beer in hand, he leaned back against the bar and waited for a lull in the conversation before asking, "What's going on? What's got folks het up?"

The question got a lively response. One old geezer, whose hair reared up straight as if he'd seen a ghost, informed Sage in hushed tones that Steele had been found with his throat cut. He next confided that a sporting girl down the street claimed she'd seen the men who'd done it. "Yup, that little ole' gal was standing at her window on the lookout for customers when two men high-tailed away down the alley right below her. There was Clancy Steele, dead as a whiskey bottle on Sunday morning, laying right in the alley's entrance." His poetic use of metaphor earned him boozy guffaws from the crowd.

"I got no faith in what that Clara says," declared a slight woman. Her transparent skin and fever-bright eye burned with obvious consumption. "She likes her opium too much. Maybe she seen what she says, maybe she didn't." The woman started hacking; crimson spots blossoming on the stained rag she'd pulled from her bodice to cover her mouth. She gulped whiskey to calm the cough. Sage slid his chair farther away.

He thought he knew who she meant. "Clara. Is that the black-haired young gal working up at Halloran's cribs?" he asked.

"Yeh, that'd be the one all right," the woman said before taking another swallow.

Another quarter hour or so of drifting from table to table yielded nothing new. So he turned toward the bartender who was slowly swishing dirty beer glasses through a bucket of gray water, his mind clearly on the wander.

"Can't say I cared much for Clancy Steele," Sage stated once the frog-faced barkeep looked up. This was a man reputed to have never stretched those long thin lips into a smile.

"No surprise you'd be saying that," the barkeep responded as he switched to smearing a dirty rag across the bar's scarred surface. "Course not liking a man is some piece from deciding to make him dead. Ain't too many folks come in here hated Clancy that much. Course then, it ain't as if he came around all that often."

"But some didn't like him?"

"There's been a few."

Sage laid down a quarter. When the barkeep returned with

another glass of beer, Sage waved away the change. The man nodded and leaned his elbows on the bar. "I suppose you heard about that young kid coming in here today?" he said.

"That red-haired boy, everybody is talking about?"

"Yup, that's the one. Now there was a boy mad as hell, that's for sure. I suppose he coulda done it, but I don't know, kinda on the scrawny side to my eye. Can't think he'd be any match for Clancy. Boy'd have to catch Clancy unawares or use some trick, and he looked to be a kid with hay still stuck to his britches."

"Folks are saying the boy came in with a friend?"

"Nah, don't think he were no friend. It was one of them regular 'bo's from the camp across the way. I think the fella just took pity on the kid and yanked him outta here before Clancy stomped him to death."

"You know the 'bo?" Sage asked.

"Now I should be able to recollect his name. Comes in here kinda regular like he travels up and down the line." The barkeep gazed into the glass eyes of a deer head mounted above the entrance doors. "Name might be Meachum, something Meachum," he said. "I see him when he has money for booze and wants the free eats. Quiet enough feller. Holds back a bit. Sorta surprised he rescued the kid like he did. Don't seem to be a man who likes calling attention to his self."

Sage shifted uncomfortably, that sounded a bit too "close ta home" as his mother would say. Like something people might say about Sage Adair, alias John Miner.

"So only the kid has threatened Clancy? Nobody else?"

"Lately, he's the only one. 'Fore that, there was another guy. He was powerful mad at Clancy. Only he was just as big as Clancy. Tough like him too. Maybe tougher."

"Angry about a woman or something?"

"Nope, tweren't no woman. From what I heard tell afterwards, this guy was a homesteader down around Silverton way until he lost his land. That government forest law took it." The barkeep's long lips twisted, and a snort rumbled in his flattened nose.

"So anyways, the government grabbed this feller's land and gave it to some timber trust. But he wasn't in the mind of being cooperative, weren't willing to pack up and leave his homestead. So, story is, ole Clancy lent the timber trust some assistance. He never said exact what he done, but it must have been something bad because that homesteader fella burst in here like a crazed hornet. Big Jed the bouncer threw him out into the street. They was busting up the chairs."

The law the barkeep was talking about was the 1898 Forest Reserve Act. Another version of a dirge sung by many a man these days, this time thanks to the greedy timber barons who used the law to shove homesteaders out of the woods and into poverty. These new-minted homeless complained that the law was nothing but legalized stealing by timber companies who got the timber land at the same time they decimated their small scale competitors. Now there's a sword that cuts both ways. No Washington politician heard the complaints. One scrawl of the president's pen and, four years later, the timber trust was well on its way to controlling every cuttable tree in the country.

Sage glanced over his shoulder at the faces of Slap Jack's patrons. More than one of them was likely trying to drown his can't-do-nothing fury over that theft of both land and livelihood.

"Remember how the politicians and the newspapers kept saying the Act would create national forest preserves for our children and their children?" he asked the barkeep.

The barkeep nodded, flicking the tip of his dirty rag in the direction of a circling housefly. "Yup. But, my sister's husband learned the hard way that law weren't nothing more than a Baumhauer timber grab. Sis don't even know where he is nowadays. Ain't nothing left of their sweet little place except acres of stumpy clear cuts. Preservation, ha!" He snapped the towel again, only this time the target was imaginary.

The name had shifted Sage's thoughts onto another track. Baumhauer, that was the company that Welker worked for. So, Baumhauer was one of the timber companies snatching up huge blocks of the "preserved" forest in the Pacific Northwest. They were paying just pennies per thousand board feet. Therein lay the trick. The federal Forest Service would only sell timber rights in huge blocks so that only the really big companies could afford to bid. This forced thousands of little gippo loggers out and on down the road.

Sage stared down into the pale murk inside his glass. It had become a night of strange coincidences. He'd never thought of Baumhauer and now the name had surfaced twice this evening, in two different contexts. These musings cut off when he realized that the barkeep was watching him–but then he saw that sympathy warmed the other's normally remote, bulging eyes. The barkeep likely surmised it was a similar sour memory that had planted the frown on Sage's face.

"When did all that happen to that Silverton feller?" Sage asked.

"'Bout three months ago or so."

"I thought Clancy'd been working as a railroad bull."

"Clancy'd work for anybody doing anything. Railroading was just one of the jobs he done. He'd a been a rich man if he hadna liked his drink and his women so much. His passin's gonna leave pockets a bit lighter around here."

"So who was that homesteader feller? He still around?"

"He's a Scot name of Colin MacKenzie. Never seen him after that time Jed threw him out. Heard Clancy say MacKenzie is working up north in the woods. Somewheres around Centralia, I think he said. Anyway, there ain't been no trouble from MacKenzie since, that I know of."

A speculative look came to the barkeep's eyes. Sage's interest in Steele and MacKenzie had become too marked. It was time to fling down a red herring. "What do you hear about work in the woods? Know of any good outfit needing help?" Sage asked.

He lingered a few minutes more, nursing the beer and jawing on about potholes and prostitutes until he thought his interest in Steele and MacKenzie had dwindled in significance. It would be safer if the barkeep didn't think to remark, later on, about how that John Miner fellow was asking pointed questions about Clancy Steele and his enemies.

❁ ❁ ❁

Midnight was long dead when Sage finally left Slap Jacks. Late as it was, he knew that Clara, the prostitute who'd seen the murderers, would still be working. She was his only hope of getting a description of Steele's killers. The establishment's namesake, Halloran, squatted just inside the door. Behind a counter that had shed its varnish years ago, the owner's doughy body overwhelmed a stool top, his short forearms crossed atop his belly in an unconvincing show of superiority. Sage tossed fifty cents at the man, forcing him to lunge for the coins. In return, Sage received grudging directions to a numbered cubicle on the second floor. He climbed the narrow stairway, trying not to touch the filthy walls. At the top, a single gas jet sputtered at each end of the long hallway, providing the only illumination. Wouldn't want to make it easy for the customers to identify each other.

Sage passed curtained doorways, barely able to read the metal numbers tacked haphazardly to their lintels. Murmurings, groans and snores filtered through the ragged curtains. Another profitable night for that bloated pig down below.

At the curtained opening into Clara's crib, Sage tugged his hat lower on his forehead before rapping his knuckles against the door frame.

A female voice, hoarse from opium use, called out, "Come in, if you please, sir."

The gloom he found behind the curtain made the hallway seem bright. Inside, the only light came from the uncovered rectangle of an open window. Sage waited until his eyes adjusted. The space was smaller than a horse stall. In one corner stood a wooden fruit crate, storage for the girl's meager possessions. Overhead, chicken wire stretched across the tops of the crib walls to discourage sneak thieves from climbing over while the girls and their customers slept. The wood partitions separating the cribs were crate-thin, less substantial than the walls in a seashore changing booth. Despair hung in the air, a mix of unwashed bodies and filthy bed linens combined with the cloying stench of opium and tobacco smoke. Still, working from a crib inside Halloran's was a better fate than plying the trade from doorways.

Rustling at his side made him turn toward the rusty iron bedstead that filled two-thirds of the narrow floor. There, a figure reclined, eyes cavernous as a skull's. The sight left him speechless until his pupils fully dilated and her features resolved into a face more distinctly human.

"Do you have a candle?" he asked.

"Yes, there's a candle but there ain't no matches. We don't need a light."

"Ah, but I'm a man who likes to see the lady he's talking to." Sage pulled a match safe from his trouser pocket, selected a few matches, and reached forward in the dark to place them in her hand. He stepped back, outside the range of flaring match and candlelight.

The flame's gold failed to gild the haggard features of the girl child who lay upon the cot. Her dark eyes looked like sunken bruises. Her nose had been broken so many times that it was bulbous above narrow lips spread wide in the trembling rictus of a smile. The ribs of her chest showed knobby white beneath the translucence of her pale, sweating skin. Her tiny breasts were exposed, drooping indifferently toward a mid section creased by dirt-blackened wrinkles. His heart clenched with pity. She could be no more than fifteen.

She bore his scrutiny for a minute, then pulled the faded dressing gown tight around her neck. "Please mister, take me. I need the money real bad."

Sage found his voice but kept it low. "Don't worry, Clara. I'm not here for sex, but I'll give you more than Halloran will pay you if you'll just talk to me."

"Talk? You want me to talk dirty?" Her smile widened, showing gums holding more gaps than ivory.

"No, not that kind of talk." He took a quarter from his pocket and tossed it toward her. Her hands scrabbled among the bedclothes to find it. When she looked up, he said, "Folks say you saw the killers running down that alley there." He gestured toward the window opening. "Tell me about them."

"They was just two men, that's all I seen."

Sage moved to the window to look down into the alley. Each end opened onto the greater illumination of a street. "Think back. How tall were they?"

The girl attempted to squeeze her eyes closed, an opium-parody of concentration. "I'm thinkin' they be one tall and one short."

Sage didn't like that description. It fit Matthew and Knute. "Is there anything else you remember about them?"

"One of them wore some kind of cap, the tall one. I saw it when they come out the alley into the street there at the end."

"Do you remember anything else?"

Clara opened her mouth as if to say something. Then her eyes widened and her gaze slid past him, focusing momentarily on someplace far outside the room. When she shifted her attention back to him she said only, "Nope, that's all I remember. Like I told the police, it were dark and they moved real fast. They was running."

Sage tried another tack. "Clara, did you know Clancy Steele?"

The girl fingered the crooked bridge of her nose. "Know him? He's one of them that gave me this nose. That Clancy Steele was mean, mean to the bone."

"Did you see him much?"

"There for a while he came around a lot, but he liked to use his fists whenever he drank. I just couldn't take it no more. 'No more,' I told Mr. Halloran." Clara raised her small pointed chin as if reliving a grand defiance.

Sage looked away, giving her that moment of remembered strength. "Before you stopped seeing Clancy, he ever talk to you about his work?" he asked.

"Did he ever. To hear him talk, he spent all his time with them fancy toffs. He always talked about their fine houses and his doin' things with 'em."

"Clancy ever say what kind of things he and these fancy toffs were doing together?"

"He never talked directly about what he was up to. He liked being mysterious. Just sometimes, when he was heading out of town, he'd brag on it being some special job for one of them that lived in a big house up on the hills."

"What about his railroad work?"

"He'd talk about that some. Used to brag about the hobos he'd beat up."

"He ever speak the name of Colin MacKenzie?"

She squeezed her eyes shut again to show an effort to remember. "Yeh, I think once he spoke that name. It were something about a fire. He laughed 'bout that. I remember that night 'cause he brought me this dressing gown here. It were new when he brought it. He was tossing money around that night."

"Is there anything else Clancy told you about the fancy toffs or about people he thought were mad at him?"

She laughed. "Nah, I told you all what I remembered about Clancy and his toffs. Everybody that knew him hated him. He liked it that way. Like I tole you, he was mean, real mean. Ain't nothing more to say about Clancy. That's all I know."

Sage accepted that declaration, thinking he could always return if he thought of any more questions. He pulled a Liberty dollar from his pocket and tossed it toward her. This time she caught the coin. "Gee, thanks, mister." For a moment, childlike wonder softened her face.

Sage looked down at her, feeling the urge to raise up her frail body and carry her from the crib, from this life, into sunshine and back to her lost childhood. Instead, he pulled his hat brim down and sidled past her to the door. "Thank you, Clara. I may be back. Let's keep our little talk a secret."

"Whatever you say, mister," she responded in a distracted voice. He was already forgotten in the anticipation of the opium to come. He let the curtain fall shut behind him.

As he headed down the hall, she raised her voice to say, "You just might want to come back later on – maybe I'll be remembering something else."

Sage paused, then descended the stairs. In the lobby he walked quickly past an unmanned front counter on his way to the street. Odd. Halloran was known to rarely leave his post – too afraid someone would hook up with one of the girls without giving him his cut. Maybe he was tending to an unruly customer, Sage thought. Yet, the place seemed quiet. More quiet than usual. Must be the lateness of the hour. Or, probably Halloran was visiting the necessary, he decided.

Outside, Sage slowly paced the alley from one end to the other, searching the mucky ground for any evidence left by the two fleeing men. On his second pass, he paused to look up at Clara's window. The candle still burned because he could see a huge black silhouette framed by its light. Sage jumped backward into the darkened doorway of an adjacent building. When he looked up again, the silhouette was gone.

A high shriek sounded before it was abruptly pinched off. It came from Clara's open window. He bolted toward Halloran's front door. As Sage charged up the stairs, he noticed Halloran was still absent from his post. Striding down the hallway, he heard the thud of running feet followed by the slam of a distant door at the far end of the corridor. Sage whipped aside the curtain into Clara's crib. Horror froze him to the spot.

Flickering candlelight glistened in the dark red blood that had gushed from a gaping wound across her throat. Sage stared at the thin face gone ghost-white beneath red smears of rouge, lipstick, and blood. Her mouth gaped slack, like a child's in sleep. His gaze wandered to her hand. Glinting between her curled fingers were the two coins he'd just given her. Tears pricked at his eyelids and his shaking hand moved to smooth her hair. Poor, poor Clara. Whose daughter was she? Would they ever know what had happened to her? Would anyone mourn her?

As he stood in the bleak silence, icy realization washed through him. He couldn't be found in this room. Too much was at stake. If he was to find the murderer and clear Matthew he needed to stay free and unidentified. Not to mention the fact that he couldn't compromise his work for St. Alban, although that mission seemed more remote with every passing minute of this awful night. Still, if he lost his anonymity, he'd be useless for both tasks.

Sage leaned down toward the dead girl. "I'll find him, little one. I promise, I'll find him, and he'll pay. You didn't deserve this," he whispered. Then he made for the stairs.

Halloran had reclaimed his post behind the counter, his head bent close to a newspaper. With luck, that low-hanging head meant the man was drunk. Sage kept his face averted and slipped into the street. Heart thudding, he headed toward the trap door and the sanctuary at tunnel's end. He moved heavily, his steps weighed down by the realization that the only person who'd seen Clancy Steele's murderers was dead. So, even if he found the killers, there'd be one hell of a problem proving it to the authorities' satisfaction.

SEVEN

SAGE STEPPED FROM behind the tapestry on the third floor into a thick quiet. Inside his room, a low flame flickered inside the oil lamp chimney next to his bed. A pitcher, basin, and fresh towels lay neatly arranged atop the bureau. His mother dozed in the rocking chair near the window. Sleep and the dim light gentled her face although, in repose, deep lines framed the slight downturn of her mouth. Not for the first time he wondered what memories shaped her dreaming. He'd lived with her until he was nine and then didn't see her again until two years ago when he'd reached thirty. Unknown to him, that had been the condition the mine owner placed on his fostering. So, in many ways this woman was a stranger.

They had arrived separately here in Portland, less than a year after their reunion. They'd been on the run from another mine owner's thugs. By their lights, Sage had been too successful in the activities in Appalachia that he'd undertaken at St. Alban's behest. Following St. Alban's instructions, Mae Clemens had arrived four weeks after Sage. She'd gone through the motions of applying for the position of dining room manager in Sage's new restaurant. To the world outside Mozart's and even to Ida and Knute, Mae Clemens appeared to be nothing more than a loyal, very competent employee. Only Fong knew about the mother-son relationship. It seemed a silly pretense but St. Alban had insisted.

Tonight, a half-mended bedsheet lay across her lap, a fallen needle glinting in its folds. Her big-knuckled hands were motionless for a change. No unguent could transform those mitts into the satiny delicate hands of a pampered society matron. They'd endured too many years of scrubbing, chopping wood, and sewing hours into the night. The mine explosion that had killed her brother and nephew had left Mae Clemens and her son on their own and destitute. There'd been no husband. Sage's father had disappeared years before.

From the sadness in her eyes, when he caught her studying him, Sage knew that, during their years of separation, she had agonized over the choice she'd been forced to make between keeping Sage with her in poverty or handing him over to the mine owner for fostering. Still, she was tough. Unlike poor Clara, Mae Clemens, had taken a different trail. Alone, impoverished and abandoned she had not yielded to despair. She'd worked hard, kept hoping and welcomed Sage with open arms and streaming eyes when he'd finally sought her out.

Not even the largess from Sage's Klondike strike changed her work ethic. She labored endlessly as she always had. When he'd teased her over it, she'd told him "some folks are born to be ants, some are born to be butterflies. I'm an ant." Regardless, over the past two years he'd come to realize that Mae Clemens was a woman of remarkable constancy—hard working, plain speaking, without pretense. In fact, as Fong might say, she was a woman who was "unbreakably" herself.

"What are you gawking at, you silly boy? Are you trying to will me awake?" Sleep still fuzzed her voice even as she straightened and carefully pulled wide her apron to find the dropped needle.

Sage started at her words, then smiled because she'd caught him at his reverie, and because she'd be embarrassed if she knew she'd been the focus of his thoughts.

"Fong have any luck finding Matthew?" he asked as he plunged his hands into the basin and began to scrub the grime from his face and hair.

"Luck called on him. One of Fong's tong members intercepted Matthew and Knute on their way back here. The man steered them to Fong's place instead. They'll be staying there until you can talk to them. Later today. After you've slept some." The emphasis she gave the last four words left no room for opposition. She must have noticed his washing hands hesitate and somehow divined that he was at a point of weary unwillingness to head out into the night again.

His exasperated sigh, therefore, was merely for show. "So, we found them before the police did. That's good news. I wish my night had been as successful." He told her of Clara's murder and of his hasty retreat from the scene to avoid the police. To his ears, his detailing of Clara's death sounded flat, emotionless. Inexplicably, he was unable to communicate the depth of sorrow, the horror he'd felt when he'd looked into the childlike face of that dead girl.

Mae Clemens was not misled. She gestured him to the table and poured a shot of whiskey. "Poor child," she said softly, putting the glass into his hand.

Sage felt momentarily confused. Was she referring to Clara or to him? A lump in his throat made him swallow hard, so that an inarticulate throat clearing was his only reply before he threw the whiskey back.

She reached across the small round table to touch his wrist, her big bony fingers strong and warm with life. "You showed her kindness, Sage. Be thankful for the kindness you showed that poor girl."

Words evaded him, and his eyes stung. He was afraid to speak. When he could speak, he sidestepped that treacherous emotional ground. "I don't know what Clara saw in the alley tonight. I think it was more than she said. The opium had her pretty bad. So, I'm thinking she wanted to string me along a bit, get more money from me later. Now I'll never know. I'll have to find some other way to discover who ran down that alley."

When, at long last, Sage slid beneath the quilted comforter, he had to pull it over his head because dawn's light was beginning to penetrate the window lace. Somehow, talking with his mother had lessened the chill that Clara's death had driven deep into his bones. His mind felt in equilibrium once again.

His last thoughts before sleep concerned the soirée and the questions it had raised. They'd talked about that. While he slept, his mother would send a cipher letter to her "Cousin Hildreth" in Telluride, Colorado. From that mail drop, the letter would find its

way to St. Alban. For two years the ruse had worked, with her letters taking less than a week to reach their true recipient. Hopefully,
St. Alban would know who Otis Welker was and, more important,
what Welker was doing in Portland.

❀ ❀ ❀

The soft clink of tableware brought Sage awake. Fong was
setting a plate of food upon the table, his shoulders moving with
customary deliberation beneath the shiny rope of his raven queue.
Each dish and utensil was precisely placed, as if the man were putting the final touch on one of his watercolors.

Fong glanced over and saw Sage watching. "Ah, good. Your
eyes open. Now you eat."

Sage threw back the covers. "Thank you, Mr. Fong. I'm so
hungry that I'm not even going to complain about your acting the
servant. So, how'd you go about locating Knute and the boy?" he
asked, sitting down to a plate of steak and eggs.

"First, I look and not find them. So, I pass word to my cousins, ask them to look. Afterwards, I come back here. Then my good
wife sent message Knute in my house, with boy. Before I could go
to them, police came here once again. This time they demand to
search the whole building from top to bottom."

"Mother didn't tell me the police came a second time." Sage
took a bite of toast and chewed it thoughtfully, "But then, we had a
lot of other things to talk about."

It seemed to Sage that Fong's eyes glowed with a sympathetic
light but the other man only said, "Could be your mother not want
for you to worry just before you sleep."

Sage reached for another piece of toast, "That's probably true.
So, tell me what happened with the police."

"They came. They said they were going to search every floor,
but your mother said no searching this floor. Many loud angry
words. In end, police searched cellar, restaurant, and Mister Knute's
floor, but of course Knute and boy not here. Your mother not let
police onto this floor. She stood at top of stair like rock." Fong
mimed Mae Clemens standing with arms folded, legs wide apart,
feet anchored to the floor, chin in the air.

Sage laughed. Fong's little dramatization was most likely accurate. "She is formidable," he agreed. "And she was right. We don't want the police searching here or thinking that they can anytime they want."

Fong nodded. "I think same thing. Maybe we should shove big wardrobe across staircase opening, here on third floor. Police will come back here soon."

As he ate, Sage thought about the secret staircase and about that rainy night last fall, when they'd learned that they had failed to keep its existence secret from Fong. On that night, near the tunnel's entrance, a violent blow had knocked Sage to the ground. Four pairs of boots had slammed into his head and ribs, ribs that still tweaked protest on damp winter mornings. Curled into a ball, his cheek scraping across alley filth, Sage realized the rhythmic kicking had ceased. From behind swelling eyelids, Sage saw the slight, unmistakable figure of Fong, his houseman, a relaxed silhouette in the alley opening. Fong advanced calmly toward Sage's attackers, hands hanging loosely by his side, his voice mildly advising the four to leave, to go away. Their response was raucous laughter.

Sage had groaned and shut his eyes, dreading the coming bloodbath. Chinese men never challenged white men and lived, especially a solitary Chinese man half the size of his four opponents. Sage struggled to raise himself, but the world swirled uncontrollably as soon as he lifted his cheek. He closed his eyes and listened helplessly as the attackers began their growling taunts.

A thud followed a gasp as a heavy body hit the alley wall. Maybe Fong was already unconscious. Maybe they'd leave off hitting the small man. Sage forced his swollen lids open. To his surprise it was not Fong's face that lay just inches from his, stink-spewing mouth agape in pain and surprise. It was the face of a bearded white man Sage had never seen before. Sage looked up from that face just in time to see Fong step forward and seemingly offer to shake the hand of another attacker. That man lunged forward, grabbing at the small hand, only to find himself flying through the air and hitting the dirt with a crunching thud. How could that be? Fong's only action had been to step aside and turn slightly away. Sage had closed his eyes, even shook his head, trying to make sense of what he was seeing. That last movement sent him spiraling into deep blackness.

When he came to, the faces of his mother and Fong hovered between his face and the ceiling of his own room. Then they smudged into haze. Full consciousness came hours later, along with pain and his demands for an explanation—which Fong gave freely. It seemed he'd known of the tunnel for months. He also knew that Sage frequently walked Portland's streets dressed as a workingman or hobo. Out of curiosity he'd been following Sage the night before. His curiosity had saved Sage from a savage beating or maybe worse.

At the end of Fong's confession, Sage and his mother exchanged a glance. Mae Clemens then told the Chinese man about their mission for St. Alban and what she and Sage were trying to accomplish. When she had finished, Fong said nothing for such a long moment that the tick of the parlor clock seemed to grow louder. Just as Sage and his mother exchanged worried looks, Fong began to talk quietly, as if to himself.

"What you say gives me problem, Mr. Adair. I planning to quit soon, open my own fine dining Chinese restaurant. It will be first one in Portland for rich white people, provide many jobs. Now, maybe my restaurant need to wait. I, Fong Kam Tong. I am warrior trained." The small man drew himself erect, pride suffusing his face. It was the first time he allowed them to see his resolve, his tremendous will.

Fong continued, "You fight against same kind of men who hurt my family and hurt my people here in 'Gold Mountain.'" His face tightened as he hissed that alternative name for America–the alluring description that had brought thousands of Chinese halfway around the world to experience lives of bitter disappointment and worse.

Sage didn't wonder what harm Fong meant. He'd seen enough of it firsthand. The Chinese in America were expendable labor, barely earning slave wages, crammed into tenements one atop the other, cut off from family, friends, and the love of women because only Chinese men were allowed to immigrate or chance illegal border crossings. Recent Chinese exclusion laws had legalized the abuse and made it worse by demonizing the Asians.

"Greedy men," Fong spat the words, "they take everything, leaving us nothing but scraps to fight over like hungry dogs. I have much anger—mountains of anger toward these men."

Fong's calm, self-possessed exterior had never hinted at the rage they were witnessing. Mae Clemens' stunned face reflected the surprise Sage himself felt.

Fong's next words were equally unexpected. "Do you think Mister St. Alban would allow me to join you in the fight?" he asked. "Would he let a Chinaman help out?" Then he looked abashed and hastily added, "That is, if you and Mrs. Clemens want my help?"

Sage responded instantly, certain of his mother's agreement, "Of course we would. We'd welcome your help." Sage reached out to grab Fong's hand and grimaced with pain. "It's evident we could use it from what these ribs of mine are telling me." Still Sage paused to consider whether St. Alban would reject a Chinese man's help. Some of the early labor organizations had led anti-Chinese riots, spurred on by sinking wages and prejudice. But no, St. Alban was one of the labor leaders who thought every worker, no matter his color, should belong to a union.

"I am sure that St. Alban would welcome your help, Mr. Fong," Sage responded confidently. "And call me 'Sage,' that's the name my friends use."

Fong smiled wide and his eyes sparkled. "So what is our next mission, Mr. Sage? Besides you getting another kick in head, I mean."

Sage laughed at Fong's joke even though laughing hurt like hell.

Thus, a deal had been struck at Sage's bedside that night. Fong shelved his plans for a fancy Chinese restaurant and became a full partner in their clandestine activities. He brought much to the enterprise. Foremost was the intelligence-gathering network he possessed in the form of his many trusty "cousins." These were men who belonged to a Chinese fraternal organization that Fong called his "tong." He also began to teach Sage the ancient Chinese fighting art called the "snake and crane." It was that seemingly effortless fighting technique that Fong had used to vanquish Sage's four attackers. Effortless only in appearance. Sage was just now, after nine months of training, starting to realize its amazing potential and the extreme challenge in doing it right.

Fong returned to the room just as Sage rose from the breakfast table and started to dress. "So, Mr. Fong, any regrets?"

Fong looked at him sharply. "Regrets?"

"You know, the fancy Chinese restaurant, still working in Mozart's, and all this late-night skulking about?"

Fong chuckled softly. "I like skulking about. Reminds me of earlier days—when I was young and new in America."

Sage paused over a button as he thought, not for the first time, that maybe it was better not to know too much about Fong's earlier days. There were times when he'd seen Fong's eyes turn as cold and black as those pebbles the Chinese moved around their game boards spread atop wooden fruit crates on Chinatown's sidewalks. Sage's fingers finished their buttoning. "Mother tells me that Knute and the boy are at your house. We'd better move them. The police might think of you, or maybe someone saw them entering Chinatown and thought it strange enough to report," he said.

"It is no problem, Mr. Sage. Mr. Knute and boy are no longer there. I moved them to my cousin's house on hill near the vegetable gardens this morning, very early."

"Well done. How did you manage to move them without anyone seeing?"

"In cousin's vegetable wagon. He deliver fresh vegetables to provision shop and carry away meat." Fong was referring to the small store he and his wife owned and that she operated a few streets away in Chinatown.

Sage glanced toward the man who was quietly stacking dishes and, sure enough, he caught the satisfied smile on Fong's face at his own sly witticism. Sage was becoming more adept at catching those slight changes of expression on a face he once believed to be impervious to all emotion.

"I'll need to talk to the boy right away."

Fong shook his head. "You must wait until darkness. No white men travel near the gardens once sun goes down. We must wait. Be safer then."

Sage wasn't happy with Fong's declaration but he accepted the reasoning. In the daylight, Sage's entry into the Chinese gardens would be noted and thought curious by the white people strolling the neighboring streets. After dark, however, whites tended to avoid the area, fearful of the "heathen" Chinese who dwelt there in patched up shanties.

So, Sage finished dressing and helped Fong drag a heavy
wardrobe across the entrance to the hidden staircase. Descending
the stairs to assume his role as the urbane restaurant host, Sage
thought about how comfortably the three of them worked together.
A small team certainly, but a team in which every member pulled
his or her weight.

Once at the ground floor, Sage paused on the stair landing
to don yet another of his roles. Smile white, wide and warm he
stepped forward to greet a group of customers arriving for mid-
afternoon tea.

Innumerable hours later, when the June dusk had faded into
moonless night, Sage and Fong left the restaurant. Sage exited down
the secret stairway. As he descended, he heard the wardrobe rumble
as his mother and Fong pulled it back across the opening. Fong
would also be leaving soon, slipping out the kitchen door. They'd
be meeting up a few blocks distant.

The man standing in an empty storefront doorway growled
in his throat when he saw the Chinese man leave by the restaurant's
kitchen door, pause to look into a neighboring shop window, and
then shuffle his slippered feet toward Chinatown. "Cocky Chink,
got himself a paying job when white men are standing on street
corners begging for work," he mumbled. "My sharp friend here sure
would like to have a go at that girly pigtail." But the man stayed put.
He knew his orders and he'd not disobey them.

The second man, the one watching the front of the restaurant,
had been standing motionless for over an hour. Above him, on the
building's third floor, gas lamplight flickered at every window. He
grumbled to himself, "This is stupid. Ain't nobody going nowhere.
They're settling in for the night." But he, too, stayed put, like his
compatriot at the kitchen door—and for the same reason. He remained in place until a half-hour after all the third floor lights were
extinguished. Then he straightened and stepped from the dark entrance of the ironworks shop. Bending to light a cigar beneath the
corner lamppost, he failed to see a lace curtain on the third floor
twitch aside, and fall back once his flipped match hit the gutter.

❀ ❀ ❀

Sage trailed Fong from the other side of the street as they both made their way toward the Chinese garden plots. Sage felt foolish as he followed the straight back of his friend and teacher. Still, white and yellow men couldn't stroll together on Portland's streets without attracting attention at a minimum or, not unfrequently, outward hostility. The two men met up at a narrow dirt lane where it began its meander among twenty or so rough-planked shanties. These one-room huts, cobbled together out of cast-off lumber, clung to a hilly slope just west of downtown Portland. Below them, neat gardens terraced downward like giant green steps. The character of this place in the moonless night was difficult to see, but the mingled scents of joss sticks, garlic, and ginger left no doubt of its oriental sensibility. They were a guarantee that he'd encounter no other white men here tonight except for Knute and the boy, Matthew.

Fong scratched softly on a door frame before entering the shanty, Sage close on his heels. Inside, the only light came from a flickering wick floating in a small bowl of oil. It sat on a rickety wooden table. Two ladder-back chairs, a tiny cookstove blackened to a sheen, a wooden soapbox, and a narrow cot against the far wall were the shanty's only other furnishings. Everything was as spotless as the old, cheap and cast-off bits allowed.

Knute and the boy sat side-by-side on the cot, their eyes wide and fearful. Undoubtably this Asian world was beyond their ken. Knute's face instantly transformed once he recognized first Fong and then Sage. "Oh thank our Lord to be. You two have finally come. I wasn't sure how much longer we could stay here in this place without jumping out from our skins. Godless chantings coming through every wall and the smells–like nothing human. The shivers have been a chasing one another up and down my spine, I'm here to tell you."

Sage glanced at Fong and was relieved to see the other man's eyes twinkling. Fong, too, caught the absurdity of Knute making such an impolite declaration while speaking in his thick singsong Swedish accent. Besides, Knute harbored no meanness. And, in fact, he'd made no secret of the abiding admiration he felt toward Mr. Fong. An admiration that continued undaunted by the strange smells of Fong's infrequent cooking or when Fong's bamboo flute sent its slow, raspy croak floating down the stairs from Fong's rooftop perch.

Sage peered into the room's dark corners. Only the four of them were in the shanty. Fong noticed Sage's caution because he said, "I tell cousin it safer if he visit other cousin. No one else here." Fong bowed to Knute and then he opened the shanty door saying, "When I left Mozart's, a man was hiding in next doorway, near the kitchen. First I smell him, then I see him. Not a good man. So better I go watch outside." He slipped away, the rough wooden door closing soundlessly behind him.

EIGHT

NOW THAT THEY were alone, the desperation radiating from the two who sat before him on the cot was palpable. Doubt flooded Sage but he fought the urge to flee and stepped closer. He tried to compose his face, to hide the awful fear, or was it certainty, that he would never find Steele's, and now Clara's, killers. "Buck up," he scolded himself mentally, "It's not your important self whose got the most serious problem here."

Lifting the lamp from the table, Sage moved it to the soapbox next to the cot. Regardless of the outcome of this interview, Sage needed to see this boy's face better. Dragging a chair toward the cot, Sage sat, stretched his legs out before him and let the silence lengthen as he studied the young man whose problems had unexpectedly become his own.

Even in the dim light Sage saw that strain had washed the color from underneath the boy's freckles. Lank red hair hung around his narrow face, and the light blue eyes looking at Sage were red-rimmed and bloodshot.

Sage's throat seemed to close with an overwhelming desire to step no farther into a world filled with this boy's problems. Then he shook the thought loose for good. There'd be no backing out. There were decisions to make. If the boy had killed Steele, a good attorney and turning himself in might be the way to go. But, say he wasn't the murderer. Turn him in or hide him? Was this country kid tough enough to survive the city jail? Could he stand up to the criminals and cops who thought anyone in jail deserved whatever horror came his way? And if Matthew was innocent, was surrendering the best solution? Telling that truth would make little difference. The police would jump on the kid like starving fleas onto a dog. And, what about the others out there who needed questioning? Like Steele's "toff" acquaintances. Were they somehow involved? If so, that meant the potential for payoffs. How many underpaid policemen would resist the offer of extra money? He just couldn't guarantee that the boy would survive this jam if he turned himself in.

Sage spoke, the words issuing from him of their own accord, laced with a calm reassurance he didn't quite feel, "Matthew, I will try my best to help you. But first I need to understand what's happened to you these last few days."

Matthew nodded. With an adolescent Adam's apple bobbing in his skinny throat, he recounted the story of the train journey north. When his tale stumbled into the brutal death of his brother, the words choked off.

Knute moved closer to the boy until his work-scarred hands were patting the boy's hunched back. As Matthew struggled for composure, Sage relived a twenty-year-old memory of a time when sobs had choked his own throat—when no words were powerful enough to withstand that sudden, aching emptiness. So Sage waited, not speaking.

Matthew's next words came from behind hands cupped over his mouth as if what he had to say was too ghastly to let out. Though muffled, the boy's guilt was unmistakable. "Billy didn't want to ride the rods. I made him do it. I promised him that he would be safe, I . . ."

Sage jumped to derail that train of thought. Leaning over he put a hand on the boy's bony knee. "Your brother is not the first fellow Clancy Steele hurt that way," Sage said, "but you could never anticipate that another man could sink as low as Steele. Most folks riding the rods have never seen something that awful happen. Matthew, I need you to look at me and listen very carefully." Once the boy's sad, tear-filled eyes met Sage's, Sage continued. "You are not to blame. Steele is, and the men who hire people like Steele," Sage said these words with deliberate, measured force. He knew that the impressions this boy grabbed onto during these crucial first days would stick with him for the rest of his life. They would either temper him, make him stronger, by opening his eyes to the world's ways, or he'd be crippled forever.

Matthew searched Sage's face with a kind of desperate hope. His bottom lip began to tremble until gasping sobs tore through him, his body rocking over his knees, his hands clutching the top of his head as if he wanted to tear scalp from skull.

Knute began patting the boy's back again, impotent concern twisting his weathered face.

Sage waited again for the sobs to subside. "Matthew, tell me what happened after you went up to bed last night," he said.

Matthew flicked tears away with the back of one hand. "I laid there in the dark, but every time I shut my eyes I saw Billy's face and that damn hunk of metal bouncing around him. Pretty soon, my only thought was to find that . . . "—hate reddened the boy's face and narrowed his eyes—"you know who. So anyway, I got up, snuck down the stairs and slipped out without anyone seeing me. I asked some folks on the street about Clancy and they pointed me toward the rail yard. Once I got there, I found that saloon where I'd seen him before. He wasn't there. I asked about him, but the feller told me Steele'd just left."

"Who'd you ask? The bartender?"

"No, the man I asked wasn't behind the bar. Someone hollered at him and called him 'Jeb' or some such name."

"I know who that man was—the bouncer. Where'd you go after that?"

"I looked in every bar down around the rail yards but Clancy Steele weren't there. So I thought I'd look in the places closer to Aunt Ida's. That's when Uncle Knute found me and we headed on back to the restaurant."

Knute nodded his agreement with Matthew's account of events, then cleared his throat. "When we come near the restaurant, a Chinese man steps out and tells us we should go to Mr. Fong's provision store instead. So we go there."

Fong must have planted his cousins around the restaurant to warn Knute and the boy away. Another example of Fong's ability to anticipate and efficiently provide exactly what they needed.

Sage spoke gently to Matthew. "So you didn't set eyes on Steele last night?"

"No sir, I never saw him but that one time right after I met up with the hobos by the rail yard." Matthew's back straightened, and he clenched his fists at his sides until they were white bones against the dark blanket. His face was set, his eyes fierce. "I ain't gonna lie, sir. If I'd found him, I would have killed him. Afore God, I held murder in my heart. I'm glad he's dead. I wish he could die twice!"

Sage believed him and sent a thankful prayer winging out into the universe—toward a deity in whom he somewhat believed. Although the boy was tall, Steele was the heavier, more experienced brawler. Matthew likely would have died had he found Steele.

Knute's steady gaze over the boy's shoulder told Sage that the other also realized how close Ida had come to losing both nephews that day.

Matthew's declaration answered one question. At fifteen years of age, he was too naive, too confident in his own immortality. He'd never survive the hardened criminals he'd encounter in the city jail, some worse than Steele, even if the police kept their fists to themselves. Sage stood up and stepped outside to think. When Fong moved out from the blackness of the porch across the lane, Sage beckoned to him. "Mr. Fong, may the boy stay here until tomorrow?"

"Yes, I already tell cousin better he stay away, make visit with other cousin last two days."

Sage indulged in a brief flare of self-pity before re-entering the shanty. Why now? Months and months of work. Making connections, planning, and dammit, succeeding at last in gaining the acceptance of Portland's high society. Now all their effort was being sidetracked by a kid who should have stayed home, slitting open fish bellies in a cannery beside a backwater bay.

Shame overcame his self-pity. Sage Adair, revolutionary hero. Running here and there rescuing the amorphous masses but turning your back on a scared kid desperate for help. If that's not a phony, just what is? Sage sighed and opened the door.

Knute still sat with his arm draped across the boy's shoulders. Normally it would have been a stretch because of their size difference. A small man with broad shoulders, a long torso and stumpy legs, Knute looked like some kindly dwarf on the pages of a children's book. Grief, however, had hunched Matthew's long frame into a knot so small that Knute could hold him. Knute's voice was a low rumble, his Swedish singsong as soothing as a lapping sea. The scene sent Sage back to those few minutes between supper and bedtime when Sage's own uncle had sat, arm around Sage's shoulders, showing Sage how to sound out the words in the paper book.

Whose to say that saving this boy's life wouldn't end up being the most important mission of his own life? There is no way to answer that question now, but, if this is what the universe has dealt, then we'll just have to play the game, and we'll play to win! Sage concluded, doubt and regrets suddenly vanquished by that blaze of determination.

Sage cleared his throat and said, "Matthew, you need to be strong tonight. I'm going to try to sort this out but it may take some time. Unfortunately, you must stay here by yourself until tomorrow." He turned toward Knute. "Knute, you must go home so your absence isn't noticed. A witness supposedly said two men, one short and one tall, killed Steele. So the police can't find the two of you together."

They acquiesced to Sage's plan without a word. Exhaustion had rendered them incapable of protest. Minutes later, the three men slipped out the end of the lane, heading east toward downtown. Behind them, the dim glow inside the shanty winked out.

"Mr. Sage, Mr. Sage, please get up." The urgency in Fong's voice snapped Sage to wakefulness.

"What is it? What is it?" Sage was out of bed and pulling on his trousers before he thought of moving.

"The police, they are downstairs. They want to search again. The lady mother, she need your help."

Sage's fingers stumbled in their buttoning. Were the police here for Matthew or, and this second thought sent chills scurrying up his spine, were the police here because, in his hasty exit from

Halloran's, Sage had not noticed a witness, someone who'd recognized him despite his disguise? He'd have to brazen it out.

Sage descended to the second floor where the air was pungent with the smell of woolens kept too long from airing. Brawny cops, outfitted in brass-buttoned dark blue uniforms and beehive helmets swarmed up and down the stairs, trudging in and out of Ida and Knute's second floor living quarters. Some carried long-handled axes. Sage paused on the staircase until he spotted an erect figure wearing the only uniform sporting two rows of shiny buttons and a gold star on its left breast. Rapid-fire orders were issuing from beneath that officer's sweeping mustache even as his imperious finger directed the men about him. Sage approached.

"Excuse me, I'm John S. Adair. What is this commotion about, if I may ask?"

The policeman's sneering examination of Sage shifted into cautionary politeness once he'd taken in the quality of Sage's suit. He said, "I'm Detective Crenshaw. Well, sir, we're looking for a murdering fugitive. We think he's hiding in this building. Are you the landlord?"

"Yes, I am the landlord." Sage hoped his face didn't show the relief he felt at learning Matthew apparently remained the only target of police interest. "So you're looking for the cook's grandson or nephew or some such relation?"

"Her nephew, sir. His name is Matthew Mason."

"I believe I heard something about, ah . . . a killing of some railroad person, is that correct?" Sage casually dipped a hand into his inside coat pocket as he spoke. Pulling out a calfskin cigar case, he flipped it open, extracted a cigar, and offered the case to the detective.

"Why, thank you, sir." Crenshaw removed a cigar and leaned forward to let Sage light it before continuing, "We want the boy for more than just the one murder. He was asking after a fella and minutes later that fella ends up dead. Now we have a witness who places him at the scene of a second murder. This time a woman, a prostitute down near the yards, working out of place called Halloran's. The boy is on a rampage of some kind."

"A ram . . . page?" Sage's stumble wasn't feigned. His mind surged into racing mode. Although, he'd been rattled when he left

Halloran's, Sage was certain that Matthew had been nowhere about. In fact, someone killed Clara long after Matthew and Knute had been hidden away in Chinatown. So how could someone claim they'd seen him, let alone describe him?

Sage became aware that Crenshaw was studying him curiously and hastened to cover the gap. "Good Lord, and you think he's hiding here with his aunt? That won't do. I can't have that sort of thing going on here!" Sage raised his voice as if hysteria were imminent, "People won't patronize a restaurant that's harboring a murderer. I hope you're going to make certain he's not here!"

"Don't you worry, Mr. Adair. My men are searching every room thoroughly. If he's here, we'll find him and take him away. I hope you won't mind if we search the ground floor and cellar a little more closely, just in case the aunt has hidden him there?"

A twinge of concern tightened Sage's fingers on the cigar. The tunnel entrance. His mother had intended to stack wooden freight boxes in front of the provision shelf where it covered the tunnel opening as an extra precaution. Had she remembered? A trickle of sweat rolled down his back. He said, "Oh, no. I would appreciate it if you would search. It's only a matter of time before this whole sordid affair gets out. I must be able to assure my patrons that they are not exposing themselves to any danger from a murdering lunatic. I welcome a clean bill of health, so to speak. But, please, no axes."

Crenshaw nodded. "It doesn't look like the axes will be necessary since my men haven't found any suspicious hidey holes yet." He gestured up the stairs with the cigar Sage had given him. "What about the third floor, sir?"

"The third floor?" Sage lengthened his upper lip trying for a mix of surprise and alarm. "The third floor is my private domain," he protested. "I do not allow the restaurant cook access to my quarters. I keep the door to the third floor locked at all times, as do my servants, so I can positively assure you that he is not hiding there. Why, I just came from there and he was nowhere in sight."

"Still, sir . . . "

"No, no, absolutely not. I cannot allow strangers to paw among my things. I give you my word of honor that there is no one on the third floor other than my servants. And, certainly not that boy."

"Well, if you are absolutely certain of that, sir . . ."

"Yes, I am quite sure." Sage turned on the haughtiness that he knew Crenshaw expected as a sign of dismissal from a man of Sage's social stature. "I must take care of pressing business but please do leave word about the results of your search in the remainder of the building, Detective." Sage lowered his voice confidingly. "She is a very good cook, but I'm just not certain that I shall keep her on after this. I mean, after all, what will people think? They'll be wondering, 'Just what kind of people does she come from?'"

"Yes, sir, I know what you mean. Can't be too careful these days. Too many strangers running about on the street. I promise if we find anything, you'll hear about it right away."

Sage nodded and started down the stairs, but paused to ask, "Tell me, why do you think this nephew boy would kill a woman?"

"That's an easy one to answer. People tell us she saw who killed Clancy Steele. The boy was looking to cover his tracks." Crenshaw picked a piece of tobacco off his lower lip, then continued. "Besides, it's no never mind why he done it. Our witness saw him flee the scene right after she got murdered, running out of Halloran's like the devil was chasing him. The body was still warm and dripping, if you catch my meaning."

Revulsion shuddered through Sage. He let the revulsion show, knowing Crenshaw would mistake it for distressed sensibility, rather than an unbearable memory surging to the fore.

Sage gave a brisk nod and started down the stairs to the restaurant floor. Pausing mid-step, he turned to ask, "Are you married, Detective Crenshaw?"

A flicker of surprise raced across the other man's face. "Why, yes, sir, I married just last year."

"Well, do bring your bride in for supper some night soon. My pleasure to serve you – at no cost, of course. My way of showing you that I appreciate your courteous efforts here."

The man removed the cigar to grin, revealing a wide gap between his two front teeth. "Why, thank you, sir. I am most obliged. My wife has spoken favorably of your restaurant. We will be delighted, I am sure, to take you up on your invite."

His confrontation with the police at an end, Sage continued downstairs. After confirming with his mother—who was calmly folding linen napkins in the dining room—that she'd stacked boxed goods before the provision shelf in the cellar, he stepped out onto the sidewalk.

Turning toward the offices of *The Daily Journal,* Sage casually glanced around, looking for the watchers Fong and his mother had spotted the previous night. A furtive movement in a neighboring doorway was his reward. He allowed himself a satisfied smile. So, Mozart's remained under surveillance. Until he got a closer glimpse, he couldn't tell if the watcher came from the police. Somehow, he didn't think so. Why would the police still be standing watch if they were in the midst of searching his building? A sideways look, as he paused to relight his cigar, rewarded Sage with the sight of a roughly dressed man stepping out from the doorway. Sage strolled up the street while his ear tracked the man's steps down the wooden sidewalk. He was keeping pace, ten or so feet back. Sage's shoulder blades involuntarily squeezed themselves together to present a bony shield until he forced them to relax. The watcher was hooked and Sage didn't want this fish shook loose until they knew more about him.

NINE

Inside *The Daily Journal* offices, three men clacked away on writing machines. They nodded at Sage without pausing in their tapping. He was a familiar figure in their newsroom. The walled office of the newspaper's publisher, Ben Johnston, filled the farthest corner. Johnston was at his desk, slashing a nubby pencil across typed sheets, his tie askew beneath his closely shaven chin. He looked up when Sage closed the door. Sandy-haired, with penetrating blue eyes that were never at rest, Ben Johnston had hit Portland with a wallop, injecting some of Eastern Oregon's rambunctious vitality into the more staid life of the State's largest city.

Ben half rose, reaching across his desk to offer an ink-stained handshake. "John Adair! You're a sight for tired eyes. It's been a while since I've seen your face around here."

"Well, my excuse is business and other distractions. What's your's? I haven't seen your face in Mozart's for some time."

"The news business has gotten more competitive. Got to work harder to pull ahead," said Johnston. The *Journal's* competition was *The Portland Gazette*, longtime voice of the city's monied interests. The *Journal*, only few months old, took a different tack, offering what Johnston billed as the "common man's" perspective. Although still in its infancy, the *Journal's* unrelenting and irreverent depiction of city bigwigs and their backroom politics seemed to be striking a chord in the heads of many readers. And, Johnston was finding himself nearly mobbed by helpful informants eager to tell him which rocks needed overturning.

"How're the numbers, Ben?" Not an idle question. Johnston had convinced Sage to sink a sizeable chunk of his Klondike gold into the fledgling newspaper.

"Looking real fine, John. Subscriptions and advertising growing day by day. You want to take a look-see at the books?" Johnston pulled open a drawer and began to extract a red ledger book.

Sage put up a hand to halt the action. "Another time, maybe. I can't stay. I'm here because I need a favor from you but I don't want anyone to know my interest in it. You understand what I mean?"

Johnston straightened up, his eyes narrowing. "Something in it for the *Journal?*"

"Could be, but coaxing a story out of it might take a while. Thing is, I need some information from the police but I can't be the one asking."

"Seems to me this is a little jig we've danced before. Let me guess . . . you want me to send one of my reporters down to the station house to nose around, right?"

Sage nodded.

"But you aren't going to tell me why you're asking or what you think is going on. Right, again.?"

Sage grinned. "Yup, that's it. You game?"

Johnston signaled his agreement with a rueful lift of his eyebrows and dip of his head. Sage continued, "Someone murdered a young prostitute last night. Down near the rail yards. She worked out of Halloran's cribs. A police detective told me there was a witness to the murder. I need to know the name of that witness but I can't ask. Do you think one of your fellas could finagle that information out of his police contacts?"

"Well, that shouldn't be too hard. We'll give it a try. How about you check with me tomorrow?"

"Thanks, Ben. I appreciate it."

"You really aren't going to tell me anything more about it?"

"Can't just yet. I will tell you that I'm no mathematician but things just aren't adding up with this girl's murder. Like that Sherlock Holmes would say, 'Something is afoot.'"

"Just remember Adair, Holmes is a fictional character. Somebody tries to spike his investigation, no real blood is ever shed." Johnston leaned back in his chair, temporarily accepting Sage's reticence. "Same deal as always? I help you out and any story is mine first?" he asked.

"Always, Ben, always." Sage touched his forehead in a two-fingered salute.

He stepped outside into the sweet scent of roses. Big pinks had been planted curbside between the streets and sidewalks everywhere throughout the city in a civic campaign to highlight Portland's mild climate. The roses flourished unless one of the horses hitched to a curbside ring got a little too hungry. Sage paused, enjoying the mild warmth of the sun while allowing his watcher, if there was one, ample time to mark his presence. Then he set off at an amble. A few blocks from Mozart's, Sage waited on the corner watching old Henry Wemme putt-putt by in his Stanley Steamer Locomobile. The auto buggy drew attention up and down the street. Wemme knew well its impact, since "Willamette Tent and Awning Co." was prominently emblazoned on both doors and the contraption's rear hatch. Wemme rolled up the street like a mechanical Moses, snorting carriage horses hastily sidestepping out of his way.

As that noise quieted, a gaggle of street musicians began their cacophony to summon up a crowd they could lead into the nearest saloon. Once they'd tooted their "catch" through the swinging double doors, the band members would be rewarded with mugs of beer and a few coins. The set up explained why the temperance ladies were fighting to get street musicians banned.

As the players and their laughing entourage began to parade through the front door, a young girl slipped out the ladies' side entrance. She carried beer in a galvanized pail, no doubt for her dad's lunch. Her cheeks grew rosy with exertion as she tried to keep the pail's contents from sloshing onto her gingham dress. Down the block, she stopped before a mason who was smoothing mortar onto bricks. The man gently tugged one of her pigtails. He looked young, strong and healthy. Portland's expansion and his own skills would keep him working.

That's a lucky little girl, Sage thought. Sure she is, as long as her daddy's health holds, retorted the ever-present cautionary voice in his head. Irritated with himself, Sage looked away from the little girl and her father. There was that tendency of his to counter the purely positive with a dash of the negative. His mother said he could scare up a cloud in the bright blue sky. She was right, he supposed. Despair isn't the universal outcome of every life. Some people have comfortable, secure lives. Unbroken lives.

Unbroken. Unbreakedness. Yet another of Fong's enigmatic sayings had been left to rattle around in Sage's head like a rock in a sluice box. Fool's gold this time or the real thing?

The thwap of the saloon door jarred Sage loose from his revery. The musicians reappeared, jangling their tambourines, beer froth in their moustaches. Musical instruments clanking and tooting, they banged down the sidewalk to take up a post before another saloon.

Sage crossed the street and when he reached the other side, he glanced behind, gratified to see that his watcher had kept up.

※ ※ ※

Afternoon tea was just beginning when Sage reached Mozart's. He glanced into the dining room, then paused, checked by an unexpected sight. Arista Dunlop and two of her female friends sat together at a small table, heads craned forward and twisting from side to side as if to ensure that no one could hear their words. They looked like three long-necked geese in a gossiping gaggle. Catching sight of Sage sauntering toward them, they sprang apart, settling back into their respective chairs with little self-conscious twitches— a curl patted here, a lace cuff straightened there.

He doffed his bowler. "Lovely to see you, Mrs. Dunlop, ladies. How nice that you have joined us this afternoon. Beautiful day, isn't it?"

Arista laughed and reintroduced her two companions, whom he'd met at her soirée. Sage took the empty seat at their table and the women ordered their tea and confections.

After the waiter departed, Sage asked, "I am most curious about your conversation before I interrupted. Tell me, was the topic wicked?"

The three tittered, exchanging glances and letting Arista answer, "Oh, Mr. Adair, you'll think us naughty." The titters burbled up again.

"A little naughtiness gives life zest," Sage assured her.

Unable to resist, Arista began, "Well, Mrs. Nelson here was telling us that the, ah, shall we say, hostess of a certain, shall we say, ah, boardinghouse goes for carriage rides with, shall we say, her employees. And . . ."

Mrs. Nelson charged into the telling. "Land sakes, Arista, there's no need to talk delicate to Mr. Adair. He's not some schoolroom miss!" She looked at Sage. "Anyway, Mr. Adair, it wasn't because this bawdyhouse madam drove through town, bold as brass, that we were talking about her. Lord knows, there's one of those shameful houses on almost every corner, and the poor creatures must venture out sometimes. No, Mr. Adair, what we want to know is how in heavens can they afford the expensive clothes they wear? Why, their customers must be starving their poor families to pay for the likes of those ensembles!"

The third woman rushed to add, "Yes, Mr. Adair, I was saying that, this morning, I saw that madam woman wearing a blue Kimberly sister's day gown. I know it was one of the Kimberly's gowns because I recently looked at that very pattern in their shop, but the cost of making it up was much too dear. So how can these bawdyhouse women afford the latest dresses when we have to make do with last season's?"

Nonplused, Sage mentally thumbed through potential responses, searching for words that would be inoffensive but still near to honest.

Arista broke the awkward silence. "Oh my, ladies, we have embarrassed Mr. Adair by our naughtiness after all."

Sage found his thought. "Oh no, Mrs. Dunlop, I am not the least embarrassed. I was merely thinking that most of these women are poor. A few, I admit, appear to do well financially, but really, very few." He flashed them his toothiest grin. "So you needn't worry. I am sure there will be a sufficient number of gowns left to make your husbands periodically clutch their hearts with one hand and their wallets with the other."

The three laughed and in the pause that followed he said, "Mrs. Dunlop, your supper party the other evening was charming. I can't think of when I've passed a more enjoyable evening."

"Why thank you kindly, Mr. Adair. Your presence brought refinement to the gathering. Not everyone has attended an esteemed university and traveled extensively in Europe like you have." The two other women nodded eagerly.

"You are too kind," he responded. "I wondered, though, that Mr. Gilcrease was not present, since I know he is an associate of your husband."

"Mr. Gilcrease? Why yes, of course, he is a business associate. Perhaps though, Mr. Adair, you are being a bit too democratic. We don't open our home to just anyone on social occasions, you know."

"Well, maybe I have confused him with someone else. I thought banking was his business, east of the mountains?"

"Oh my, you are mistaken there. Mr. Gilcrease is some government functionary having to do with land or some such thing, right here in Portland."

"I must have mistaken him for someone else, then. By the way, that rib roast you served was absolutely delicious. Any chance Mozart's could have the recipe?"

❀ ❀ ❀

When Sage climbed to the third floor, Fong had already returned and was puttering about in Sage's room. Tossing his bowler onto the hat rack, Sage flung himself into a chair and propped his feet on the fender of the unlit potbellied stove. He stared gloomily at the vase of yellow roses atop its cold metal surface. Usually, flowers lightened his mood. These didn't.

Fong noticed. "Problem?" he asked.

"Nope. Everything is going quite well. I just talked with Arista Dunlop downstairs. You remember me telling you about that Gilcrease somebody they were whispering about? Got her to tell me who he was. She never even suspected that I was fishing."

"Ah." Fong's typical response.

"If it weren't for Arista Dunlop's frequent and favorable recommendations, Mozart's wouldn't have become so popular and I wouldn't be receiving invites to select soirées. The woman's gone out of her way to be kind."

"Ah." Fong said again and took the chair opposite Sage, an unusual action for him. He usually preferred to remain standing, both feet firmly planted.

"Yup. Our Mrs. Dunlop has been very helpful yet again. She has no idea her helpfulness might get her a stab in the back." Sage's long fingers fiddled with the paper knife that had been lying beside the vase. He stopped fiddling and looked at Fong. "So tell me, Mr. Fong, why, instead of being elated that I winkled the information from her, do I feel lower than a grass snake's belly?"

The fine lines around Fong's eyes deepened with sympathy. He sighed and said, "I have two thoughts. First thought is that to repay kindness with deception brings no honor. Second thought is that all war is deception."

Sage thought that over. "Both those thoughts seem true, Mr. Fong, yet contradictory. How does a person reconcile them inside himself?"

"Reconcile? What is the meaning of that word?" Fong asked.

"Maybe, I mean to be comfortable being deceptive, in acting without honor, in war."

Fong leaned forward to stroke a rose petal with the tip of his finger. "Uncomfortable is a better place to be, I think. Discomfort reminds man of responsibility. You must not forget. If you betray the lady's trust for a dishonorable outcome, then honor cannot be . . . recaptured."

"'Redeemed,' I think you mean."

"Ah yes, redemption."

"Mr. Fong, this conversation is not making me feel better."

"Sometimes that is how it is," Fong responded. "Maybe talking of other matter will make you feel better. You know how you like to mope."

"Good suggestion. So, tell me, did you see the little shadow trailing me on my walk about?"

"Ah yes, he followed you all morning. So I followed the man following you—a little dragon parade of three." Fong allowed himself a slight smile. "He was not the one from outside the kitchen door, the one whose smell goes before him. I think he is man your good mother saw standing across street from restaurant."

"Police, do you think?"

"No, I think not. When you came inside restaurant he walked to Portland Hotel, not to police station."

"Portland Hotel? That's where that man Welker is staying." Sage stared off into the distance, thinking about Welker and wondering what the Baumhauer agent was up to. "Well, whoever the man is, he can't follow me when I head out the next time because I've got to move the boy. Out of town I think. The police are being a little too tenacious in their hunting. I've got a plan but I'll need your help because it's complicated."

Fong was still thinking about the man he'd followed to the Portland Hotel because he said, "Mr. Solomon might be able to tell us something about watcher and about Mr. Welker."

Sage saw the wisdom in Fong's idea immediately. Angus Solomon was the black maitre'd in charge of the Portland Hotel's elegant dining room. He'd assisted Sage and Fong before. Solomon never asked them for anything more than a minimal assurance that whatever task they assigned to him would either make life uncomfortable for the powerful or easier on the poor. Fong had become a particular fan of Angus Solomon's. Sage suspected they got together sometimes, sitting and nodding like two old wise men, not speaking very often but each word weighty when they did.

"Good idea Mr. Fong. I'll go see him as soon as I've moved the boy into hiding." Sage paused, wondering whether Fong still agreed that Matthew was their first priority.

"Yes, he come first," Fong said, sending a shiver down Sage's spine. Did the man read his mind?

As Sage began to pack a valise, Fong departed for the livery stable. There he was to rent a covered trade van and leave it in the usual place, its horse's reins tied to a steel ring embedded in the curb. The location was one block behind an elite establishment operated by a certain bawdy house madam, Miz Lucinda Collins. Someone his mother would call a warm friend of his—very warm indeed.

TEN

ONCE OUTSIDE MOZART'S front door, Sage headed west, ambling toward the park that stretched for many blocks along the downtown's western edge. Nearing the park, he stopped at a flower vendor's. From among the buckets filled with vibrant roses, Sage selected a variety of buds and gave them to the vendor to wrap in tissue paper. As he waited, Sage peered between the slats of the stall at a man who stood about halfway down the block. As he feared, it was the same man who'd been following Sage earlier that day. Hand on a lamppost, the man was pretending to inspect the heel of his shoe.

More wary, Sage tucked the bouquet under his arm and strolled south along the park until he reached Lucinda Collins' exclusive parlor house. Ivy tendrils encircling mullioned windows softened its brick face. Four baroque columns supported a small porch roof, allowing just room enough for two to pass. A green mansard roof swooped gracefully three stories above, its border edged with scrolled loops of wrought iron. Many well-dressed men had climbed these wide granite steps to drop the polished horsehead knocker upon that shiny black door.

He too dropped the knocker and the door opened immediately. Lucinda's maid, Elmira, stood in the doorway. Her black dress and starched white apron were stylish, her smile was wide.

"Mister Adair, you all do come in. Miz Lucinda, she'll be mighty glad to see you. Let me show you into the front lounge." Elmira took the bouquet of roses. She lowered her voice conspiratorially, "I'll put these in Miz Lucinda's room as usual." He handed the flowers over and followed her through the entrance hallway toward the open archway into the parlor.

Lucinda's lilting voice came from within the room so Sage paused, waiting for an opening. "Now, Marila, when you converse with a gentleman, sit like a lady, not a logger. Keep your feet together on the floor or, if you cross your legs, do so only at the ankle. Additionally, last evening you used the word 'shit' in mixed company. I have told you before, and this is the last time, our ladies never use that word in the parlor. Our guests expect to have social exchange with intelligent, cultured, flirtatious ladies. If you cannot change your behavior to reflect that standard, then I'll have to ask you to leave us."

"Oh, Miss Lucinda, I promise I will try harder. I want so to stay. This place is my dream. Carriage rides like today, shopping for fine clothes, always safe. I can't go back to the streets again, please don't make me go."

Lucinda sighed heavily then said, "All right, dear. You do have an appealing nature. No more slip-ups, though. Go along." Lucinda caught sight of Sage standing in the doorway as she turned to watch the girl leave.

Her face brightened then dimmed. "John, it's good to see you." She got to her feet and advanced. "Too much time has passed."

Sage looked around for the flowers he'd brought, but Elmira had taken them and disappeared. The woman stood before him elegantly attired in a shadow-blue lace dress, the same color of her eyes, that fit her round and flat places like fuzz on a peach. The gown, no doubt, was a new creation of the Kimberly sisters.

Sage took her outstretched hands and kissed the knuckles of her topmost one. "Would you really throw her out?"

She laughed. "No, she's here to stay. Though in what capacity remains uncertain."

As one they stepped over to sit on the plush red settee. For an instant his thoughts flashed back to his first love, Mary. Another parlor. Another firm hand, warm to the touch. A hand attached to a body that surrounded an untrustworthy heart. Mary, daughter of a wealthy merchant, had been eager to marry him until he told her he was nothing more than a miner's lucky son. That personal history proved a price too dear for her social ambitions.

This woman, Lucinda, was different. She cared nothing about his origins. Mary had been looking to sell herself to the man who could offer her high social standing. He didn't think Lucinda sold herself anymore for any reason. Certainly, he'd never paid. She'd brushed aside his initial offer of money with such vehemence that he'd never asked again. So their relationship was no business transaction. Whatever it was remained uncertain, but at least it was more honest than what he'd had with Mary.

He shifted and a tube of paper laying on the settee rolled against his thigh. Drafting paper. He picked it up and pulled it open. "What is this? A house plan? Are you going to build a new house?"

"No, that is the plan of this house. The electric man just delivered it to show me where the wires would run." Her slim hand swept through the air. "I'm thinking of installing electric light to make the rooms brighter. Also, with the electric lights, the air wouldn't reek so of gas fumes. What do you think?" She leaned away from him, her eyes slightly narrowed. She looked more interested in seeing his reaction than in hearing his answer.

Sage studied the parlor. It held comfortable settees, patterned wallpaper, and lacquered wood detailing around doors, windows and mantelpiece. At night gaslight gilded the room with a warm, flickering glow. "I find I don't like electric light," he said. "It's too harsh. We've only a couple of light globes in Mozart's kitchen. Still, people seem to prefer the convenience. They're stringing more and more of that ugly wire up and down the streets. What's got you thinking about it?"

"I am hoping it will improve the property's value. In case I decide to sell the place." Watchfulness, like a dog's stare from beneath the dining table, was in her eyes.

His thoughts warred. Was she going to leave the city? Did he want her to? What answer did she expect from him? "Sell it?" he asked. "Why would you want to sell? Yours is the most exclusive parlor house in the city." He cleared his throat, somehow knowing he'd strayed down the wrong trail but not seeing a way back, he continued in the same direction. "No madam can rival your hospitality or style. You'll be a success for years to come."

He watched her face lose light and expression. When she smiled, deepened lines around her mouth made the smile brittle.

She said nothing, only ran languid fingers over her temple and across her hair, leaning and turning away from him as she did so. "Well, John. Happy as I am to see you, I doubt you are here because of my irresistible allure," she said.

Her feelings were hurt, Sage realized and he fumbled for a response that would comfort. He settled on an oily approach, and felt shame flood his cheeks even as he spoke, "Lucinda, love, while you are always irresistible, unfortunately, I do need to use the escape route through your cellar. There's a man outside, waiting for me and I don't think he means me well."

Lucinda's eyebrows rose, ever so slightly, toward the widow's peak in her honey brown hair. Without thinking, he found himself leaning forward to press his lips against hers. She purred in the back of her throat and wrapped her arms about him.

Everything shrunk down into a pinpoint that held the smell of her perfume, the warmth of her skin and the swirl of his thoughts circling aimlessly. Her whisper next to his ear brought him back. "Just how long do you have, John, before you need to use that escape route?"

He pulled away and sat up, straightening his tie and hating himself for doing it, knowing he was again going to disappoint her.

"Unfortunately, only a few minutes," he answered. "There's a wagon waiting the next street over. It'll attract attention if I leave it standing unattended too long. Believe me, I'd surely stay otherwise." His kiss was swift but thorough, as he tried to communicate the intensity of his sudden need to hold her and to forget everything else.

This time it was Lucinda who sighed, sat up, patting her upswept hair back into place. "Wagon? That means you'll require an apparel change. You'd be conspicuous driving a wagon wearing an afternoon walking suit." She stood up and moved toward the door.

"You're right," he stood to follow her. "People do notice who goes about in conveyances," he said, thinking of Arista and her friends' comments. Lucinda was a proud woman and would not appreciate hearing the speculations voiced by those women. "My changes of clothes still here?" he asked.

"Yes, John. Your various farmer, hobo, and other outfits hang in my closet. When I have nothing better to do, I fantasize on how I will explain their presence if we're raided."

"Ha! And fantasy is what that is." Sage swept his arm in an encompassing arc. "A raid on this establishment. That's supremely unlikely, isn't it?"

He didn't have to explain. The judicial, legal, commercial and monied leaders of the city who frequented Lucinda's were unlikely to expose each other to such an embarrassment. Even the chief of police was rumored to frequent Lucinda's house.

Her lips compressed as she initially took offense. Then a sparkle lightened her eyes. "Hmm . . . can't you just see the coppers trying to puzzle out which one of our esteemed guests likes to dress as a farmer–complete with straw hat?" They both laughed.

Ten minutes later Sage, wearing faded farming clothes and straw hat, was stumbling through Lucinda's crowded and many-roomed cellar looking for the archway that led into the cellar of the adjoining building. Lucinda owned both buildings. This second building housed a millinery shop with housekeeping rooms on the second floor. That was where many of the seamstresses lived.

The milliner's cheap rent and the seamstress' reasonable room rates were conditioned on Lucinda's guests being able to exit via the shop's side door without comment or recollection and on the milliner's providing a job to any woman Lucinda thought ill-suited to the sporting life.

Sage climbed the wooden steps into the workroom of the millinery. From there it was only five steps to the outside door. He paused to glance about the room. Ten women sat hunched over sewing machines, their feet furiously treadling while their hands pushed colorful fabric under the stabbing needles. Not one of them looked up as he slipped out.

Halfway down the block, a brown horse waited in the traces of a trade van, his reins tied to an iron sidewalk ring. Fong had succeeded in finding a horse to rent. Sage quickly untied the reins, mounted the wagon, and clucked the horse into action.

"You there, Mr. Fong?" Sage asked in a low voice tossed over his shoulder.

Fong's voice was equally soft. "I'm here. Boy's clothes here. Boy knows we are coming."

Taking care not to be seen by the man who skulked outside Lucinda's house, Sage drove the van northwest toward the terraced Chinese gardens. Once there, Fong slipped out of the van. Minutes later he returned, accompanied by Matthew. The boy clambered over the tailgate into the back as the van began to roll. Sage tipped his wide-brimmed straw farmer's hat to Fong, who stood in the dirt lane, his face impassive.

The placid horse plodded down Morrison Street, its iron-shod hooves ringing on the trolley rails embedded in the cobblestones. Whenever a motorman's foot hit the trolley bell pedal, the horse calmly moved toward the curb and halted until the trolley rumbled past. Horse and van traveled across the Morrison Bridge, high above whistling steamboats, tugs herding log rafts, tin-roofed warehouses and bustling river wharves. Aromatic smoke circled above sawmill teepee burners along the river's eastern edge, casting a gray plume across the water. At the bridge's far end, the buildings of East Portland's commercial district clustered together. When the van rolled off the bridge planks onto solid ground, Sage turned the van southward, heading upriver into the scattering of villages and extensive farmland that eventually opened into the hundred-mile-long river valley. As the surroundings turned more rural, the horse discovered a burst of speed. Sage loosed the reins, giving the horse its head and it began trotting down the dirt road. Sage relaxed and enjoyed the breeze on his face, musing that, although Fong refused to ride on a horse's back, somehow, the Chinese man could always pick out a good one to rent.

They rolled through the town of Milwaukie without slowing. On one side fruit orchards spread eastward while, on the other side, an industrious brick works hunkered down beside the river bog. Sage, bouncing atop his seat, responded to the various greetings of his fellow teamsters--the wave of a laundry-van driver, the doffed cap of an old man atop a wood wagon, a curt nod from a dour-faced fellow on the seat of a brewer's dray. Sage welcomed these sociable expressions of affinity. Each one of his roles had a way of reaping its own rewards. A sneering voice inside his head erased that positive thought by deliberately misquoting a hoary old adage, "Jack of all lives, master of none." He pushed it aside. Too bright a June day for that kind of gloom.

Ahead, the wagon traffic had halted. A herd of dairy cows, shepherded by a farmer and his dog, ambled from one side of the road to the other, creating an effective bovine blockade. Nearby a man and a young boy were clearing fallen branches in an apple orchard. Wearing identical denim overalls, the two worked together as a team—the man wielding a long-handled rake while the boy of seven or so carried the rakings to a burn pile, away from the trees. As Sage idly watched the two, a woman and a small girl came into view, far down the long row of trees. The woman was carrying a large jar of lemonade, the girl a basket. Before the family met, however, the cow herd cleared the road and the van rolled forward.

Land, a wife, and children. Getting up every morning knowing what the day held. The rough of clean denim overalls, son at his side, watching as a smiling wife and daughter walked toward him beneath the trees. For a moment Sage let himself picture Lucinda as that wife in her faded gingham dress, a breeze mussing her hair.

The vision failed. He couldn't insert either one of them into that bucolic setting. Not them. They were both seekers of something different in life. Lured onward by a grail impossible to define, their quest's outcome forever uncertain.

"Matthew," he called into the van at his back, "it'd be all right if you'd like to come on out now."

The boy crawled out of the stuffy box and onto the wagon seat with alacrity, sweat beading his forehead. He wiped it dry with a red kerchief before tying it back around his neck.

After a few comments on the day and the scenery, Sage turned to thinking about the fact that there'd been a witness who claimed he'd seen a lanky, red-haired kid running from Halloran's. "Matthew, what time did you hook up with Knute the night before last?" Sage asked and then watched the boy from the corner of his eye. Matthew scrunched his face in the effort to remember. "I don't rightly know. I don't carry a pocket watch. But I do remember Uncle Knute saying when we met up with that China fellow that he hoped near to eleven o'clock weren't too late to bother Mrs. Fong. So, it musta been before eleven."

Clara's murder happened after midnight. Besides, Knute would never take part in a murder. Sage'd stake his life and everything he owned on that fact. So that meant Matthew was nowhere near Halloran's cribs when Clara died. Still, the word of the accused boy, his uncle, and that of a Chinese woman who barely spoke English would carry little weight with a jury. He needed better evidence to save this boy. "Did you stay inside Mrs. Fong's house once you got there?" Sage asked.

"Oh, lordy me, I surely did. It was too darn scary to go out and about. That Chinatown is enough to make a feller dive under the bed. Except there weren't any beds, just these mats on the floor."

Sage smiled, imagining Chinatown's impact on this youngster from a remote coastal village. Sweet heavy incense wafted out of small joss houses to mingle with the other exotic China scents in what must have been an assault on a nose that had no reference in the world this boy had always known. On all sides, at all hours, Chinese men crowded the sidewalk, their aggressive speech making no sense whatever to the boy's ears. Equally strange for his eyes to see, were the clumps of men wearing thin black tunics over pajama-like trousers, watching as others like them shuffled along in slippers or clumped by in elevated wooden clogs. Each man's long black hair dangling down his back in a single braid, tied off with a little red bow. But no one looking into their piercing black eyes would fail to take them seriously on this, their own territory.

Maybe the boy seen the severed human hands hanging overhead from wooden poles out second-story windows. That sight still took him aback despite Fong's explanation. Sage understood that the Chinese wanted their bones returned to China upon their death. He also understood that the high cost of such transportation meant that only their dried hands made the journey. But still, on a warm summer night, shriveling hands dangling overhead was a sight a bit more exotic than he cared to see.

The police didn't like such sights either but the Chinese got away with it in Chinatown. Most days, the few white people traveling Chinatown's streets were unlikely to complain. That scarcity of

European faces, changed, of course during the Chinese New Year celebration. On that day hundreds of Europeans and Asians lined the few blocks to watch the colorful paper dragon, with its human legs and feet, sway its way from curb to curb, its passage heralded and trailed by flutes and gongs, while firecrackers exploded without pause until the smoke choked the parade watchers' throats. Overhead, those same poles still jutted, but on parade day, Chinatown's residents wisely removed the grisly fruit, replacing it with bright red flags.

"Would anyone have seen you if you'd left Mrs. Fong's?"

"Well, yes. Uncle Knute. He lay right there beside me. I think Mrs. Fong slept outside our room. Anyway, I stayed there, sir, I did. I didn't even leave to use the necessary." His face wrinkled in puzzlement. "Besides, you told us that someone killed Clancy Steele before Uncle Knute found me, not afterwards," he said.

Sage told him about Clara's murder. Matthew's face blanched so white his freckles looked like bee pollen floating on milk. That reaction made his shocked protestations unnecessary. Clearly the boy was not involved in Clara's death. Yet, a witness had described Matthew to the police. Curious. He hoped Ben's reporter found that witness's name—it could be his first real lead.

Shortly before dusk, after passing through the tiny town of Zion, the van rolled up a long driveway toward a tall, spare farmhouse. Nearing the house, Sage slowed the wagon and half-turned to the boy. "Matthew, you committed violence only in your thoughts, and no one can blame you for that. So I'm going to ask these folks to keep you here until I get some answers about who killed Clancy and Clara. There's no point in you going to jail. I don't think you'd enjoy being locked up with a bunch of criminals. Here I know you'll be safe. Do you mind working hard, Matthew?"

The boy gulped but answered, "No, sir, I'm used to working hard. I saved thirty bucks to leave home, five more than Billy." His face clouded. "Anyway, I'd expect to help out if they let me stay here," he said, his voice subdued.

Sage clapped him on the shoulder. "I think you'll be fine. These are good folks but a little different. Since you'll be their guest, you'll need to respect their ways. All right?"

"Yes, sir. But how are they . . ." Then he saw the farmer, his wife, and their children standing on the wraparound porch. "Oh," he said quietly as the wagon drew to a halt, "these folks are some of those Mennonites."

Indeed, everyone on the porch wore somber black. The woman and three young girls wore snowy white aprons over their long dresses, while the man and four boys wore trousers and shirts fastened with hooks instead of buttons. They all smiled but watched in silence until Sage had stepped down off the driver's perch.

"Brother John. Hast thou come to fetch thine own vegetables?" asked the bearded man who'd moved to stand on the top step.

"Why yes, Brother Jonas, I have indeed. I have also come to ask a favor," Sage responded.

"What favor does thou request?"

"My young friend Matthew, here, is in need of a safe place to stay for a short while. I'm hoping you'll let me board him with you. He promises he'll help out around the place. He's a good worker."

"Matthew is an honest Biblical name. Come sit while I think on your request." Jonas gestured toward a fir bench and then turned toward one of the boys. "Jacob, you and the others take Mr. Adair's young friend to the barn and show him the cows and horses. Take that wagon horse with thee. He looks in need of water and oats."

The rest of the family dispersed as Sage and Jonas sat on the bench, Sage leaning back against the clapboards to ease his tired back. A long ride atop a bouncing wagon seat defeated even the strongest muscles. "Thanks to you, Jonas. That horse is thirsty, I'm sure."

One of the daughters returned with a cool glass of well water for each of them. Sage drank gratefully.

Jonas waited until Sage had emptied the glass before saying, "John, is there more to this than thee has said?"

"Yes," Sage admitted, "there is. The boy's been accused of something he didn't do, and I'm trying to keep him out of jail until I find the guilty party. He's just a country boy. The city jail is no place for him." Sage told the entire tale of Matthew's journey and the subsequent events, leaving out only his own meeting with Clara.

Jonas gazed out across his fields where vegetable and berry shoots were pushing up through the dark loamy soil. "Poor child.

To lose a brother like that," he said softly. "Since thee believes the boy innocent, we welcome him beneath our roof. But, I cannot raise my hand if they come for him. Thee knows that?"

"I know that. That's why I brought him here. Everyone knows you Mennonites reject violence. I figure if they do come for him, they won't come trigger-happy." Sage drank and said, "Jonas, if you want to say 'no' because of danger to your family, that's okay. I'll understand. It won't alter things between you and me."

Just then Jacob and Matthew returned. Jonas said to Matthew, "Matthew boy, thee may sleep in the barn with Jacob. Help him keep watch on the animals. We've been having a bit of trouble with the foxes, since they are with kits this time of year and hungry." His face remained gentle as he said, "May I ask thee to remove that red from around thy neck? We do not abide decorations that gratify lusting eyes and turn our thoughts from God."

Matthew flushed pink. He removed the offending kerchief, burying it deep in his overall pocket. "Yes, sir, thank you sir," he mumbled.

Sage visited a few minutes longer but refused a bed for the night. The last glimmers of a red sun were fanning outward from somewhere beyond the horizon when the van rolled back down the lane. Reaching the road, Sage reined the horse further southward, toward Silverton.

ELEVEN

LESS THAN AN hour later, the horse's hooves thudded down Silverton's wood-planked main street. The timber-mill town lay against the foothills of the Cascades at the point where the valley floor began its upward tilt. Frequent rain, slope runoff and heavy timber wagons would churn a dirt street into mire most months of the year. One and two story whitewashed wood-frame buildings, some squared off by false fronts, stood along wooden boardwalks that ran the length of both sides of the street. Wood smoke and the smell of horse dung thickened the air.

People who lived in these small timber towns were the salt of the earth. Every day a struggle, disaster always possible, and yet, hopeful flowers poked from pots and the boardwalks were well-swept. This little center of commerce even had a minuscule bandstand set back from the street, ready to come to life when the community needed a celebration.

Sage left the horse and an extra dollar with the liveryman, asking that the stalwart animal receive a good rubdown and an extra measure of oats before being stabled for the night. Of the many saloons lining the street, he chose one with windows facing the livery stable.

The spikes of countless caulked logging boots had gouged

the saloon's wooden floor. Every face turned toward him as he entered the haze created by after-supper, hand-rolled smokes. Most everyone stood at the bar, wearing the sturdy overalls of loggers, their trouser legs shortened at least three inches at the bottom. The odd length prevented stray branches from snagging the fabric and pitching them into the path of a moving log or in amongst the cable rigging.

A white bearded, suspendered man stood behind the bar. Sage climbed onto a stool.

"Howdy, son. What's your pleasure?" asked the man, his gap-toothed smile friendly beneath bright green eyes.

"I'd surely appreciate some food. I been driving all day delivering. Just finished," Sage gestured out the window toward his unhitched van. "I'm powerful hungry."

"The wife will fix you up something right quick. You want a beer? I brew my own."

"A beer sounds mighty all right," Sage said. Soon he was forking into a plate of venison, potatoes, and turnips. He didn't fake his enthusiasm. The food tasted good and so did the beer. After wiping up the last of the gravy with his bread, Sage leaned back to sip the last of his beer.

When the barkeep came to take away his plate, Sage asked his question. "You know, I once met a fella who lived down here in Silverton, name of Colin MacKenzie. Don't suppose you know where I might find him, do you?"

"MacKenzie? He's not in these parts no more."

"I don't understand. He told me he was logging timber on his own place. He seemed set to stay. I'm surprised he up and sold out."

"Sold out, hell. They drove him out." The comment was an angry growl from a man sitting to Sage's right. When Sage looked interested, the man continued talking.

"MacKenzie's place was real nice, way up the Silverton River, right on the water. During the spring floods he could float the logs down to the mills here. His piece totaled one hundred and sixty acres, tens of trees to each acre. Repaired himself a used steam donkey engine to haul the logs to the river, had some rigging wire and a bunkhouse. He was sitting real good."

"That's exactly what he told me. So what happened? Why isn't he here anymore?"

"Well, first, they brung in squatters to claim the land around and behind him. 'Twas a sorry bunch of drunks hauled in off the streets of Portland. They went up to the woods, chopped down a few trees, built a shack you wouldn't stable your horse in, and settled in to drink themselves damn silly. Then they went down to the land office and filed a claim on the one-hundred-sixty acres of home-stead land. Blinkity-blink they got a deed in just a few months. Now MacKenzie and the rest of us, we waited five years or more for our deeds, but these sorry so-and-so's, why they got their deeds right away. Once they had the deeds, they transferred them to these big time investors—we never learned their names. 'Course, the investors were behind the whole damn scheme from the get-go."

"Sounds like some kind of con game, but I can't say I under-stand how it made MacKenzie pull up stakes and leave his own land behind."

"That's because you've only heard the first half of the story." The man's tone was bitter. "You ever hear of the Forest Reserve Act?"

"Someone mentioned it, but I'm not sure I know rightly what it is."

"I'll tell you. Homesteaders like MacKenzie were cutting big-ger and better trees, cheaper than what them timber trusts could cut back East and down South. And our Pacific Northwest lumber was outselling the big boys' lumber in the Midwest. So, those Mid-west timber barons muscled through the Forest Reserve Act. They got them crooks in Washington D.C. to declare big hunks of home-steaders' timber land 'forest reserve.'"

The barkeep, in sonorous tones, began proclaiming from memory, "'Yes, my fellow citizens. Without the Forest Reserve Act future generations will find themselves without timber, with water-sheds denuded, and drought and floods. All the certain result if our public land continues to be exploited for private gain.'" He punctu-ated his performance by slamming a beer mug onto the bar.

"Einer! Don't be getting yourself excited! You know what the doctor said," his wife shouted from the kitchen.

The barkeep continued, ignoring her shout, "Yah, that's what they claimed. So the Forest Service drew lines on maps and told the homesteaders to move out. Then the so-called Forest Service 'manages' the reserves by selling the trees to the timber trusts for a few cents a thousand foot. 'Course, none of the locals could compete—couldn't afford to bid on them big units of timber. Silverton River's turning into a mud run, thanks to all their logging. For the first time, we have to worry about our drinking water being clean."

"Didn't that hurt those investors who bought the fake homesteaders' deeds?" Sage asked.

The man to his right took up the tale again. "Not at all. See, the Forest Act let a landowner, who knew how to, trade his land in the forest reserve for government land somewhere's else. Better land, even. Problem is, nobody told the rest of us about the deal while there was still land available, so just the investors made out."

"So, that's why MacKenzie moved out?"

"Nope, not MacKenzie. He wasn't going to move. He made that clear. It was going to take an army. Then one night, while he visited here in town, someone dynamited his donkey engine to kingdom come. Set the rest of his place afire. Nothing was left. Barely a tree worth cutting. He took a look, packed up and rode away. Guess he decided to start over. Ain't nobody heard from him since that day."

The barkeep chimed back in, voice heavy with sarcasm, "Well of course, we all know that the fire was just one of those pecuLiar 'acts of God.'" Here he gave a broad wink to Sage. "Leastways, that's what the local law said." He flicked the end of his bar rag at an errant fly before continuing, "Funny though, how them kinds of acts of God only been happening to the independents and the cooperatives and never to the timber trusts." Silence reigned in the aftermath of that comment, leaving Sage to wonder how many of the ten or so men now in the saloon might have had their own visitations from "God."

Sage took another plunge. "Sounds like something Clancy Steele'd be mixed up in."

The barkeep and other man looked at him with narrowed eyes, their faces stiffening. "You know Clancy Steele?" the barkeep asked, this time without his toothy smile.

"Know him and don't like him. Had a few run-ins with him."

"He's the hired thug who brought them drunks in here to homestead for those investors," grumbled the man beside Sage. "Don't know of nobody in this town having kind feelings toward that man. Most of us think he's the one that burnt MacKenzie's place, but no way to prove it."

Sage backed off. He'd pumped this particular well dry. Any further inquiry increased the risk they'd get suspicious and somehow warn MacKenzie. Maybe they didn't know where the man was, or maybe they did. These people had tasted betrayal enough to have learned caution. And, pleasurable as it would have been to tell them Steele was dead, wisdom dictated that was a pleasure that needed to go to someone else. He couldn't risk MacKenzie being warned of Sage's interest in his affairs.

Sage bought beers for his two new friends and arranged to rent a room from the barkeep. He climbed the narrow stairs, expecting to settle in for a good night's sleep. Instead he lay there, propped against the iron bedstead, watching while the rising moon cast a dim light across the acres of tree stumps that crowned the neighboring hillside.

If Steele burnt MacKenzie out, then MacKenzie had good reason to kill Steele. How to find MacKenzie? And, even if Sage found the former homesteader, how could he prove MacKenzie was Steele's murderer? Then there was Clara. Who'd killed that child prostitute? MacKenzie? That made no sense. The men who knew MacKenzie clearly respected and liked him. But if not MacKenzie, then who?

Sage and the horse set out early in the morning, the empty van rattling behind. The horse was frisky with the morning and a belly full of oats. Sage had eaten enough pancakes and bacon to keep him for a week. He stopped at Jonas's farm to collect fresh peas, lettuce and stored potatoes for the restaurant. No sense wasting the trip or the van. He and the farmer talked while the boys loaded the van with root vegetables, early strawberries and tomatoes from the hothouse behind the barn.

"He's a willing worker, that Matthew," Jonas said in a low voice as they watched the boys finish their task and disappear around the corner of the house. "Gets along good with Jacob. Is well-mannered."

"I'm glad to hear that, Jonas. That's what I suspected, but your saying it makes me a whole lot more comfortable about foisting him off on you."

"Thought it might."

Sage found Matthew in the barn, forking fresh hay into the stalls. "You going to be all right staying here, son?"

"Yes, sir. I'll be fine. Me and Jacob, we talk a lot, and the food's real good, and the work's nothing I can't handle."

"Is there anything for me to send out to you, clothes or something?"

"Mr. Jonas wants me to wear some of Jacob's clothes so that I won't be so noticeable. But sir, I surely would appreciate a book. These folks don't believe in book learning, excepting the Good Book, and I've read it so many times I can practically recite it."

"You like to read, Matthew?"

"Oh, yes sir, more than anything. I hope to make my way in life using book learning."

"You're in luck, then. I tucked a book into my valise that I'll lend you. Just make sure that you don't neglect your work for Mr. Jonas." Sage pulled out Charles Dickens's *Great Expectations.*

"Oh crikey, Charles Dickens." Matthew breathed the words as he traced the title's gold indentations. His fingers, scarred from slips of the fish knife, gently paged through the book as if it were made of silk. "Don't worry, sir, I'll read this after my chores are all done. It'll be something to look forward to. Charles Dickens. I only read one of his stories by installments in the newspaper, but I liked how he put his words together on the page. You could see it all happening."

When Sage clicked the horse into action, the boy was still standing there, slowly turning the pages of the book. Sage settled back on the seat. Interesting that boy. Not afraid of hard work, polite and loves to read. It feels right to help him. Just hope I can land on the right track and ride it to the end.

❀ ❀ ❀

Sage crossed the Morrison Bridge back into town as the sun was setting. The laden van had meant a slower return trip. The frisk finally worked out of the horse. "It's all right, ole fella, you'll be home soon. Just two more stops," Sage called to the plodding horse who snorted but kept up his pace. He knew his stable was near.

Tying the horse to the same curb ring where first he'd met the trusty beast, Sage patted its head before entering the millinery shop's side door. The women looked exactly the same except, because of the fading light, all sat hunched closer to their sewing machines.

Lucinda was not at home Sage discovered once he entered her house from the cellar. In her bedroom, he dressed in his town attire, leaving her both his farm clothes and a note. Then he waltzed straight out the front door just like a regular customer. He thought he saw, in his peripheral vision, a dark figure step back into the shelter of a tree trunk in the park across the way, but Sage was careful not to stare in that direction. Hope that fella had to sleep in the park overnight, Sage thought.

His pace was brisk. He planned to gobble one of Ida's entrees, maybe two. He'd dine in Mozart's elegant dining room, midst all the trappings of material success--crystal, china, and silver and people to wait on him

At a glance, Mozart's appeared normal and full of diners. But, he'd expected to see his mother either circulating among the tables confirming all was well or greeting patrons as they entered. She was nowhere in sight.

Sage worked his way across the room, nodding and exchanging greetings with people he knew. On the opposite side of the swinging kitchen doors he found his mother. She was standing at the big black stove, an apron tied around her waist.

"Mrs. Clemens, how is it that you are here at the stove?" he said, aware that the kitchen help had gone silent when he entered.

She turned to look at him, rolled her eyes to the ceiling, pushed back a wisp of straggling hair with her forearm, and said, "They arrested Knute. Ida's in pieces. The doctor dosed her with laudanum. Fong left the minute he saw you enter the dining room."

She gestured with her head toward the kitchen sink. "To top it off, our dishwasher didn't show. So, right now, we need some plates washed."

❀ ❀ ❀

His parlor clock was chiming one a.m. when Sage climbed to the third floor. Although Fong had returned earlier to take over the dishwashing, they'd all been too busy to converse. As Sage entered his unlighted room, he saw Fong standing at the window, eyeing the street through a narrow gap in the curtain.

"Still there, Mr. Fong?"

"Yes. Only a shadow in the doorway, like before. He is thick dark that moves in thinner dark. Easy to spot."

"Did you find the time to take some of that produce I brought back to Miss Lucinda's?"

Fong turned from his watching, his eyes pushed into crescents by his smiling cheeks. "Yes. Miss Lucinda very happy. She say strawberries look very good. She said to tell you to come visit soon. She says she'll show you something very special with strawberries."

Sage wasn't certain, but he thought he saw a lusty glint in the other man's eyes. A hot blush flowed up his neck.

"Ah, well," he said, "I'm likely to be too busy to visit her for a while." He dropped collar and cuffs on the bureau and began to unbutton his shirt.

"The rest of the produce is still in the van as we planned?"

"Yes, produce is in van at livery stable."

"Good. Tomorrow, I need to depart in the daylight without anyone seeing. That produce wagon is my best bet. We'll back it up to the kitchen door so tight that our watching friend won't be able to see what goes in or out of it."

Sage noticed that Fong was still watching him, a slight smile lifting the corners of his lips. "What's so funny?"

Fong glided toward the door before he answered. As he reached the threshold, he turned, the smile coming again. "Strawberries," he said, then went out.

TWELVE

John Adair strolled up the semicircular drive of the elegant Portland Hotel wearing a frock coat, double-breasted vest, and tan subtly striped trousers. On three sides, curtains of ivy draped the stone railings of the hotel's second-story veranda. The hotel's brass band tootled as it tuned up in the courtyard, preparing to play as it usually did on summer afternoons. Across the street, people sat on the low courthouse wall, laughing, enjoying an almost party atmosphere as they waited for the free concert to begin. The mild summer heat had sent crowds into the neighboring streets. Sage had noticed that Portlanders reveled in the sun, like spring flowers thrusting aside winter's unrelenting gloom.

When it came to being the city's most elegant restaurant, the Portland Hotel was Mozart's nearest competitor. Of course, the menu was different. Mozart's fare was less exotic, never offering green turtle soup, deviled Maryland crab, or "crousades" of sweetbreads. Overall though, Ida's food was still the more tasty. Thoughts of Ida led straight to the vision of Matthew's strained face in the light of that flickering oil lamp. The day around Sage seemed to dim. He shook it off. Nothing he could do about the boy right now, he told himself. All was set in motion and until it was time, he needed to attend to this other matter, St. Alban's mission.

Angus Solomon stood behind the walnut podium at the dining room's entrance. From that position he presided over the dining room like a circus ring master. His job was one of the most prestigious a black man could hold in Portland. Tall and slender, Solomon's smooth skin was the color of burnished acorn. His smile brightened his deep brown eyes and his high cheekbones bespoke some Carolina Indian blood.

To the hotel patrons, this distinguished black man was nothing more than an elegantly proper servant. Sage knew, however, that like himself, Solomon played more than one role. When he wasn't at work here in the Portland Hotel, Solomon ran a small North End hotel called the "New Elijah." That establishment catered to black railroad workers and other travelers of color who were unwelcome in the "white" hotels. As part owner of the New Elijah, Solomon was a gentleman of substance, his net worth probably greater than that of many of the patrons he served in this dining room. Sage smiled at the thought. Sometimes the ironies inherent in living a double life tickled his fancy.

Today, the mirrored dining room was half full. Wearing colorful afternoon walking clothes, the guests occupied the various linen-draped tables tucked among the pots of imported jungle plants.

After a greeting of, "Good afternoon, Mr. Adair." Solomon led Sage to a table within the embrasure of a small bay window, somewhat apart from the other tables. He gestured, saying loud enough for others to hear, "Mr. Adair, I trust this window table is acceptable?"

"Yes, Mr. Solomon, it is precisely the table I had hoped for."

Laying a damask napkin in Sage's lap, Solomon paused as if to pass the time of day—a custom of his when seating dining patrons.

To someone watching, the smile on Solomon's face would have appeared relaxed but his murmured words came quickly, "Mr. Fong, your most estimable man, spoke to me of the gentleman in whom you have expressed an interest. I, in turn, have conversed with the staff. We'll monitor to whom the man speaks. I must say, the staff has an unfavorable impression of him—very demanding, without courtesy." Solomon's fastidious diction was pure Carolina high society. In fact, it had been the opportunity to manage the dining room of the new Portland Hotel which had lured Solomon away from extended service in the South Carolina governor's mansion.

"Please express my gratitude to them for their assistance," Sage said as he slid folded greenbacks onto the snowy white table linen. Sage opened his menu with a flourish covering the whisk of money into Solomon's pocket.

A party of guests passed close by the table. Solomon raised his voice, "Thank you, Mr. Adair. May your day be pleasant also, sir. If there is anything you need, please don't hesitate to ask."

"I never do, Mr. Solomon. Thank you. As always, I am most grateful for your assistance."

As Sage ate, he idly watched a small, gray-haired, light brown waiter clear, then efficiently lay, place settings on nearby tables. A salesman occupied a neighboring table, his sample case sitting snugly against his leg, as if thievery were imminent. Mustard-colored plaid covered the salesman's broad back which billowed out beyond the sides of his chair. He'd overdone his pomade application, the excess grease making comb tracks in his orange hair so distinct that they looked like furrows in a field. Sage turned away from that sight to gaze out the window seeking, but not finding, Welker's distinctive face among those enjoying the mild sunshine on the hotel's veranda.

The insistent ping of silver on glass drew Sage's attention back to the salesman even as the man's booming voice caused the other diners to stare. "Hey there, boy!" He was calling to the waiter who'd been setting the tables. "Why aren't you bringing me my meal? They told me that this is supposed to be a fine dining establishment!"

The waiter froze for a split second, a muscle bunching in his jaw before he carefully laid aside the cutlery. Hurrying toward the irate salesman he said, "I am so sorry, sir, for any delay. I'm not your waiter, but I will locate him for you."

"What do you mean, you're not my waiter?" The man's unrelenting belligerence froze all conversation in the room. "I gave you my order, didn't I?"

Just then a young, round, very dark-skinned waiter came out of the kitchen, carrying a full plate in his hands. The older waiter gestured toward the one approaching. "No, sir. This is your waiter. It appears he has your order."

The salesman's eyes were already fixed on the approaching plate, but his tone remained mulish. "Oh, well, it's hard to tell you boys apart."

"Yes, sir," the older man said as he backed away from the table, his face impassive.

Embarrassment prickled across Sage's scalp. He glanced toward the other waiters in the room but saw only stony faces, with eyes focused on nothing. Not one of them showed an obvious reaction to the salesman's behavior.

Sage turned back to his food and chewed thoughtfully. Easy to forget that other people had to play roles. These waiters for example. But unlike Sage, their roles were forced upon them. As John S. Adair, he could express his opinion and nothing all that bad would happen. Not so these men. White hostility and arrogance was an ever-present danger. Whenever these men stepped from their homes into the wider world, they had to don whatever submissive role the circumstances demanded.

Shame at belonging to the same race made Sage want to tell the salesman off. But like these waiters he had to stifle the impulse. He wasn't only John S. Adair. He was also John Miner and whomever else his mission might require. The people dining around him would remember and remark on anything he said in these circumstances, imperiling his carefully constructed John Adair role. He'd have to channel his disgust into merely leaving an excessive tip for the wait staff.

A voice at his elbow jolted him from this reverie, "Pardon me, sir, would you care for more coffee?"

"Yes, thank you very kindly," Sage said to the gray-haired waiter who'd slipped up beside him. "That man over there . . ."

The waiter's face tightened and closed. "Pay no mind, sir. Will there be anything else?"

Back at Mozart's, Philander Gray was inhaling his dinner, a napkin neatly tucked into the collar beneath his jutting chin. "Did they let you in to see Knute?" Sage asked, after taking a seat at the lawyer's table.

Gray gulped some wine, then answered. "They didn't want to at first, but I made some noise, so they let me talk to him."

"Privately?"

"Yup. A bit of folding paper encouraged the turnkey to toddle off on some errand or another. So we talked. He's doing okay, steady as a rock. I gave him your message. He's not said anything about the boy. And he told the police he knew nothing about any murders. Knute didn't know who it was that twigged him out as having been with the boy, maybe nobody. Might be a bluff." Gray returned to his attack on the bloody steak. Sage thought, not for the first time, how amazing it was that Gray's voracious appetite failed to add even an ounce to his stringy frame.

"When can we bail him out? Ida's frantic with worry. You're lucky you received a meal, the way her nerves are working."

Gray carefully dabbed a napkin tip to the greasy corners of his mouth. "Looks like the judge is going to drag his heels about setting the bail. Murder, you know. Like I said, Knute's holding up fine. Wanted me to reassure his wife. Asked me to tell you not to worry . . . he knows you'll fix things."

That bit of information fizzed like sarsparilla in Sage's stomach. "Philander, I wish I felt that confident," he said. "The boy's safe for now, but it's going to take some time to look into this. The clues are complicated. I feel like I'm trying to untangle a ball of string that a cat's been fighting. I have to be away for a few days, following up on some things. While I'm gone, you'll keep a lookout over Knute?"

Gray washed down the final morsel of food with his last swig of wine and swallowed a burp before responding, "Yup. Long as you're paying me, you don't have to worry. Just go on about your business. They can't hold him too long because no one ever claimed to have seen him anywhere near Halloran's when either Clara or Clancy died. Only thing they know is that he went missing same time as the boy so the police figure they were together. If Knute sticks to his denial he should come out all right, eventually."

Gray liked to act like money was his primary motivation but Sage knew better. Trustworthy, discreet, and widely known for his charitable acts, Gray was a good man to have in your corner. Sage rose to shake hands just as a waiter approached with pieces of pie on two plates, one apple, the other cherry.

Gray's eyes lit up and he smiled broadly. "I do love Miz Ida's cooking. If the woman wasn't already married, I'd ask her myself," he said as he reached with both hands to take the plates. As Sage turned to leave, Gray picked up a fork and aimed it at the apple piece.

❀ ❀ ❀

Sage found Fong scrubbing the bathing room floor on his hands and knees. Seeing Sage, Fong rocked back on his heels, then rose to his feet supple as a young mountain lion.

"Mr. Sage, you speak with Mr. Solomon?"

"Yes Mr. Fong, he was there and had done his job. Thank you for talking with him."

"He very smart man, Mr. Solomon."

A rare compliment from Fong. And Solomon had called Fong "estimable." It was no surprise that these two men, though seemingly dissimilar, admired one another. Both had achieved success in a strange world that was exceedingly hard on their kind.

Sage began stripping off his finery. "That's true," he said. "We're lucky Solomon's our friend." Weariness washed over Sage at the thought of donning yet another disguise. Still, there was no choice. "Mr. Fong, I must go out right away. Would you kindly fetch the logger trunk?"

When Fong returned, Sage asked, "Mr. Fong, the other day when you said my being John Miner might be a problem . . . were you talking about that breakedness thing again?"

Fong, unloading the trunk, paused to nod. "I think on it, too, since then. John Miner is person other people see. Danger happens when a person turns into only what others see. This because person changes to be every new person. Like that lizard, chameleon. Maybe when person turn into that lizard the soul gets broken. You see the problem?"

Sage thought he understood at last. "If you always let others define yourself, you lose yourself?" he offered. That might explain the problem, but it was no answer. "But, Mr. Fong, what if you need to play roles like I do or you are forced to play them in order to survive. How can you remain yourself–you know, unbreakable?"

"Ah," said Fong as he continued pulling clothes from the trunk, "that question is for another day."

Sage laughed. "You must want me to figure it out myself. I'm learning your ways, Mr. Fong."

Fong raised one eyebrow. "So, Mr. Sage, answer me. Which journey is more memorable? The one I tell you about or the one you travel?"

That question put an end to the lesson. Sage changed into long underwear, dungaree trousers, suspenders, and the thick soled logger boots. He slung the rope handle of a bindle over his shoulder. Inside were an extra pair of clothes and a few other essentials. Minutes later, followed by Fong, he slipped into the kitchen from the basement stairs, then out the door into the produce wagon where it stood at an angle against the stoop, blocking sight of the door to anyone standing in the street. It was too risky using the tunnel in the daylight. As planned, his mother had gathered the kitchen help together at the far end of the kitchen for instructions, so none of them saw him.

Fong clucked the horse into action, and the wagon rattled away from Mozart's. A few turns later, Fong's voice floated into the hot, stuffy van from his perch on the driver's seat. "Same smelly man was again outside the kitchen door. He look at our wagon but did not move. We trick him."

Once at the livery stable, Fong pushed the empty van backward so that its rear butted against the yard fence. While Fong paid for the horse and van, Sage pulled open the doors and slipped away.

THIRTEEN

SAGE TRUDGED UP Burnside Street, bindle dangling from his shoulder. This street marked the boundary between the commercial downtown business district and the North End's seedier operations. The North End was a mix of saloons, prostitute cribs and fringe businesses that served those down on their luck, in addition to the more sedate businesses that serviced Portland's black and Asian communities.

Burnside Street was where the unemployed congregated. Here no store sold to bank clerks, businessmen or ordinary housewives. No sparkling shop windows enticed passersby with displays of current fashions. Instead, the dirty storefronts offered tools--axes, screw jacks, seven-foot saws sporting enormous teeth. The apparel for sale was equally functional: hogskin gloves to protect hands from wire ropes, caulk boots bristling with spikes to anchor into tree trunks, copper-riveted dungaree trousers guaranteed to withstand hard physical labor, and, for those days of endless rain, woolen mittens, oilskins, durable woven coarse wool coats or the cheaper shoddy coats made of pressed wool scraps. He'd seen more than one of the latter dissolve beneath the onslaught of the Northwest's winter downpours.

The job sharks also plied their trade here on Burnside Street.

Sandwiched here and there between the goods merchants and the saloons, their narrow storefronts promised work to hungry men. Inside, their business was conducted from behind tall counters, the available jobs chalked on the blackboards that hung on the walls. Those who could read, or at least knew the important words, could see both the open jobs and daily wages, "Buckers, $3.50; Swampers, $1.50."

The sharks matched men with jobs, reaping profits far exceeding their effort. Profits off the desperate men that the sharks derisively called "timber beasts." Maybe they used the "timber beasts" name as a way of justifying their heartless exploitation. Whatever the reason, Sage had never met a shark who possessed a whit of mercy in his cold greedy heart.

His target on this foray was the Burnside sharks, but he wasn't quite ready. Sage needed information. But first he needed a few minutes to recapture how it felt to live inside the skin of a "timber beast." So he leaned against the warm bricks of a building front and breathed deeply. There was no scent of roses here. Instead, dust and stale urine intermingled to form the smell of impoverished lives falling in a downward spiral. Single men, their accents and dress hailing from many different countries, drifted back and forth across the busy street, gazing into windows or lounging in curbside groups. A few strode more purposefully, obviously decked out in their going-to-town clothes. They'd recently been paid off and had a little money in their pockets. Most, however, wore tattered dungarees and scruffy work boots like he did–shuffling along with only lint lining their pockets. Sage stood, absorbing the rhythm of that life. Remembered again how it felt to wander homeless, his belly empty. The memory was sharp. He'd experienced some hard years once he'd severed ties with his foster father and before he'd panned gold in the Yukon basin's Rabbit Creek.

At last, he was ready. He pushed off from the brick wall and sauntered into a saloon that advertised "Beer 2¢." Inside, he paused to let his eyes adjust to the smoky gloom. Men stood at the chest-high bar or sat at rough wooden tables scattered across a floor stained black by hawked tobacco. Loggers chewed tobacco instead of smoking because wildfires in the woods meant loss of work or even death. When they came to town, they brought the habit with them. Sage was used to seeing men spit streams of brown juice and executed a lively sidestep to avoid one such arc on his way to the bar.

Watered down beer in hand, Sage moved among the drinkers. He'd learned in Silverton that MacKenzie could work at any logging job. And also, that he was determined to buy more land. So, MacKenzie would go after the highest-paying jobs, like running the donkey engine or topping trees. It took him an hour but Sage left the saloon with a list of the job sharks who'd recently advertised those two jobs.

Sage discovered MacKenzie's trail on his sixth foray into a job shark's den. The storefront was only ten feet wide by twenty feet deep. Light filtered in through the grimy front window. The man behind the counter watched with narrowed eyes as Sage made his way to the counter. The man's cold eyes were spaced close together, crowding a long nose that, in turn, hooked over a wispy mustache that failed to hide the two large, yellow teeth that pushed resolutely forward.

"You can't be looking for work in the woods. You look like some kind of greenhorn to me," the man said, his nasally whine undercutting the contempt he sought to convey.

"I'm stronger than I look and I'm a hard worker, but you're right, I've only worked in the woods on my family's farm before we lost it," Sage answered with the naive eagerness he'd been perfecting during his search among the job sharks.

"Hell, you sound like an American. Why you want to go into the woods and work with them dirty foreigners?"

This wasn't the first job shark to ask that question. Thirty thousand people had landed in Portland during the last two years, many of them foreign-born, many seeking work in the woods.

"I'm working my way up from California, hoping to meet up with my cousin. I'm looking to work as a swamper," Sage said, knowing swamping was the least skilled job in the woods. A swamper lopped limbs off the felled trees, turning them into the smooth sided logs that the donkey steam engine could skid out of the woods. Swamping demanded only that the man could endlessly swing an axe without cutting off his own leg. The job also paid the least, so turnover was high. Swamper jobs were always open except when the woods were closed because of fire danger.

"We got swamper jobs. They don't pay but $1.50 per day plus grub and a bunk. Cost you two bucks for the referral." Referrals were one way the shark made his money. Additionally, the sharks had you-scratch-my-back-I'll-scratch-yours arrangements with the camp bosses, who, for a cut of the referral money, exercised a brutal control that ensured turnover remained high in the woods.

"I guess that'd be okay if there's an opening in the camp where my cousin, Colin MacKenzie, works."

"This is your lucky day. I just sold a referral to MacKenzie last Tuesday."

Excitement raced through Sage. Tuesday was the day Clancy Steele had died. "Are you sure it was last Tuesday? I heard he's been in the woods all this last month. Maybe it was some other MacKenzie?"

"Big, tall fella, black hair, blue eyes, talks Scotch?" It was the description given to Sage by Slap Jacks' bartender.

"That sure enough sounds like my cousin . . ." Sage allowed his sentence to trail off into doubtful silence.

The man yanked open a counter drawer and began pawing through a scattering of white cards. "Hell, I got his card right here in my drawer. Yup, here it is. 'Colin MacKenzie, donkey engine, last Tuesday.' Like I said." He tossed the card back in the drawer and slammed it shut with satisfaction. "You aiming to follow after your cousin or not?"

"That's what I been hoping. Does his crew need a swamper?"

The man bared his yellow teeth in a smile that looked more predatory than humorous. "Oh, that crew's always needing a swamper. Cost you two dollars for referral and another three for rail transport out to the crew."

The man overcharged for transportation, but Sage accepted the job with the eagerness of a bumpkin who'd just stepped from behind the plow. After being told to present himself at one o'clock the next afternoon to pick up his ticket and directions, Sage headed toward the rail yards. He would soon find Colin MacKenzie. Now to find Meachum, the helpful hobo who'd rescued Matthew from Clancy's boot. Once he'd talked to Meachum, Sage was heading for a bath. He needed to soak away all the disgust he'd accumulated during the day. Once clean, well, might be he'd go see a lady about her strawberries.

❀ ❀ ❀

Dusk was melding into night when Sage shuffled into the first hobo camp, one of two near the rail yards. A grizzled old tramp had once advised Sage that three types of men rode the rails: drunks who drank and wandered; hobos who worked and wandered; and tramps who dreamed and wandered.

One whiff of this first camp informed Sage that this was where the wandering drunks were bedding down. No hobos or tramps here. Trash heaps dotted the clearing and stink wafted in from the mounds and pools of excrement that lay only a few paces back into the trees. He tried to ask questions but most of these men were too drunk to do more than give him either a slack-mouthed stare or an irritated snarl. The few who managed to mumble a response had never heard of Meachum.

In the second camp, deeper into the alder grove, people were bustling about. A battered basin of water with a sliver of cake soap next to it, sat atop a tree stump where some were scrubbing grime from face and hands. To one side, a small campfire burned beneath a cut down metal barrel that was sending steam rising into the still evening air. Two men were using a stick to stir the clothes inside the barrel. It was the hobos' washing machine and killer of lice. Holding the center of the clearing was the main fire where large black-bottomed cooking pots rested among the coals. It was around this fire the men would later arrange themselves to sleep, the unspoken agreement being that the most frail would hold the positions closest to the dying embers. Sage immediately joined those men who were combing the grove for dry wood.

Once their communal meal of beans and bread was finished, twelve men found seats on crates and wood blocks, resting their shabby boots on the rocks encircling the fire until the heat on their soles penetrated into their socks. The summer evening was chill, a reminder that Spring had not let loose her hold. As they sipped the gritty coffee brewed from boiled grounds, the story telling began. As always, work was the common theme.

"There is a farmer down the valley, nearby Newberg, named Simple. He pays fair to men who work hard," offered a lean man with a narrow face, white teeth, and a German accent.

"There's a farmer down the valley named of Crosby," coun-
tered another man. "He's looking for men but he sure don't pay fair.
Starves you to death with the wormy vittles. His last crew got so
all-fired mad they planted every one of his fruit trees upside down."
The group guffawed.

"So what'd he do when he found out about the trees?"

"Well, 'course he fired 'em all. So they went to the nearest 'bo
camp and told the story. Next morning another crew turned up
to work. Lunchtime come, he serves them moldy bread and meat
so tough the cow must have trotted all the way from Texas—eatin'
nothing but sagebrush and cactus the whole way."

"Whoo wee. What'd that second group do?" asked another,
playing along.

"Same darn thing—planted the trees headfirst. Farmer Crosby was fit to be tied," the storyteller responded.

The stories continued as the dark thickened. Most of their
tales were about hobos getting even with miserly bosses, in ways
that mixed spite with humor. Sage laughed along with them, feeling
the pain as well as reliving those others' minor triumphs.

"I hear the bulls have been pretty rough up and down the valley here," came the tentative voice of a Negro who'd ridden the rails
down from Seattle.

Faces turned somber. "It's been bad," a man agreed. "Young
boy was murdered just the other day."

"Least this time the sonofabitch that murdered him got murdered himself. Damn his soul to hell," said another man, his voice a
low, raspy Scots burr. "It's about time we start fighting back. Them
railroad bulls and hijackers, they're killing people. Train out of The
Dalles, last week, highjackers dropped a rope ladder down from the
deck into the boxcar and killed three hobos for their week's pay.
None of the bo's were carrying weapons."

Sage couldn't see that speaker, who was sitting back from the
fire, at light's edge.

"Yah, we ought to start teaching them bastards a lesson,"
piped a kid's reedy voice still in the process of changing.

"I hear tell some men are doing just that. There's a group
calling itself the Flying Squadron traveling the rails, going wherever

there are bad bulls and hijackers." Again this came from the Scotsman in the shadows.

"Oh hey, I heard of that group when I was 'boing the Midwest. They out West here too?" asked a man who'd nicked his chin while shaving in front of a broken mirror tacked to a tree trunk. He sported a piece of stickum on his chin to stop the bleeding. Being clean shaven was hard under these conditions, but sometimes appearance was what decided whether a man found work or not.

"Maybe so. Someone told me that a week or so ago, outside Pocatello, that Flying Squadron cornered one of them bad bulls and stripped him naked before tossing him off on a slow turn. Their way of warning him. 'Bo's on that train said it was the most relaxing run they'd ever had into Boise." This information came from a man who'd been quiet till then. The others laughed like they knew exactly what he meant.

Here was the opportunity. Sage said, "You think that Squadron fixed the bull who killed the kid?"

"Could be. He deserved it. Clancy Steele was hard as a railroad spike. Like a lot of the railroad bulls, he'd make a special point of robbing you before he threw you off the train. Never spared the punches. Maybe the Squadron heard about him and what he did and took care of him," suggested the German.

"So, the Flying Squadron don't advertise what it does?" Sage asked.

"Depends. They might let out the word. Sometimes the bulls tell and it gets back to us. Mostly, we just add two and two together. Maybe they done it, maybe they didn't," another offered.

Sage waited until the conversation drifted back to work opportunities then asked, "Say, I don't suppose anyone here knows a fella by the name of Meachum? Someone said he came through here a few days back. I'm trying to hook up with him."

The young kid said, "Meachum? Yah, I run into that guy a time or two. Said he was heading up to Seat . . ."

He didn't finish the sentence because the Scotsman sitting behind him planted a swift boot in the kid's backside, interrupting, "Why are you looking for him? Pardon my curiosity but we don't know you, mister, you just kind of appeared here," he said, turning the camaraderie abruptly cold.

"I had a partner riding the rods with me," Sage explained, "and he said he was supposed to meet this Meachum guy here in Portland but wasn't going to make it. Wanted me to tell him."

"Yah? What was that partner's name?"

"Grady O'Dell." Sage supplied the first name that came to mind. Last he knew, Grady O'Dell was running one of the Yukon's log cabin drinking holes in a place that took two days of snowshoeing and a mighty strong thirst to find. It was unlikely they'd ever heard the name.

"Well, if this fella Meachum passes through, we'll give him Mister O'Dell's message," the man said.

Sage sat around until the fire died down and men began drifting away to roll up in their blankets. Sage followed suit, moving to the outskirts of the camp. Once snores started filling the night, he picked up his blanket and set off toward town. After stepping into the darkness beneath the trees, he looked back. Moonlight caught on a white oval face. It showed only black holes where the closed eyes should have been. The skeletal stare was coming from where the Scotsman had bedded down. The prickle of that stare stayed in the center of Sage's back long after he'd slipped away beneath the trees.

FOURTEEN

FIVE HOURS LATER, Sage was again walking through the night, this time heading home from Lucinda's. Every sinew, every muscle, every joint in his body seemed to move in perfect synchronicity. Satisfying lovemaking, nothing better. But, to be honest, his mind was really on their talk afterward. For the first time in a very long time, he'd told someone else about his childhood. He hadn't planned to. But his damn nightmare had woke them both up. And he was feeling close to her. So, as the moonlight came through the window, he told her.

"I was eight when I started working as a breaker boy at the mine."

"Oh John, eight years old?"

"I was lucky. Most children in that mining town started working as early as six. My mother kept me away from the mine as long as she could. The time came, however, when we needed the forty cents a day I could earn."

"What's a breaker boy?"

"We'd crouch over the coal chutes and pick out pieces of slate and rock as the coal moved past heading toward the washers. Made us round-shouldered, real quick. Few months of that and we walked like wizened old men. It was filthy dirty and dangerous. The anthracite coal smashed fingers, crushed hands. Sometimes a boy would fall in and he'd smother before we could pull him out."

"Dear Mother of God," she whispered.

"We worked from dawn to dusk in the breaker shed. My mother too. I didn't know there was any different life." Sage sighed, then said, "I'd just turned nine when they sent me down below, into the mine. I hated it—the noise, the dust, the smell of paraffin, blasting caps cracking, dynamite rumbling the ground. Mostly, I hated the dark and the musty smell of dirt." The hand that had been stroking her shoulder clenched. "I hated the dark," he repeated, "and I hated the god awful weight of the walls, the roof. That weight is like a living thing, always bearing down, trying to crush a body, even now when I sleep."

He rose onto one elbow. "Lucinda, when you were a child, were there monsters in your dreams?"

Her body tensed, memory blanking her eyes before she answered, "The worst monster in my childhood came after me when I was awake. Sleep was my escape."

He pulled her closer. "I think I understand. It was that way for me too. I turned terrified the instant the elevator started down the shaft."

"How did you endure the fear?" She rolled onto a hip to watch his face.

He thought a moment and then smiled. "My mother, bless her heart, loved flowers. My uncle built her window boxes for our three windows. Of course, it wasn't our house. We paid rent to the mine. Too much rent. Anyway, she always kept flowers in those window boxes. In the winter, she'd tie bits of colored kerchiefs to the sticks. So when I'd be scared going underground, I'd put the image of one of her flowers in my mind. The more afraid I got, the harder I'd think of that flower."

He glanced at Lucinda. In the moonlight from the window he saw the glisten of tears on her cheeks. She was looking across the room at the vase of roses he'd brought. "You bring flowers, John, you always bring flowers."

His head dropped back onto the pillow. "You know, I don't think I ever made that connection." He was silent for a moment, then took up the story again, "Anyway, when I was still nine, they had me working beneath the base of a coal wall. They used us boys to dig a narrow slit deep into the bottom of the coal face. Next we'd plant the dynamite at the back of the slit. Once we crawled back out, they'd set it off. The coal face would drop into a pile of rubble for the men to pick through and load.

"'Anyways,' as my mother would say, one day the mine owner's son and his six-year-old grandson rode the elevator to the bottom of the shaft. His grandson was touring the mine for the first time. Guess the idea was to let him see all that he would inherit–the mine, the machinery, the men." Sage paused, his mind reaching back.

"Ventilation's not too good in those deep mines. Methane gas can build up and explode. That's what happened. Everything exploded. I lived only because I was digging way back in the slit. When I came to, my back was sliced deep but that was all. I had to push aside a lot of rocks to crawl out. Luckily, the coal face didn't fall in the explosion, if it had . . ." He'd reached the heart of his recurring nightmare.

He cleared his throat and continued, "Everyone else I could find was dead, except that little boy, the mine owner's grandson. He was hurt, though, and the tunnel had collapsed. There was no passage to the elevator. There was no way out until I remembered a ventilation shaft deeper in. I tied the boy's arms around my neck with my overalls and found the shaft. It was narrow, but once I cleared an opening into it, I saw sky. Bright blue sky, way up above. I was skinny enough to fit carrying the boy. So I started climbing, the boy tied to my chest. I climbed until sweat ran down my face and dripped off my chin, until my arms and legs trembled so bad I didn't think I could climb one more step. The rock cut my hands and my bare feet, and blood ran from the cut on my back. Every time the boy's weight shifted, the cut on my back ripped wider. I'm crying the whole time because my uncle and my cousin were both dead down below. So, I keep hauling us up and up and up. I keep staring at that light, way up at the top—a bright square of daylight. Finally, we made it. I climbed out."

He rolled to face her, his fingers moving a strand of hair away from her eyes. "Me and that little boy were the only ones who lived. Everyone else remained in that mine. It's still their tomb, far as I know. Twenty-seven hard rock miners and the mine owner's only son."

Lucinda didn't say anything, just moved closer to him and wrapped an arm around him. He gazed at the shaft of moonlight where it lay across their feet. For a long minute he said nothing. Then he continued. This next part was no easier.

"The mine owner felt beholden because I'd carried his grandson out alive. The boy was all he had left. So he took me into his house, raised me with his grandson. He had me schooled, all the way through university. I learned how to hold a teacup, engage in frivolous discourse and wear a stylish suit of clothes.

"It was a long time before I realized how much that mine owner hated me. I'd catch him watching me, staring at me like he'd never understand why this mine rat lived when his own son had died. Maybe that's when first I learned how to play the roles. I tried so hard to convince him I was worth it."

He looked into her eyes. "So, Lucinda, now you know. I am not the gentleman you might think I am. I'm just a coal miner who got lucky."

"Your father, did he die too?"

"I guess you could say that my father was dead to me and my mother long before that mine explosion. I'll tell you about him sometime, but not tonight."

Lucinda's fingertips brushed the strands of dark hair from his forehead. "Thank you for telling me. You've always seemed different, better than the others. There's more to you somehow. And I think your secret childhood connects to your other secrets, like why you are really here in Portland." He started to shake his head in denial but she stopped him with gentle fingers across his lips. "I don't need to know anymore, John. Not now, my love." So softly were the last two words said, that he wasn't certain he'd really heard them.

He wrapped his arms around her and squeezed her tight. He spoke into her sweet-scented neck, "Lucinda, when we're alone, would you call me 'Sage?'"

She tilted her head away from him so she could look into his face. Tears trembled in her eyes. "Sage," she said, giving the name a try. "I like that. How did you get that name?"

His laugh was faint. "My dear mother saddled me with the middle name of 'Sagacity.'"

"'Sagacity.' There's a new one. So your friends don't call you 'John?'"

"Not my real friends. I don't really like it. My father's name was 'John.'"

"Mmmm...Sagacity," she mused. "That is an odd name."

"Actually it's an old family name on my grandmother's side."

"Your mother liked it?"

"Not so much liked the name as liked its meaning. She says she didn't want me to ever forget where I came from—who my people were or what my obligation was in the world."

Lucinda slowly traced the smooth curve of his jaw line. "She sounds tough. Why did she think you'd forget?"

Sage laughed. "She's tough alright and a mother. I was her only child. She was convinced I'd eventually go out into the world and leave that gritty mining town behind. She was right as it turned out. Just happened sooner than she expected."

"And do you ever forget the people you came from?"

Sage laughed, captured her hand and kissed her finger tips. "No. I can honestly say that the legacy of that original Sagacity might be traveling with me. Family legend has it he was advisor to a warrior chieftain who died in a lost battle against Ireland's invaders." He didn't elaborate.

Sleep eluded him after their conversation. So, once Lucinda was breathing softly, he slipped from her side to head home along the edge of the park blocks. Inside the park, moonlight filtered through the leaves and he paused to sniff the sweet smell of mown grass.

Suddenly, someone jerked his arms behind him. The unmistakable icy barrel of a revolver jammed into the soft hollow beneath his right ear. He tamped down the urge to struggle or run. Fong's voice sounded in his mind. "Do not try to outrun bullet. When situation turn bad, relax. Let opportunity present itself." Sage loosened his muscles and waited.

A whispered voice spoke in his ear, "Stop sticking your nose where it don't belong. This is your only warning." Before Sage could reply, the revolver lifted off only to slam back into the side of his head so hard that bright light flared behind his eyes. Sage's knees buckled and he would have fallen except for the hands squeezing his arms, dragging him backward into an alley. Once off the street, they dropped him. A boot slammed into his head and blackness roared into his world.

❀ ❀ ❀

A sharp nip on Sage's finger jerked him back to consciousness. His eyes fluttered open in time to see the beady, unblinking eyes of a rat staring into his from its crouch above his smarting finger. He bellowed and the rat scuttled away. Sitting up, he grabbed his head with both hands, trying to contain the explosion until the pain lessened. He staggered to his feet only to have the world swoop then dive. Holding onto the alley's brick wall, he fought the vertigo that swept through him every time he moved. Mozart's was too far. Lucinda was two blocks away. Lucinda, then.

The stairs to her front door, when he reached them, seemed steeper, higher and plunging like the deck of a ship. Hard to believe how easily he'd mounted them just hours before. Leaning against the door frame, he struggled to reach and then drop the knocker. He never heard the door open.

❀ ❀ ❀

Pain hammered Sage's head in a dozen different places. Then he smelled Lucinda's scent on the pillow. He opened his eyes. She was there, sitting beside him, watching his face, worry etching a deep vertical crease between her brows. When he reached up to smooth the wrinkle, his hand escaped his control, so he let it drop to the blanket.

From the other side of him, a cool wet cloth was smoothed across his forehead. He rolled his head on the pillow, closed his eyes at the pain and then opened them to see his mother. She smiled.

They peppered him with questions that hurt his head to answer. At last, they were satisfied. Lucinda gathered up the soiled rags. Gently, she kissed him on his brow, saying, "Sage, I'll leave you with your mother, now that I know you'll be all right."

He said nothing. She left the room—winking at him just before the door closed.

"You told her you're my mother?" Sage asked.

"Didn't need to. She took one look at the two of us and told me who I was. Smart gal."

"I can't believe you're here."

"Why wouldn't I be? She sent for Fong. Fong told me. Where else would I go? I'm your mother."

"Yes, but it's a house that ah, ah . . . "

"Don't be such a snob. She's a businesswoman." She twisted the rag dry again and smoothed it across his forehead. "Don't forget, we come from poor folk. There's more than one working girl in our family line. I'd never turn a one of them away from my table."

Sage smiled. "You like her?"

"So far, I like what I've seen."

Sage recalled the whispering voice. There had been a burr, as if the man was Scottish. There had been a familiar smell. He knew that smell. "Mother, why would a man smell like camphor?"

"Camphor's something people use for colds, sniffles and chest congestion. Some folks are clogged up all the time." Her voice seemed to be coming from somewhere far away and then there was silence.

Noon sunlight slanted through the leaves outside the window. Sage groaned then flipped back the covers, swinging his legs to the floor.

"What are you doing? Get back into bed! You shouldn't be up," his mother spoke sharply from the chair next to the bed.

"I've got to. I have to be somewhere at one o'clock. Did Mr. Fong bring my clothes?"

Exasperation laced her sigh. "Of course he did. He figured you'd still want to head off into the woods." She knelt down to draw his stockings over his feet, since his face, when he'd stood to pull on his trousers, signaled he'd probably puke if he had to bend over. Through eyes slitted against the pain, Sage looked down at her graying head and wondered if he'd be returning to see her.

FIFTEEN

SAGE STEPPED INTO the railway car only to find a conductor blocking the aisle. "I am sorry," the man announced with his hand raised to halt Sage's passage, "we only allow first-class passengers in the lounge car." He spoke loud enough for the entire car to hear. Although shorter in stature, the man's tone of voice managed to convey a superior look down his nose while his over-sized mutton-chop whiskers quivered with importance.

Riding the jouncing wood benches in the third-class car would make his head pound like hell. So, Sage had sought the comfort of first class. He showed the conductor the ticket he'd gotten from the job shark. "How much to upgrade this?" he asked.

The conductor leaned forward to sniff discreetly as he read the destination. Then he held out a hand, palm up and said, "Just to Chehalis? Sixty miles, one dollar."

Sage passed over the coin and the conductor stepped aside. The lounge car was railroading at its most luxurious. Heavy wicker chairs with blue velvet cushions ranged along either side of the aisle. Jeweled daylight streamed through narrow stained-glass windows inserted into a rectangular roof cupola that ran the length of the car. Small brass light fixtures swung from the cupola's center, their glass globes an exact match to those swaying on the car's walls. His logging boots scuffed a plush carpet patterned in red and green diamonds.

The aching in his head didn't stop Sage from pondering the fact that his fellow passengers, riding amidst this opulence, could care less that the people who crafted these beautiful surroundings could never afford to ride in them. Nor were these train passengers going to wonder whether some hobo rode beneath their feet, clutching for dear life to one of the car's supporting rods. Someone like Billy, Matthew's dead brother.

As he stumbled his way forward, the scattering of passengers turned as one to stare out their respective windows, the backs of their heads a deliberate rebuff. None of them welcomed his scruffy presence, he thought and smiled with grim satisfaction. A little reality is good for their souls. Reaching the farthest corner, Sage gingerly lowered himself into a chair and turned it in toward the wall. He didn't care to look at them either. Stuffing his bindle beneath the chair, he wadded up his coat for a pillow, pulled his hat low and closed his eyes. Sleep offered the only escape from his headache.

Behind his closed eyes he mentally took his place beside Ida, Knute, his mother and Fong. They'd be at the burial about now, in the shade of the Lone Fir Cemetery. Sorrow at Billy's death stabbed and held Sage as fiercely as the pain in his head. Finally, somewhere north of Vancouver, he drifted off to the lulling rhythm of the train wheels' click-clack in his ears.

❀ ❀ ❀

"Mister, wake up. We're pulling into Chehalis. Your stop." The conductor was poking his shoulder with a stiff finger.

His head still throbbed but not as intensely. Sage thanked the conductor and reached for his bindle. No one else disembarked although, further down the platform, a few men climbed aboard the train. As he stood gazing in the direction of the steam locomotive, a gravelly voice sounded from behind him. He turned to see a white-haired man with a hawkish face and piercing brown eyes looking at him. "I said, you sent here by McCurdy to work?"

"I was if McCurdy looks like a wharf rat and has a storefront in Portland."

"Wharf rat. Yup, that's a good description all right." The man cackled. "The wharf rat's telegram said he was sending someone up here to work in the Plunkett Camp. I'm the cook there, came to town for supplies. Name's Homer. Come on, the wagon's over here." The man pointed toward a farm wagon where two big mules stood in the traces. "I'll be right back. Got to get the mail. You go on ahead and climb in back. You're looking a little bit peaked. Drank too much your last night in town I expect. You can sleep it off on the flour sacks, leastwise till the road gets bumpy." He cackled again.

Sage watched the old man clump away, noticing that the hitch in his gait was because the man had legs of differing lengths. Clambering over the tailgate, Sage made himself a nest among the stuffed cotton provision sacks. A few minutes later the wagon dipped to one side as Homer climbed aboard. "You're lucky, young fellow. Plunkett Camp's not a bad place to work. That's 'cause the food's pretty good—course, I'm the cook." He cackled again and clucked the mules into action.

Sage dozed until the wagon tipped into a deep rut and jostled up out of it. He sat up, thinking his head might hurt less if he held it erect. The road had become rougher as it began meandering across fields filled with stumps, scrub brush and young alder trees. Here and there a crude house of hand-planed lumber stood midst a few acres of fields tilled around stumps too big to pull out. These were the stump farmers, families struggling to raise milk cows and grow crops on land that, just a few short years ago, was covered in fir, cedar, hemlock and big leaf maple. Back breaking work for a meager living. It took imagination to believe this tough land was capable of transformation into rich productive farms like those found back East. Certainly more imagination than he would be willing to back with years of sweat and heartache.

Plunkett Camp. So that was his destination. McCurdy was cagey; he'd kept the name of the camp secret. Didn't want to risk having men find the work on their own. McCurdy had enjoyed lording it over Sage: "You look like hell, boy. Don't know if I oughta inflict you on the log boss. Can't hold your likker?"

Sage had made no response, wordlessly handing over his five dollars and taking a rail ticket in return. No point in responding to the goad since they both knew the job shark would never jeopardize his additional two-buck referral fee from the logging camp owner. McCurdy'd send Sage out on that train so long as he was breathing and could walk on his own.

As Sage bounced atop the flour sacks, one hand clutching the back of the buckboard, his thoughts kept returning to the attack outside Lucinda's. Obviously, he'd gotten too close to knowing something. Maybe they'd overheard him asking about the Scot, MacKenzie. It was a Scot who had cracked his noggin. The memory of that hissed burr was as sharp as that rat's bite. He tried to remember where he'd asked about MacKenzie. In least seven job shark storefronts and a couple saloons. Men looking for work had crowded into the storefronts. So, that was probably it. One of MacKenzie's friends overheard Sage asking after the Scot and decided to scare him off. That made sense.

Or maybe his attacker was that fellow who'd watched him sneak away from the hobo camp. That man had spoken with a Scots burr. So MacKenzie or Meachum? Which man was the one they were protecting and why? The attack made sense only if one of the two had murdered Clancy Steele. Sage mulled over both possibilities but couldn't settle on either man as the more likely. Though, if he was forced to draw the "likely straw," MacKenzie would be his choice. But then, where had Meachum disappeared to and why?

Then again, maybe it was neither of them. After all, there were plenty of Scots walking around Portland. No telling who the man was or who he was protecting. Another memory, this one a blur, tugged at his thoughts. His reaching for it only chased it farther away. He let it go.

All the thinking made his headache worse so he turned his attention to his surroundings. The wagon had begun bumping through a recently logged area. Here the stump tops were still bright yellow with amber colored pitch dribbling down their sides. Mounds of lopped evergreen limbs marked where the trees had fallen, leaving behind crushed ferns, moss, and shrubs in the churned up dirt.

"There it be," Homer called over his shoulder.

Sage twisted to look forward for his first sight of Plunkett Camp. A cluster of shingle-roofed shacks sat a few hundred yards up slope on the side of what folks back in Pennsylvania would call a "mountain." Out here, though, it was a "hill" and not a very big one at that. Higher up, Sage could see the edge of the cut where hundreds of tree trunks soared into the sky. Those'd be the next to fall.

Closer to the camp it was obvious that the movable shacks had been set up without making them plumb because two of the shabbiest listed toward the downhill side. Those would be the bunkhouses. An open-sided lean-to provided shelter for the mules. A smaller, better constructed and level shack, standing apart from the rest, probably housed the log boss. All and all it looked like every logging camp Sage had ever worked in.

Homer stopped the wagon in front of a fourth building, where smoke curled from a stovepipe that jutted out its side. He twisted in his seat to look at Sage. "This be the cookhouse—I'd appreciate some help unloading if you can handle it," Homer said, his eyes sympathetic.

"No problem," Sage said. He jumped down, the jar of the landing making him immediately regret the move. Unlatching the tailgate, Sage started carrying wooden boxes and cotton sacks into the building where Homer began swiftly stowing the provisions on shelves and in bins.

"Howdy. You the man McCurdy sent out?" asked a man standing by the cookhouse door when Sage turned from chaining up the wagon's tailgate. The stranger was tall, his barrel chest clothed in worn blue plaid flannel, his graying black hair hanging lank to just below his ears, while stubble tracked the contours of his craggy face. "Name's Plunkett," he said. "I'm the owner and the log boss here. What work can you do? Your shoulders look a mite under worked for you to be a faller or a bucker."

"Name's John Miner. I've swamped, graded, and helped on the donkey engine, but, like you say, I don't have much experience falling or bucking," Sage replied.

"Well, the donkey died yesterday. The donkey doctor just hopped today's train to Tacoma to fetch a part. Don't know if he'll need help or not when he comes back. We can always use swampers. They don't stay around long." The man looked Sage up and down as if Sage were a horse at auction. "You sure you're up to the work? You're looking kinda peaked."

"I'm stronger than I look, just ran into a little tussle last night is all. I'll be fine." Sage said, even as he fought to suppress a groan at the sudden stab of pain behind his eyes.

"Well, you're here. We'll give you a try. Because the donkey's down, we're working a shorter day. So we don't need you to start. You just rest today. Your pay will start tomorrow. McCurdy told you we work a six-day week, ten-hour day, didn't he? I'll give you one-dollar fifty a day, plus grub and a bunk. You'll be bunking over there," he said pointing at the leaning bunkhouse standing closest to the kitchen. At Sage's nod in agreement, Plunkett entered the cookhouse leaving Sage to find a bunk on his own.

Sage grabbed his bindle from the wagon and headed for the bunkhouse. Damn, MacKenzie had to be the donkey doctor. He must have been one of the men getting on the train at Chehalis. Missed him by one day. Now he'd have to wait in this logging camp until MacKenzie returned. And being a traveling operation, this was one rude camp. Traveling log camps moved with the tree line. As the trees were cleared and it started taking too much time to get to the timber, the shacks were loaded onto skids and pulled closer. No one bothered building outhouses in these temporary camps. His nose made that abundantly clear. Only the tree stumps provided men privacy. A warm summer day, like today, made the air ripe with the stench of human waste. Sage hoped the drinking water came from somewhere well away and uphill from the camp.

The inside of the ten-by-fourteen-foot bunkhouse looked exactly as he expected. Three tiers of plank bunks extended along walls that let light glimmer through the gaps between boards. It would be brittle cold in the spring and fall. A sizable wood stove squatted in the center. About seven feet up, wires were strung from wall to wall. These were for drying wet clothes overnight. Sage examined what appeared to be an unclaimed, third-tier bunk and felt the mattress. Hay-stuffed sacking and none too clean. Bedbugs and lice guaranteed. Just as he thought this, a tiny brown wedge with six legs skittered across the back of his hand where it rested on the mattress. He jerked his hand away, shook the bug to the floor, and squashed it. Fighting the pain, he rolled up his sleeves, picked up the mattress, and carried it outside, holding it well away from his body. He'd be sticking to the blankets in his bindle and hard planks while he was here.

Sage dozed on his bunk until the sounds of men entering the bunkhouse woke him. The smell of sweat and unwashed clothes filled the room. All thirteen of the loggers were tall, apparently Scandinavians or Slavs. Rudimentary English was their common language. His bunkhouse mates greeted him, asked his name, but left him alone while they continued to josh each other.

At the triangle's metal clang, the men trooped to the cookhouse. It was one big room filled with two rough plank tables and backless benches. The far corner contained a compact cooking area, dominated by a giant wood burning cookstove. The crowd of men divided itself into two groups to sit at tables which had room for fifteen or so. Homer plunked down hot platters of venison, potatoes, greens, and cornbread. Although the food was simple, it was plentiful and tasty. In near silence, the men loaded their tin plates and fell to eating. Sage caught Homer's eye and lifted a hunk of cornbread in salute. Homer responded with a pleased, gap-toothed grin.

After supper a few men sat outside on stumps while others lay in their bunks exchanging a few words, dozing or writing letters. A few were reading. A small group was squeezed together on one side, listening as one of their mates read from the Bible. Sage lay on his bunk, staring at the roof timbers overhead and thought about the attack. He didn't try to be conversational. He knew from experience that these men wouldn't spend time getting to know him until he'd shown that he could do his share of the work. Logging was a hard, transient life. These men had no energy to spare on fleeting friendships or laggards who made their work harder. Even before the twilight deepened into night, snores were issuing from most of the bunks. Work would start before dawn the next day. Sage, his head still a dull ache, also drifted off.

Drizzling rain came with the day. Upslope, white tendrils of fog slithered through the tree crowns. Far below, a sullen mass of the same gray fog hid the river bottom. Bellies full of pancakes, potatoes, eggs, salt pork, and coffee, the men climbed through the predawn gloom toward the dark line of trees.

Work began without much talk. The men knew their jobs. Someone handed Sage a five-foot axe that he used to chop the limbs off trees that had been felled the day before. His muscles were strong because of his fight training with Fong. Still his hands, although protected by heavy hogskin gloves, were getting blisters.

As always, Sage paused momentarily to marvel at the woodmen's skill. Two tall, powerful Swedes were felling trees together. Standing on planks jutting out from the tree trunk five feet above the ground, they alternated waist level swings of six-foot axes. Swing by swing they made the undercut, on the side where the tree was to fall. Halfway through, a stream of golden sap began to flow from the cut and down the trunk. Chips flying, they made a higher cut in the other side. The faller's cry echoed through the woods. The giant tree thundered downward, taking smaller trees with it.

Next, two buckers attacked the downed tree with their sixteen-foot crosscut saw. They cut it into uniform lengths for skidding down a road constructed of debarked logs, lying side by side. Sage labored near the buckers, racing to lop off the limbs before the buckers were ready to move to their next cut.

Although Sage was unhappy that he'd missed MacKenzie, he was fortunate the donkey engine was inoperable because it freed up a rigger. The rigger helped Sage by carting off the limbs Sage whacked off. Once the engine was fixed, the rigger would be back to snugging the wire around the logs so that the steam-powered cable could drag them over the skids down to the loading area. Once in the loading area, another engine would winch the logs onto a wagon on pulled either by mules or oxen. Horses couldn't stand up to the work. Plunkett Camp, like most logging operations, used a number of wagons—a few owned and driven by independent teamsters. Those wagons hauled the logs to the nearest pond. There rope and wire would cinch the logs into a raft for floating down to the mill. Grueling labor, every part of it.

Sage worked hard the whole day. With the rest of the men, at the five-hour mark, he took a break right where he stood, wolfing down slabs of bread and meat. Five hours later, they stopped work for the day. He plodded down the hill, aching everywhere but feeling like he'd managed to pull his share of the load. The others seemed to think so too—making friendly comments and offering him chewing tobacco, which he declined. Halfway to camp, the descending woodsmen met up with a lone man trudging uphill toward the forest, a small iron gear in one hand and a box of tools in the other. The man was big, well-muscled, with black curling hair and a clean-shaven face. Straight teeth flashed white as he greeted the tired workers.

"Hey, MacKenzie, did you enjoy your day off? Bet you never gave one thought to us here, slaving away!"

"Day off, I'll be gonna to hell. My butt doesna have any feeling from those third-class train slats and after that log wagon I canna say where my legs begin. Whoa, after that ride I'll no' sit easy for days. And here I am, hungry enough to eat my boots, but Plunkett said this part gets installed in yon donkey before I get fed, so do pardon me if I don't stop to palaver." He moved on past them but shouted back over his shoulder, "Now don't you be forgetting, that there's one more pig heading to yon trough. You better be leaving some for me."

As the other woodsmen laughed and continued downhill, Sage paused to watch as MacKenzie picked his way among the stumps and disappeared into the underbrush.

SIXTEEN

Sage groaned when he attempted to roll out of his bunk the next morning. A night on the hard planks after a day's hard labor left him feeling as if he'd been pulled through a knothole backward.

His bunkhouse mates cast knowing smiles in his direction. They remembered how it felt the first day back in the woods after time spent in the city. He hobbled to the tin basin to rinse his face. Like the other men, he didn't try shaving in the ice-cold water.

Men were already shoveling in the food when Sage clambered over a bench to take his place at the table. MacKenzie sat at the same table, just a few men away.

"Hey, doc, is that donkey running?" asked someone from further down the table.

"Installed that pesky cog last night just a wee bit before dark. She's raring to heehaw this morning," MacKenzie said as he forked a pancake dripping with syrup into his mouth.

"We dropped a passel of trees, so you'll need to work hard for a change to catch up to us," said one of the fallers, raising his head from his plate to flash MacKenzie a toothy grin.

"Ain't nothing me and the donkey canna' handle, so don't try lollygagging on that springboard, dreaming of your "houses" and "lots,'" MacKenzie retorted. Those within earshot roared with laughter at MacKenzie's sly reference to the common practice of those hitting town after payday–that of visiting "houses" of prostitution while drinking "lots" of whiskey.

When Sage left the cookhouse, he was puzzling over how to strike up a conversation with MacKenzie. Then he became aware that someone was calling his alias—'Miner.' Sage turned. It was MacKenzie.

"Mr. Miner, you a wee bit hard of hearing?" MacKenzie asked, but he didn't wait for the answer. "Plunkett tells me you're an experienced donkey man, and I'm short a hand today. How about you working for me?"

"Okay, I'd rather ride herd on the donkey than swamp any day," Sage said slowing his steps to match MacKenzie's as they climbed toward the engine. From a distance, the donkey engine looked like a gigantic rusted whiskey bottle propped upright among the stumps. Its rusted smoke stack poked up through a shake roof. Large steel cables snaked out the front end into the logging area. Boiler, engine, cable drums and roof were bolted onto a large platform, twenty by twelve feet. The platform sat on huge wooden runners it used to winch itself across the forest floor when it needed to set up in a new location.

"Hope you're up to hauling wood and water all day," MacKenzie said. The donkey engine burned the wood to boil the water to build the steam that moved the pistons which, in turn, enabled the drums to reel in the steel cable, pulling the logs through the underbrush.

In short order, the donkey's furnace was roaring and the engine began panting like a tired dog, as it waited to take on its first load. Overhead, steam and smoke drifted into the dawn sky. Meanwhile, the rigger headed out into the downed logs, choosing the first one to tie to the steel cables for its journey to the loading area. Sage busied himself filling barrels with water from the closest stream and stockpiling short sticks of firewood. MacKenzie adjusted dials and checked engine gauges.

"Where you hail from, Miner?" asked MacKenzie as they waited for the rigger's shout to signal it was time to engage the engine.

"I grew up in Pennsylvania. Mined some up north. Traveled south to California and then headed back up here to the Northwest. I've worked the woods in Alaska, California, and Oregon. How about yourself?"

"Edinburgh is my birthplace. Came to America about ten years ago. Stayed awhile in the East before heading west with a wee stake to make my fortune." MacKenzie's lips twisted in a rueful smile.

"What happened?"

"I owned a hundred and sixty acres of homestead timberland down near Silverton, Oregon. Worked it real careful. I had the full setup—donkey engine and all. Then the timber trusts decided they wanted my land." MacKenzie broke the stick he was holding over his thigh with a sharp crack before tossing it on the woodpile. "So, the bastards burnt me out."

"How'd you know it was the timber barons who burned you out?"

MacKenzie sighed. "They used a front man named Clancy Steele to finagle timber land for them. My land sat in the middle of their patch. Clancy is the kind of man who likes to brag. Wasn't hard to figure out."

"So where's Clancy now?"

"He's around. Still does some work for the timber barons, but mainly he's working as a railroad bull. Mean bastard, I'll be betting he likes the work."

The rigger yelled so they jumped to task. The pressure had built up so that the engine was puffing like an angry beast. Smoke swirled in great billows overhead. With screeches and groans the drums began to reel in a heavy steel cable that twanged under the strain of an unseen log attached to its far end. That taut wire cable was deadly. A snapped cable became a writhing snake that could cut a man in two. Or else, sometimes, the log being pulled snagged, only to break loose and bound toward the donkey with such force that it flattened any woodsman caught in its path.

Sage worked without stopping, minding the rigging, fetching water and wood. The metallic shriek of the wire over the drum was deafening. His only relief from the din came when he trudged, buckets in hand, to the muddy stream that tumbled down through the cut zone, about an eighth of a mile from the engine. He and MacKenzie spoke during the few lulls, but mostly they worked hard to keep the cable taut and moving freely. All day, the logs bounded toward them over the rise of a slight hillock.

Near day's end, Sage helped the riggers wrap the cable around some standing trees at the edge of the cut. Building up a head of steam, the donkey engine began reeling in the cable, winching itself along on its platform runners toward the next day's location. Halfway there, one runner encountered a boulder too high for it to slide over.

Sage jumped to the boulder, pickaxe in hand, trying to dislodge it so the runner could push it aside. Over the steam engine's huffing, the whine of the drum and the shrieking of the cable, Sage heard MacKenzie shout. A flying body hit him, knocking him flat, pushing his face into the musty earth. Simultaneously, there was a loud crack. Out of the corner of his eye he saw the steel cable flick into a tree stump next to his head before whipping back in the other direction. The engine spun into the high whine of revved machinery suddenly released from a heavy load. Then silence pinched off the noise.

In that silence he heard the faint chirp of evening birds in the fir crowns. At middle distance, near the now-silent engine, men cursed. Near his ear, labored breathing came from the body atop his own. Sage lay motionless unable to move beneath the weight. The body lifted, and he rolled over to see MacKenzie grinning at him.

"That was a close one," MacKenzie said, nodding toward the tree stump. There was a two-inch-deep gouge made by the lashing cable along the entire side of the three-foot-wide stump. If that cable had hit Sage, it would have sliced right through him. The man grinning at him had just saved his life.

MacKenzie acknowledged Sage's words of gratitude with a shrug before climbing back atop the platform. They rigged the cables again and finished hauling the donkey engine to its new location on the slope.

Food had never tasted better than it did that night, even though the fare was exactly the same as the night before. Sage had seen men delimbed and decapitated by snapped cables. In the woods, where there was no doctor, death was almost a certainty when the cable struck.

The men who'd seen the cable snap that day told the story. They congratulated Sage on his good luck, while praising MacKenzie for his quick action. The men's words rang sincere. Each one knew he might be next. Each one hoped there'd be a MacKenzie standing nearby.

After the meal, the men straggled outside to sit on stumps to smoke or chew or to jaw over the events of the day. MacKenzie sat alone, near the door. When he saw Sage step out of the cookhouse, he stood up.

"John, let me show you some of the local sights hereabouts. There's a good view of the valley up that trail over there that you might like to see." MacKenzie pointed at a trail winding around the hillside away from the camp. They set off, MacKenzie in the lead. They followed a narrow deer track that meandered between the stumps and then into a forest not yet touched by axes. Giant trees formed a dense canopy pierced by shafts of fading sunlight. All around, massive trunks rose like the marble columns he'd once seen soaring into the dim reaches of European cathedrals. Beneath the canopy, there was a mixture of moss, fern, and a prickly-leafed plant some called Oregon grape. The warm air smelled sweetly of berries, wild flowers and sun-warmed fir needles. Seconds after stepping into the forest, the camp sounds were gone.

They walked in the wooded silence for ten minutes until emerging into a sloped clearing. Fire had swept through. The tree trunks were scorched black and most lay on the ground. The hillside, exposed to the setting sun, was a collection of terraced granite platforms edged by sheer drops of fifty feet or more.

MacKenzie stepped onto a platform, raising his hand to point upriver to a line of snow-dusted peaks encircling the valley. "You ever see a sight this beautiful in Pennsylvania?" he asked.

Sage turned to look up the valley. The Pocono Mountains in Pennsylvania were beautiful, particularly in the fall when the hardwood forest flamed red and yellow. But these mountains were different. Rugged upthrusts of the Earth's mantle, created by cataclysms violent beyond all imagining. It was easy to answer honestly. "No, Pennsylvania cannot boast of this wonder," he said.

In that instant he felt the cold unyielding jab of a steel point prick his rib. MacKenzie stood at his left side and behind, a knife in his hand. Sage didn't move.

"You should thank me, Miner, if that really is your name. That beautiful sight is the last thing you'll see in this lifetime."

"What are you talking about?" Sage tried to step backward from the edge, but the knife pricked sharper. He stopped.

For the first time, MacKenzie's soft Scots burr sounded unfriendly. "When I rode into camp yesterday, Plunkett handed me a note from McCurdy. It came up with you in the mail. He let me know he was doing me a favor—sending me my 'cousin.' Since we both know we're no relation—who the hell are you? Your answer better be good, or you're going to be flying into that great beyond right there in front of your boots."

"My name is John Adair."

"You a Dickensen?"

It took Sage aback momentarily to discover that MacKenzie thought him an agent of that notorious detective agency. Working people reviled the Dickensens, but last he knew, those hired thugs seldom worked for timber barons. Usually they made a living beating up people on behalf of the steel barons, mining companies, and railroad trusts.

"Believe me, the last thing I am is a Dickensen. I'm here be cause there's a young boy accused of a murder he didn't commit."

"What's that got to do with me? Why are you interested in me?"

"I'm interested in you because the murdered man was Clancy Steele."

The knife fell away. Sage stepped sideways, away from the knife, until he was standing well back from the precipice. Then he looked at MacKenzie who had dropped the knife to his side, his forehead creased in a vertical line of puzzlement. "Steele is dead? Someone killed him?" His voice rose on the last word. Either he was genuinely dumbfounded or else a mighty fine actor.

Sage sat down on the granite shelf, well back from the edge. He gestured to the rock beside him. MacKenzie also sat.

"So if you thought I was a Dickensen, why'd you risk your life to save me today?" Sage asked as he handed the other man a machine-rolled cigarette. Sage seldom smoked, saving it for times when his nerves jangled. Now was the time for a smoke alright.

MacKenzie lit up, blew out a stream of smoke, and squinted toward the snow-capped peak straddling the head of the river valley. "No mystery there. Canna let a man die just because I suspected him of being no good and out to cause me trouble. I wasn't even going to shove you off the edge here, no matter what you said. Just wanted to scare you into telling the truth. I've never done anything in my life that would call for me to kill a man just because he seemed too interested in my business."

"You admit you hated Clancy Steele."

"Aye. To be sure I hated him. I'd built up my operation so that it was just starting to turn a profit. When Steele turned up, I lost everything I'd spent seven years building. I hated him so much that the last time I visited Portland I looked for him."

"Did you find him?"

"He was in Erickson's, that big saloon there on Second—off Burnside. He was so drunk and full of himself that he never saw me."

"Did you talk to him?"

"No, I didn't. He was drunk and in a mean mood. Besides, I wanted to listen to him brag. I know it wasn't his idea to burn my operation. Even if I was stupid enough to kill someone, it'd be the man Steele took his orders from. Steele's just one more bully without much brain. Those type of men are thick on the ground. Killing one of them wouldn't save the next guy's sawmill. But you say someone murdered him. How'd it happen?"

"A witness said that two men surprised him and one of them slashed his throat."

MacKenzie's nose wrinkled in distaste. "Well, I'm no hypocrite. I'm glad the bastard's dead. But I sure the hell didn't kill him."

"When did you arrive in camp from Portland?"

"I arrived here last Tuesday at six o'clock in the evening with Homer and a few other fellas. When was Steele killed?"

"That night around nine o'clock," Sage said, knowing MacKenzie had told the truth because his alibi could be easily checked.

"You said you overheard Steele bragging. What did he brag about?"

"Well, he was yammering on about how he would be riding high in the saddle real soon. That he would be getting his share. My impression was that he had something on someone but I couldna tell who or what. I thought on that at the time because I try to keep up with Steele's doings whenever I get to town. Well, at least I tried to. I suppose that's over now." MacKenzie mashed his cigarette out on the granite before dropping the butt into his shirt pocket like a responsible woodsman.

"MacKenzie, who did Steele run with when he was in town? Do you know?"

"Aye, I saw him many a time with McCurdy, the job shark. McCurdy had a brave mouth when Steele was around. It was McCurdy that supplied the drunkards Steele planted on different homesteads to claim the deeds. I suppose those two had what passes for friendship among their kind."

Sage stood up and so did MacKenzie. "I'm real sorry I suspected you, MacKenzie. I'd heard what Steele did to you. I figured you had good reason to kill him, and McCurdy said you'd been in town that day. Now I know you had nothing to do with it. Please accept my apology. I'd be proud to shake your hand if you're willing."

MacKenzie grinned and thrust out his hand. "I don't hold your suspicions against you. Man's got to be careful these days."

The two men shook hands, the snow-laden peak at the valley's end the only witness.

SEVENTEEN

THE NEXT MORNING Sage rolled out of his bunk and slipped out of the bunkhouse while the birds still slept. He didn't bother collecting the three dollars he'd earned. In the predawn light, the trees and sky, bushes and stumps were shades of black and gray. Bindle looped over one shoulder, Sage carried a stout stick. He was alert but not too concerned. By this time of year, the bear and cougar had trailed the grazing deer into the higher altitudes.

Dawn rolled over the snow-covered ridges and crept across the valley floor, dogging his heels as he hiked down the rutted logging road. Alongside him, gray glacial waters plunged over a rocky riverbed. Near to seven o'clock he'd reached the first farmhouse, its rough-plank boards silvered by the morning light. Sage stopped to speak to the farmer who was leading his cows out to graze among the stumps in the field. For a dime, Sage got a slab of cold meat between two pieces of thick bread. He ate as he walked, thinking about Plunkett's camp and the men working there.

Just three days ago he'd traveled this road hoping to find a murderer; instead, he'd discovered a man he wanted to call "friend." He liked MacKenzie's certainty of purpose and ready laughter. He'd miss his flashing smile. Still, real friendship with a man like MacKenzie wasn't possible. There was too much about Sage himself that had to stay secret. Real friendship required an openness he couldn't afford to show. "Oh dammit it to hell," he said aloud, only to jump, then hoot with laughter as a startled squirrel skittered first toward him and then away.

Noon struck the courthouse clock just as Sage jumped down from a farmer's wagon onto the main street of Chehalis. He hunted for the post office, finding it tucked inside a dry goods store. Waiting for him was an envelope from his mother. She wrote that she'd heard from her "cousin" in Denver and was enclosing the letter. It was in Vincent St. Alban's script and confirmed Sage's suspicions about Otis Welker:

> The man about whom you inquired acts on behalf of his employers whenever there is underhanded business to be done. His appearance does not bode well. Death seems to follow him around. His presence means something illegal or violent is involved. We'd like to know what. Be very careful. He never travels alone. There are thugs about him that people don't see until it's too late.
>
> On another note, it is with deep dismay that I must inform you that a Dickensen slithered past our defenses and infiltrated our organization. Not at the top, but maybe close enough to learn the names of those in the field. If he learned your real name, Welker may have it, too. I'm sorry. I pray you are not endangered. Take care. My very best regards in solidarity, V.

His mother's letter related restaurant news and told him the police had not returned. She closed her letter with:

> Dear Boy, I'm sure I don't have to tell you how I've come to love our home here. Still, I would gladly leave it all behind rather than risk losing you. Take care and don't be concerned about me. They're not going to bother an old housekeeper. Your always loving mother, Mae.

Sage's eyes stung as he stared at those last five words. Seeing them for the first time in print made him think again about her years of sacrifice and wonder what she felt when she wrote them. He read both letters once again before tearing them into small pieces and setting them afire atop a stone wall. Once they'd turned to ash, he slipped off the sun-warmed wall and headed toward the telegraph office at the rail depot. The telegraph operator sent a message to Fong, care of the Union Station in Portland. The message stated Sage was heading north but expected to return in a few days. After eating his fill of meat and potatoes in the railway hotel's dining room, Sage shouldered his bindle and began walking north along the tracks.

The sky was a low hanging steel grey and the weather had deteriorated into a drizzle that a steady wind made cold. Sage looked for a fir with low-hanging branches. After some minutes' walk, he finally found one he could crouch under and still watch the tracks.

Two hours later he was still sitting under the tree, shivering with the cold and disgusted with the day. Was any of this nonsense helping St. Alban? He couldn't see how. Besides, for whatever reason, somebody was watching his every move and then bashing at his head. And that thumping hadn't been because of St. Alban. Not likely. Instead of fighting the good fight against economic oppression here he was, out in the middle of nowhere, traveling even farther from home just to save a big-eared, freckle-faced kid he didn't even know. And, so far, he was failing in that relatively simple task.

Even without Matthew's problem, would it really matter? Sometimes he wondered whether the whole St. Alban caper was nonsense. Did he have a need to see himself as being important or singularly wise in a world gone crazy? A need so unbalanced that it deluded him into thinking he, Sage Adair, could change the world? God knew it wasn't like he getting paid for the chances he took. But then, he didn't need money. He had his own—plenty of it. Still, right now, it would be deuced hard to explain to a rational listener why he chose to squat underneath a dripping tree, miles from home, waiting to jump a train so he could ride like Don Quixote into who knows what situation.

The rain dripped, his morose thoughts keeping time as they circled round and round, taking his spirits down and down. A brisk wind flew up the tracks, spinning white blossoms from the wild apple tree into the air like oversized, soggy snowflakes and sending a vision of two little girls slithering into his thoughts. Their fingers dead white against the snow they brushed away so they could reach the dust bin's latch and the scraps of discarded food. Tiny faces, pinched with cold, rags wrapped around their boots to keep their feet from freezing. Beyond them, their father waited with a group of other men, as he had been waiting day after day. Like unmoving rocks of misery around which other people flowed, they'd stood before the factory gates. Closer to home was his Uncle Shaun, who'd hacked the sun awake, spotting his raggedly kerchief bloody. The mine explosion was a merciful deliverance. Sage had seen coal miners die from the two-headed devil, black lung and starvation, hacking their lives away in the shadows of the damp porches dotting the ravines outside the company towns. Death came calling on those porches, in the form of hunger and disease. And the coal companies wouldn't pay a nickle more to ease the suffering they caused.

Sage shifted. The rain was steadily falling, as if a sky high water tap had been carelessly left open. Yet, those memories had fanned his internal fire back to life. Too bad there was no way to purge them of their evil. Or wall them up. Like those medieval penitents in the churches who lived on food passed to them through small holes in the stone walls. If the memories would only vanish, maybe he could turn his back on St. Alban and dank, lonely places like this one.

Sage snorted loudly, sending some creature in the nearby brush scuttling away. Forgetting would be as "likely as cows trotting milk into butter," as Mae Clemens liked to say. It wasn't only those memories that kept him going. It was Mae Clemens herself, what she taught him and how she had lived.

He picked a tight fir cone from those scattered about his feet. Such complex, beautiful symmetry he mused, turning it round and round in his hand, flicking the seed tails with his finger. The natural world abounded with perfection while humanity was as irregular as rocks in a pile. He sniffed the cone only to jerk back when a glob of pitch snagged his mustache hairs. That's what he got for being fanciful. He'd be smelling fir pitch for hours to come. It'd be a devil of a time getting it out.

A rumble rolled up the tracks. A train was coming. It would slow for the curve. Sage grabbed his bindle and stepped into the bushes so that no one on the big locomotive could see him. The long line of cars swayed past, moving at about ten miles an hour. The names of the various railroads—B & O, Great Northern, Southern Pacific, Rock Island Line—in big black letters were emblazoned on their wood-slatted sides.

A railcar with an open door was swaying toward him, its metal suspension beginning to screech as it rounded the curve. Amid the deafening noise of cars, pouring rain and whip of wind, Sage sprinted out of the bushes to the open door, leapt to grab at the floor planks and pulled himself up and into the car. Even before he gained his feet, he sensed the faces peering at him from the gloom. Sage nodded at the men before squeezing into the corner at the other end, tucking himself out of the sight of any railroad bull who might look in the door.

A glance from beneath his hat brim at the other men in the car eased his mind. None looked familiar. He hadn't seen any of them at hobo camp in Portland three nights ago. His stealthy departure would have been cause for comment around the campfire.

"Hey, what's your moniker?" one of the men called.

"John Miner," Sage responded and, sensing welcome, he scrambled across the vibrating floorboards to sit beside the group of five who had a deck of cards and pile of unspent matches in play.

"Where you coming from, John Miner?" asked the same man, apparently the spokesman for the group.

"Plunkett's logging camp. Up there swamping, but I lit on out of there this morning." Sage deliberately borrowed MacKenzie's joke, "I decided time had come to visit some houses and drink lots," he explained. The men laughed. For awhile, they played cards for match sticks and swapped stories about life on the road. Later, they all fell silent, staring out the open doors at the wet green countryside, rough little towns and isolated farms, each man adrift in memory or thought. Tension took over whenever the train stopped at a depot or water tank. As the brakes began squealing and the train slowed, they wordlessly gathered up their belongings and sneaked peeks out the open doors on each side, their ears straining for the sounds of danger. All were ready to shout an alert and leap out if a bull appeared at either open doorway or if boots started thudding atop the steel roof. It was the usual drill. One every experienced hobo knew whenever the train was pulling in.

Sage finally caught up on the sleep he'd lost heading out of Plunkett's so early in the day. On the final leg into Seattle, feeling safe among his companions, Sage stuffed his bindle behind his neck and closed his eyes, letting the sway of the train and the soft murmur of their travel-weary voices lull him to sleep.

Twilight had leached color from the day when the train began its slow slide into the Seattle rail yard. The summer rain was over, leaving the air sweet and the sky a fading blue. Sage, like the others, jumped out at the yard's edge, while the train was still traveling at a fairly fast clip. Hobos hated to "jump and flip" but they were more afraid of getting too close to the railroad bulls in the yard who usually lay in wait for those riding the trains. A smart 'bo never entered the yard if he could help it.

Hitting the hard ground and rolling, Sage gained his feet, snatched up his bindle then paused for a second to watch as other men and bindles flew out boxcar doors all up and down the train like fleas off a carcass. Then he scrambled down off the rail bed. Within a block he was in Seattle's Chinatown. Supper was a warming and tasty ten-cent bowl of seasoned noodles.

Sage waited until darkness had securely descended before entering the hobo jungle. He wanted a chance to study the faces around the fire before he stepped into the light.

Like its Portland counterpart, this camp was also well organized. These were the working hobos and here he was most likely to find Meachum. Supper was over, but the men offered him bread and cheese, which he declined, and coffee, which he accepted. He reciprocated by handing around the pouch of tobacco and rolling papers he'd just bought.

The talk around the fire was about the few men hired that day to work on the docks.

"How much does a man earn in a day on the Seattle docks?" Sage asked.

"They're paying 50-cents an hour. Ten-hour day, six-day week." A lilting Scandinavian accent colored the words spoken by a man they all called Big Swede.

"Hey, that's darn good," Sage said, thinking of the dollar-fifty a day he'd been earning as a swamper at Plunkett's.

"Ya." Big Swede responded, "You want to get that money, though, you must join the longshoremen's union. Only union jobs on the docks pay good. Me, I join union in Frisco. I have a union card," he patted his breast pocket, "I can work on any union dock on the West Coast."

"How much to join?" asked a whip-thin man who called himself "Prairie Slim."

"Ten dollars initiation, fifty cents a month plus twenty-five cents for funeral benefits," Big Swede responded. "But the work. It is very hard. Most longshoremen are big men, like me."

Other men, as tall and bulky as Big Swede, nodded agreement.

"What are you doing for that fifty cents an hour?" Sage asked.

"Today we loaded fifty-pound flour sacks. I stay down there in the hold. Sacks slide down the planks, I pick up two on my shoulder and stow them in stacks against the bulkhead. Ten of us, we maybe load three to four thousand sacks all day. My shoulders are real sore," Big Swede said, using his gnarled hand to knead his shoulder.

"You looking to work on the docks, John Miner?" Big Swede asked. He looked doubtful, like Sage's six-foot frame was short on brawn.

"Nope, I'm not cut out for that kind of work. Actually, I hoped to hitch up with a friend of mine, name of Meachum. You seen him around?" There was a stir to his left as a man rose and slipped into the surrounding darkness.

"No, never heard of the man," said Big Swede. There was murmured agreement from those hunkered down around the fire.

❀ ❀ ❀

Later, once he'd spread out his bedroll, Sage headed for the trench latrine dug in a small clearing well away from the camp. He'd just buttoned his trousers when rough hands shoved him from behind, making him jump the trench to avoid falling in. He nearly didn't make it.

Sage steadied himself in his boots before looking around to see four hulking men surrounding him. Maybe not longshoremen but big enough even so. He felt somewhat reassured because, in the faint light, there was no glint of metal. Their menacing stances told him, however, that they intended to pummel him senseless with their bare fists.

Fong's familiar refrain flashed through his head: "When force superior, first—run away quick. Second—talk fast. Third—fight smart."

Running away quick wasn't possible—they had him surrounded on three sides and that malodorous trench was at his back. Maybe number two. "Hey, what's going . . . ," Sage began, only to have his breath escape him in an 'umph' as the men rushed him and knocked him to the ground before he finished the sentence. He sat in the dirt, carefully flicking the small wood bits off his palms. "Fight smart" it was then.

Sage swiftly regained his footing and settled into the bow stance, his front leg slightly bent, his rear leg straight. He raised his hands, lowered his shoulders, and told himself to relax. While he was no Fong Kam Tong, he might be able to do some damage before they brought him down.

The biggest man charged at him, his arm moving in a swinging roundhouse from the left. Sage shifted forward, clasped the man's forearm, and rocked back, using his assailant's momentum to send him, arms flailing, to Sage's right. The man hit the dirt with a satisfying thud, having to scramble to avoid tumbling into the trench.

A second man rushed in from the right. "Grasp bird's tail, single whip," Sage told himself even as he raised his right hand, wrist hooked down, fingers touching. Turning at his waist, he swept the hooked hand toward the sky. It hit the man squarely beneath the chin, knocking him backward.

Feet rooted in the ground, Sage continued moving through various forms of the snake and crane, each one diverting his attackers' force away from him. "White crane spreads its wings" unbalanced a two-handed clutch from the right. "Hand strums the lute" transformed a meaty fist heading for Sage's chest into a man on his knees whimpering from a dislocated elbow. "Brush knee, twist step" protected Sage's crotch and knocked the wind from the last man standing. Sage's attackers crawled back, staggered to their feet and clustered together, well away from him. He heard them muttering as they tried to decide their next attack. Sage was pleased to realize that he stood no more than two feet from where he'd begun his defense. A cooling sheen of sweat coated his face. Still he wasn't panting, even though his attackers were sucking in great gulps of air. Fong would have been pleased.

As the four turned toward him, Sage lowered his shoulders and relaxed his muscles in preparation for the charge. One of the men had picked up a heavy stick. With a yowl he rushed at Sage, who again dropped into the bow stance.

"Enough!" The sharp command cracked out from the tree line. A man stepped into the clearing. This time, something metal did glint in the faint light. Sage froze, as did the charging man who immediately lowered his stick and straightened.

"Can't you see this man's going to break every one of your bones if you keep at it? Leave him be, I tell you!" the man ordered Sage's attackers.

"Meach, he's a slippery character, but we'll take him. We ain't been hurt that much."

"That's because he's chosen not to hurt you, not because he can't. I've seen this kind of fighting before. Stand down, I tell you."

The man stepped farther into the clearing and spoke to Sage. He still held the revolver at the ready. "Sorry about the fellas here. They're a mite protective. That's a most peculiar way to fight, mister. You managed to hold off the whole Squad."

"I take it you're Meachum," Sage said.

"Who are you? You better give me an answer I like, or maybe I'll have to use this here gun," the man replied, waggling the gun barrel for emphasis. A slouch-brimmed hat shadowed the man's face and hid the intent in his eyes.

Meachum had called Sage's attackers "the Squad." Taking a chance, Sage said, "It's not who I am, it's what I am that matters. Let's just say I believe in marching with the Saint and all his angels." There was a sharp intake of breath from one of his attackers and the man holding the gun lowered it to his side. He stepped closer, pushing his hat back on his head so that his face showed.

"You know St. Alban?" Meachum asked.

"I'm one of his men," Sage replied. "So are you fellas, I suspect."

EIGHTEEN

THE SHADOWS ON Meachum's face emphasized jutting brows, a sharp nose and canyon deep lines alongside his mouth. The thick swath of hair across his forehead suggested a young man, but those were silver strands glinting in the light. He was the man who'd left the campfire when Sage asked after "Meachum."

"Is there a message for me from the Saint?" Meachum asked.

Sage lowered his hands and rose from the wide stance of the bow step. "No. When I started looking for you, I had no idea you were with the Flying Squadron," he said.

"Why were you looking for me?"

Sage glanced toward the four men, who were standing nearby rigid as the tree trunks crowding the clearing. "I think, maybe, that matter is just for the two of us."

Meachum's eyes narrowed, his calculating look a sensation moving across Sage's face. Sage met the look, allowed his face to relax, opening to the other man's scrutiny.

Meachum turned to the others, "Men, I need to speak with this fella. Go bed down. I'll give a call if I need you."

"Is that a good idea? What if. . . ." An undertone of alarm accompanied the words one of the men spoke.

"Go ahead on. This man and I need to talk private." Meachum's voice was firm as he waved the four away, toward the camp where the other hobos could be heard snoring in their bedrolls. Grudgingly the men moved in the direction Meachum indicated, but each man in the Squadron paused to glare at Sage. He got the message. Anything bad happened to Meachum, they'd hunt Sage down like he was a rabid dog.

"Come on. I know a more comfortable place for us to talk private," Meachum said, moving toward the rail yard. Sage trailed him across the tracks into a neighborhood of clapboard shacks tucked against a hill. They approached a one-room structure that closely fronted the dirt road, squeezed within a row of shabby wooden buildings. On each side, sounds spilled out of the lighted windows and clapboard gaps – shrill laughter, loud talk and other, more private, noises. But the building they approached was silent, its darkened window partially covered by a swag of tattered cloth. Sage gazed at the name "Angel" someone had scrawled on the door lintel in crude black script, wondering what they were doing at a prostitute's door. Meachum used his knuckles to tap lightly on the glass. A woman's querulous, slurred voice responded, "Go away. I ain't working tonight."

Meachum leaned close, speaking quietly into the crack of the door, "Angie, it's Meachum. May I come in?"

"Harry!" came a soft exclamation. The door was snatched open, and a white hand reached out to grab Meachum's arm and draw him in. Meachum resisted.

"Angie, my dear, I've someone with me. Can we both come in?" Meachum asked in a low tone.

"Of course you can." The door opened wider, and a dressing gown fluttered in the gloom as the woman noisily groped for matches. As the match flared, he saw the thickened figure of a middle-aged woman outlined in light as she fumbled to light the lamp wick. She turned to set the lamp on an unpainted wooden table against one wall of the room. The lamplight exposed a face puffy from too much drink, her hair scraggly despite the frantic combing of her stubby fingers. Yet, there was also a suggestion of a once pretty woman, for her nose was small and straight, her eyes large and dark, her chin the tip of a blurry heart-shaped face.

Her hand nervously waved them toward the only two chairs in the small room. "Sit, sit. Can I fix you a cup of tea? I gathered me a few bits of coal from beside the tracks today, so I can get my Acme a-going." She pointed to a small cast-iron stove squatting in one corner. "'Tis a bit chilly in here."

"How's Mary?" Never pausing for an answer, the woman flitted from one side of the shack to the other, yanking and smoothing the rough blanket, kicking a pair of scuffed hightop boots beneath the bed and snatching up discarded clothes that she clutched to her chest as she looked for a place to put them. "Just give me a minute to tidy up," she said.

"Mary's real fine, Angie. Please don't go to any trouble. Come sit. There's a favor I want to ask of you." Meachum stood and gestured toward the spindle-backed chair he'd just vacated.

Obediently, Angie dropped the clothes onto the bed and took the seat, her face raised to Meachum. In the near light of the kerosene lamp, Sage got his first good look at her face. She seemed forty or so. Dark smudges that seemed part fatigue and part eye blackening, pooled beneath large, dark brown eyes.

"Angie, this man and I need to talk somewhere private, and I wondered if we might talk here at your place. That is, if you wouldn't mind leaving us for a bit."

She jumped up. "Oh, no, I don't mind at all. Just let me get on my clothes. Can't go walking about in the street like this."

Meachum reached in his pocket. "Is there a warm place close by you can go to, Angie?" he asked as he laid a few coins on the table's worn surface.

She eyed the coins, a look of yearning racing across her face. "The Tipsy Seagull's probably still open."

"Then we'll step outside for a bit so you can get dressed." Meachum headed for the door with Sage at his heels.

Once Angie had set off down the road, the men re-entered and sat again at the table. For a moment, they both gazed around the room. She'd stuffed wadded newspaper into gaps around the door and the single window frame. If Angie was still here, still alive next winter, ice cold drafts would slither past those paper defenses and chill Angie's hunched shoulders no matter how many gleaned coal bits she fed to her Acme. Sage shivered.

"Angie wasn't always in this fix," Meachum said, a heavy sigh punctuating his words. "I knew her husband. He was killed early on when the Squad was heading out to work the wheat fields in Eastern Washington. Bulls shot him. No reason, just got him alone. They didn't even know he was part of the Squadron. When Angie learned he was dead, she lost their baby. After that, she just gave up. I try to help her, but she's pretty far gone."

Sage said nothing. Throughout the West, grieving Angies struggled to survive in village and town. Their numbers had reached epidemic proportions.

Meachum cleared his throat signaling it was time to get down to business. "Okay, so what's your name and why were you looking for me?"

Sage didn't hesitate. "I've been going by John Miner, but my real name's John Sagacity Adair. My friends in the cause know me as "Sage Adair."

"Well, Mr. Adair, what do you want with me? People tell me that you were asking about me in Portland. Where else have you been looking?"

"Just back in Portland and now here, in Seattle." Sage shifted in the creaking chair trying to determine how to politely accuse this craggy-faced man of murder.

Sage hesitated, but then followed his inclination which told him, "We're on the same side. He's owed straight talk until he proves otherwise." So Sage said, "A railroad bull name of Clancy Steele is why I'm here. Someone murdered him the same day he killed that boy who was riding the rods up from Roseburg."

Meachum cleared his throat to say something, but Sage halted him with a raised hand. "Before you say anything, I want you to know that I was acquainted with Clancy Steele and his activities. A sorrier human being has never existed. To my way of thinking, it was just a matter of time before Steele got sent to his Maker. So, if you found yourself in a situation where you had to kill him, I'll not say a word against you. The problem I have is that the police are of a mind that the dead boy's brother murdered Steele. I know he didn't and I've got to somehow prove he had nothing to do with it."

Meachum's face revealed neither fear nor alarm, only intent interest. He leaned forward. "Brother? Are you talking about that boy whose aunt works as a cook in that fancy restaurant? The boy

I pulled off Steele in Slap Jacks? 'Matthew,' I think his name was. How do you know him? Is he a relation of yours?"

"That's my restaurant. His aunt's my cook," Sage said and watched surprise change the other man's expression.

"Hmm, your restaurant? Your's must be quite a story to tell." But Meachum didn't wait for a response. "Well, a part of me wishes I could say you've found the murderer. But, I didn't kill Steele and neither did my men. The lad seemed a fine boy. I can understand you wanting to help him." Meachum leaned back, his thumb and forefinger stroking his stubbled chin. "Maybe I can do something for you, though. You twigged to the Squadron."

It was a statement not a question but Sage nodded anyway. When Meachum had said the word "Squad" in that clearing by the latrine, Sage knew who his attackers must be. Meachum led one of the Saint's Flying Squadrons that were traveling the rails, defending the hobos.

"I was down in Portland on Squadron business," Meachum said.

"Was Clancy Steele part of that business?"

"A real big part. We'd been hearing that the bulls were turning meaner up here in the Pacific Northwest. Story is that they've been working in gangs, running atop boxcars, swinging down into the cars to rob folks. I came on ahead of my boys to see if the rumors were true and to try to identify those bulls who were involved."

"Was Steele one of the men you were looking for?"

"Turns out he was. Didn't know that until I talked to some of the bo's there in Portland. Fact is, young Matthew's situation opened the floodgates. When I got back to the camp after seeing Matthew into his aunt's arms, the men had plenty to say. Seems Clancy Steele was spurring the other bulls on and it was getting out of hand. So, he was more than just involved. Near as I could discover, Steele wasn't agile enough to drop down from atop the decks to rob folks. The coupler pin and rope, like what killed that boy's brother, now that was definitely Steele's signature trick. He'd hurt quite a few 'bo's that way but the boy was the first folks knew of Steele killing somebody."

Meachum compressed his lips and shook his head. "There's no point to reasoning with a person like that. Leastways, when those scum drop down into the car to rob they're getting something for it. Steele's using the coupler pin and rope was nothing but murdering meanness."

"So, even after you heard what Steele did to Matthew's brother, the Squad didn't take any action?"

Meachum shook his head. "I was in Portland by myself. Met up with the men here in Seattle. We were going to all head back down that way tomorrow." Meachum leaned forward, his elbows on the table. "Adair, the Saint doesn't want the Squad involved in killings. My Squad's never killed anyone and won't, except maybe in self-defense though I hope never to see that day. Now, we might throw a deck crawler off the train onto a soft patch when the train's moving slow 'round a curve. Put the fear of God into him. But that's all. And, we don't stray too far from the rails. So, Steele's death wasn't our work. Not that we didn't plan on doing something to him—looks like we just didn't get the chance."

Sage exhaled, not aware until that moment that he'd been holding his breath. "Meachum, I got to admit I'm feeling a bit mixed. On one hand I'm glad the Squad isn't involved, but on the other hand I've just run out of likely suspects."

"Well, Adair," Meachum said, "You're not the only fellow who knows how to give out that he's somebody different. I rode the cushions into Portland. I didn't arrive as a hobo. I wanted to get to know the railroad bulls, drink with them, figure out who might be involved. So I hung around saloons down near the yards, buying folks drinks, listening to them talk. That's where I first saw Steele. He'd come in off a trip down to Frisco. Something happened on that run. First thing he said after belting back a few was, 'Boys, that was a train ride right into the Promised Land.' He kept crowing about how he'd hit the mother lode. He even sprung for some folks' beers."

"Did he describe the nature of this 'mother lode?'"

"No, I listened hard for that. He kept snickering like he'd gotten one over on someone. One comment he made, though, made me think the men he had in a tight spot were his so-called social betters. I remember he said, 'They'll soon be learning what happens when they look down their noses at me.'"

Sage also leaned forward across the table. "What'd he mean by that, do you suppose?"

"That's what I wanted to know. I tried to figure out what happened on his trip up from Frisco. I talked to the bo's that rode the rods that trip and they said after Redding or so, things seemed real quiet. They didn't see Steele nor any other bull the whole rest of the trip. Not even when they stopped for water. One man said he saw Steele jump down from the locomotive when the train pulled into Portland and disappear right quick into the train station. That wasn't his usual practice. Normally he was one for walking the length of the train to thump on any stragglers he could find."

"Sounds like something might have happened in the passenger cars."

"That was my conclusion. And, as you know, if something did happen in the passenger cars, a hobo wouldn't hear about it."

Having heard the total of Meachum's information on Steele, Sage changed the subject. "So, how'd your boys get wise to me there in the camp?" Sage asked.

Meachum laughed. "It's not a good idea to call yourself a friend of someone who's sitting not more than six feet from you."

Sage laughed, too, even as he felt his cheeks flush. "So you were that fella who slid away, off to the side."

"Yup. Leastways I got moving once I got over the shock of hearing a stranger call himself my friend. Don't feel bad. I've peeled my own orange a time or two. Once, I tried to pass as an orchardist down in California. I was looking into the potential of union organizing the fruit-packing industry. So, here I am, standing around in this orchard, surrounded by these fruit farmers. They show me these shriveled leaves and I call it 'blight.' Problem was, I learned later that it was codling moth afflicting those trees, something even a novice orchardist would have known. I saw those men exchange looks and knew the time had come for me to skedaddle. I swear I felt the little feet of that codling moth skitter right up my spine. I scooted out of that town faster than hell can scorch a feather. That was a real close one." Meachum shook his head with the memory.

"How do you go about being able to pass yourself off as so many different kinds of folks? Mostly I'm either running a restaurant or I'm living rough. I've never tried a skilled trade like orchardist."

"Way I do it successfully is to study the real ones. Figure out their lingo and what concerns they have in common. You talk the same concerns, they think you're one of them. Just don't get lost in the rigamarole of the game."

"What do you mean?"

"You got to be careful to spend enough time in your own skin. Otherwise, one day you wake up and you're just one twirling ball of different people."

Sage sat back in the chair, startled. It sounded like Meachum was talking about Fong's mysterious "unbreakedness" thing. Had this "breakedness" thing always been around without his noticing or was it turning out to be the coincidental theme of the month? He shook the question loose and returned to the moment. "So, you think getting confused about who you are is a danger in our work?"

"You bet it is, and it happens before you know it. Sneaks up on you. Next thing you know you're thinking about taking actions that aren't true to yourself or what you believe. Then you have the guilt to deal with, the realization you are no better than the sorry bastards we're fighting. So, you either leave the game or you start lying to yourself. None of that is for me. Nope. To quote ole Ben Franklin, 'One ounce of prevention is worth a pound of cure.'"

Sage felt his eyebrows rise of their own accord. Prevention? "What kind of prevention?" he asked.

"It boils down to a few things. First, be yourself every chance you get and stay as much of yourself as the role will bear. Don't get carried away with being a thespian. Second, spend time around folks who know the real you and will remind you of who you are. Maybe most important, find something you like doing that has nothing to do with this crazy work of ours."

"Like what?"

"Well, take me for instance. Few months, every wintertime, I stay at home with my wife and son in Denver. There's a small shop attached to my house where I build furniture. Not fancy furniture, but I try to make it nice. Wife tells me I'm getting better at it." Meachum's long fingers stroked the warped table grain as he talked, a bemused half-smile deepening the creases bracketing his mouth.

"Aren't you afraid you might lose your edge, if you don't stay intent on our work? Don't you need to keep the fire stoked?"

Meachum shook his head. "About seven years ago, I realized a fella in this work could either blaze through like one of those comets, or figure out how to pace himself to stay in it for life. I started thinking 'slow and steady like the turtle' was how to stay with it." Meachum gave a shrug. "Who knows? I just take each day as it comes. Every once and awhile I take stock, decide all over again whether to stay in the work."

Meachum rose to fire up Angie's Acme stove and boil coffee. Hot cups warming their hands, the two men traded stories about their work for the Saint. Beyond the window the neighborhood quieted as sleep overtook residents and customers alike. While Sage enjoyed the talk, in the back of his mind, he kept turning over Meachum's advice about prevention, wondering when and where he was truly Sage Adair. Not often and not in too many places he concluded.

As they left the small crib, Sage laid a gold piece by his cup accompanied by a silent prayer that Angie would find her way before it was too late. When Meachum and Sage parted outside Angie's, they did so as friends—friends who held few secrets from each other. They'd arranged a way of communicating. Sage realized he was looking forward to seeing the Flying Squadron's leader when Meachum next passed through Portland.

An hour later, Sage lay submerged up to his nose in a hotel's deep porcelain tub, the warm water sluicing away the grime of lumber camp, wagon bed and boxcar. His sleepy brain gently turned over the events of the past five days. In the end, he concluded that it hadn't been a wasted trip. He was heading home with something further to investigate, thanks to Meachum. If Steele had threatened powerful men, they might have killed him. So it was back to Portland. Time to start all over. He'd been looking down the social ladder for the murderer. Now he was going to start looking up. It was time for Mr. John Adair, Mozart's dapper owner, to get busy on behalf of Matthew.

NINETEEN

CAVERNOUS UNION STATION magnified the locomotive's hisses coming from beyond the doors, the cries of cranky children, and the general hubbub of the traveling public. Sage, wearing a new worsted suit and clean felt bowler fit right in, looking like just another businessman as he strode across the marble floor, deftly sidestepping to allow an overloaded luggage truck to pass. The black porter was carefully rolling his burden between the passengers, face clenched in concentration. As Sage watched the luggage truck's progress toward the train platform, he saw that most of those hurrying past barely noticed the porter and his truck. That invisibility made the porter's job all the more difficult.

❀ ❀ ❀

Mozart's was in that quiet lull before the start of the supper trade. The dining room's only sound was the metallic snick of the silverware being polished by Horace, the gnome-like waiter who'd worked at Mozart's since it opened. Horace nodded at Sage and pointed toward the kitchen. "Miz Clemens is in the kitchen. It's good to see you back, Mr. Adair. Hope your business trip was successful."

"Thank you, Horace. Has all gone well in my absence?"

"No problems that I know of," the waiter answered.

Fong and Sage's mother stood at the stove, cooking. Or rather, she was watching Fong prepare a Chinese dish. Both looked up, then smiled broadly when they saw Sage pushing through the swinging doors.

While Sage and Fong ate the oriental concoction, Sage's mother kept Horace busy in the dining room. Fong's dish was much more flavorful than the oriental noodles he'd shoveled down in Seattle.

Fong told him that the men watching the restaurant disappeared the day after Sage left town. In their absence, Fong had made a quick trip out to Brother Jonas's farm.

"Mr. Jonas say Matthew is hard worker, well mannered, but that boy reads too much, prays too little," Fong reported. "I took out more books like you said. The boy was grateful."

Sage was glad Fong had followed through with the books. It was one thing to respect a host's customs, but religious conversion was a bit too much to ask. "What about Knute? Is he still in jail?"

"Mr. Gray bailed him out. Mr. Knute is back at work. Mrs. Knute is back in kitchen."

Sage relaxed and rubbed his stomach. "Mmm, that was good, Mr. Fong. If that's a sample of the food you intend to serve one day in your restaurant, I'm in for some competition in the fancy dining department." Then his smile faded. "Well, Mr. Fong, if we're lucky, those two men will be back at their post once they hear I've returned."

"Why lucky?" his mother asked, as she came back into the kitchen. "Before you went to Seattle, you tried to avoid those two men."

"Because, thanks to my travels, I'm certain that neither MacKenzie nor Meachum were involved in Steele's death. So I think those two skulking men outside might lead me to whoever it is that doesn't want me to find Steele's killer." Sage stood up and carried his plate to the sink. "My plan is to head out onto the streets so one and all can see me," he declared as he clapped his new bowler onto his head.

❀ ❀ ❀

The band was blasting forth a robust Sousa tune as Sage strode up the Portland Hotel's circular drive. Groups of men and women crowded the terrace, dressed in their afternoon finery, listening to the music while they drank and ate the hotel's version of afternoon tea—coffee and frosted cake.

In the dining room, Solomon glided among the tables with their snowy tablecloths. Seeing Sage, the maitre'd waved his assistant away, saying, "I'll seat Mr. Adair, William. You go see to the terrace guests."

Solomon placed Sage at a table near the kitchen door, behind a drooping palm, then positioned himself so he stood with his face concealed from the other diners' view.

"Mr. Fong informed me you'd gone out of town, so I gave my report to him," he said.

"Yes, I understand our gentleman has been busy entertaining the cream of Portland's financial community."

"That is correct. The room attendants tell me that everybody who claims to be anybody visits your Mr. Welker."

"Thank you, Mr. Solomon. Can you say whether any one person is a more frequent visitor of that gentleman than others?"

"Senator Hipple seems to spend considerable time with the gentleman, either in his room or in the hotel's bar. They conduct quiet conversations there in the bar. Too quiet to overhear, unfortunately."

"So nobody's gotten an earful?"

"Unfortunately, no. The two take great care to discuss the weather whenever any staff is about. Most secretive," he said, raising one eyebrow.

"Mr. Solomon, there are two other requests I need to make of you, if it's not too much of an imposition."

"Mr. Adair, I find this inquiry entertaining. Provides a bit of variety to my otherwise somewhat monotonous activities. Pray, tell me what you need."

"First, I need to speak to a porter or someone who worked the Frisco to Portland train run on May seventh. Second, I wondered whether staff people, those working late at night, might have ever seen two men visiting our Mr. Welker. Men who none call 'gentlemen.'"

Solomon's forehead crinkled into thoughtful furrows. "I did not query the late-night staff. Some of them are my friends, so I shall ask them. Two men, you say?"

"Yes. According to Mr. Fong, one has a funny smell, while the other one smokes cigars."

After glancing around to ascertain if they were under observation, Solomon gave a dignified nod as if receiving Adair's order while he said in a low voice, "About this other matter of the porter, Mr. Adair. I believe I am acquainted with the gentleman you are seeking. He stays at my hotel whenever he has a stopover. I will inquire whether he is the one you seek. I'll send word to you if he's the man."

This business concluded, Sage ordered a flute of champagne that he carried with him as he moved among the tables visiting with various acquaintances. As he strolled from group to group on the terrace, he caught sight of Otis Welker. The sharp-featured man sat alone at a terrace table against the hotel's stone wall, a newspaper unfolded before his face. Welker gave a slight nod of recognition but no invitation to converse when he saw Sage look in his direction. Sage paused, returned the nod, and moved on.

※ ※ ※

From the hotel, Sage moseyed up the street to *The Daily Journal*. Ben Johnston sat hunched over writing paper, his last furious scribble punctuated by a stabbing period. "There! That'll make Mr. High and Mighty Williams choke on his breakfast steak tomorrow morning." Johnston looked up and grinned.

"John, good to see you! Take a seat. I hear you've been away from town this past week. Anything to do with our little story?" Not for the first time, Sage admired Johnston's ferret-like persistence when it came to uncovering the secrets of the powerful.

"As a matter of fact, I'm starting to think there might be a helluva story—I'm just not sure what it is. Were you able to discover who it was that claimed to have seen Clara's murderer?"

"Yup. It was Halloran, the man running the cribs. Claimed he was at his hotel counter that night and saw a red-haired boy go up then run back down covered in blood."

Sage mentally ran through the sequence of events as he remembered them. "Did you learn whether Halloran claimed he left his post at any time that night?"

"As a matter of fact, they showed my reporter Halloran's signed statement. The statement said he was manning the counter from nine o'clock until the murder, never leaving–not even to visit the necessary. Halloran was quite definite about that."

"Well, Ben. One thing for certain, Halloran is a damn liar."

"You sure about that, John? Why would he lie?"

"I'm beyond sure. Can't say why he'd lie either, but there's a reason because that is exactly what he's doing." After a moment's pause, Sage asked, "Ben, you heard anything about a man named Otis Welker—a new visitor in town?"

"Mr. Welker has been attending various exclusive social events. I believe he is here representing the interests of the Baumhauer Corporation. Looking to buy up more federal timber, I suspect. Of course, I'm not exactly a welcome guest at the Blue Book affairs these days, so, what I hear about those folks is secondhand."

"You might want to dig a little, see what you can learn about Mr. Welker, Ben. I'm beginning to think he might be involved in our mystery—maybe deeply involved."

Johnston scratched a note on a piece of paper. "This is getting better and better," he muttered to himself.

Sage smiled. If the newspaperman weren't holding a pen, he'd be rubbing his palms together.

Solomon had sent word by the time Sage ambled back to his restaurant, adopting his "see-and-be-seen" stroll. "Mr. Solomon said railroad porter will be at his hotel, nine o'clock sharp tonight," Fong reported. "If you there, he will talk to you. The porter leaving tomorrow morning very early."

Promptly at nine, Sage entered Solomon's New Elijah Hotel. It was the last wood-frame hotel built in Portland. In its short heyday, it had been the city's most elegant hostelry. The lobby's worn carpet, faded red velvet curtains, and smoke-dulled wallpaper paid homage to that bygone era. Solomon and his partners saw to it that the mahogany wainscoting was polished mirror slick. Hotel customers conversed with well-dressed clerks. A carved front desk served as the command center. Its walnut expanse had been carved by an Italian craftsman who had remained in Portland after he'd finished embellishing various city mansions.

Sage entered the small dining room to find a solitary black man sitting at a table. The stranger rose deferentially, "Mr. Adair?" he asked.

"Yes, I'm John Adair." Sage extended his hand to shake.

"My name's Nathan Brown," the other man said, tentatively stretching his hand out in return. His was more a touch than a shake.

"I appreciate your talking to me, Mr. Brown. I'll try not to take too much of your time. I know you must rise very early tomorrow."

Brown nodded but stayed silent. His face was small and round with a finely formed mouth. Sage thought that when Brown smiled, his face must be all smile. Brown, however, wasn't smiling.

"I'm trying to find out if anything of note occurred on a train trip from Frisco to Portland last month."

"What day last month?"

"The seventh."

Brown's dark eyes focused on the middle distance. A slight horizontal line creased his smooth forehead. "I ought to remember that trip. My granddaughter's first birthday was the next day."

The two men sat for a moment in silence. When Brown spoke again his words came in the slow cadence of the deep South, "Why, yes, I do recall something happening. A gentleman claimed someone stole his hand case from his berth. He was quite upset."

"Who was he? What did he say was in the case?"

"I don't remember his name. He'd been in the dining car, drinking bourbon. He was quite drunk. I remember thinking he came from Portland. He kept yelling that when he arrived home to Portland he would report the incident to the railroad."

"What kind of case was it? What did he carry in it?"

"He said it was a flat one for carrying papers, so I thought he'd lost papers."

"Was the man's case ever found?"

"No, we made quite a search. He insisted. We believed that one of his companions or another passenger stole his case. He, of course, immediately assumed it was one of us." Brown's tight facial expression said it was an affront neither forgotten nor forgiven.

"He traveled with others?"

"Yes, he was one of a party of three men. I think they all lived in Portland. I know all of them got off the train at this depot."

"You don't know the names of these men?"

"No, sir, the tickets don't have names on them, and I was relatively new to this line. I'm just now learning the names of the regular travelers."

"You think they were regular travelers then?"

"Well, from their clothes and their gold watches and fobs, I believed they were men of business and substance. So I assumed they were regular travelers."

"Tell me, Mr. Brown. If you saw these men again, do you think you'd recognize them?"

"I am certain that I would."

Sage gave a satisfied smile. "When's your next stopover in Portland?"

"I'll be staying here at the New Elijah three days from tomorrow."

"I wonder if you'd kindly do me a favor when you return. I'll pay you well for your time, and it shouldn't take but a few hours or so."

As anticipated, Brown's broad smile was reward in itself. "Mr. Solomon asked me to help you. I'd be happy to oblige any way I can."

Sage told the train porter what he needed, and the two parted, Brown climbing the stairs to his bed, Sage heading home to plan a party.

TWENTY

SAGE CALLED UPON the Baker Theater's owner and found the man sweeping out the lobby. Despite what appeared to be a serious hangover, the man was agreeable to Sage's request. Afterward, returning to Mozart's, hungry for a leisurely breakfast in the kitchen, Sage found Ida Knuteson back at her stove, handling meal preparations with her customary cheery efficiency.

By one forty-five that afternoon, Sage stood beneath the Dunlop mansion's portico fighting the fleeting thought that he was once again the country cousin come calling with cow dung on his shoes. The butler, however, didn't toss him out. Instead, he ushered Sage into the drawing room where Arista stood, one hand on the oak mantelpiece, her delicate face rice-powder smooth and faintly rouged. She looked ethereal in a lilac dress, the muslin clinging to her slender frame. Her unguarded look of pleasure at seeing him triggered a snip of shame that he pushed aside.

Gently mocking a continental gallant, he raised her hand to his lips and smiled as engagingly as he knew how. She laughed at his game, listening to his excuses with an arched eyebrow. "I apologize for disturbing you before the hour appropriate to your receiving at-home calls. But, I must speak to you before your first callers arrive," he said.

Arista tilted her head, giving him a lopsided smile, "Oh, my goodness, doesn't that sound intriguing. Come, take a seat, John. Such a titillating introduction to your visit. First, though, we'll talk of other things until the tea arrives. Actually, my women's club is gathering here soon, so I am glad you came early."

"Ah. What good works have the ladies of the club adopted this season?" Such clubs were a rising trend across the country. Apparently bored with unrelenting leisure and uncountable possessions, upper class women had begun involving themselves in civic affairs. Nothing so crass as attacking whiskey barrels with upraised axes. That harridan role was left to other women. Rather, the upper class woman had begun wielding her domestic axe against the attitudes she found in her drawing room, parlor and likely the conjugal bed chamber. Her efforts had won laws creating separate prisons for juvenile delinquents. Current among the Portland women's low key crusades was the demand that ownership plaques be placed on all downtown buildings. The intent was to make public the names of the men who owned the brothels. The irony inherent in that particular crusade threatened to make him smile. More than one of the fervent do-gooders would be in for a rude awakening when they saw their own family name affixed to these buildings. Lucinda's throaty chuckle seemed to echo in his ear.

Arista remained oblivious to Sage's ruminations. "We've taken up the foundling home," she told him, as if this act was on par with "taking up" knitting or maybe tennis. "They find such dear sweet babies abandoned on its doorstep. It horrified us to learn from the home's superintendent that many of these innocents arrive malnourished and addicted to opium." Her face twisted and she asked with real wonder, "How can a woman do that to her child?" He remembered then. Arista had lost her only child. A sharp jab of compassion nearly knocked Sage off course. For an instant the thought flitted through his brain that if Arista knew the truth, knew what he was trying to do, she would agree to help him. It took some effort to check his impulse to tell her. That revelation wasn't his risk to take. Matthew's life depended on Sage being successful. More importantly, unless he was reading the signs wrong, there was every likelihood Arista's husband was up to his knees in some dirty business. He just didn't know what. So subterfuge it was, the necessary evil. Still, that didn't mean Sage had to like it.

"I suppose it's an act of love," he managed to answer her question.

"Love? I must say, John, you have a most peculiar view of what constitutes motherly love."

A flash of exasperation shoved guilt aside but he kept his voice kindly. After all, as his mother would say, "Can't blame a man for not knowing how to milk a cow if he's never seen one."

"Arista," he said, "It's fortunate that you've never had to face terrible choices. Opium is less expensive and easier to come by than food. Poor mothers sometimes ease their baby's hunger pangs with a dose of opium."

She wasn't having any of it, indignation lifting her chin high. "Why ever do they place themselves in that position in the first place? The mothers must get themselves addicted," she punctuated her statement with a grimace and shake of her head.

"Some are addicted, most aren't. They're poor, Arista. Dirt poor. Most of them start out as innocent, inexperienced country girls. Newspaper ads asking for housekeepers or nurses or companions to the sick lure them into the big city. I'm sure you've seen those advertisements. The ones that say, 'Young girls wanted—good wages.'"

She nodded, her eyes turning thoughtful.

"Many of those ads are deliberate lies. Once the girls are here, their need for food and shelter makes them easy prey for the procurers. Other women find themselves in dire straits overnight. One day they are respectable married ladies packing lunch pails for their husbands. The next day, they are widows or abandoned wives with too many mouths to feed." She needed to see, really see. "Arista, you've seen the countless sickly faces of these women on the street."

She seemed to be thinking, maybe remembering, but she only said, "John, it surprises me to know that a man of your station would know about, let alone think of, such things." Admiration warmed her words.

The thought that he intended to take advantage of this well-meaning woman made him hesitate. She was already key to his plan for finding those responsible for Steele's death. Did he also need to play the missionary? Still, this woman and her friends were in a better position to force social change than he was. That's what his uncle would say. When Sage had been eight, he'd been watching his uncle toss pebbles of varying sizes into the black depths of the tailings pond. Together, they'd counted out loud the seconds it took for the ripples to stop. The biggest pebbles had the longest effect. That lesson had stayed with him. So here was Arista, sitting in her fine house, imbued with social influence in the small pond that was Portland, a fairly big pebble in her own right.

"Let me explain about the opium," he began. "We can thank England for that. Since pillaging China, our English relatives have distributed opium all along the Pacific lands. A small bottle of liquid opium, just so," he spread thumb and pointer finger to form a two-inch gap. "It costs less than one meal and lasts a lot longer. Some may become addicted, but some use the drug to soothe hungry bellies. Still mother's love, Arista, desperate in a way you and I cannot imagine." At the sight of her stricken face, Sage hastily corrected himself, "One, I cannot imagine anyway. You, I think, know it."

Arista fumbled for a handkerchief, turned away and carefully blotted the corners of her eyes. The tick of the pendulum clock on the mantel seemed to grow louder, as he regretted the wound he'd just given her. She'd lost her son to diphtheria the year before.

But when she swivelled back to face him, her face was composed and resolute. "John, I had no idea. You must think me an ignorant boob. Those poor women," she said. A spasm of pain washed across her face, empathy she could feel despite her privileged life. She smiled ruefully. "So what you're telling me is that we've misjudged these poor women. Well, I thank you for that. The other ladies will hear of it when we meet today. Maybe we should do something to help the mothers of these babies as well."

A heavily laden tea tray arrived and was placed upon the low table before the sofa by a silent maid who quickly departed. At last it was time to talk about the purpose of Sage's visit. Given the empathy and kindness she had just displayed, he found it difficult to lay out his scheme, knowing he was hiding the most crucial fact from her–that he was laying a trap for her husband and his friends.

"I am here to ask you a favor," he said. Her finely shaped eyebrows raised in expectation and he continued, "In New York, the finer restaurants host private after-theater parties for their special patrons and the performers. I'd like Mozart's to introduce this custom in Portland. Friday evening, following the premiere performance at the Baker Theater, I want to host a little gathering. It would, of course, be gratis to those attending. I hope to determine whether it may be a custom that catches hold with the more select people and thespians in the city."

"Oh, what a wonderful idea!" Arista said, clapping her hands together, her eyes shining. "I think our crowd will love it. So cosmopolitan. How do you want me to help?"

"I'm hoping you'll urge people to attend the event. The individuals you invited to your soirée are the very type of people I want to attract. My thought is to invite them, with perhaps a few other guests, as well as the performers from the theater. I hope you'll urge acceptance of my invitation when you speak with the ladies this afternoon and give me a list of those I should invite. The invitation will be of such short notice that people may think it unseemly to accept."

"Oh, you'll have no trouble attracting the ladies to your little event, John. No matter how short the notice. Although I suspect your real interest is directed more toward their husbands' fat wallets."

Sage laughed. "Arista, you understand me completely. The restaurant is ideally located for an event of this sort—it's just a few blocks from at least two theaters. If our after-theater parties become fashionable, Mozart's will certainly benefit financially."

Arista twisted her lips in mock distaste but the sparkle in her eyes meant she was on board. They spent some minutes discussing the event—listing who to invite and what to serve. When the butler appeared to announce that the first women's club guest was arriving, Sage tucked the list into his coat pocket and took his leave. Arista would do her best to advance his plans. Still, he left her mansion feeling shame over the way he'd maneuvered her into helping him out.

❁ ❁ ❁

Two hours later found Sage once again leaning against the sun-warmed bricks along Burnside Street, the tattered flannel shirt and faded denims soft against his skin. He watched as McCurdy's storefront slowly emptied itself of gaunt-faced job seekers. Each time a man slouched out, his face reflected a mixture of anger and relief. Anger at the high cost of getting a low paying job. Relief that wages were at last in the offing.

Inside, McCurdy sat on his stool behind the counter, cleaning his fingernails with a small knife. He glanced up and then straightened. "Oh, boy! It didn't take you long to get fired. I suppose you want me to find you another job? It'll cost you extra. You messing things up means I won't get any business from that timber boss for awhile. You didn't even stay the week. He'll want his money back." Despite McCurdy's chiding tone, the involuntary lick he gave his lips said that he what he really foresaw was another two-dollar fee finding its way into his till.

Sage reached the counter and leaned an elbow on its scarred, unpainted surface. "Plunkett didn't fire me. I quit. Here's something to make up for my leaving Plunkett's early," He said, tossing a silver two-dollar coin on the counter. "Now you ain't been hurt at all, have you, McCurdy?"

McCurdy's mouth went slack in surprise. Taking a gulp that bobbled his Adams apple, he said, "Ain't nobody ever done that afore."

"How'd you like five of them?"

"Ten dollars! Are you fooling with me? Where'd a swamper get ten dollars to give away?"

"Don't matter about where the money comes from, McCurdy. What matters is whether you're willing to give me some information and keep your lip buttoned about me asking."

McCurdy narrowed his eyes, his normal rat-like cunning taking hold. "What kind of information are you talking about?" He strove to sound disinterested but his fixed gaze on the coin gave him away.

Sage covered the coin with his palm. "No. It's either 'yay' or 'nay.' You decide. Whatever you decide, you'll have to live by it. Ten dollars or nothing." Sage leaned across the counter so that his unwavering dark blue eyes were within inches of McCurdy's alarmed mud-brown ones. "But I should warn you. You might suffer certain consequences if you decide not to talk."

McCurdy stepped back. His eyes drifted down to the coin that lay uncovered once again on the counter. "Four more of those? Okay, I'll answer your questions and won't tell nobody. But what if I don't know nothing?"

Sage straightened, "Oh, you will. You see, my questions are about your friend Clancy Steele."

"Clancy? Clancy—he's dead," the other man's confusion was real.

"Where was he living when he died?"

That question seemed to ring no warning bells in McCurdy's mind, though he bought time by planting his butt back on the stool and striking a match to a cigarette before answering, "He stayed up at a rooming house on Hoyt, at the corner of Eighteenth. Been there awhile," the words rolled out lazy as the smoke dribbling from his nostrils. Sage fought the urge to punch the man's face.

"Who'd he work for?" he snapped instead.

"Why, the railroad. Everybody knows that."

"He also worked for other people, didn't he?"

"Well, he done some work for one of them timber companies. Sometimes he'd work special jobs, but I don't know nothing about that. We wasn't what you'd call friends, more like business acquaintances. He'd didn't tell me none of his secrets."

"What happened on his last trip to Frisco?"

For the first time during their exchange, McCurdy's face closed, a tic in his cheek suggesting he was trying to suppress a reaction. Sage saw the fingers around the cigarette momentarily tighten.

Sage reached across the counter to grab and twist McCurdy's shirt front until the collar choked the man's scrawny neck red. "Don't try to bluff me, McCurdy. I already know some of what happened on that trip. You don't tell me the truth, I'm going to know it and I won't like it."

McCurdy twisted his lips to one side as if itching his nose with the motion and jerked loose. Smoothing down his shirt front he said, "Clancy didn't tell me exactly what happened. But I figured like maybe he got hold of a paper that could make him rich. I tried to make him tell me what he got but he wouldn't."

"If he took a paper off that train, where would he hide it?"

"I've been thinking of that since the morning I heard he was dead. Only place I thought of was his rooming house. I've been trying to figure out how to get in to see his room."

Sage rode the trolley car up to the corner of Eighteenth and Glisan. From there he walked a block farther north until he stood in front of the only boardinghouse at that intersection. It was a drab, three-story building, its footprint on the lot enlarged over time by cobbled together additions that tilted off its every side. It must take endless work to maintain just one floor of this old rambler, he thought. Wonder how many servants the landlady keeps? Not enough, he answered his own question upon seeing the paper scraps snagged in the drooping rose bushes that lined the walkway. Someone had stuck a handwritten "Room to Let" card inside the window next to the door.

Sage knocked on the faded door. A woman of sufficient height and heft to join ranks with the longshoremen opened the door. An apron wound about her thick waist and more frizzy graying hair tumbled out of the bun atop her head than she had tucked into it.

"You here about room?" Her East European accent was thick but the phrase still rang familiar. He'd heard it spoken in a multitude of accents.

"Are you the landlady?" he asked. At her nod, he answered her question, "Not exactly, ma'am. May I have a moment of your time?"

Disappointment changed her face, anxiety deepening its lines. Sage glanced at her hands and spotted a worn gold wedding band on her right hand. She's a widow then. An infant's wail sounded in a room somewhere near the end of the passage that seemed to stretch clear to the back of the house alongside the stairway to the second floor. An outraged toddler shrieked and older children started yelling. The woman shot a glance behind her, then turned back to him. "I got five of them to raise, all under ten years," she told him.

He smiled sympathetically. "Please, ma'am, it will only take a moment. I promise I will make it worth your while even though I'm not interested in taking the room."

The woman sighed heavily but stepped out of his way, allowing him passage into the house. To one side was the parlor, spartan but clean. A card table stood near the potbellied stove so that her roomers could play their games in relative comfort.

"I wanted to ask if you'd let me look at the room you have for rent. I understand it was Mr. Steele's room."

He strained to understand her response, the words larded with that accent. Then he caught the rhythm. "So many people, they come to see that room but no one want to rent. Maybe I should charge a nickel a peek, like nickelodeon." She wrinkled her nose. "No one would pay. Nothing to see. The police have already been here. Took most of his things. Only old clothes left. Vultures, in this country just like back home. When you knocked I was going to clean upstairs while children ate." She paused, looked at him quietly, taking his measure. Then she shrugged and picked up a dust mop leaning against the stairway newel post. "You might as well come along. Instead of nickel, maybe you help me flip mattress? My back, it is always hurting."

Seeing his smile she turned away and began climbing to the second floor, gesturing for him to follow with a flip of the rag in her hand. Dutifully, he trailed her broad backside and the soft squeak of her thick-soled shoes up the stairs.

She opened a door right at the top of the stairway. "This is room. There is mattress. You grab other end?"

Once the mattress was flipped, she headed for the door. The noise below had increased to the caterwauling stage. "You look around, mister. Please, do not take things. I must go see to noisy children," she said and was gone. The noise downstairs increased to a shrill crescendo.

Sage waited in the middle of the room until the woman's heavy footfalls faded. Sunlight slid past the worn weave of a blue gingham curtain, dust motes raised by the mattress flip drifting through its beam. A four-dollar iron bedstead was centered against the wall opposite the door, effectively bisecting the square room. On one side stood a small bedside table, a wardrobe, and a dresser with a chipped ceramic water pitcher sitting on its stained top. On the other side there was a mostly empty bookshelf and a naked clothes tree. He stepped closer, noting that the shelf's few books were religious in nature. Probably the only kind of proselytizing the tired landlady has time for, Sage mused.

Your typical short-term-tenancy room. Despite being flipped, the mattress center still sagged. Countless bodies had left their indent as they sought respite in sleep. That was it for the room's contents. If this house has an inside commode, it'll be a shared one down the hall.

Sage began with the wardrobe and drawers. There were two well-worn suits, while the dresser's top drawer held an undisciplined jumble of grimy throwaway collars and cuffs. The wardrobe contained only working clothes; stained winter underwear, heavy work trousers, and dingy shirts. The leavings of an unremarkable life– but then, what would a searcher determine about Sage's life from the room where he sleep? Not that much more, Sage thought.

Despite upending drawers and wiggling underneath the bed to stare up through the bedsprings, Sage found nothing but a single dust ball that he slipped into his pocket least the landlady suffer mortification at its presence. He found no paper of any kind.

When Sage quit the room, he followed the children's chirping voices down into the kitchen. There a gaggle of tow-headed children sat on chairs, crawled about on the floor or in the case of the youngest, sat tied by a dishtowel to a chair, its small fist jammed into an even smaller mouth, its eyes wide and observing. The landlady stood at an ironing board, a wicker basket of clothes on the chair at her side. In one hand she held a heavy iron. Close by another iron was heating on the cooking range. More tendrils of sweaty hair curled out from her bun. The flush on her cheeks and the soft white glow of her skin hinted at the girl she must have once been.

The smell of fresh baked bread made Sage's mouth water but he took care not to look at the loaf cooling on a nearby rack. People like this woman tended toward generosity. He stepped closer, saying, "Excuse me, ma'am. You said that others have looked at the room. Who were they?"

"The police come just after poor Mr. Steele, he was killed. Next his brother, he comes."

"Are you sure it was his brother?"

"That is what he says to me. Afterward, I think he not look like Mr. Steele. Courteous fellow, but he smelled strong."

"Smelled? What kind of smell? Like he needed a bath?"

"Oh, no. He look clean. He smell like medicine. It is a name I cannot remember. I use it for the children's chests."

"Do you mean he smelled of camphor?"

"Yes, that's it. Camphor." She apparently liked the word because she said it again. "Yes, he smell like 'camphor.'"

"Did he carry anything away with him?" More than likely the mysterious "paper" had walked out the door and was either back with its owner or ash.

She was shaking her head. "No, I think that he did not. He came very soon after Mr. Steele died. I had no time to look over Mr. Steele's things after police left. So I stayed there. Watched like hawk." She felt the need to explain her zeal, "I worry that the Steele family might say I took something so I watch that man, I do."

"Was he just looking at everything or did you think he was looking for something in particular?"

She stopped pushing the iron to and fro for the first time. "Let me think." There was a pause while she thought. "He was looking for one thing. He poke under the drawer paper and wiggle under mattress. Funny places to look for your brother's things, I think."

"Did Mr. Steele ever mention a brother or any other kin?"

She shook her head. "To me he never said nothing like that. I don't know about his family."

A stooped old man walked slowly into the kitchen, red suspenders tight across his narrow shoulders. She smiled at him. "Ah, Mr. Goldberg. This gentleman is . . ." She looked at Sage.

"Hello, my name's John Miner," Sage said, stepping forward to shake the older man's gnarled hand.

"Mr. Goldberg, he maybe tell you something. He sometimes played the cards with Mr. Steele." She looked at the elderly man. "You miss Mr. Steele, I think, Mr. Goldberg." She returned her gaze to Sage. "The two of them take turns making up stories about growing up on a farm. They are silly stories sometimes. I do not think all of them were true."

The old man laughed and turned bright, interested eyes in Sage's direction. "So, you are wanting to know about our Mr. Steele, is that so?" he asked.

"I'm trying to find out if he had family here. I need to speak with them if he did."

The old man raised a hand to stroke a wrinkled, sparsely whiskered chin. "I'm thinking there was a wife and a couple of kids hereabouts. Saw the two of them arguing on the front porch a while back. Overheard her saying the kids needed clothes and that she needed money for a ticket to ride back home to them that night. That led me to thinking she was his wife, 'cause why else would she be asking for money from him just like he owed her? I thought she lived nearby because only the suburban railways ran that late in the afternoon."

The old man might be slow moving, but his brain worked fine. "Do you recall when it was that you saw Steele talking to this woman?"

"Spring, early on, I think. Air still had the nip of mountain snow fields to it. I peeked out the curtain. Remember thinking she looked mighty cold and tired. One of those worn-out women. Wondered why he didn't ask her in."

Sage said goodbye to the amiable old man and the harried boardinghouse landlady after sliding a silver dollar onto the table. They'd given him much to think about. Sage wanted to track down that smelly man. Either there were excessive numbers of camphor-scented men in town, or else the same man kept turning up in interesting places-like across from Mozart's, in dark alleys and now here at Steele's boarding house. Also, there was the woman Mr. Goldberg had seen. Who was she? Where was she?

TWENTY ONE

STEELE'S WIFE WAS proving hard to find. Another night of nursing stale beers at Slap Jacks saloon bore no fruit. No one knew anything about the woman. Sage began to wonder whether old man Goldberg had imagined a wife when none existed.

The theater-party plans for the next evening were all in place. Arista Dunlop's blessing of the event guaranteed his key targets would attend. Social hounds like them couldn't stay away from the premiere of what might become the city's newest top drawer social event. If nothing else, his years of living with the mine owner had schooled him well in the bored elite's desperate need to find novel distractions.

Sunrise had just finished rimming the jagged pinnacle of the distant Mount Hood when Sage climbed to the fourth-floor attic. From the outside, the space appeared disused, its windows blank, opaque with dirt. Inside, however, it was spotless and unlike any place Sage had ever seen before. Fong had varnished the wood floor to a high gloss. Red silk banners hung across stark white walls. Black-dyed sacking covered the windows. A diffuse light glowed downward from the skylight Fong had inserted into the roof. In this stark, soothing space, Fong reigned as undisputed master.

Fong was already there. Sage watched the Chinese man flow across the shiny wood floor, Fong's body seemingly weightless, akin to the drifting clouds he often talked about. These graceful movements formed Fong's fighting art. His moves were generations old, passed down from teacher to student. Their power disguised in flexible attack and strategic retreat. It was this fighting technique that Sage had used to keep the Flying Squadron at bay when they were bent on heaving him into the latrine or worse.

Fong appeared unimpressed by Sage's exploit. Instead of praise, Sage received yet another lesson. "Like the snake and crane, you must learn to anticipate surprise attack, so enemy's first blow never hit you," Fong began. "The eye, ear, skin must feel attack first. Eyes must be trained. Like this." Fong flashed his hand toward Sage. Sage jerked his head back, too late. Fong's palm smacked Sage's forehead, hard enough to make rocks rattle.

"Ah! You see? You must learn to keep eye moving, know what is at side and never close eyes in unsafe place." That began an hour of moving to intercept, connect, and repel attacks. Through it all, Fong continually targeted Sage's forehead. By the end of the drill, Sage was starting to anticipate in sufficient time to deflect the flashing hand away from his face. This success came with a cost. He didn't appreciate the growing headache.

At the session's end Fong said, "Two times surprise takes you. That only happens if eyes, ears, nose, and skin are not alert. Eyes should see light flicker. Ears should hear sound of attacker's breath. Nose should smell attacker's sweat. Skin should feel body pushing against air. Next time we drill on these things." Fong was breathing normally, as relaxed as if he'd just laid aside a book. In contrast, sweat dripped off Sage's face and his legs quivered with exhaustion. He bowed. "Many thanks, Mr. Fong. This has been most instructive. I'm going downstairs to wash up and get my aching head as far away from that damned hand of yours as I can possibly take it."

"I see you down there." Fong raised a cautionary finger. "Remember, no bath until your body cool, otherwise will wash away chi force. Not good for health. You need to react more, think less," he added before turning away.

❁ ❁ ❁

A note sat propped against Sage's bureau mirror. Since Chinese characters covered the paper, he made no attempt to read it. Hopefully, the note contained the good news that the elusive Mrs. Steele had been located. Fong had sent word to his tong contacts in outlying towns, asking them to find the woman. Maybe his efforts had met with success. Sage paced the room, cooling down, impatient for Fong to descend.

When Fong appeared, he confirmed Sage's hunch about the note. "Cousin who is washhouse man in Forest Grove say a woman name of Steele live outside village."

That would fit, Sage thought. Forest Grove was a farming town that lay next to the Coast Range's wooded foothills. Not that far away. But, getting there would require yet another train trip. No choice about that. He needed to talk to the woman. Yup, another train ride. Ever since his recent pledge to avoid trains, he'd had to ride one after the other. At least this trip to Forest Grove would be the last train ride he'd have to take for awhile.

"How do I find this cousin of your's once I get to Forest Grove?" he asked.

"Forest Grove small place. He work in only Chinese washhouse. Behind train station."

Before setting off for the train, Sage mulled over how best to elude his shadows. He didn't want to have them trailing along as he tracked down his only lead on Steele's secret horde. Luck awaited him in the street. A patrolman rounded the corner just as Sage stepped out Mozart's front door. The hefty uniformed figure, with its shock of thick blond hair and wide shiny forehead, was a welcome sight. Patrolman Hanke, the local beat cop and unabashed devotee of Ida Knuteson's cooking, was on the job. Hanke had eaten his fill more than once at the table in Mozart's kitchen.

As they neared each other, Sage haled the other man, "Ah, Patrolman Hanke, I wondered if I might solicit a favor from you?"

Hanke's broad face broke into a smile. "Anything you need, Mr. Adair. I'll be happy to oblige unless, of course, you ask me to break the law," he corrected, his face suddenly somber.

Sage hastened to reassure, "That I would never ask. No, my problem is a bit unusual. There's been a strange person watching the front of the restaurant. I don't know that he means harm, but it is a bit troubling. He's there now. If you look over my shoulder, behind me, you will see him loitering in the entrance to Kelso's ironworks shop. Might you, as part of your duties, find out what business he's about?"

Sage thought he saw the patrolman's big ears twitch. Hanke was ever eager to exercise his police authority. "Aye, I see the man. He's wearing a dark coat and a black fedora? Is that the man, Mr. Adair?"

"Yes, that's the fellow."

"He looks suspicious to me, all right." Hanke's hand wandered to the smooth head of his wooden baton. Sage spent a moment wondering just how much he'd mind it if the club encountered the stranger's noggin, given that Sage was now fairly sure the stranger in the doorway was the same man who'd coshed him in that alley outside Lucinda's.

Hanke tensed. "I think he knows we're talking about him. He's starting to sidle off in the other direction. I best be going, Mr. Adair, if I'm going to find out who he is and what he's about before he skedaddles." Hanke headed off without waiting for a response, fixed on his quarry like a dog on a squirrel.

Sage didn't wait to see what happened next. Instead, he quickly turned in the other direction. As he neared the far corner, he heard Hanke shout. Two pairs of heavy boots began running down the wooden boardwalk away from him. Sage grinned as he rounded the corner. That should throw them off long enough for him to disappear. Now for the train station.

Ten minutes later, Sage was loitering in an inconspicuous corner of the platform, waiting for the S & P to Hillsboro to arrive. Less than an hour after that, he was getting his backside bruised by the wooden seats of the interurban line as it chugged up the canyon heading west toward the Tualatin River valley. At last the train crested the final hill and began dropping down onto the wide fertile plain spreading toward the dark bulk of the Coast Range that rose about thirty miles distant.

Once the train broke free of the canyon, there were few tall trees. Sage gazed out window, trying to imagine how it must have looked sixty years ago when Indian bark houses dotted the valley. During the 1849 California gold rush, all the old firs left unburned by Indian fires had fallen to farmers' axes in their rush to plant crops to feed the miners. By then the Indians had disappeared, most dying from white man's diseases. Now, more than fifty years later, the valley was a patchwork of fields where farmers labored amid stalks of early summer grain and the trees of young orchards. The farm housewives were equally industrious. Rows of washing snapped in the breeze beside the prosperous looking farmhouses. What he was seeing was civilization, progress. But was it really? He could almost see the ghosts of those vanished Indians, men, women and children, walking beneath the firs or wading through thigh-high prairie grasses. Who and what was civilization, anyway?

At last the train had chugged its way through Cedar Hills and Beaverton and over the longer stretch into Hillsboro, the county seat. There, Sage left the train to find a stable. Forest Grove lay six miles or so beyond Hillsboro. He didn't think there was anyone following but Sage didn't want to arrive in Forest Grove on the train, hire a horse and take the risk of leading someone directly to Clancy's widow. Better for any potential tracker to believe Hillsboro was the destination.

At the livery stable, the hostler offered Sage two choices. Either a wild-eyed roan gelding or an ancient swayback paint. The paint's bloodshot brown eyes were eying him with dread so he took pity on it. He turned toward the sidestepping roan, thinking fondly of the placid horse that had pulled the produce van to Silverton. Pushing hesitation aside, he grabbed the reins and hauled himself onto the gelding.

An hour and many backward glances later, Sage dismounted with relief. The horse had fought him the whole way and his arms ached with the effort of controlling it. He knotted the reins of the skittish horse to the hitching post in front of a dry goods store. Enough of fighting that four-hoofed devil. He'd find Fong's cousin on foot.

It didn't take long. The business section of Forest Grove covered only a few square blocks. Sage found the washhouse tucked behind the rail depot. It was a one-room, one-story, fir-sided structure, not unlike those he'd seen in Plunkett's logging camp. The door stood ajar. The front windows, closed at night by down-swinging shutters, stood open, the shutters roped up for ventilation. Inside, four Chinese men were working. They worked naked from the waist up, their bottom halves clothed in black drawstring trousers. Above the trousers, they were so thin that their knobby spines caught at the black queues trailing down their backs.

He wondered which man was Fong's "cousin." Against the back wall, one man turned an iron handle, to make a copper drum twirl. Another man lifted and plunged fabric inside a huge washtub. The third man worked a wringer contraption, rotating a wheel so that the rollers squeezed cascades of gray water from the clothes he was feeding between them. Near the laundry's front windows, the fourth man stood beside a blazing cookstove, a variety of irons atop its glowing burners. The man was rapidly ironing a white shirt that lay on a padded board. Sweat sheened his face and torso. Even though Sage stood just inside the door, the air was a thick, steamy mix of soap and carbolic.

The man at the wringer, who faced toward the door, said something in rapid Chinese. The man at the ironing board looked up from his work and set down his iron. Grabbing a cloth, he wiped his face as he came forward, inquiry in his dark eyes. "May I help you, sir?" he asked in thickly accented English.

"I hope so. Mr. Fong sent me," Sage said and saw the man's shoulders relax. "Mr. Fong said that Mr. Tuck Lum could help me find a woman named Mrs. Steele who lives somewhere near town."

"I am Tuck Lum," the man said with a quick dip of his head. "When message come from Mr. Fong, I think of this lady. She stays outside town at the Abbott farm, only one mile. She helps them. I think her name is Steele."

"Does this Mrs. Steele have children?"

The Chinese man narrowed his eyes in thought. "I think that maybe she does. She comes to town with children, but Abbotts also have children. Still, I think she has children, one boy and maybe a girl."

After getting directions from Lum and leaving a few coins in return, Sage trudged back to the gelding. The horse stayed docile as Sage mounted and reined him northward at a slow walk. To the west, the mountains rose in deep green ranks. Although the coastal range was smaller than the Cascades, its topmost ridges were frosted white. In a few weeks, the snow would be gone and the deer would return to the high meadows. On either side of the road, the vivid green of sprouting grain marched in rows across the fields. There'd be a good yield this year, unless heavy summer rains brought rust.

A white farmhouse, sitting in the midst of old, bigleaf maples, came into view. A windmill for pulling up well water, stood at the yard's edge, its blades unmoving. Sage rode up the dirt track between two well-tended fences. As he and the horse clopped into the yard, a long-haired black dog whipped around the corner in full bark. Sage's horse immediately lost his placidity and plunged into a frenzy of shying and backing. While he fought to stay in the saddle, Sage heard a sharp command, and the dog ceased barking. When he could finally look up, Sage saw two women standing together on the wide porch that fronted the house.

"Strange horse, just rented him," Sage said by way of explanation as he slid from saddle, hitting firm ground with a jolt. Holding the reins, he moved within a few feet of the porch. A rosy-cheeked, rounded woman who reminded him of Ida Knuteson, stood at the top of the steps. Her bright blue eyes glinted with amusement and welcome. Behind her, in the tense stance of a deer about to bolt, stood a tall, angular woman. Etched lines ran across her forehead, circled her fearful, deep-set brown eyes, and framed her long slash of a mouth. She looked as if she'd never known a single moment of carefree youth. Sage addressed himself to this woman, certain she was Clancy's wife.

"I am sorry to disturb you, Mrs. Steele. My name is John Miner. I have traveled from Portland to talk to you about your husband, Clancy."

TWENTY TWO

THE GASP ESCAPED before her hand could cover her mouth. She remained silent, frozen, save for the involuntary twitch of her fingers against her lips.

The other woman sent Sage a sharp look, her eyes darkening with concern and wariness. She moved toward the shocked woman. "There, there, Bess, let's sit down here for a bit." Her plump arm circled the taller woman's waist as she steered her toward a bench along the wall. Once seated, they both looked toward Sage.

Bess Steele's brown eyes were wide and staring. Then she focused on Sage, her voice cracking as she asked, "He's dead, isn't he, Mister?"

Sage felt a spasm of self-disgust. During the long ride out on the train and then the horse, he had never once considered that Steele's wife might be ignorant of his death. Now he thought, how would she know? Living as she does well away from town, a closely guarded secret. Who would have known to tell her?

"I'm so sorry, Ma'am. I thought you knew." Sage moved to stand before her on the porch. He looked toward the plump woman. "Mrs. Abbott?"

She nodded, "Yes, I am Mrs. Abbott."

Both women said nothing, waiting for him to continue. "Someone killed him about two weeks ago, but the police don't know who," he said.

"Was he shot?" Bess Steele asked.

"No, ma'am, someone stabbed him in the street. He didn't suffer." That was all he was going to say about Steele's mortal wound.

Her dark eyes filled with tears. Abruptly, she rose from the wooden bench and stepped off the porch to stumble through knee-high dandelions toward the windmill tower. Sage and Mrs. Abbott watched her go.

Mrs. Abbott spoke. "No matter how badly they treat you, they're still your children's father," she said.

"He treated her bad?"

Her pleasant mouth twisted. "The worst, near as I can tell from what little she's told me. I met the man, a big, violent bully. It comes as no surprise at all that someone killed him—was a matter of time, to my way of thinking. Just glad Bess didn't do it, what with those two little ones she has to raise."

Sage looked across the side yard. Bess Steele sat with her long back against the tower leg, staring away across the field.

Mrs. Abbott touched his forearm, gesturing him to the bench. "I think you and me should drink some lemonade. Give Bess a little bit of time. Please, take a seat. The lemonade's already made." She disappeared through the screen door.

True to her word, she returned in minutes with three full glasses on a tray. "We'll just sit and drink ours. I expect Bess'll be ready for hers when we're done," she said as she settled into an old reed rocker.

They sipped while grasshoppers, with papery whirs, jumped between glistening grass stems. Closer at hand, bees worked the honeysuckle blossoms winding up the yellow porch posts. Sage learned that Mr. Abbott was off with the children searching for a cow. Mrs. Abbott chatted on about the canning she planned and about the quality of fruit growing in the small orchard next to the barn. At last, she reached for his empty glass. "You best go talk to her now. The children will be returning soon." She handed him the full glass of lemonade, and Sage set off across the grass toward Bess Steele, who sat motionless at the base of the windmill tower.

When he was within five paces, she turned her head toward him. Her eyes were dry. He handed her the lemonade, which she took from him after a moment's hesitation. He dropped into the long grass near her feet.

Looking away, across the field of ripening oats, she sipped the lemonade and then seemed to forget she held it. "I always knew he'd end up killed or hung." Her voice was soft, musing.

Sage said nothing, waiting for her to continue. With a metallic chitter, the canted blades overhead began a slow turn.

Not looking at Sage, Bess Steele spoke in a low voice, almost as if she were telling herself the story. "Clancy and I grew up in the same part of Ohio. My dad gave me to him in marriage when I was but sixteen. I don't blame Pa none. He was trying to feed a lot of mouths.

"After we married, we headed out here to the West. Clancy couldn't wait to shake the Ohio dust from his boots. He said we'd be rich one day." She paused for a beat or two, then continued.

"That train ride was something special. We sat for days just staring out those windows at all the towns and farms. When we saw the Rocky Mountains—my, my. We thought that gods must live on top of those mountains. You know, like in the Greek stories." Bess Steele's face softened, memory quirking her lips into a wistful smile. The smile faded as she went on. "We came here to Oregon because Clancy heard there was work in the woods, and land we could homestead.

"At first, it looked like our life was going real fine. Clancy worked at a logging job out Oregon City way. I had Timothy, and we started proving up a homestead. Then Clancy took to drinking. When he drinks . . ." She sighed and set the lemonade down in the grass. "When he drank, he was mean—real mean. Anyway, he started to fight all the time, and he lost his job. After a while, nobody'd hire him. They thought he was trouble."

She paused, swallowing hard as if a bone had lodged in her throat. "Things got real bad with us. Annabelle was born. Clancy was doing some kind of work for the timber men. I could never tell what he did for them. I thought him having that job might settle him some. You know, that he'd stop drinking and fighting. But he didn't, he just got worse."

Here she paused, her chin trembling as she picked a wild ox-eye daisy, its "eye" a velvet brown. As Sage watched, her long fingers plucked the pure white petals from the stem, one at a time as thoughtfully as if each one had meaning. When they were all gone, she sighed and let the stem drop into the grass. She looked up at him and said, "So when he left on one of his mystery trips, I took what money we had and came out here to Forest Grove. The money wouldn't take us no farther. We were so poor. Anyway, I started waiting tables in a restaurant. We had an awful hard time until the Abbotts took us in. They're real good people."

Sage waited to make sure she'd finished before asking, "When's the last time you saw your husband, Mrs. Steele?"

"He hauled himself out here about three weeks ago," she said, her voice hard with some remembered grievance.

"Why did he come out?"

"I couldn't figure that out. He didn't seem to be interested in seeing me or the kids. He brought us a bit of money, but he could have sent that. He did sometimes."

"What happened when he came here?"

"He rode up just before supper. Mr. Abbott stood out on the porch with me until he saw Clancy wasn't drunk."

"Did he usually come drunk?"

"He never usually came at all." Bitterness laced her voice. "When he did come, yes, he was often drunk. Mr. Abbott would've asked him to leave if he'd been drunk. Like I said, Clancy'd be mean, and Mr. Abbott doesn't hold for none of that in front of his missus and the kids. He's a prohibitionist and pretty strong about it."

"But, this last time Clancy hadn't been drinking?"

"Well, I don't think I can say that. I could smell the spirits. But he wasn't drunk."

"Then what happened?"

"He asked if we could go talk in our little place over yonder." She pointed toward a cottage behind the farmhouse. "That's where me and the kids stay. The Abbotts let us live there. They say we need a home of our own. They're good people, the Abbotts," she said again.

"You weren't afraid to be alone with him?"

"No, not unless he was drunk. You see, Timothy could have run for help if I needed it. Anyway, I gave him some coffee and he talked to the kids. He'd even remembered to bring them some candy and small presents. A whistle for Timothy, a little baby doll for Annabelle."

Sage began to wonder if his long trip out from town was going to end in failure. "Did he talk about anything in particular?"

"Oh, he bragged a little, but he always did that. He talked about his rich, important friends, places he saw, things like that."

"Is that what he talked about this last time?"

"Yes, pretty much."

Sage suppressed a surge of exasperation. "Mrs. Steele," he said, "it's very important that I know exactly what Clancy said that day."

The shocked look left her face and her gaze became direct, as if she had just realized that she had no idea who Sage was or why he was asking questions. Before she could ask, he said, "I'm trying to find out who killed your husband. They think it was a young boy, the nephew of a friend of mine. I know the boy did not do it, so I need to find out who did."

For all her previous vagueness, she caught on quick. "You and the police are thinking different on this?"

"Yes, the police are taking the easy way out. They think they know who killed your husband, so they're not even looking for anyone else."

"Humph," she said, then fell silent a moment before saying, "I don't put much faith in the police anymore. They never protected me and the kids when we needed it. Lazy, that's what they are. Let me see if I remember his words." She tilted her chin down and gnawed on her knuckle while she thought.

Recalling slowed her voice as she spoke, "He talked about how his train had finally pulled into the station. He seemed to think how he said it was funny. He said people would have to look up to him instead of down, like they'd been doing. More things like that."

"Did he say who?"

"No, Clancy never mentioned names. He was kinda secretive that way."

"Did he give you anything to keep for him?"

She shook her head. "No, he didn't give me anything."

"Did he go into any room by himself where he might've hid something?"

"No, he sure didn't. He stayed right in the front room. There are just two rooms in our cottage."

Sage gave up. It did seem like he'd made the trip for nothing. He stood and held out his hand to help her rise. Just as she reached her feet, five children in stair-step sizes ran around the corner of the house. One peeled off and disappeared behind the cottage. Seconds later, Sage heard the unmistakable thwap of an outhouse door slapping shut.

Sage said his goodbye. Then a thought stopped him. "This is going to sound like a peculiar question, Mrs. Steele. When Clancy last visited, did he use the outhouse?"

Her nose wrinkled in surprise. "Well, yes, I guess he did."

"May I visit it before I go?"

Her eyes widened in curiosity, but she was too polite to comment. "Well, I . . . why, certainly you can. It's round back of the cottage."

Sage headed where her finger pointed. A small, black-haired girl of five or so was just coming out of the one-holer, smoothing down her dress. Her bright brown eyes widened in surprise when she saw the unexpected stranger coming toward her.

"Hello there, Annabelle. My name is Mr. Miner, and I'm looking to use your outhouse here if I may."

She stepped sideways, a bit off the path before nodding a solemn assent.

He entered the tight space, automatically breathing through his mouth instead of his nose. As he stood looking around in the small gloomy structure, he could hear Annabelle's little boots thud down the path as she ran toward her mama.

TWENTY THREE

A SURVEY OF the small, spider-webbed outhouse yielded nothing. Sage reached up to run his fingers along the top of the wall headers. Nothing but dust. He'd been afraid of that. He stuck his head out the door and sucked in a lung full of clean air. Then, in one smooth motion he turned, knelt, lifted the toilet seat, and leaned in.

Seconds later he backed out, his hand against the outhouse, fighting the urge to retch. "Damn," he thought, "damn that Clancy."

Sage had seen what he'd been afraid he'd see–a red tobacco tin lying on the wooden frame that supported the toilet seat. The only way to retrieve it was to lean in and reach for it.

He shook his head, trying to shake the stench from his nostrils. "If anyone's watching me from the house, they're sure going to wonder." He lit up the cigar he'd purchased at the train station. It took a few vigorous puffs before tobacco smoke formed a wreath around his head. Clamping his teeth tight, Sage plunged back into the gloom. Using a foot to keep the door propped partially open he dropped to his knees, inserting his head and one arm into the hole. Smoke roiled as black flies buzzed their outrage at his intrusion. He strained, his fingers reaching until they felt the smooth tin. Carefully he withdrew it. He didn't know what he'd do if it fell into the pit. Sage wrapped the tin in hastily snatched outhouse paper and dropped it in his pocket. As he turned to flee out the door, he almost trampled a boy of about nine who was standing there, brown eyes wide, mouth agape.

"I'm finished, son. You might tell your mama the privy needs a bit of lime," Sage said, heading toward the front of the farmhouse. At the corner, Sage looked back. The boy had neither moved his feet nor changed expression, only turned his head so his eyes could follow Sage.

Sage gave a carefree wave, thinking he knew why the boy was speechless. Probably saw me through the door while my head was in the hole. That'll be some story he tells them.

Bess Steele and the Abbotts stood clustered on the porch. After polite goodbyes Sage grabbed the reins of his horse, which immediately began to crow-hop sideways. Embarrassing moments later, a mounted Sage bounced away down the lane. Glancing over his shoulder, he saw the young boy entertaining the older folks, his small body bent at the waist, his arm reaching down to the ground. As one, the faces looked from the boy toward Sage, who straightened his spine and jauntily waved as he and the horse rounded the bend.

Farther on, Sage reined the gelding to a halt in the shade of a leafy maple. The horse seemed content to drop his head and graze. Sage didn't bother dismounting. Sitting in the saddle, he pulled the tin box from his pocket. Something clanked inside it. Opening the lid, he dumped out the object. It was a brass key, with a round head and a shaft longer than a normal key's. It showed no identifying marks whatsoever. Nothing else was in the box.

Dandy, just dandy. He tugged loose his key ring. After hooking the mystery key with others on the ring, he dropped them back in his pocket. The tobacco tin went into the empty saddle bag. Taking up the reins, he headed toward Hillsboro at rapid pace, since he wanted to catch the last train of the day.

❀ ❀ ❀

Thursday morning dawned clear, promising a dry night for his theater party. Sage's surreptitious search from a third-story window revealed no watching men. Their absence likely due to the solid bulk of Patrolman Hanke, who had occupied the watcher's station in the ironworks entrance through most of yesterday according to his mother. The night before, when Sage had arrived back at Mozart's, there'd been another patrolman standing in the same spot.

When he'd commented on the patrolman to his mother, she had informed Sage that Patrolman Hanke had taken evening supper in the restaurant kitchen. Over steak and potatoes he'd vowed to catch their fleet-footed mystery man. She quoted Hanke as opining that "there weren't no point in him running unless he's thinking on breaking the law." She drily observed that it appeared Mozart's would be "the unofficial feed bag for members of the Portland police force for the time being."

This morning, yet a third patrolman was standing below on the sidewalk. "That fella down there looks like a real big eater," Sage muttered to himself as the lace curtain fell back into place. "Better order extra supplies for a few days."

Sage knew the skulkers' absence was illusory. For all he knew, they were sprawled in comfortable armchairs watching Mozart's through the windows of that six-story building across the street.

Two hours later, his mother's arrangements for the evening reviewed and approved, Sage ventured out. The sun was just beginning to penetrate between the buildings. The street sweeper, however, had not made his rounds, so Sage cautiously tread across wooden paving blocks still slippery with horse dung.

He didn't bother looking to see whether anyone followed him. A midmorning attack was unlikely in the city's business district. Moreover, they might be more interested in knowing his destination than in giving him another clout.

Minutes later, he pushed though the glass doors into City Hall's rotunda. No one followed him inside. After pausing to obtain a location, he strode along the marble hallways until he came to where "Property Tax Department" arched in black letters across a frosted door window. Inside, behind a high counter, a pale man with thinning blond hair, his thick spectacles making his brown eyes owlish, looked up, his face inquiring. His tongue swiped across his thin upper lip before he asked, "May I help you, sir?"

"I am trying to find out who owns a piece of property here in town. I was hoping you'd have a record of the ownership," Sage said.

The man straightened. This was clearly a question he felt competent to answer. "Why, yes, sir. This office has that information. If you would be so kind as to give me the address, I'll retrieve it for you right away."

Sage gave the address of Halloran's cribs.

The clerk hesitated a moment. His mouth opened as if he would question the address, then he snapped it shut and pulled a thick ledger from beneath the counter. Running an ink-stained finger down the list, he stopped, read a line and closed the book.

"We show that building as owned by a Mr. Jasper Keating."

"'Jasper Keating?'" Sage asked in surprise. "He's a leasing agent. He doesn't own buildings." Sage had met Keating while he was in the market for a building to house Mozart's.

The clerk pursed his lips. "Nevertheless, the records show Mr. Keating as the owner. We have him registered as the owner of many buildings in the North End."

Sage understood. "I see. But of course there is nothing to show whether, in some lawyer's office, there isn't a paper saying that, in fact, Mr. Keating is not the owner and that someone else is. Who do you suppose would be that lawyer?"

"I am sure I wouldn't know, sir."

Sage gave up. After thanking the marginally helpful clerk, he left. On impulse, he stood beside the door a few seconds, then opened it. The clerk stood at the wall telephone, cranking a summons to the operator. He began speaking into the mouthpiece. Hearing the door click open, the clerk looked over his shoulder. When he saw Sage, he slammed the earpiece onto the hook without saying another word.

Sage smiled. "Sorry, I thought perhaps I'd forgotten my walking stick here, but I see that I didn't."

"Wa . . . Walking stick? I don't recall seeing you carry a walking stick."

"Oh, well, maybe not. Perhaps I'm confused, or maybe I forgot it somewhere else. So sorry for the interruption."

The clerk stood as if frozen, while Sage once again made his departure.

Sage left City Hall through the west door to the driveway. He paused in the deep shade of the portico, looking for a follower. He saw none.

Stepping smartly up the street, he was knocking at Lucinda's front door within ten minutes. When Elmira ushered him to the parlor doorway, Lucinda was alone, sitting at the shawl-draped piano against the far wall. Her fingers were playing a slow, melancholy tune. He stood for a moment, listening. "Lucinda dear," he said only slightly louder than the music.

She stopped playing. Her hand lifted to her eyes and dropped before she swivelled on the stool, standing to face him with a bright smile on her lips. Her eyes were sad and rimmed in smeary black. Stepping forward, he took the balled white handkerchief from her hand and wiped the smudges from beneath her eyes.

"Trouble, Lucy?"

"Oh Sage, I don't know. Sometimes I wish my life were something else. Just feeling sorry for myself, I guess. Maybe I spend too much time here, ever the enterprising business woman." Her tone was bitter.

He chucked her under the chin. "Lucy, you know that a domestic life would bore you."

She looked at him, a flicker of hurt in her eyes but she only said, "I'm sure you're right, Sage. This is where I belong."

Sage shifted, uncomfortable. "Well, how about you head out with me, girl? We'll stroll the Park Blocks and drink some tea in that new shop near the Cabot Club."

Sparkle returned to her eyes. His invitation pleased her. Not many of the men who visited this house would want anyone to see them with Lucinda Collins on their arm. "I'll go get my shawl," she said, almost skipping from the room. She called out as she ascended the stairs, "Elmira! Please fetch my Gainsborough hat, the Japanese silk with pink poppies. Mr. Adair and I are walking out!"

Sage was waiting at the front door when Lucinda appeared on the stairs, a woman as lovely and stylish as any in Portland. When he told her so, she blushed as if unaccustomed to compliments.

They strolled beneath the oaks in the Park Blocks, south to the end before returning north. Along the way, they encountered men one or the other knew. If the men were alone, they'd nod and sometimes stop to speak. When the man's wife or other female was with him, his nod became near imperceptible. Once, following one of these furtive greetings, Sage and Lucinda heard a furious hissing from the woman, followed by a defensive rumble from the man.

Reaching the tea shop, they settled at a table near the window. Once they'd ordered, Sage made an effort to entertain her with tales of his Klondike gold rush adventure from five years before. "The Mounties wouldn't let Americans descend into Canada on the other side unless we each carried at least twelve hundred pounds of provisions. So we had to make trip after trip up that golden staircase to the top of Chilkoot Pass. We climbed almost four thousand feet at a forty-degree slope, a single line of us trailing up narrow steps carved out of ice all loaded down like donkeys. Straight up to the top. I didn't know whether my heart, my lungs, or my legs would give out first."

"Golden staircase? You said they made the steps in the snow. Did they call it 'golden' because it was leading them to gold?"

"Oh, no, nothing as fanciful as that. Think about it. It took hours to climb to the summit. People ate and drank along the way. It was steep. There was no place to step off, no rock to hide behind and cold enough to freeze liquid in an instant."

Lucinda's eyes widened and a loud chortle escaped her that she instantly muffled with her gloved hand. "I guess you men got pretty direct out there in the wilds. Still, you must have made it up that staircase."

"That I did." Sage touched the white streak where it swept back from his right temple. "Not without problems, though. From the crest, we slid seven miles down the other side to Carter Lake. The sled ran away with me and I hit a tree that knocked me out. This white in my hair and a bit of gold are my only two Klondike souvenirs."

As their teapot came close to empty, Sage worked the conversation around to the question of who owned Halloran's cribs.

His casual inquiry didn't fool Lucinda. "So that's why we're having such a lovely afternoon, Sage?" she asked, her mouth quirked in a sardonic smile. "Well, if so, the price you've paid is more than the information is worth. This has been a lovely afternoon, and I feel ever so much better."

She paused to take a sip of tea, seeming to savor its taste before saying. "Halloran's building is owned by the oh-so-proper Arista Dunlop's husband."

Sage wasn't certain but it seemed she'd imparted that bit of information with more relish than it deserved.

"Edward Dunlop?" he asked, playing dumb.

"Yes, Sage. None other than Mr. Edward Dunlop– husband of that Arista Dunlop, who, I understand, is a particular friend of yours." Her eyebrow arched, but her smile didn't reach her eyes. "Other than a few houses owned by women like me, the rich men of this town own most of the lower-class sporting establishments. Isn't that clever of them?"

Lucinda poured the last of the tea into his cup, set the pot down, gave him an innocent smile, and folded her hands demurely on the table. But her eyes flashed fire. "I suspect that's how some of them can afford to keep their respectable wives, such as your Mrs. Dunlop, so elegantly gowned," she said.

TWENTY FOUR

MOZART'S SUPPERTIME PATRONS were graciously but unmistakably hustled out the door promptly at nine o'clock. No lingering over coffee or wine. Even before the last satiated customer left, the staff began readying the restaurant for the theater party. Clean tablecloths snapped across the tables, the wall sconce chimneys were vigorously scoured. Like a field commander, Mrs. Clemens stood at the kitchen doors directing the placement of platters and bowls of meats, cheeses, salads, breads, berries, and cream cakes onto a buffet. Catching Sage watching her, admiration in his eyes, she blushed, then flapped her hand to shoo him upstairs to change his suit.

Stringed instruments squawked from the balcony overhead as the musicians readied to play. Glancing up, Sage confirmed that the train porter, Mr. Brown, had a comfortable seat in the balcony, positioned so he'd see everyone who entered the restaurant. Balancing an overflowing plate on his knee. Brown saluted him with a bread roll to signify his appreciation of the food.

"Let the play begin," Sage murmured. There were times when Life seemed to unwind as if tossed out by an invisible but friendly prankster—one lucky happenstance abutting another. Most times, though, Life hurled a man along as if he was buckled onto those wood slats the snow-crazy Scandinavians rode down mountainsides. Sometimes, it was all a man could do to keep his feet under him until the ride ended.

One hour later, Sage swung wide the front door to greet his invited guests who first trickled and then crowded in. Soon, the actors themselves swooped onto the scene, their bright colors, showy gestures and theatrical laughter filling the room. Sage began to drift between chattering groups, listening here and there, but always attune to that group of men clustered around Otis Welker. Sage wanted to eavesdrop on that conversation but it was impossible. Maybe someday he could rig the dining room with hidden speaking tubes that piped down into the cellar. An impractical idea he had to admit. Too bad. Whatever Welker's group was discussing, their tense expressions were at odds with the evening's gala. He decided to wander in their direction. Maybe Perry had drunk enough champagne by now to raise his voice.

" . . . Mr. Gompers's speech was most edifying," came the pubescent voice of a young man named 'Charlie.' He was speaking to a group that included his parents, who were themselves, frequent customers. Sage paused to listen, interested in what Charlie might think of the labor leader.

"Mr. Gompers is trying to stir up more of that union rabblement. I don't know why you even listened to him," said Charlie's father.

"Father, if you had only heard him. He told us about the appalling conditions in New York sweatshops. Young women, girls, children even, are . . . "

"That's in New York. It has nothing to do with Portland, what goes on . . .," responded his father in a repressive tone. He wanted no further discussion of the matter.

His effort failed because Charlie's earnest voice interrupted, "Yes it does! We sell goods made in those sweatshops in our store! Mr. Gompers told how the New York Consumers' Union is calling for a nationwide consumer boycott of a whole long list of goods."

"A boycott! Charlie, if you want to go to the university, you'd best not urge a boycott of your father's store," a stout woman admonished, her hand nervously flicking an open fan before her face.

Another man in the group, his face already flushed from the champagne, chimed in. "Yeah, Charlie. You could end up working in a sweatshop your own self!" He snickered and leaned closer to the boy, speaking in an exaggerated, confidential tone, "Careful what you ask for, Charley boy, you just might get it!"

The group laughed and the young man's face flushed crimson above his snowy white collar. Sage moved on in the direction of Welker's group but not before winking at the discomfitted boy, who offered a grateful look in return. Welker was frowning at Perry who was waving his arms, and talking loudly, but not loudly enough for Sage to distinguish the words.

Perry settled down. As one, all the conspirators turned to stare at Sage, their expressions speculative. Now was clearly not the time to insert himself into their midst. Sage instead paused at the next exchange he encountered, one between the leading actor and a well-dressed couple. The three greeted him and then continued their conversation.

"Tell me, Mr. Floyd, you have performed in Portland before, as I recall?" spoke the fluttering voice of the matron whose ample curves were cinched into a tight bodice. Sage wondered whether it was her corset or Mozart's free drinks that had turned her face rosy.

"Why, yes, madam. I am flattered you remember." The actor's accent sounded British but beneath them was the trace of New York City, Hell's Kitchen maybe.

"I say there, Floyd, I noticed that in the Heilig Theater, the boxes are situated right next to the stage. At the Baker tonight, the boxes were farther away on the balcony. Tell me, which of the setups do you like playing to best?" came the self-important voice of the matron's husband, proprietor of the city's most exclusive haberdashery.

"Ah, no one has ever asked me such an interesting question," this time the player's sonorous voice was further enriched by a theatrically suppressed chuckle. "I think perhaps I prefer boxes close to the stage. That allows me to draw inspiration from my audience, such as that provided by your lovely wife," said the actor as he bowed to the woman, presenting her with the pink rose he whipped out of his lapel. A sideways glance followed her soft squeal. No doubt checking to see if others had noted Floyd's gesture.

Unable to stomach anymore of the exchange, Sage moved toward the buffet table, where Knute, who'd been pressed into service, was refilling the bowls.

"All is well, Knute?"

"Very well, Mr. Adair," Knute responded, then continued in a lower tone. "A letter came today. Our boy is working hard but he's fine. Sounds bored. He was looking to leave the country life behind him when he left home."

"When we've got this mess settled, Knute, we'll find a place for him. I've been thinking on that and I've some ideas."

"Thank you, Mr. Adair. I'm sorry about bringing our family troubles to you."

"No trouble, Knute. I find your problems a nice change from an otherwise dull life. Just sorry it happened to your family."

Sage glanced up at the musicians' balcony. His eyes caught an excited gleam in Mr. Brown's. The porter gave three deliberate nods. He'd spotted them. Every one of the mystery men from the train ride was in the room.

Sage continued strolling from group to group, always angling in the direction of Welker's table. As he neared it, Welker said something to his companions who simultaneously rose to wander off toward their respective spouses. Sage paused until Welker gestured toward a vacant chair. "Please sit down. I seem to have lost my friends to their wives." Above his thin-lipped smile, Welker's blue eyes were cold, like those of a fish on ice.

As Sage took a seat, one of Fong's oblique homilies came to his mind. "Crane, one foot raised, stands motionless waiting for Snake to come to him. Snake does not see." Sage decided to be still like Crane just to see if it would force Welker to speak first. It did.

"Mr. Adair, it appears that your little foray into cosmopolitan practices has met with success tonight."

Ah. Welker intended to make small talk then, despite the nearly overt hostility in his eyes. Sage larded his reply with equal banality, "Yes, people do seem to be enjoying themselves. I hope that they'll want to continue gathering here after future premiere theatrical performances. Of course, I'll be charging then."

"I would think that very likely, since Mrs. Dunlop has affixed her stamp of approval on the enterprise."

"Mrs. Dunlop has been most supportive," Sage agreed.

"After-theater parties, I believe, are quite common in New York, Boston, and other Eastern cities. Is that where you are from? Though I seem to recall hearing that you hailed from Colorado. Denver, I believe."

"No, Mr. Welker, I've never had the pleasure of visiting Denver, although I understand it is situated with a fine view of the Rockies." He told the truth. He and the Saint never met in Denver because the Dickensens swarmed over that town, thick as the flies in Bess Steele's outhouse. "I hail from many places, Mr. Welker, the East being one of them."

Welker's chuckle lacked humor. "I am sure that is true. Where were you born?"

"In Pennsylvania," Sage answered truthfully, "but I've lived many places since then. How about yourself, Mr. Welker? Are you from Wisconsin originally? Is that how you came to be employed by Baumhauer?"

"No, Mr. Adair. Like yourself, I've lived many places."

"I presume, Mr. Welker, that you are here on business for Baumhauer. Perhaps you are hoping to buy additional timberland? I understand Baumhauer made a purchase near Silverton not so long ago."

Welker leaned back in his chair and seemed to be studying the tip of his unlit cigar. "Well, when one represents the timber industry, one is always ready to buy. Actually, however, I am here visiting friends. So tell me, the admirable Mrs. Clemens, is she a relation?" Welker nodded his head toward Sage's mother, who stood scrutinizing the buffet table. She directed a waiter toward the spare champagne bottles sitting on the sideboard in a tub of ice. The waiter jumped to fetch a new bottle.

Sweat suddenly filmed Sage's forehead. "No, she's no relation. We are most fortunate that she came to us."

"Where does she come from? I would think the two of you related. There seems to be a resemblance."

"Really? But, no. She, I think, comes from, ah, from somewhere in the Midwest if I recall. Would you care for more champagne?" Without waiting for an answer, Sage raised an arm to catch the waiter's eye, gesturing toward Welker's glass. The waiter hustled over.

Welker lit the black cheroot and exhaled smoke toward the tin ceiling's embossed swirls. Then he said, "I understand you have been much out of town of late, Mr. Adair." The eyes were hooded but alert. The Snake waiting to strike. The Crane was not invisible at all.

Sage arranged his face to display what he hoped was disinterest and replied, "Yes, I travel frequently, on business for the most part."

"Business? I would not think a restaurant, even one so fine as Mozart's, would require much travel."

"My business interests are more varied. I have investments and property in other locations that demand my time." The other man's interrogation was beginning to stray into the impolite. Apparently Welker realized this because he switched tracks but still pressed forward.

"Oh, so you have financial interests in one of the delightful towns to the west?"

Momentarily Sage flailed before realizing from Welker's phrasing that one of Welker's minions must have seen him at the train depot the night before, not long after the Tualatin Valley interurban line arrived.

Partial truth was always better than a total lie. "As a matter of fact, yes, I traveled to Beaverton yesterday." Sage responded. "That, however, actually was restaurant business. I've located a new source of fruit preserves. It's canning season, so I was making arrangements to obtain a farm woman's product for Mozart's."

Welker arched one of his pale eyebrows. "How industrious of you, searching out the local fruit. I trust your mission met with success?"

At that moment Knute approached the table, cutting off any further grilling. Knute said Sage was needed in the kitchen. When Sage stood, so did Welker so he could lean across the table to shake hands. Welker's hand was chilly and too tight to be friendly. Sage responded with the broad smile of the obsequious host before hurrying into the kitchen. He moved quickly, spurred on by the need to escape the chill of those hostile eyes drilling into his back.

There was no emergency, just his mother's intuition. "I saw that you were squirming, thought maybe you'd welcome a rescue," was her only comment as she handed him a stack of clean plates to carry back out into the dining room.

❁ ❁ ❁

It was one o'clock before the last of the partygoers trickled out the door and Mr. Brown could descend from the balcony. The porter identified Louis Perry as the man who'd lost the case on the train. He described Hipple and Gardiner as the other two men riding on the train with Perry. Sage paid Mr. Brown well for his time and locked the door behind him. He was glad the day was finally over.

When Sage slid beneath a summer quilt, his body was achingly tired but his mind was restless. Thoughts chased each other endlessly around in his head. Welker, Perry, Dunlop, Hipple, Gardiner—it all spelled money. Lots of money. Gilcrease, a government bureaucrat. Gilcrease and money. Clancy Steele and timber interests and phoney homesteaders. Timber and Welker. So, land deals, money, and Portland's richest men. Then there was the camphor man and Clancy Steele being murdered. Which led to Perry's being frantic about his case being stolen while he was riding on the same train as Steele. Later, Steele elated, bragging about coming into money and prestige. All the bits of the answer were there, if he could just figure out how the bits fit together. There had to be a key. Well, and that was part of it. There was a key, a real key. On his key ring, as a matter of fact. But it was a key to what?

❁ ❁ ❁

Sage woke to the sound of faint, frantic cries. He sat up, ears straining until the sounds sorted out into Chinese-accented words of "Fire, fire!"

Fong! Sage leapt from bed, tugging on his trousers as he opened his door. At hall's end, a smoky haze pooled above the stairwell. He ran to his mother's room, but even as he raised his fist to pound on the door it opened and she stood there, clothed, clutching keepsakes bundled in a bedsheet.

Quickly they descended the main staircase, encountering Knute and Ida on the second-floor landing, both in nightclothes

– Ida clutching her cat. At the bottom of the stairs, Fong was beating at burning carpet with a wet tablecloth. Knute grabbed up a loose rug and joined him. Fong pointed toward the kitchen. "Fire in kitchen, too, Mr. Sage."

Smoke was indeed seeping from around the swinging doors. Sage ran to push open one of the doors. Smoke roiled out, close to the floor. Sage grabbed a linen napkin from the sideboard, pressed it over his nose and mouth, and plunged inside. His smarting eyes strained to adjust to a kitchen made fantastic by swirling smoke. Here, too, the floor was afire.

A tall metal milk jug full of water his mother insisted on keeping in the kitchen stood near. He tugged it toward the blazing floor boards, then tipped it over. As the whooshing flood of water hit the flames there was a sizzling snap and the fire blacked out.

After making sure that everything was soaked, Sage whirled back out through the doors, relieved to find that the floor by the front door was no longer burning. Outside a fire-wagon bell clanged and horse shoes clattered. The rolling ruckus halted before Mozart's, firemen clinging to every handhold on the wagon.

The firemen weren't disappointed to discover the fire extinguished. They bustled about, checking Mozart's and the surrounding buildings for any burning embers. Inspection completed, the men mounted the wagon for a sedate rumble back to their firehouse beds. Only the fire chief remained behind.

The chief's face was serious beneath the shell of his helmet as he motioned Sage aside. "Mr. Adair, you look a pretty smart fellow to me. I'm sure I don't need to tell you this was arson. It's too peculiar, having two fires in different places at the same time."

Sage nodded. "That's what I figure. Question is, how'd they do it? Both doors were still locked."

"I've looked at that. I'm quite certain that here at the front door they just opened the message slot, poured in some paraffin, and topped it off with a match. I notice there's a small open window next to the kitchen door. Looks like someone broke it and poured paraffin in there. Dribbled a bit on the wall, I'm thinking, because there was a long burn stripe coming up from the floor. Not a lot of damage but it could have been worse. Much worse. Lucky your Chinaman was up and about."

They were standing in the middle of the now quiet street, both studying the building's ornate ironwork facade. The fire chief cleared his throat to speak. "It, ah, well, ah, it looks like someone hoped you folks wouldn't find a way out. Like they wanted you trapped inside. Now that's a worrisome thought. I'll be talking to the police tomorrow. Maybe you best be thinking about who might wish you harm and take a few precautions. They might give it another go, maybe try something different next time."

Sage's thoughts had already rabbited down that trail, except that he was pretty certain he knew who was behind this latest personal attack.

His warning issued, the fire chief bid goodnight and went on his way. Sage gazed up and down the street before going inside. No one was in sight. But then, they could be anywhere. Maybe behind one of those darkened windows of the building across the street. As Sage reentered Mozart's, he told himself that the icy prick in the middle of his back was just another flight of his "fancy-filled" mind that his mother liked to tease him about.

She was waiting inside, along with Knute, Ida, and Fong. They sat around the nearest table not speaking, sipping and studying the camomile tea Ida had brewed as soon as the firemen allowed her back into the kitchen.

The cook was not drinking her tea. Instead, Ida was kneading her hands together, stopping the motion when she realized he stood in the threshold. "Oh, Mr. Adair, we're the reason this happened. Somebody wanted to punish us because they think Matthew killed that awful man." Ida wailed, tears filling her blue eyes. At her side, Knute sat with smoke-blackened hands gripping a mug, his face long and glum.

Sage grabbed a chair, whirling it around so he could sit astraddle. "Ida," he began, "You can forget thinking that you are responsible for this. I've been busy learning things and I think I know why there was a fire. Believe me, this is not about Matthew. I can't tell you what is going on. But you'll have to trust me that I know what I'm talking about."

The couple relaxed at his words. Minutes later, weariness took over and Ida, Knute and Mae mounted the stairs hoping to get in some sleep before dawn and the beginning of the workday.

Sage's mother paused to hug a startled but pleased Fong before she, too, left for bed.

Sage and Fong sat quietly until Sage said, "We are damn lucky you decided to stay in your room here instead of going home tonight," Sage said. "How'd you smell that smoke, all the way up on the third floor?"

"I not on third floor when fire start. Not able to sleep, so I went to talk to Mr. Solomon at his hotel. I know he stay up late. When I come back, before I go down in tunnel, I walk by front of restaurant to see if anybody watching there. I see smoke, so I yell "fire," in street, run through tunnel, grab tablecloth, hit fire and try to wake everyone up."

"Was anyone in the street or the alley?"

"I think no, but not sure. Just before I enter alley, I think there is movement at other end of building, running away."

"Did they see you go in the tunnel?" Sage hated the idea of losing the secrecy of that entrance.

"No, they disappear before I reach alley. No way they know what happened to me."

The two men sat in silence, Sage replaying the events of the fire in his mind until he thought to ask, "Mr. Solomon have anything to say?"

Fong's weary face cracked into one of his toothy grins. "He say that men working in hotel tell him that a smelly man visits Welker man every night after hallways mostly empty. Same smell. Camphor."

TWENTY FIVE

RAIN SPLATTED AGAINST the windows where Sage, Mae, and Fong sat in Sage's small third-floor alcove. Early morning dray traffic rattled in the street below, its volume increasing with every minute. The noise of commerce would continue growing until the wagon rumbles, horse clops and the calls of men became a cacophony that wouldn't start diminishing until dusk.

"It's time we put this whole mess of facts together," Sage said. "There are a number of reasons to conclude that someone working for Welker's little group killed Clancy. We know that Clancy bragged that he had something on the rich men that he thought would bring him money in the future. So he couldn't have been talking about money or jewels because both are easily converted into cash and blackmail wasn't necessary. And we know that Perry, the man who lost whatever it was, claimed it was kept in a hand case. So, I'm thinking it's a document of some sort. What we don't know is what that writing said or who killed Clancy for it, though I'm betting he was murdered by the two men who've been watching us. And, we know they haven't found what Clancy stole, because they're still interested in our doings and now they've tried to burn us out. So, they are still feeling threatened by our interest in Clancy Steele and whatever he was holding over them."

"Sage, do you suppose if we knew why this Gilcrease fellow is important and exactly what he does, that we might be able figure out what those scoundrels are up to?" Mae Clemens asked.

"Yes, that's a really good question. Who is Gilcrease? And, we also need to find out what lock that key fits. I know it's not to a bank safety-deposit box, because I've rented boxes in every Portland bank, in case of fire or bank failure. I checked my safety deposit keys. Steele's key doesn't look like any of them."

Fong was looking thoughtful, his brow creased. "Maybe I can find where key fits," he suggested. "Members of my tong work many places. Maybe they have seen key that looks the same. I can draw picture of it. Show it around."

"That's a good idea, Mr. Fong. While you're doing that, I'll try to find out more about Gilcrease." Sage started to stand.

"What should I do?" his mother asked, keen interest making her eyes bright.

"We need you to keep things running smoothly here, Ma," Sage said.

"Humph," was all she said but her face said a lot more. Sage merely patted her shoulder as he left the room. He'd be getting a tongue-lashing a few hours down the road.

After Sage and Fong left, Mae Clemens sat rumminating. Then she slapped her hand on the table and stood. "Keep things running, my fanny," she said to the empty room.

❀ ❀ ❀

Sage was visiting the *Journal* offices once again where he found his friend Ben Johnston bent over copy, his pencil furiously scratching away. He laid the pencil aside at Sage's question.

"Gilcrease, Gilcrease, that name sounds familiar. If he's in the timber business, Roscoe's the man you need to talk to." Johnston stood to go to his open door and holler, "Roscoe, come in here, if you would."

A small, wiry man hurried up the aisle into Johnston's office, his brown eyes snapping with lively curiosity.

"Yes, sir?" he said in a clear, piping voice.

"Roscoe, take a seat. My friend here wants to know something about a fella called Gilcrease, James Gilcrease. You heard that name around?"

The man's forehead wrinkled in concentration before smoothing out when recognition hit. "Yes, I've heard of him. He works at the federal Forest Service office here in town. I believe he's pretty high up in that office—might even be running a department, as a matter of fact."

"Is there anyone you know in the Forest Service that you can ask? My friend here wants to know, and I suspect there'll be a story in it for us," Johnston said, raising an inquiring eyebrow toward Sage. Sage nodded just once.

"I think I can find that information. I've cultivated an acquaintance in that office. I'll give him a jingle on the squawk box." Roscoe hurried away.

"Energetic fellow," Sage observed.

"Yup. He's going to go a long way in this business. He's like a terrier. Gets an idea in his head and won't let go. Sometimes he lacks sense, though. That'll come with experience, if he doesn't get himself killed first."

The two men waited, talking about nothing in particular until Roscoe reappeared at the door. "Gilcrease is in charge of the federal forest reserve program. Buys and trades land. He travels all over the Northwest. My acquaintance doesn't think much of him. He wouldn't give me any specifics."

"Thanks, Roscoe," Johnston said with finality, letting the reporter know he'd been dismissed. Roscoe left, disappointment writ large across his face.

Johnston looked at Sage, who said, "Well, that fits. Makes sense that the bad guys are involved in some kind of land deal. They've been pulling off shady land deals for years." Sage told Ben about the drunks being paid to prove up homestead claims only to sell them to the timber interests as soon as they received title.

Ben wasn't impressed. "That's an old story. Any timberland homesteader tells of one or another instance of it. Doesn't sound like that would be sufficient for someone to murder Steele. In fact, we wrote a story on that a while back when you were gone on one of your mysterious trips. Anyway, we tried to gin up pressure on the local federal prosecutor to take some action, but so far, nothing. I suspect he's in league with the whole kit-and-caboodle."

"So, if the conspirators have the federal prosecutor in their pocket, why would they care about anything Steele might have on them?" Sage asked. "Even if Steele produced some document proving the homestead scam, they are protected by the crooked prosecutor."

Johnston leaned back in his chair and stared up toward the ceiling. "Well," he said, "a guy could always take the evidence down to San Francisco's federal prosecutor. He's supposed to be an honest bulldog who despises the one we got here. One thing's for sure, I don't believe that whatever it is has happened yet, from what you've told me."

"What do you mean, Ben?" Sage's pulse quickened.

"You said they are meeting with this Welker fellow and acting nervous. Since they have nothing to fear from the local prosecutor, then maybe we need to ask what else might make them anxious." Johnston raised an eyebrow waiting for Sage's response. When one didn't come, Johnston answered his own question. "It's an easy one John. Money, plain ole filthy lucre. I'll bet they invested a lot of money in some scheme that Steele's information would ruin. Now, if Gilcrease is involved, the scheme must involve federal forest land. And, because of Welker, it must also involve the timber interests. So then the question to answer is "just what is their little moneymaking scheme?"

Johnston had to be right. It all fit. "Maybe we need to find out more about what this Gilcrease bureaucrat has been doing lately," Sage said.

Johnston was ready to join in. "There might be something there. I'll get Roscoe onto that idea as well. Maybe between the two of us, we'll acquire enough information to add things up. Hell's bells, could be I'll finally get that story you've been dangling in front of my nose these past few weeks!" Both men laughed and Sage left to track down Gilcrease, knowing that Johnston's analysis had hit the target square on. Everything revolved around money and trees.

Success eluded him. Gilcrease was not in his office. As things turned out, the man's absence proved a bit of luck.

❀ ❀ ❀

The woman carrying the string bag full of soap bars drew little attention as she wandered past the cribs and cabins occupied by the so-called "soiled doves." A faded calico dress showed through the torn gaps in the woolen shawl draped over her stooped shoulders. Salt-and-pepper hair straggled from the untidy bun at the nape of her neck.

At each stop she offered the women "Frenchified" sweet-smelling soap at an uncommonly reasonable price. Sight of the satiny bar brightened otherwise dimmed eyes. There were many takers. In each instance, the soap seller rattled on about her own personal disaster.

"Ah, miss, thank you for thinking of buying my soap. I make it myself, you see. Still, it's a mighty fine soap to soothe the rough spots and leave a touch of sweet scent."

As the purchasers pressed their noses into the bars, the woman prattled on. "I learned how to make it in a fine house. I worked there many a year. Anyways, they turned me out into the street when my master took against me. I don't know why. I have always been a hard worker and caused no trouble. It may be you know of him, Mr. Gilcrease . . . Mr. James Gilcrease?"

The hours passed. The woman sold her bag empty a number of times. Each time that happened, she'd walk south into the business district to buy scented soap from Portland's largest department store. Then, sitting on a low stone wall, she'd unwrap the soap and drop it into her bag before heading north to sell it at a loss.

Late afternoon, her fortitude was rewarded. "Why, dearie, you oughta be right happy to be shut of that James Gilcrease. You look to be a decent woman who shouldn't be about that kind of person," a woman said while her dirty-nailed fingers mindlessly scratched at insect bites dotting her scrawny arms. "I can tell you stuff about that disgusting man that would curl your hair."

It took some time and a shot of whiskey inside the nearby saloon, but at last Mae had the woman's story to carry home.

❀ ❀ ❀

Sage returned to Mozart's just before the noontime dinner hour. A rug hid the scorch marks by the front door and the faint smokey smell blended nicely with Ida's fry up in the kitchen. But, there was no Mae Clemens and no one could tell him where she'd gone. An hour later, a mild panic was starting to flutter in the top of his throat. He could do nothing about it. The patrons kept arriving and someone had to seat them. By four o'clock when the pace let up. Sage knew what it meant to "sweat" over something. It wasn't just a figure of speech.

Sage climbed to the third floor to examine Mae's room. The dress she'd been wearing lay on her bed. Inside her wardrobe, every one of her dresses seemed to be there. Well, she surely wasn't stark naked when she left Mozart's. That thought lessened the weight of concern. Thoroughly puzzled, Sage returned to the kitchen.

Fong had finished washing the dishes. "Mr. Fong, I'm afraid that . . . ," Sage started, only to stop at the slap of the kitchen door. Turning, he saw his mother. She wore a tattered dress and shawl that he'd thought she'd long ago dropped into the trash bin. Apparently he wasn't the only one in the building who maintained an alternate wardrobe.

Then he remembered how late she was. He advanced toward her, saying with a hiss that surprised him, "Where have you been?"

She looked up from folding her tattered shawl. "Why, I've been out, Mr. Adair. Ida had things here well in hand and running smoothly when I left."

He felt his face redden with the suppressed urge to yell at her. Five hours late! And she'd done it the day after Welker's not so veiled threat about their relationship and just hours after a fire that nearly burnt them to death. He couldn't give vent to his anger. To everyone in the kitchen, except Fong, Mae was merely an employee. So he kept his voice mild but let his eyes flash. "Well, ah, next time please inform someone when you intend to be absent from your post."

"Certainly, Mr. Adair," she responded meekly but her eyes snapped with fire. She moved past him and out the swinging doors, her lips tightly compressed until they went white. He followed her.

They ascended the stairs in silence. Once the door to Sage's room had closed behind them, Sage exploded. "You knew I'd be worried. Didn't you think about how I'd feel when I found you missing? Good God, Mother! Welker's men have been sniffing around here like a pack of starving wolves!"

She wasn't cowed. "Oh, so now you're thinking you want to talk about feelings? Well, then. How do you think I felt when you ran off. How dare you tell me my job is to 'make sure things ran smoothly?'" Sarcasm clotted her last two words.

He didn't care. "Mother, it's not your fight, it's mine!" Sage's voice rose, the increasing volume releasing the pent up fear he'd been feeling all the hours past.

Her head snapped erect, her blue eyes darkening as she enunciated carefully, "Is that so? Who was it said this is just *your* fight? Was it *your* father who got killed by those cowardly Dickensens because he wanted decency? Is it *your* brother and *your* sister's son who lie buried under a mountain? How many of *your* friends, the people you played with as a kid, hacked up black coal dust until finally there was nothing left but the dirt hitting their coffins? How many times did you clean behind your so-called betters just to keep a leaky roof above your head and a hunk of coal in the stove?" A rush of unshed tears glittered in her eyes. "Sage, did you give up your child," she paused, her eyes vacant from pain before she looked at him fully to say, "Your only child, to a damn greedy mine owner, never knowing if that boy would ever claim you again? Don't you dare tell *me* this is *your* fight!"

He didn't speak. Her fury was like falling into the icy Yukon. Mae Clemens rarely let her anger show. He reached toward her but she jerked away. He backed off and held his hands up in supplication. "I'm sorry, Mother, you're right. It is our fight. Our fight together. That's what we agreed. I forgot. I wasn't thinking. I'm sorry. I was just so worried."

She turned to lay her folded shawl in a bureau drawer. She shut the drawer and stood there, back rigid as a brick. He waited.

When she turned to face him, she was smiling, her eyes bright. "All right then, it's settled and over. Anyways, I think I've found out why your Mr. Gilcrease is so helpful to Welker and his friends. It should come in very handy."

TWENTY SIX

LUCINDA LOOKED LIKE an ordinary housewife early the next morning. Tendrils of fine hair wisped from beneath her calico kerchief and her waist was cinched tight by the narrow white strings of a butcher's apron. Her long fingers were spreading stove black on top of her kitchen's cookstove. For a moment, Sage found it easy to envision her in some cottage kitchen, children playing near her feet. She turned to grab a cloth from the table and saw him. When she lifted a hand to brush back her hair, a streak of stove black appeared on her cheek. "Oh damn," she said snatching up a dish towel to wipe away the smudge.

"No worry, Lucinda. You look fetching."

"Very funny. Well, you've caught me with my secret indulgence. I like to clean." Swiftly she whipped off the apron, dropped the kerchief and dish towel and grabbed Sage's forearm, steering him toward the parlor. Later, after a brisk, cheerful Elmira had served them coffee, Sage asked Lucinda about Gilcrease's secret. She thought a moment before saying, "Well, of course, there are houses that cater to men who are interested in other men. You must know that, after the fuss the newspapers made when that English Mr. Wilde went to court. People don't bandy it about, but only the ignorant wouldn't know."

Sage distinctly remembered Oscar Wilde's jailing. Even though deep in the winter snow of the Yukon Territory, Sage had heard the talk and seen more than a few sly glances exchanged. So, she was right. Men preferring the company of men didn't seem shocking enough to be of much use with blackmail.

He noticed Lucinda had fallen quiet. He saw her take a deep breath. "And then, there are those who like children, like Gilcrease." She said.

"There are such houses? How could they advertise what they offer?" he asked.

"Oh, Sage, and here I've always thought you worldly. There are at least four hundred so-called bawdy houses in this city. Did it never occur to you that a few of them might trade in unusual preferences, ones as awful as Gilcrease's?" As she said the name for the second time repulsion twisted her face.

"Where do they find the children?"

Her laugh was bitter. "That's no secret, either. Just think, where is there a collection of young boys that no one cares about?"

A response flitted through his mind, but Sage let it go because it was preposterous.

Lucinda had read him, though. "You figured it out but you don't want to believe it. Boys' Christian Shelter, the BCS. They pluck the boys from there like ripe fruit off a tree. A promise of work and maybe a few dollars to the BCS manager, is all it takes for the purveyors to get their pick. The bastards."

"So how many of these hell-holes exist in the city? The houses that sell children to men?"

"Maybe four for girls, two for boys." Abruptly, Lucinda reached for her now cold coffee where it rested on the table before the settee. As she brought the cup to her lips, the liquid's dark surface quivered.

"Lucinda, I didn't realize . . . "

She raised her palm before his face. "Sage, never mind. I can't talk about it now." Lucinda's cup clattered in the saucer as she put both down on the table. Turning to face him, she said, "There are two houses that specialize in young boys. Your man Gilcrease likely visits Lynch's. That's south of town near Carruthers Street. From what I hear, the despicable stoat running it has decorated it in red velvet. Gilcrease, being one of our so-called betters, would appreciate that touch. He'd think the other house beneath him, though how he could sink lower than he is, I'm sure I can't say."

An hour later Sage crouched under the boughs of a cedar tree, not sure why he was there. Across the street stood Lynch's. A tall, narrow house, its clapboard peeling blue. Heavy drapes at every smeared window blocked the outside world. The porch was small, tucked high up on one side. Three boys sprawled on various steps of the long wooden stairs, their ages ranging from ten to maybe thirteen. Their movements lacked youthful vigor. Their legs, boney beneath ragged blue coveralls, lay motionless along the steps. A tow-haired fourth boy, the youngest, sat on the concrete landing at the bottom of the stairs, his sallow cheek pressed against his knees.

The red front door opened behind the boys. None of them looked around to see the newcomer. It was a teenage girl, her lips crimson, her cheeks rosy with cosmetics. She clutched a thin, brightly patterned wrapper close to her slight body. She stomped to the edge of the top step and jammed her hands onto her hips, allowing the wrapper to gape open above the waist. With a shock, Sage realized that this too, was a boy, his pale chest flat and hairless. The girlish boy spoke sharply to the others with no effect. They ignored him and he retreated with an irritated flounce. After the door slammed, the four boys remained motionless, staring off into the distance, each in a different direction.

The red door opened again, this time much wider to accommodate the bulk of an enormous man who lumbered onto the porch. He too advanced to the top of the steps. The boys didn't look at him but they drew themselves upright and their bodies became rigid as he spoke. The man waddled back inside. The boys stood slowly and climbed the steps, each moving like an elderly man with arthritic joints. Sage watched until their small backsides disappeared into the house.

"I'll get that bastard Lynch if it's the last thing I do," Sage muttered to himself as he uncurled his fists and pushed up from the ground.

"Sonny, I hope to dear God that you find yourself a way to accomplish that goal," a frail voice tweeted from behind his shoulder.

Sage started and turned. A wizened old man sat on the bench slightly behind the tree. Sage spoke the thought that had a hold on his mind. "How in the hell is this abomination allowed to go on? Don't the neighbors care? Doesn't anyone complain?"

"Of course we care and we complain. Does no good. Lynch must be paying somebody off because nothing happens. At first, we tried to help those unfortunate boys, but you can't trust them. They steal our things. Terrible situation all right. So let's see whether you just walk off from it. Wonder how long it will take you to forget how bad you feel right now." The old man got up and shuffled away across the grass.

The gold of fading sunlight hit the enameled door on the other side of the street. What unspeakable horrors took place behind that gleaming red surface? "One battle at a time, Sage ole' boy, one battle at the time," Sage cautioned himself. "But I will not forget," he added.

❀ ❀ ❀

When Sage opened the door to Gilcrease's office he found a clerk sitting at a desk immediately inside. "I am here to see Mr. Gilcrease," Sage said, carefully keeping his voice business-like.

"What time is your appointment, sir?" the young man asked.

"I don't have an appointment. Just tell Mr. Gilcrease that Mr. Lynch sent me. I'm sure he'll find the time."

The young clerk swallowed, timidity and indecisiveness struggling for control of his face. "Mr. Gilcrease never sees anyone unless they have an appointment."

Better to make it easy for him to decide. "Either you tell Gilcrease I'm here or I shall." Sage's sharp tone spurred the clerk into action. He near trotted toward a door at the back of the office. Stepping inside, he closed the door. Through the frosted glass, Sage heard the muffled sound of a voice rising in anger and the quieter murmurs of the clerk's response. When he came out, the clerk's face was pale. He nodded toward the rear office and returned to his desk, where he picked up a large map with trembling hands.

A pervert and a bully. I'm going to really like dealing with this bastard. Anger surged with each step Sage took toward Gilcrease's office. Sage didn't have to wonder how he was going to handle the man, his fury pushed any deliberateness aside.

The nattily dressed man jumped to his feet when Sage entered and slammed the door shut behind him. Gilcrease's smooth-shaven face flushed raspberry. His round cheeks crowded an upturned nose giving him a porcine aspect. Thin brown hair swept back from a high forehead coated with sweat. His small, receding chin was tucked into the folds of a spotlessly white cravat anchored to his collar by an emerald pin.

"I am sure I don't know any Mr. Lynch," he said, trying for imperious and achieving a squeak.

Sage stepped around the desk to grab the man's vest front. "I won't fool around with you, you perverted pig. You know Lynch, and I'll make sure this whole town knows it unless you tell me what I want to know." Sage released his hold so abruptly that Gilcrease stumbled backward into his chair.

"What, what . . . ?"

Despite his polished exterior, Gilcrease appeared to have an aversion to both dentist and toothbrush because his gasping mouth offered a row of blackened teeth. Disgust twisted Sage's gut.

"You either tell me what you've got going with Otis Welker and his friends, or everyone in this town will hear about your filthy little secret. About the children you molest. Is that plain enough for you?"

Gilcrease's face drained to dead white. "Welker . . . Welker . . . he's on his way here. If he sees you, I'm dead." The man's lips quivered; his entire face paled and began to shine with sweat.

"Why's he coming here?"

"He said he had some things to tie up. Oh dear God, if he sees you, I'm dead," he said again, this time the words shrilly urgent.

"You know who I am?"

"You're that man from the restaurant, Adair. Welker talks about you."

"What's he said? Tell me." He stepped toward Gilcrease, whose eyes stayed riveted on Sage's clenched fists.

"I can't. Not now. For God's sake, man. I'll tell you later.

You've got to leave now. He'll be here any minute. Please go. Go! I'll
... I'll meet you at ten tonight down on the farmers' wharf, near the
bridge. Please. Go ... go! He said he'd kill my family."

The man's terror was genuine. Fright had him by the throat
and he wasn't going to talk. "All right, I'll go now, but you be there
at ten o'clock, and I'd better not find one of Welker's men coming
at me with a knife."

Gilcrease jumped up, his hands fluttering in the direction of
the door. "Yes, yes, I promise. Just go, just go. Please."

Sage left. Outside the building, he thought he saw Welker
round the corner. Turning his face away, Sage hurried in the opposite direction.

A block from Mozart's, Sage was startled by a hand reaching out from a doorway to grab his forearm. It was one of Fong's
cousins, who gestured sharply. Sage stepped into the shelter of the
building's entry columns. "Mister Adair ... you come with me now.
Not go to restaurant. Police there looking for you."

Sage thanked the man and soon entered the back door of
Fong's shop. Inside bundles of dried fungi hung from exposed raf-
ters and stacks of paper-wrapped packets exuded strange smells.

Mrs. Fong bowed to him before leading him into the parlor.
She was tiny, but held her head high, her glistening black hair twisted upward at the nape of her delicate neck. The parlor had polished
wood floors and a muted red carpet upon which sat large bronze
urns holding plumes of red and black silk flowers. Mrs. Fong offered Sage one of the room's two chairs. Ebony in color, the chair's
carved surface was a Gorgon's knot of snake and crane filigrees.

Pantomiming the drinking of tea, Ms. Fong bowed low and
glided from the room. She returned minutes later with an orange
lacquer tray that held a black teapot and cup. Kneeling at a low
table, she poured the tea and offered it to Sage, deferentially inclin-
ing her head.

As always, the tea was sweet and smooth, needing none of
the cream and sugar Occidentials used to improve the taste of
their brew. He smiled at her and nodded his thanks. She smiled
faintly and returned the nod. Mrs. Fong was an enigma to Sage.
Such a tiny person. Yet she had journeyed far to start a new life.
Even more than Fong, she seemed a center of calm content. All

Fong ever said about his wife was that she was very smart and a hard worker.

The distant tinkle of a shop bell interrupted his musings. With a departing bow, Mrs. Fong went into the store, leaving Sage to sip his tea amidst the strange colored flowers.

Fong entered the room and took the chair across the tea table. He didn't bother with a preamble. "Matthew is in jail. So is Mr. Knute."

Sage straightened. "How in the world . . . ?"

"Police say Matthew sent letter from farm. Silly boy wrote the return address on the envelope. Someone saw envelope and told police. Patrolman Hanke came to warn you before other police came. He was very scared but he came to tell us anyway."

"Welker."

"I also think it was Welker. The police now looking for you. They want to know how boy ended up staying on the restaurant's vegetable farm. I asked Mr. Gray, the lawyer, to talk to the boy and to Mr. Knute."

"Damn, damn, damn." There was nothing else to say. He was on the brink of figuring out what was going on. He could feel the answer forming like a huge storm cloud. He also sensed, somehow, that time was running out. But a change was in the offing and if he didn't hurry, he might never learn the truth. Tonight, Gilcrease would tell Sage what he needed to know. And, they would find the lock that key fitted. Except, to do that, he needed to stay out of jail.

"Mr. Fong, any luck on that key?"

"It is not key for bank box. Maybe it is post office key. Before the police came, I was going to take trolley to a post office in Rose City. A cousin told me key drawing I showed him look like key from that post office."

"You'd best be heading out then," Sage said, glad to know there might be progress with the key. "If you don't mind, I'll wait here until later tonight, when I'm supposed to meet Gilcrease unless the police come for me beforehand. "

"Where you be after?" Fong asked.

"I'll head to either Solomon's New Elijah Hotel, to Lucinda's, or back up to your cousin's garden place on the hill. Depends on which one feels the safest."

"Good. I will look in those places for you tonight." Fong stood and started toward the door.

"Mr. Fong!" Sage called. "What happened to the farmer where Matthew was staying–to Brother Jonas and his family?"

"Don't know. Didn't want to ask police. I ask Mr. Gray to find out for us."

After Fong left, Sage puzzled over all the pieces that seemed related to one another. Anxiety and frustration roiled inside him. He couldn't shake the heavy weight of impending doom that seemed to be settling over him like fog creeping up a piney wood holler. That crane had better step out pretty damn quick or the snake would slither away, leaving nothing but cracked egg shells behind. Exhaustion overtook him. Sage abandoned the chair to lay down on the floor. Head cradled on his arms, he fell instantly asleep, never moving when the blanket was draped atop him minutes later.

TWENTY SEVEN

THE FARMERS' WHARF stretched empty and deserted except for a few wooden crates stacked here and there. A produce wagon stood next to the farthest stack of crates, its shafts empty. Somewhere, a farmer was touring the town on his plodding farm animal, or else the horse was in a stall, munching hay.

Sage scanned the street leading down to the wharf. A block away, the bottom of a whiskey bottle glinted as three men took turns tilting it toward the darkening, overcast sky. Nearby the only sound was the wet slap of water hitting the heavy wharf piers as the river raced past in a snow-fed freshet.

Stepping from beneath the warehouse overhang, Sage was glad to escape the stink of the raw cowhides he'd been hiding behind. The hides were no doubt awaiting transport down river to the tannery in the village of St Johns. Soon, it was the wet smell of the wharf that hit his senses. Beginning at dawn, farmers' wagons rumbled over its thick wooden planks to transfer produce onto the ocean going ships that would steam down river and south along the coast to San Francisco and points beyond. The dry summer days had let the horse manure settle into the cracks between the planks, so that barnyard and tangy river smells mingled to scent the night air.

As he crossed the wharf, Sage couldn't see Gilcrease shelter-
ing beside any of the crates. He expected to find him in the farthest
corner, near the abandoned wagon and the tallest stack of crates.
Ten steps from the crates, Sage stopped, aware of a movement on
the wagon bed. Narrowing his eyes in the gloom, he stared in that
direction. He could make out a line of odd shapes perched on the
edge of the wagon's box. One bobbed. He was looking at a row
of seagulls, each one intently staring downward or else they were
asleep. The head of the closest seagull swivelled until its black button of an eye stared unblinkingly at Sage. The other birds did not
move. Foreboding began its cold creep up his spine. He stepped
closer. The birds remained fixated on a black hump that lay wedged
between the wagon's wheel and the crates.

The seagulls stayed motionless until Sage came within three
feet. With a thwap of wings they rose slightly, only to land again on
the farther side of the wagon box. They weren't about to willingly
abandon whatever it was they'd found.

Sage looked at the seagulls. Their cold black eyes stared back.
He looked across the black ripples of the flowing water at the dim
flicker of lights in the small buildings and houses on the river's eastern bank. Behind them, he could make out farm fields, their neat
lines softened by dense clusters of evergreens. He sighed, reaching
into his vest pocket for his matchbox.

Squatting down, he felt the hump of black. His hand confirmed that it was a body. Striking a match, Sage reached out to tug
on what he knew to be a shoulder. The body rolled onto its back. In
the dim flare of the match, the brutal devastation of the man's face
caused Sage to shift his squat back a pace. He moved forward again,
trying to see past the blood and split flesh to the features. His gaze
traveled from the crown of the ruined face to the chin. Around the
neck, a once-white cravat, now drenched in black wetness, failed
to conceal the horizontal line beneath an insignificant jut of chin.
An emerald pin glittered within the bloodied folds of the cravat.
Gilcrease. It was Gilcrease. Sage dropped the match when its flame
nipped his fingers.

The pain snapped him back to the present so that he heard
the thudding of boots on the planks behind him. Three dark forms
were running straight toward him. Against the dark sky, he saw the

unmistakable outlines of policemen's beehive helmets. Sage leapt
to the other side of the body, his sudden movement startling the
seagulls into flight. They couldn't catch him here. He needed to stay
free. Looking down into the flowing blackness, a curse on his lips,
he held his nose and stepped off. Just before his feet hit the water
he thought he heard a cry of "Adair! Stop!" As the freezing spring
water sucked the heat from his body and carried away his hat, Sage
felt momentary confusion that they'd recognized him in the dark.
Then he was clawing for the surface, wishing he'd thought to pull
off his shoes.

An hour later Sage was a shivering knot of bone and flesh,
crouching beneath the concealing leaves of a rhododendron tree.
The chill of his soddened clothes had mingled with the sweat of his
furtive flight up from the river. He had to clench his jaw to stop his
teeth from chattering out his presence to passersby. His eyes stayed
fixed on Lucinda's front door, across the green lawn of the Park
Blocks. Half an hour before, he'd been heading for its sanctuary.
Just in time, he saw the chief of police mounting her steps trailed by
two men in suits and one uniformed patrolman. It was not a social
visit.

The door opened and Sage leaned forward to peer across the
park. The chief and the two men in suits set off down the steps.
Good. That left only the patrolman. Lucinda would see to it that
he'd be distracted long enough for Sage to slip inside. He began to
imagine the heat of a warm drink and dry clothes on his clammy
skin. As the three men reached the sidewalk, the chief and one man
turned north. The third man stepped across the street and entered
the park. Sage drew back further under the bush.

The man took up a post against the darkened trunk of a tall
elm. So the chief was posting guards inside and out. After making
sure no late-night strollers were about, Sage moved from bush to
bush until he reached the corner of the building. Then he turned
his back on the park.

Ten minutes of cautious circling brought him to the side
door of the milliner's shop. He slid his knife blade between casing

and door to lift the latch. Opening the door, he stepped inside and closed it. Around him stood the distinctive metal hulks of the sewing machines, their treadles, bobbins, and wheels silent for those few hours between deep dusk and dawn light.

He grabbed a candle and matches from a shelf before descending into the cellar where the smell of moldy earth pervaded the air and scuttling came from the blackness that lay just beyond his candle light. Stealthily, he climbed the stairs and eased open the door into Lucinda's kitchen. His twitch of alarm nearly yanked it shut when he saw the broad blue serge of a patrolman's back not three feet away. As it was, he froze, not even breathing, transfixed as the patrolman lifted a heavy white mug of coffee to his lips. In between hoists of the mug, the patrolman talked to the equally broad back of the cook who was noisily lifting and plunging dirty dishes inside the big enamel sink. "So, anyway, me and my boy, we like to fish over there at Sullivan's Gulch. There be trout and sometimes salmon in season," he was saying, his words laced with an Irish lilt.

Sage pondered what to do but could think of nothing. He'd have to descend back into the dank cellar and wait the patrolman out. The door leading into the rest of the house opened abruptly, causing him to pull the cellar door nearly shut until he saw it was Elmira. She crossed the kitchen to stand facing the patrolman as she said, "Now, a big fellow like you needs you some pie or maybe a sandwich I am sure . . . " Sage took a chance and opened the door wider, hoping the movement wouldn't create a draft to alert the patrolman.

Elmira spotted him instantly. Only a single, slow blink of surprise revealed she had registered his presence. Her honey gold face stayed impassive, her voice warmly animated as she continued, "Now, while the cook here prepares you something to eat, how about you come help me shift a small table in the back parlor? It's not too big, but, as you can see, I'm on the small side. Folks like to do some dancing around the Graphophone and the table needs moving, to make ready . . ." Sage marveled at her quick thinking. The patrolman cheerfully clambered to his feet and Sage eased the cellar door shut. He opened it only after the closing kitchen door muffled their voices.

He pushed the cellar door wider and gratefully stepped into

the welcome warmth of the kitchen. "Hazel," he whispered. The pan the cook was drying clattered onto the wooden counter.

"Oh, Mister Adair, the police were . . . "

"Yes, I know. Can you smuggle me up to Miss Lucinda's room?" When she hesitated, he said, "I mean, unless she has someone with her."

She gave him a wide smile. "Oh no, Mr. Adair. She's in the parlor. We can go up the servants' staircase. It's just that we'll have to be careful. There's a full house tonight, and we best not run into any of the guests. The police chief made sure to tell all our guests that they are looking for you."

Hazel acted as scout until Sage reached the safety of Lucinda's room. While Hazel bustled off to fetch hot water for the basin, Sage stripped off his wet clothes and climbed beneath the comforter, hoping to warm his shriveled flesh.

Lucinda entered the room as he was standing at the bureau, a towel wrapped around his waist, reveling in the feel of warm water on his face and arms. Since it was the late-evening peak of the night, she looked elegant. The satin sheen of her red dress highlighted the thick swirl of her golden hair.

She took up a post just inside the door, hands on her hips, head tilted to the side. "Just like that you invade my boudoir . . . with nary an invite, I might add." The relief lighting her eyes belied her chiding.

"I apologize, ma'am, for the inconvenience. It seems the entire police force is intent upon finding me."

"Why yes, the presence of a patrolman in my kitchen gave me some clue to that fact. Not to mention the politically careful search our police chief just conducted of the house."

She perched on the comforter after he had crawled back beneath it. He told the story of what had awaited him on the wharf. She immediately focused on the aspect of the incident he found most troubling.

"You say that the police were calling your name when you jumped off the wharf?"

"Yes. That's right. I can't figure how they could have recognized me from that distance and in the dark." Sage replayed the entire scene once more in his head.

She patted his hand and pulled the comforter up high on his neck. "Let me try to find out about that. Before he left, the chief slipped the word that he'd be returning later tonight in his private capacity. Maybe he'll tell me how they knew it was you on the wharf."

She leaned over and kissed his forehead and his eyelids, her perfume sweet and warm in the air. "Go to sleep, my love." Sage snuggled deeper into the warmth of her bed. He was heading into sleep when she blew out the lamp and slipped out into the hallway.

TWENTY EIGHT

MUCH AS HE hated to do it, Sage slid from beneath the comforter at the first twitter of the dawn birds.

His farmer clothes hung in Lucinda's closet, cleaned and patched by Elmira's skilled hands no doubt. Lucinda was lucky to have the woman, as Lucinda herself had said more than once. After dressing, Sage stood beside the bed, looking down at her sleeping face. Eye black and rouge smudged the surface of her white skin like smears of dirt on window glass. He touched her cheek with the back of his hand. In repose, her expression was somehow wistful. She stirred at his touch but did not waken.

He departed through the milliner's store unobserved. Fortunately for him and for them, seamstresses generally didn't begin their workday until after dawn broke. Fifteen minutes later he joined a small army of others crossing the river, their work boots making muffled thunder as they traveled the bridge's wooden planks. Ahead of them, sunrise outlined the distant mountain as its warmth began to wash gold across the city. In that moment, Sage forgot the danger of pursuit, forgot that it was imperative he intercept Philander Gray before the lawyer left his house, and simply mused about the soft nature of summer morning light.

The sight of patrolmen halting the trolleys, walking through them from one end to the other, snapped him back to the present. The fact they were searching the trolleys was good news. That meant they were searching for the well-heeled John Adair, someone they could expect to make his escape in relative comfort. Sage glanced over the railing toward the farmer's wharf. The police were being equally diligent in following that angle. Men in rowboats leaned out with grappling hooks to stab beneath the racing opaque water. He shivered, reliving the chill. Maybe rivers should be added to his list of things to avoid. Better not, given that putting trains on that list had somehow resulted in trains being a persistent presence these past few days.

At last, the overhead girders of the Morrison Bridge turned into a long open trestle spanning the riverside marshland. Reeds and brushy hummocks channeled the runoff from the Hawthorne springs into the river. Hunting in the shallows were scores of blue herons, their eyes focused on piercing through the water flowing around their stick-thin legs. Good luck to them. He wished he had their patience.

At last his boots hit dry land at Seventh Street. From there, he walked a block east, caught an electric trolley upon which no policeman rode and traveled in comfort for the remaining twenty blocks. Ole' John Adair wasn't wrong in his appreciation for comfort, Sage told himself.

Gray's large white house abutted the Ladd farm, one of the eastside farms that were visible from the slopes west of the city center. He knew that farther east were scattered farms and two-story frame buildings, clustered together at various crossroads sporting names like Sunnyside, Montevilla and Rose City.

Coming here was a long shot. But Gray had once told Sage that he always smoked his morning pipe while sitting on his veranda since his wife, Amanda, refused to let him to smoke indoors. Gray said he didn't mind because he enjoyed starting his day by admiring Amanda's flowers. Sage wondered what Gray had to say about that prohibition come winter time. This morning, however, he was mostly hoping Gray hadn't changed his habits.

The absence of near neighbors made it easy for Sage to slip into the alcove formed where the veranda met the house wall. He barely got settled when the screen door screeched opened and slapped shut.

Gray's low rumble and Amanda's soft voice advanced toward the end of the veranda where Sage was hiding. He squatted and waited while china clinked onto a table, a rocking chair creaked under a heavy burden and Amanda's light step retreated into the house.

"Psst . . . Philander." Sage rose from his crouch until his eyes were level with the veranda floor.

Gray waved a careless hand for Sage to join him, as if Sage were merely a neighbor come calling on a lazy summer morning. "I thought you'd be along sometime this morning," he said. "Glad you could make it. The *Gazette* reports the police have launched a manhunt. Sling yourself on up here. Amanda has provided coffee and something to eat." The lanky man gestured toward the table beside him.

Sage clambered over the railing and grabbed a seat in the empty rocker beside Gray. His stomach growled when his eyes caught sight of a heaping plate of bacon and toast, a pot of strawberry jam, two china cups, and a silver coffee server. Sage helped himself. Bacon and toast had never tasted better.

Gray let him munch a few minutes then launched into his report as if having clients climb over his veranda rail at the crack of dawn was an everyday occurrence. "They won't let me bail the boy out, needless to say. He's considered a flight risk. Knute, on the other hand, maybe him I can get released. He was at work the day the boy arrived at the farm. Now nobody at the farm is saying who brought the boy out there." Gray paused to look at Sage over his half-lens glasses. "I'm sure I don't have to tell you that those folks are in for some powerful grief if someone doesn't step forward and take the blame on that count. But for now, they aren't talking and they aren't in jail. Just remember, though, they're not going to lie. Against their religion I suspect."

Yes, Sage knew that. And he knew he couldn't leave Brother Jonas in that fix, not if he wanted to look the man in the face again. Gray was right that Brother Jonas would never lie. Nor would he allow anyone in his family to lie. Which meant it was good that the police had not arrested Brother Jonas and forced him to tell. But how long would that reprieve last?

"Are the police still convinced the killer was Matthew?" Sage asked around a mouthful of toast and jam, the crisp bacon strips having already disappeared into his stomach.

"They haven't bothered to look for anyone else, near as I can ascertain."

"Philander, what kind of evidence do you need to prove Matthew's innocence?"

"Well, we either make Halloran admit he lied about seeing the boy when Clara was killed, or somehow I get the name of the real murderer and proof he did it. Otherwise, Matthew is in serious trouble." Gray sucked noisily on his pipe and in the ensuing silence, both men watched a red-breasted robin splash birdbath water into the air.

"How's the boy looking?" Sage was afraid he knew the answer.

Gray took a sip of milky coffee before he answered, his words coming in what for him, was a hesitant way. "Well, of course, I didn't know him before. Strikes me as a boy who used to laugh often and who believed that life held more good than bad. Don't think he still thinks that. He's by himself in a cell, but he can't help but see what's going on around him. He's scared. Worse, he also seems resigned—as if something inside is breaking down, letting go. I didn't like leaving him there."

Sage squeezed his eyes shut at an image of that innocent freckle-faced boy locked away in the police station's dank cellar. Given what that boy had been through, anybody's spirits would be at the point of giving up. In just a short time, Matthew had left home, seen his brother brutally murdered, run for his life, gotten caught and now was in a cage, totally dependent on strangers' good intentions to save him from hanging. There was no need to make this observation out loud. Philander knew it already. So, instead Sage spoke to reassure himself as well as Gray, "Matthew's a good boy. Smart. He wants to make something of himself. He can overcome this but we need to act quick. He's at an age where he could go adrift and never make it back to shore."

Sage leaned toward the other man. "So, Philander, I've an idea about how we can get that evidence you need." The other man straightened in his chair, showing more eagerness than normal for him. "You'll have to give me a hand, if you're willing. Your reputation is at risk if it doesn't go exactly right, if I've guessed wrong about the situation," Sage cautioned him.

The big man smiled wide around the pipe stem clamped between his teeth. "You know me, Sage. I like a little excitement now and again," he said.

"Okay. Two things. First, find Patrolman Hanke and get him to meet us tonight. Tell him that, if all goes as planned, there could be a promotion in it for him. The second thing I need for you to do, is arrange for a closed carriage to be waiting outside Halloran's cribs in the North End about 8:30 p.m. Make sure the driver is someone you can trust. Someone who will look the other direction if his passengers act a little strange. You do those two things, and I think I can get you the evidence you need."

Gray agreed and, with that assurance, Sage headed back toward town.

❀ ❀ ❀

Around eight o'clock that night, Sage and Fong had taken up posts in darkened doorways, waiting for a slowing of the foot traffic through Halloran's front door. At last, it appeared that most of the girls were upstairs, busy with customers. When Sage and Fong slipped through the front door, they saw that the lobby counter was unmanned. A high-pitched shriek and a man's lascivious chortle came from the open door behind the counter. With swift, silent strides Sage and Fong passed behind the counter and into the office before Halloran could withdraw his liver-spotted hand from inside the bodice of a very young girl's dress.

"What . . . ?"

Sage strode over, grabbed the girl's wrist and yanked her off the old man's knee. He handed her a coin. "You go on upstairs until we call you." Gesturing to Fong, Sage said to her, "My friend here will be watching to see that you stay put."

The girl shot a startled look in Fong's direction and scuttled from the room. Fong trailed close behind.

Halloran began rising from the armchair until Sage shoved him back down. Halloran's wheezing filled the small, windowless room. Fong appeared in the doorway. He nodded at Sage as he stepped inside, closing the door. Then he tugged a meat cleaver from inside his commodious black tunic, waggling it to catch the lamplight on its steel edge. Halloran whimpered.

"Take my money," he begged. "Take whatever you want. Just don't let that yellow bastard near me."

Sage leaned down to grab the front of Halloran's food-mucked shirt, his nose wrinkling in disgust at the man's fetid breath and rank body odor. "My friend's parentage is impeccable, which, I am sure, is more than you can say, you miserable degenerate," he said, his voice tight as he twisted the shirt. "Also, I like to think of him as golden, not yellow."

"Whatever you say, mister. Just keep him the hell away from me."

"I'm glad you think like that, Halloran, because my friend here, he doesn't much like miscreants like you. They've caused him a lot of trouble. Isn't that right?" Sage turned to Fong.

Fong showed Halloran an expanse of large yellow teeth, bared in a crazy grin beneath glittering eyes. He lifted the cleaver and ran a fingertip up and down the blade, theatrically testing its edge. "Miscreants very bad," he hissed.

Halloran whimpered again.

"So, Halloran, if you want to keep your ugly head attached to your pathetic body, I suggest you cooperate with me and my friend here."

"Wha. . . . what do you want? Whatever you want."

"What I want, Halloran, is for you to tell us why you lied about seeing that young kid in here the night Clara's throat was slit."

Halloran's eyes, above the twist of his shirt, glanced off toward the ceiling as if looking for an escape route. Fong took a step toward him, and Halloran refocused on Sage's face.

"I got a note from the owner. He told me that the man who brought the note was going to tell me what to say and that I better go along. So I did."

"Who is this owner?" Sage asked, already knowing the answer.

"It's Mr. Dunlop. Mr. Edward Dunlop," Halloran said.

"Who came to see you and brought you the note?"

"He was a stranger. I didn't know him."

"Describe him."

"Ah . . . , a Scottish accent. About thirty or so. His eyes were scary. They was like staring into marbles . . . dead-like. His hair was under a cap but I think he's a carrot top."

"Did he smell?"

"You mean like he needed a bath?"

Sage tightened his twist on the shirt. "No, you idiot. Did you notice any kind of smell on him?"

A drool of spittle ran from the corner of Halloran's mouth. He used a fat red tongue to lick it up. "Now that you mention it . . . he smelled like that stuff people put on when they're coughing."

"Camphor?"

"Yes, that's it . . . I told you everything. There's nothing more I can do to help you men." Halloran's voice shook as his stubby fingers started smoothing his shirtfront Sage had released.

"Oh, but you're wrong there, Halloran. You are going to take a little trip with us." Sage grabbed the man's wrist and elbow and pulled him from the chair.

When the three men came out of the cribs, an enclosed carriage stood waiting, black curtains hiding its interior from view. Halloran opened his mouth, then snapped it shut as Fong stepped up to dig a sharp fingernail into the man's sweat-soaked back. In no time the carriage was rolling down the cobbled street, turning first west and then south.

❀ ❀ ❀

Minutes later, the three men stepped down onto a quiet residential street. Philander Gray and Patrolman Hanke were already there. Hanke's mouth dropped open. "Mr. Adair . . . ," was all he could say. Gray stepped up to the driver, said something in a quiet voice, and handed him a coin. The driver nodded, tied the reins to the seat board, and settled back, tilting his hat over his eyes.

"Patrolman Hanke," Sage said, "thank you for coming. In a few minutes you will understand why you're here, and you'll have information that will impress your chief."

Sage turned to Halloran. "You say one word and I will let my friend have at you. Do you understand?"

Halloran nodded so vigorously that his cheeks wobbled. His relief at seeing the two more respectable additions to the party was evident.

They walked half a block to the Dunlop mansion. The butler who opened the black lacquered door was unable to hide his surprise when he saw the motley group standing on the doorstep. He asked them to wait until he learned whether the Dunlops were receiving. They ignored him and shuffled across the threshold. Fong remained outside. Sage strode past the empty formal parlor toward the back of the house to the room where he and Arista had discussed the plight of the foundlings and their mothers. The butler followed behind, tugging at his coat sleeve.

A domestic tableau greeted their eyes. Arista Dunlop sat close by a lamp, a length of tatting lace in her fingers, steel-rimmed glasses perched on her nose. When she saw there were visitors, she snatched off the glasses and tucked them beside her skirt. Edward Dunlop sat across from her, a newspaper held up to his face. At their entry he first lowered the paper, then dropped it and stood. Alarm mixed with outrage on his face.

"I beg your pardon. I don't remember that we were expecting guests this evening . . . Why, Mr. Adair!" he exclaimed.

At this exclamation, Arista also stood. "John, John, are you all right?" She brushed past her husband, crossing to Sage.

"Yes, Arista, I am fine. Everything is fine. We just need to speak to your husband—alone, if you don't mind."

She looked over her shoulder at her husband, but Dunlop's eyes were riveted on Halloran, the color draining from his face.

"Edward, Edward, what is it?" she asked, panic turning her voice shrill.

Dunlop cleared his throat and said, without taking his eyes from Halloran, "It's, it's all right, dear. You go on. Let me talk to these men."

Arista turned toward Sage, who nodded at her and smiled reassuringly. Too polite to protest before strangers, Arista gathered up her lace work and swept from the room with her head held high.

TWENTY NINE

THE SECOND THE door shut, Dunlop launched into bluster. "I have no idea why you men have come here and frightened my wife, but I'll . . . "

"Dunlop! Sit down!" Sage's voice was low but intense. Dunlop's mouth flew open in a surprised "Oh" but he sat. This was not the deference he'd come to expect from John Adair.

"We'll not take much of your time, Dunlop, but you are going to tell this patrolman here why you instructed Halloran to claim he saw the young boy at the cribs the night that girl Clara was murdered."

Dunlop's mouth slackened in shock. He started to protest. "I don't know . . . "

"Dunlop, don't bother. Mr. Halloran has already told us about the note and the visit from your friend."

"What visit? What friend? He was no friend of mine!" Dunlop said, making it clear that he knew exactly who Sage meant.

"You know Dunlop. The thug you had carrying your messages around town."

"I can't tell you."

"You don't have a choice. This patrolman here can arrest you outright for impeding a police investigation. You instructed a witness to lie. Think of Arista, for God's sake! How will she feel when your name hits the front page of *The Daily Journal* as the real owner of Halloran's cribs of prostitution? Respectable people like you are supposed to keep that kind of thing quiet, aren't you? The public's not supposed to know about all your dirty little investments around town."

Dunlop's face turned the color of bleached muslin. "We'd be ostracized. Our friends would have nothing to do with us. I . . . we . . . we couldn't show our faces in public."

"So tell us what we need to know, and maybe no one will find out about your little side businesses."

Dunlop pointed to an oak sideboard. "Can I get a drink first?" When Sage nodded, Dunlop crossed the room to pour whiskey into a glass and returned to his chair. His hand was shaking as he lifted the glass to his lips. Sage snuffed the flush of pity he was starting to feel by focusing on the lives this weak-kneed excuse for a man had demolished for personal gain.

Sage looked toward Patrolman Hanke who shook his head almost imperceptibly. Gray also declined. Sage steered Halloran onto the far corner of a brocade settee, poured whiskey into a glass and handed it to Halloran who took it with both hands and drank greedily.

Sage took the chair Arista had vacated. Gray sat down at the other end of the settee from Halloran. Hanke remained standing near the doorway, his face stolid but his eye's keen

"You have your drink, Dunlop. Now start talking," Sage said.

Dunlop cleared his throat then said, "An awful man came to me early on the morning after that girl in the North End was murdered. I was at my office. I always get there early." He fixed his look on Sage and continued, "I didn't know a thing about the murder that morning. The man didn't say there'd been a murder down at the property. He just said there'd been trouble. I only found out about the girl's death later."

Dunlop gulped whiskey and said, "He told me that I was to write this note to Halloran and that he'd personally deliver it. I told him 'No.' Then . . . then he hit me. He socked me right in my middle." Dunlop's tone conveyed shock at the idea someone had the temerity to actually hit him. No doubt Dunlop considered himself someone to whom no one would be rude—let alone violent.

"Yes? What did he do next?" Sage prodded.

"He told me what to write."

"What did he tell you to write?"

"He said that Halloran was to tell the police what the messenger said he was to tell them and that he was to do so immediately. Something about him saying he'd seen a kid with red hair going up and down the stairs the night before. And to say anything else the man bringing the message told him to say." Dunlop gulped the rest of his whiskey.

Sage looked at Halloran, who nodded his agreement with Dunlop's rendition of the note.

Sage turned back to Dunlop. "So why didn't you go to the police?"

"He said that my pretty wife could get hurt if I did that."

"You would have gotten protection. You could have sent Arista away until everything worked out. Why didn't you go to the police?"

For the first time during the interview, Dunlop was about to take a stab at lying, because the man's eyes slid away from Sage and toward the empty fireplace.

"No other reason. I was just worried about . . ."

Sage was out of his chair and inches from the man's face before Dunlop could finish the sentence. "Tell us the truth! We know there's more to it." With his Fong-trained peripheral vision, Sage saw Hanke start forward then stop when Gray gestured him to halt.

Sage gripped Dunlop's wrist, while pushing his face even closer to that of the sitting man. "You will tell us the whole story. We may not have to tell the police everything, but you will tell the four of us. Do you understand?"

Dunlop nodded vigorously. Sage released his hold and returned to his chair.

As Dunlop spoke, he fixed his gaze on the swirling flower pattern of the Brussels rug beneath his polished shoes. "I've put most of our money, from a house mortgage and all, into a land deal that a group of us have been working on. If it goes bad, we'll lose everything–all of us will." Dunlop looked up, his eyes anxious. "Arista doesn't know anything about it. None of the wives do. It was a pact we all made."

Sage spoke without forethought. "That was a stupid mistake right there. Go on, Dunlop. Tell us the rest of it."

"Well, this man told me that if I didn't write the note and keep my mouth shut about it, I was going to lose all the money I put into the land deal."

"How did he know about the land deal? Did he say?"

"No. That's what I wanted to know. He was a complete stranger, and yet he knew how to ruin me." Once again, Dunlop's wondering tone made the claim credible.

"So you went along with it?" Gray's contemptuous voice rolled across the carpet.

Dunlop started, as if he'd forgotten that he and Sage were not alone in the room.

"It was everything we had!" The man's voice was shrill.

Gray's outrage was palpable. "You elevated your damn possessions over an innocent boy's life? You let that damnable lie continue, even after you learned of the murder?" The rise in his voice signaled outrage about to erupt.

Sage hastily interceded, using his voice to cut Gray off. "Just what is this land deal, Dunlop?"

"It's got nothing to do with that girl getting killed." For the first time, Dunlop's tone was mulish.

"We think her death has everything to do with your damn deal," Sage responded with barely contained fury.

"I'm not telling you anything about it." Here Dunlop sat back in his chair, folded his arms across his chest and clamped his thin lips tight. Clearly, a threat of violence would be ineffectual. Besides, Sage was certain that Hanke would feel compelled to intervene if Sage stepped across the line. The big German police officer might be willing to stray a few steps beyond orders but no way he'd countenance Sage's manhandling someone, let alone one of the city's richest merchants.

"Tell us about the man who came to you and told you to write the note."

"He was Scottish, his hair was orange, and he was big. That's all I remember."

"Did he have a peculiar smell?"

"Smell?" Dunlop started to shake his head, then stopped.

"Yes. When he hit me, when he was close . . . I guess he did smell. He smelled of camphor."

The confirmation was no surprise. Sage had gotten all he needed. "That's it, Dunlop," he said. "You need to go down to the police station with Patrolman Hanke, Mr. Gray, and Halloran here and tell them about the note."

"Police station. I can't . . . "

"You've already told Patrolman Hanke everything. You go now or he'll come back with a warrant and a passel of his fellow officers. You want a scene like that in this neighborhood?" Dunlop looked toward Hanke, who nodded. Dunlop's shoulders drooped. "All right, I'll go."

As he left the room, Dunlop hissed at Sage, "Don't you ever expect me to darken the door of your damn restaurant again!"

At the outside door, Sage glanced up. Arista stood on the stair landing, her face inquiring, strained. "It will be all right," he mouthed at her. Her look of concern did not lessen. He thought she'd be spared any public scandal from Dunlop's confession. The police chief would see to that. What Sage didn't know was whether she was strong enough to survive the financial storm that would burst about her ears if Sage's efforts to uncover the land deal came to fruition. Poverty was a calamity impossible to associate with Arista Dunlop.

He saw from the flare in her eyes and the tightening around her lips that she didn't believe him. Her words spat at him like icy bullets. "The butler will see you out Mr. Adair. I'll thank you to never visit my home again." With that she whipped her skirt aside, whirled around and headed back up the stairs, her back stiff with rage. Even though the loss of her friendship had always been inevitable, it didn't prevent Sage from suffering an intense pang of regret.

Once outside, Sage stood on the steps of the mansion and watched while the four men climbed into the carriage and rolled away down the road. His shoulder still tingled from the slap it had received as Gray had passed him on his way to the street. "You've done it, my boy. It'll soon be over. In a few hours the lad and his uncle will be sitting there in Mozart's eating one of the divine Miz Ida's berry pies." No doubt Gray would be joining the two jailbirds over that pie, if Sage knew Philander Gray.

Sage smiled grimly. The crisis might be over for Matthew and Knute, but there was still the matter of the three murders and that mysterious land deal at the bottom of it all. The way ahead might have a few less obstacles, but there was still a chance for fatal missteps while that damnable Welker and his hirelings remained on the loose.

❀ ❀ ❀

Lucinda's kitchen was empty when Sage nudged the cellar door open. He crossed the room, crept up the back stairs and down the carpeted hall. As he expected, she was in the parlor below, entertaining her guests, her sweet soprano soaring above the piano notes. Seconds later he was safe inside her room.

He woke when the covers slithered off his naked shoulder. Her body snuggled next to his. "What a nice surprise," she murmured as she wrapped her arm over him and wiggled against his back which had the effect of summoning him further from sleep.

Afterwards, Lucinda told him what she'd learned from the police chief.

"He said that a man ran up to a patrolman in the area. He told the patrolman he thought there was going to be a murder down on the docks."

"So how'd those coppers know my name?"

"Because the same man said he'd seen it was you pushing the victim toward the wharf with a knife at his throat."

"The police chief bought that? He knows me. He thinks I'd walk down the street with a knife to some man's throat?"

"Well, you know, I think he was so willing to be free with his thoughts because he found it a little hard to swallow himself. He gave me to believe that after he learned the specifics, he wasn't going to be looking quite so hard for you. Our police chief seems more interested in finding the man who spoke to that patrolman on the street. I think you'll be safe here now."

"Did he give you an idea of what those 'specifics' were? I mean, besides our convenient man in the street?"

"Yes." An emotion Sage couldn't place made her voice sound small as she continued. "He said that the poor man on the wharf was cold to the touch. He said the timing didn't fit."

Sage rolled over to wrap his arms around her bleakness. "Lucinda, it will come out all right. I'll be fine."

"Are you sure, Sage? I'm afraid. They have killed so many people, and we still don't know why."

"I'm sure everything will be fine," Sage said, his own fear imbuing steel to his words. "Just go to sleep. I think we're close to the end."

As they were drifting off to the sound of dawn birds, Lucinda mumbled. "Oh, Mr. Fong was here earlier tonight. All he said to tell you was, 'Nielsen's apothecary store in Rose City.'"

THIRTY

AN HOUR LATER, Sage once again crossed to the east side of the Willamette River. Seeing no patrolmen intercepting trolleys, he rode one until he reached the livery stable at the end of the bridge. The horse he rented was an experienced city horse, unruffled by noise or smells or the goings on around him. Just a comfortable old plug who'd seen and done it all. Neither a heel nudge nor twitch of the reins could spur the horse into changing his plodding pace. In fact such inducements seemed to slow the beast. So the two of them ambled north, toward Barr Road, the one diagonal street in the city. Legend was that the road followed an old Indian trail between the Willamette and Columbia rivers. When he reached Barr Road, Sage reined the horse eastward into the sun, toward the village of Rose City.

Small two-story wooden buildings, clustering at each cross-road, marked his eastward progress. Frame houses also dotted farmland that undulated northward until it reached a low east-west ridge. The financial speculator in Sage dwelled for some minutes on the wisdom of buying a large tract of land this far from town. Someday this city might grow as big as the cities back East with family homes, apartment houses and businesses covering all these open fields. Still, who would want to live so far from the commercial center? Land speculation was probably a bad idea.

Not certain where the apothecary was located, Sage surveyed the storefront of every building he passed. At last he saw a bay window that had "Nielsen's Apothecary" in arching letters across its glass expanse. Sage lowered himself from the broad back of the docile horse, tied it up, and patted its nose, grateful it had yet to display any temperamental oddities in behavior.

He stood outside the shop, studying the window display of a neighboring dry goods store until he made certain the clerk was busy with customers. The air inside the apothecary's one room was fragrantly medicinal. On either side, tall glass-fronted shelves displayed row upon row of boxes and bottles tucked inside small cubbies. The apothecary apparently valued orderliness. Sage stepped up to one of the glass fronts, idly scanning the concoction's labels: Dandelion Root, Heldenias Root, Soap Tree Bark, Comfrey Root, Calmuda Root . . . must be the root section. The apothecary himself was working behind a high counter at the back of the store, tapping powder into the basin of a small metal scale. At his back were row upon row of colorfully labeled dark-brown bottles, forming an impressive wall of danger. These were the poisons and other restricted drugs.

To one side at the back, brass post office boxes filled part of the wall. Sage moved toward them as if he knew what he was about, hoping that the clerk would keep talking with the red-faced woman and that the apothecary would continue to weigh and measure. The key in his pocket didn't show a box number, so he'd have to try each keyhole until he found the right one. If he was lucky, the key would fit after one or two tries.

Two insertions and turns of the key met immovable resistance. Then he realized the shop had gone so silent that the noise of horse clops and rattling wagons passing by outside seemed loud.

An aggressive woman's voice spoke at his elbow. "Excuse me, sir. Can I help you with something?"

Sage turned to find the clerk looking up at him with narrowed eyes and compressed lips.

"Why yes, ma'am. My cousin, who is feeling poorly at home, sent me to get his mail and I've forgotten his box number, though I have the key here." Sage held up the key he'd retrieved from the outhouse.

The woman's face relaxed into a smile as she said, "Tell me the name of your cousin, sir and maybe I can locate the box."

"Clancy Steele," he said, hoping that the woman hadn't read the city newspapers and that Steele's cautious nature hadn't led him to use an alias.

The woman looked thoughtful. "Yes, that name does sound familiar. Let me look at our records." She lifted a wooden flap to pass into the work area behind the counter, saying nothing to the apothecary, who was vigorously mashing his pestle into some resisting substance. The woman consulted a list, then returned to Sage after carefully lowering the counter flap back into place behind her.

"Your cousin's box is number 17." She pointed toward a box, and Sage stepped up, inserted the key, and turned it. It moved with a satisfying click of the latch. He smiled at the clerk, who smiled back before returning to her customer.

The small metal door swung open on oiled hinges. Sage realized he was holding his breath only when he let it out at the sight of the long white envelope laying inside the box. He pulled it out. It was thin, containing no more than a few sheets of paper. His heart was pounding. Maybe this insignificant thin envelope had triggered everything. He slipped the envelope into his breast pocket before carefully shutting the door and turning the key. Nodding to the clerk, he left the store.

Sage climbed aboard the placid horse and turned its head west, toward the city. His mind was on the envelope. Did it contain the answer to the question of who had killed Steele and, more importantly, why?

The horse nickered, causing Sage to look around. Otherwise, he would have never seen the woman's body that lay beneath dense bushes at the roadside. Her dark dress blended into the shadows so well that it was only her pale hands and the back of her white neck that drew attention. He quickly dismounted and, with reins in hand, advanced toward the prone figure, his mind already racing ahead to the question of where he could take her for help. As he bent over her, she gave a small moan—the last sound he heard before a much louder crack ripped through his head and the world before his eyes turned black.

❀ ❀ ❀

The painful chasm in his head widened every time his body jostled. He heard a moan then realized it came from him. He kept his eyes shut as he tried to rise above the wall of pain that split his head. Immobility and a burning at his wrists meant a rough rope tied his hands together. The jostling, the firmly cushioned seats, the creak of wood and squeak of leather harnesses told him he was in a coach. An overpowering smell of camphor filled his nose. Unbidden, a steady string of epitaphs flooded his aching head. He stopped the flow because the intensity was making his head hurt worse. Another moan escaped his lips.

He heard a familiar voice. "Did you pay the woman off? Will she keep her mouth shut?" That was Welker's voice.

"Aye, that I did. Don't worry, she'll not tell anyone of her part in this." It was that same Scot's voice that he'd heard in his ear once before.

Welker spoke again. "We are fortunate you spotted our boy here crossing the bridge and followed him. Your telephone call caught me just as I was checking out of the hotel."

Then his voice came closer to Sage, as if Welker had leaned to get a look at his prisoner. "He's coming to. Looks like you didn't kill him after all, Ian, my boy."

"I didn't want to or else he'd be dead."

"As it turns out, my heavy-handed friend, it wouldn't have mattered. At last our Mr. Adair has found what we've been looking for. So now he's just a bother to us."

Sage opened his eyes. "Welker." It came out in a croak.

"Hello there, Adair." The other man's rapacious face smirked in satisfaction. "So we are, at last, meeting as our true selves. I want to thank you for finding our little document here. Clancy proved a bit trickier than I expected. Ah well, no matter. Now we have it, thanks to you." Welker waved the white envelope, moving the close air of the coach before relaxing back against the cushions. He pulled a black cheroot from his pocket and touched a match to its tip. Sage gagged at the wafting smoke. Welker's smile was sardonic.

"Ah yes, I've noticed that a blow to the head tends to make the stomach feel touchy." He smiled again and exhaled another cloud in Sage's direction.

"Don't worry, Adair. We have the perfect cure for a touchy stomach, don't we, Ian?" he said to a big man, who looked as if he'd stand at least six foot three. Ginger-colored hair topped a freckled face. Small pale blue irises, surrounded by an inordinately large field of white, looked out from beneath eyelashes so light they seemed invisible. The reek of camphor wafted from his pinstriped suit.

"Oh, aye, Mr. Welker that we surely do, we surely do," he responded with snide heartiness.

"Going to slit my throat, are you, Ian?" Sage asked around the throbbing in his head.

"That is Ian's preferred method. He is so very skilled at it. He tells me that he learned it working in the Chicago stockyards right after he first arrived from Scotland." Welker carefully knocked ash onto the coach floor, studied the cigar tip, and said, "Enough of him, though. You are the star here, Mr. Adair." Welker inhaled deeply. As he exhaled, he said, "Tell me. Are you working for Vincent St. Alban and his rabble? We know he has someone assigned to Portland. It strikes me that you are the most likely candidate."

Sage said nothing.

"Not going to tell us anything, is that it?" Welker's tone remained mild. "Well, never you mind. In a short while the answer to that question will be moot." The tempo of the coach's rocking changed, and Welker lifted the edge of the leather window curtain.

"Oh good, we've reached the lane into the pasture. So thoughtful of you to transport yourself into the suburbs for us. Makes disposal so much easier."

As the coach came to a halt, a nicker came from a horse that was apparently hitched to the vehicle's back end. His own livery horse, no doubt. He'd sort of liked that horse. Sage suppressed a chuckle at the irony—he was having warm thoughts about a horse at a time like this? He didn't much like horses. He intended to buy one of those automobiles. Must be the knock on his noggin.

Welker's voice intruded into these distracted musings. "Here, you deserve to read this, after all you went through just to find it for us." Welker held out a piece of white paper. Sage reached for the paper with his bound hands, needing to bring it close to his eyes in the dim light of the coach.

It was an agreement. At the bottom he saw the signatures: Dunlop, Hipple, Gardiner, Perry, and a few others that were indecipherable. The agreement was short and to the point. The signatories agreed to pool their money to buy acres of land in some place called "Easter Valley." They further agreed they would either sell or exchange the land for federal land. The allocation percentages listed seemed tied to the signatories' relative dollar contributions to the purchasing pool. That was all.

Sage looked up from the letter, puzzled. Welker smiled benignly. "You still don't understand, do you? Just think, you'll die without knowing why. Ironic, don't you think? Especially when you went to so much trouble. You almost made it. If Ian hadn't spotted you on that trolley crossing the Morrison Bridge, followed you, and called me, well, you might have eventually answered most of your questions. You are a persistent snoop, I'll give you that." Still smiling Welker took the paper from Sage's bound hands and touched it to the tip of the cheroot. Sage watched a brown circle appear, then flare into a gaping hole. Welker dropped it to the floor where it quickly became a dusting of gray ash.

Welker smiled that mirthless smile again. "That's that, I'd say." His smile faded. He started to open the coach door until a sharp call from the driver's perch arrested his action. A new voice sounded outside the coach.

"Hey, you there! What are you doing on my land? Does this look like a park to you? You be getting on your way or me and my boys will move you on ourselves."

As Sage started to cry out, Ian clapped a hand over his mouth. Sage heard the driver's apologetic responses, and the coach began to bounce back along the dirt track.

Across from him, Welker settled back against the seat, his jaw clenched, irritation cracking his composure. Once the coach returned to the smoother surface of Barr Road, Ian removed his hand. Sage twisted to swipe his mouth across his own shoulder.

"Don't like the taste of Ian, Mr. Adair?" Welker chuckled and wagged the burning of cheroot in Sage's direction, saying, "Well now, if you keep quiet, Ian will keep his hands to himself."

The three rode in silence until Welker straightened and stopped the carriage by rapping on the coach roof with his knuckles.

"Go to the Albina rail yards," Welker shouted and the coach jerked back into motion.

Welker gave Sage another lipless smile. "Just a small delay. You'll go for a train ride, after which you'll be supper for the fish. Neater that way, I think. All's for the best."

Sage turned his thoughts to the Albina train yard. It lay along the Willamette River's east bank, across the electric trolley tracks that ran down Williams Avenue. He knew it provided the terminus for the Southern Pacific tracks and was the place where the railway shunted its train cars for repairs.

Welker spoke to the silent Ian. "Perhaps, Ian, you might give our Mr. Adair here a wee bit of a tap. We can't have him making noise, now that the road's becoming more crowded."

Ian must have obliged because the world went black in one searing jolt.

THIRTY ONE

Sage stirred this time as the coach's steel rimmed wheels clattered across railroad tracks. He continued to slouch against the seat corner, keeping his eyes closed as he explored the pain in his head. It wasn't that much worse. Could be, with all the coshing it had been experiencing, that the ole pumpkin was becoming immune to pain.

As the coach jolted to a stop, Welker said, "Ian, go find our friend. Tell him we'll need a special train. Just the engine and a few boxcars is all—it just has to cross the river to the depot and come back. And, tell that moron Harold to keep a sharp lookout and rap on the roof if he sees anything."

The coach springs compressed then sprang up as the big Scotsman apparently exited the coach. Sage opened his eyes only to squint as even the dim light struck like daggers.

Welker was watching him. "I was thinking it was about time you came back to us. Sorry for the delay," he said. Sage wanted to punch that smug face and then groaned at the pain his passion stirred up.

Welker shifted in his seat. "We'll wait here a bit until Ian finalizes the arrangements."

"Seems like I deserve to know the reason why you're having me killed," Sage said, surprised when his voice came out in a raspy croak. One thing he knew from experience is that the bad guy either felt compelled to gloat about his superiority or else try to justify his venal actions. Welker would be a gloater, no question about it.

Welker reached inside his coat to remove a silver flask. He twisted off its top, tilted it to his lips and swallowed. He offered it to Sage who balanced it between the palms of his tied hands. "Gentleman should share a drink at a time like this, don't you think?" Welker asked.

The whiskey was warm as it flowed across Sage's tongue and down his throat into his stomach, which lurched, then settled. Sage handed the flask back to Welker, wishing he'd swallowed more. "I'm not drinking with a gentleman, but the whiskey's not bad," he said. "You going to tell me how clever you've been or not?"

"Yes, well," Welker paused to light another cheroot, "let's say that Portland's leading citizens purchased something of value that my company has now bought from them. We'll leave it at that."

"This has something to do with the Forest Reserve law doesn't it?" Sage asked.

"Perhaps. No matter. Soon you won't care in the least about the specifics of our petty little dealings here on earth."

Disgust made Sage shake his throbbing head. "How can you do it?"

Welker understood the question. "As Darwin said, it's 'survival of the fittest.'"

"Darwin? Welker, I'd have thought you better educated. Anyway, it was Huxley who applied that theory to the human condition . . . not Darwin."

"The principle's the same," Welker snapped before taking an angry pull at the flask.

"No, it isn't. What's 'fit' for the human species? We're supposedly the only animal possessing a conscience. So, is the caveman who clubs the fellow next to him for more than his share of the kill a 'fitter' human? Or how about the knight who bludgeons his neighbors into serfdom? Or closer to home, how about a capitalist like Carnegie who drains the life from his workers, then builds libraries so other people will sing his praises? What exactly is a 'fit' human being, Welker? The man who is willing to sport the bloodiest tooth and claw?"

Welker gave a constricted smile. "My, my, your eloquence betrays you, Mr. Adair. That pretty little speech tells me that you really are St. Alban's man like I suspected. I might pass that on when I give my report—maybe it will give me a little extra credit with my employers."

Sage stayed silent.

Boots approached the coach. Then Ian's voice came from outside. "I found him and he says now's the time. So we best get to moving."

Welker touched a parting finger to his hat and opened the door. The livery horse stood nearby, its head dipped low as if it was asleep. Welker climbed astride its back without another word to Sage. As he reined the horse away from the coach, Welker gouged his boot heels into the animal's ribs. The horse stopped dead. Welker kicked harder but the animal didn't move.

Welker's sallow face flushed bright crimson. He kicked the animal with even more force. Still no movement. He shouted, "Goddamn you, you . . ."

"Quiet! Someone will hear you and look over here!" Ian's voice was sharp with anxiety.

Welker compressed his lips with effort while he used the reins to lash at the horse's ears and pounded his heels into its ribs.

The horse sat its rump down.

At that sight, Sage guffawed only to stop when his head felt like it split down the middle. Welker was clutching the horse's mane in a vain effort to keep his seat on its sloping back. Then, cursing, Welker slid sideways off the sitting horse. When the animal felt the absence of Welker's weight, it stood up. Its great brown eyes gazed into the far distance as if it were contemplating a grass pasture empty of bothersome humans.

"Say, Welker, didn't they teach you how to ride back there in Minnesota? I wouldn't stand so close to my friend's hind leg if I were you," Sage choked out.

Welker glared at him then snatched up the reins and began walking down the tracks with the animal plodding behind at its customary speed.

Ian yanked Sage's arm, spilling him from the coach onto the ground. "Tie it up, Harold. We're going for a train ride."

The man atop the coach jumped down from the box.

Clambering to his feet from the gravel roadbed, Sage looked around. The yard buildings were far away. Near the river, crying gulls wheeled above the half-submerged piers of a derelict dock. In front of him stood three linked boxcars, much like the other boxcars scattered about the yard. A locomotive engine near the buildings started chugging its way toward full power. No one was in sight.

He looked down the tracks toward town in time to see Welker hoist himself back into the saddle. This time, Welker didn't use his heels. Instead, he twitched the reins and the horse began its sedate walk. Welker's back was rigid with frustration, but his heels stayed far out from the horse's ribs.

Ian hustled Sage toward a boxcar's open door and shoved him chest-first onto its floor. He grabbed and slung Sage's legs after him so that he lay among bits of paper and straw. Ian and the coachman, Harold, hefted themselves into the car and tugged the sliding door shut until only a three-foot gap remained. The car jerked as the engine backed into its automatic coupler. Seconds later, the train began rolling south, its solitary whistle toot sounding across the empty railyard.

Sage watched as the yard and then warehouses, slid past the open door. They were heading for the Steel Bridge across the Willamette River. He studied the two men sitting across from him against the boxcar's wooden wall.

Ian's skin was sun-reddened. His freckled fingers looked monstrous as they piled tobacco onto a cigarette paper, then rolled it tight. When he glanced up at Sage, his glassy blue eyes twitched. Then he smiled. Sage shivered.

The second man, Harold, was smaller. His hair was greasy black above a round, flat face. While his yellow teeth gnawed dirty fingernails, his eyes rolled in their sockets like a crazed animal. His darting looks went everywhere except in Sage's direction, his teeth gnawing ferociously all the while, like a starving dog's at a meatless bone. And yet, it is the hardworking, rarely murderous loggers who get saddled with the nickname "timber beasts." Welker and his forest-destroying masters, killers of all that stood in their way, they were the real "timber beasts."

Sage let that thought go for some later day, should he have any more days ahead of him. Right now he had to extricate himself from this pickle or there wouldn't be later days. Death was guaranteed if he threw himself out the open door with tied hands while the train was gaining speed. Fong's words came to him. "It is best for your opponent to believe you are no threat. A fish sees only two upright stems in water before the bill swoops down." Sage allowed his head to loll sideways as if he had returned to semi-consciousness.

Feigning weakness worked. Ian scooted across to him, pulling out a knife to slice the rope from around his wrists. Sage's shift in position, although slight, was still enough to elicit an alarmed response from Harold.

"Do you think it's smart to free him like that?" Harold's voice squeaked from his big round face.

"Hah! I've already taken this pipsqueak twice. Besides, the boss says when they fish Adair out of the river, it has to look like he just hit his head and fell in . . . an accident. 'Can't have one of the city's prominent men turning up murdered,' he says. We won't have much time once we're on the bridge. Southbound's due in half an hour, so we have to be off that bridge onto the sidetrack well before then." Ian scooted back to his place against the wall.

Sage worked at becoming more of a pipsqueak, allowing his back to hunch into the wooden wall and letting his aching head bounce loosely with the movement of the car. He needed to act soon, but it was too far to the door and equally far to Ian. When the train stopped, Ian would move closer to manhandle him out the door. Sage focused on breathing his energy into his center of gravity, his mind traveling to each of his muscles, relaxing them, one at a time. In a few minutes his softness was no longer feigned. He'd allowed his body to gather what Fong called his "chi" energy. He felt a peace as calm and solid as a forest boulder. There'd be just one chance and he'd need that energy at full strength.

His eyelids drooped almost shut. Lucinda's laughing face appeared in his thoughts before transforming into the still, sleeping face he'd watched that dawn. A sudden sting of tears brought the realization that his feelings toward Lucinda had changed in recent days. She'd become someone he needed. Needing someone was uncomfortable, frightening in a way. Then, in quick succession, thoughts of his mother, Fong, Solomon, St. Alban, and even Meachum swirled through his mind. He recognized that, over the last two years, each of them had become a piece of his satisfaction with his life. So had, to a lessor extent, Ida and Knute, the newspaperman Ben and Philander, the ever-ready lawyer. Each had become someone he'd come to care about and even need. All were the people who knew a part of him that was genuine, some seeing more of him than others. Maybe it was these people who Meachum had been talking about . . . friends who'd tell him if he ever started losing himself in the game.

His eyes snapped nearly open with the realization that Fong and Meachum had both told him the same thing, using different words–that a person–no, that he, Sage, should learn to be strong in who he truly was. Otherwise, he could become lost in the amalgamation of his roles. Fong had said a "soul needed unbreakedness," Fong's way of saying that a soul needs a center to wrap around. But not just any center. Where a center holds nothing but venal ambition and greed, a man's soul becomes unsubstantial, lost. It yields men like Welker and Dunlop. Men who destroy lives, trampling what comes between them and their desires, acting with vicious satisfaction or callous disregard. They'd lost their affinity with others. Sage didn't want to become like them–to turn into the very kind of man he hated. But he was starting to understand what kind of man he wanted to become, if he had the chance.

His thoughts jerked back to the boxcar as the train banked onto the trestle that crossed high above the marshes at the river's edge. They wouldn't drop him in the marshes–too shallow and too many people who'd see. No, they'd knock him unconscious and drop him to his death above the main river channel. The train slowed as the grade steepened to arch above the river. Sage focused on staying relaxed and loose, letting fear flow out with each exhale.

The train rattled off the trestle onto the main span. As it neared the middle, Sage heard the metallic screech of braking. The train rolled to a halt. The chug of the locomotive sounded at least three boxcars ahead. Good. He wouldn't have to worry about fighting off the engineer and fireman as well. Sage took a deep slow breath then, let it flow out through his nostrils. He was ready.

Ian reached down, grabbed Sage's forearm, jerking him to his feet. Sage flew up with no more resistence than a thistledown, so light that he just kept going, allowing his elbow to jab Ian's throat as he flew past and out of the big man's grasp.

Ian slewed around, his arms flailing, as he tried to grab Sage. "You son of a . . . ," he choked out. Sage grabbed for the man's right wrist, pulling Ian off balance while hooking with his right foot and sweeping it to the left. Ian toppled with a thud. Outraged pale blue eyes glared up from where Ian had landed at Sage's feet. The big man rolled away and came at Sage again, raising his right fist to strike downward. Sage grabbed the upraised wrist and elbow, held them and kicked hard into Ian's groin. Fong's "seven stars," thank you very much!

Sage's eye caught a movement at his side. Harold had decided to wade into the fray. Before Harold moved close enough to throw a punch, a blur of black hurtled through the open door from the roof. Fong!

The slight man stepped in front of Harold, putting his hand forward as if to offer a handshake. The moon-faced man flew five feet before he slammed into the boxcar wall and slid to the floor.

At Sage's feet, Ian writhed, still gasping from the excruciating effect of the seven stars. Sage turned to Fong, "What took you so long? How did you find me?"

"We had to wait until you start ruckus. How we found you is long story . . . no time now." With that, Fong reached out a hand and pushed Sage to one side. While Sage staggered in an effort to keep his footing, he saw that Ian had risen from the floor and was lunging toward him, a knife in his upraised fist, his lips curling back from his teeth like a vicious dog's.

With Sage out of reach, Ian transferred his intent to Fong, continuing the blade's downward arc toward Fong's head. Fong reached up, grasped the big man's sweeping wrist, stepped to the side and twisted from his waist. Ian sailed out the open door over the head of a startled Patrolman Hanke, who was trying to heft himself into the boxcar. With a sound like the splat of a melon hitting a tree, Ian smacked head first into a bridge girder, bounced off it and dropped from sight.

Fong, Sage, and the patrolman all stared at the empty patch of summer sky where they'd last seen the killer.

"You haven't taught me that move, Mr. Fong," Sage said at last.

"Too advanced for you," Fong answered.

THIRTY TWO

THE BOXCAR JERKED as the train moved forward again. Hanke grabbed for the car floor as Sage and Fong hauled the big cop aboard on his belly.

"Hello there, Mr. Adair," Hanke said, dusting dirt and straw from the front of his uniform. "Who was that man I just saw go off the bridge?"

"A hired thug named Ian," Sage answered. "I think he's the one that killed Steele, that girl Clara, and Gilcrease. I'm guessing," Sage reached down to lift the narrow-bladed knife from the floor and hand it to the patrolman, "he used this."

A scuttling movement in the corner of the boxcar caused all three men to turn toward Harold, who whined, "I didn't know he was gonna kill none of them folks. I tell you, I didn't know, I didn't know."

In the few minutes it took for the train to reach the railroad depot's sidetrack, Harold told all he knew. He said Steele's death had surprised him. He'd thought they were just going to jump him and teach him a lesson. "But Ian, 'stead of hitting him, slit his throat. Right there before my eyes! He said if I told, he'd do the same to me. After that I didn't stay around when he was trying to make a point with folks."

Fong and Sage exchanged looks at the man's inadvertent pun. "So you weren't around when he murdered Clara?" Sage asked.

"No, sir. I found out about her being killed the day after, when he bragged on it and about how he framed that boy."

"What about Mr. Gilcrease?" Patrolman Hanke asked.

"I, ah, the last time I saw him, he was alive. Him and Ian walked down toward the river, but I stayed with the coach."

"Did you snatch him off the street?"

"I just drove the coach, following along beside Ian, like he told me to. Next thing I knew, he grabbed that man right off the street and shoved him in the coach. He made me drive around until he yelled at me to stop. Next I know, the two of them were setting off down toward the river. I drove off and never saw that Mr. Gilcrease again."

"So what did you think Ian planned on doing to me, there in the middle of that railroad bridge?" Sage asked not bothering to suppress his sarcasm.

"I, ah, well I, ah, I was scared of him. I was scared he was going to kill me too."

"What do you know about Welker?"

"Who's Welker?"

"The other man in the coach, you dolt!" Sage was exasperated.

"Him? No, I never saw him before. I didn't see him too good today. Ian told me it was better that I not get a good look at him, so I kept my eyes turned somewheres else." Harold hunched his shoulders and shuddered.

Sage looked at Hanke. "That enough for you, Patrolman, to bring charges?"

"Yes, sir, Mr. Adair. I think you've solved the murders, and this guy here will be telling his story to my chief, just as soon as I can reach a telephone."

"You might want to talk to the men on the engine. From what Welker said, this isn't the first time they've taken out one of what he called a 'special' train at Welker's behest," Sage said, his head throbbing, his muscles watery from the release of tension.

He gestured the patrolman to move closer so Harold couldn't hear them.

"Yes, sir, Mr. Adair?"

"I'd just as soon you forget the part Mr. Fong and I played in all this mess. Let your chief think that you followed me and uncovered the solution on your own. Will you do that?"

Two vertical lines creased the patrolman's wide forehead. "I'm not sure that's right, because you and Mr. Fong did all the work. I just went where Mr. Fong took me, and I didn't do anything to subdue the prisoner."

"Patrolman Hanke, you'd be doing us a real big favor. I operate a classy restaurant. This kind of publicity would scare people away. It'll hurt my business."

"Well . . . I guess, in that case, I can take the credit," Hanke said slowly, his big face brightening into a sudden smile, "and be glad of it. My chief's going to think I'm one smart street patrolman, solving three murders in two days."

"You are smart. You trusted your intuition that Mr. Fong and I knew what we were doing, and you risked your job to follow that intuition. No one else on the police force would have done the same thing. You deserve the credit."

Hanke's smile widened. "Well, I guess that's right. I knew you wouldn't slit nobody's throat, Mr. Adair. If you wanted to do away with them, you'd just poison their food."

Patrolman Hanke didn't attend the private supper party at Mozart's two days later. A "Closed" sign was on the door, and the dark green curtains were drawn across the windows. Inside, tables were pushed together, letting the diners feast boardinghouse style, passing dishes from hand to hand. It was an unusual gathering of guests: Sage and his mother, Knute and Ida, redheaded Matthew, Fong and his wife, Lucinda and Ben Johnston. If any one of them thought the group's composition socially awkward, their behavior didn't show it.

Sage finally interrupted the talk and laughter. "Mr. Fong, you've told me how you found me on that train but tell everyone else the story. Tell them about you and Patrolman Hanke."

"Ah," Fong responded, then took a sip of wine and nodded his head. "Mr. Adair told me follow that Welker man, so I did that. Welker checked out of hotel very quickly and got picked up by coach. I follow on foot. I very lucky. Many horses, wagons, and trolleys clogging roads, so I keep up with coach until on other side of river. There I jump on back of wagon going same way. Then I lost coach. Still, I think they going the same place as Mr. Adair–up Barr Road to Rose City village. So I follow along Barr Road. Then I see that man Ian shoving Mr. Adair into coach. I follow at dog trot and watch as they drive into a field."

"Where they were going to kill me, I might add. Why the heck didn't you rescue me then?"

"The field was flat–wide open. I'm small but not so small I can hide among short grasses. No matter. I rescued you anyway."

"What do you mean? It was the farmer coming along just in time who rescued me."

"Who you think told farmer about the strange coach in his field?"

"Oh," Sage said.

"So when coach drove from field and headed toward river, I followed. Then I stopped at cousin's house. He speaks English very good. I ask him run to telephone and call Patrolman Hanke at police station and say he should hurry up Barr Road. I meet him and we keep following Barr Road. He asked along way about coach–with one horse tied behind, many people noticed it. We decided coach was going to rail yard on east side. We go there by shorter way down gully path and watch coach arrive. We saw that Ian man talk to locomotive engineer, so we hid behind boxcars. When they put Mr. Adair in boxcar, we climbed on top. Patrolman Hanke not like that. Also . . . " Fong's face let the others relive those anxious moments. "Patrolman Hanke must learn how to move like cat. He is very noisy, clumsy. Lucky they didn't hear him and that he didn't fall off.

"Anyway, we stayed on top of boxcar until it stop on bridge. When Mr. Adair started ruckus, I swing into boxcar. That is all."

Fong allowed himself to look somewhat smug as he took another sip of his wine. Everyone else laughed and clapped. Fong's wife looked proud, even though Sage knew she'd understood only a few of the words. The admiration for her husband, showing on the listeners' faces, said all she needed to know.

Lucinda spoke as the clapping died down. "Why? Why all the killing? What was it all about?"

"That part I'm not real clear on. Ben here," Sage nodded at Johnston, who leaned back in his chair, a look of bemusement on his face, "has been working on the 'why.' All I know is that the so-called leading lights of the city pooled their money and bought some land in a place called Easter Valley and that they signed a paper agreeing to sell it in a block. I haven't figured anything else out."

Johnston shifted forward, his elbows on the table. "I can help there. Once you told me they'd bought in Easter Valley, our man at the land office knew what to look for. It turns out that our departed friend, Mr. Gilcrease, helped Baumhauer work a big land swindle against the Forest Service. First Senator Hipple and a California senator got Easter Valley declared a national forest preserve—right after our local boys bought the land. Gilcrease helped in two ways. He vouched to the Forest Service that Easter Valley was a forest. Then, once Hipple got it declared a forest reserve, Gilcrease adjusted the boundaries to make sure they included all the land our friends had purchased. That way, under the Forest Reserve Act, the federal government could either buy it back or trade straight across for some other land. In this case, our hometown boys made a land trade, their Easter Valley holdings for an equal number of heavily-timbered acres in the Cascade range."

Lucinda interrupted. "Even so, that doesn't sound like a reason to kill three people."

Johnston gave her a wide smile. "It does if Easter Valley is desert land that is being swapped for land covered in virgin timber."

"Ah," said Sage, "so that's where the Baumhauer Corporation and Welker come in. They bought the swapped land to cut its timber."

"Yup, that's the deal they made. Desert land bought at cents an acre by our local boys, who swapped it for rich timberland that they then sold to Baumhauer at below-market price. It was a sweet deal. They all stood to make a lot of money."

"So that's what Steele was holding over them. No wonder they killed him. He tried horning in on the middle of their deal without contributing any of the money or taking any of the risk," Sage said and for a minute, his mind went back to the mental image of Clancy and Bess Steele as a young married couple traveling westward on the train, their hopes for the future pinned on the lush green mountains of Oregon. Instead, they found violence, poverty and death in a gutter.

Mae Clemens spoke up. "So what's happened? Were those rascals stopped before the deal went through?"

Johnston shook his head. "Nope. The day before Gilcrease died, he transferred title of the timbered land to our little group of leading citizens. The next day, they sold it all to Baumhauer. You,"—here he nodded at Sage—"were just a loose end Welker wanted to snip off before he left town on the next train. While you headed across the Willamette on Welker's bridge special, he was on his way to board a train heading south, riding in his own Pullman car."

Lucinda was outraged. "That's it? Three people are dead and they all get rich?"

"Nope, not quite. According to the U.S. Attorney in San Francisco," Ben took a swallow from his wineglass before he continued, "it'll take some time, but he's going to bring our local boys and the Senator up on fraud charges and undo the deal."

Mr. Fong spoke. "What about that bad man Welker? Does he get away with it?"

Johnston didn't smile at this question. "Well, yes, since the only man who could tie him to the murders flew off the bridge into the river. Still, Welker maybe didn't get away with it. The land swap with the Forest Service made for Easter Valley will be voided, and Baumhauer stands to lose everything it paid for the timberland. That won't make Welker's bosses happy with him, since it was his job to guarantee that the deal happened without a hitch." Johnston let there be a beat of silence before he broke the real news. Pulling a scrap of newsprint from his vest pocket he said, "Yesterday's San Francisco paper reports that 'a Mr. Otis Welker, formally of New York City, was unfortunately run over by a coach and killed a few days ago. His death is considered a homicide since it appears he was deliberately propelled into the street. Someone shoved him from behind. The police are investigating.'"

Sage read the news story and found that he didn't feel much satisfaction at its report but seconds later he had to admit to feeling somewhat heartened that the cosmos had seen to it that Welker reaped what he'd sown. Three people were dead on his orders, after all. Still, it wasn't cause for celebration. Sage said nothing, just stared into his glass and thought. A murky kind of justice at best, he concluded. After tossing back the last of his wine, and pouring another glass, he rejoined the conversation flowing around him.

❀ ❀ ❀

After seeing Johnston and Lucinda into a carriage and the Fongs on their way home, Sage re-entered the restaurant. He felt satisfied with the small steps he'd just taken to move his soul further away from the dangers inherent in a state of "breakedness." Lucinda had accepted his invitation to take the excursion boat over to Ross Island the next day for a picnic, with lemonade, beneath the trees. Yes, of course, she assured him though her eyes shone bright with curiosity, she did indeed own a gingham dress she could wear. The mingled confusion and pleasure on her face when he handed her into the carriage caused him to laugh aloud.

He'd also enjoyed Fong's look of surprise when Sage requested his assistance in constructing a rooftop flower garden. The surprise in Fong's face had been fleeting, however, replaced by a wide smile of understanding. "Ah yes, Mister Sage, flowers are most good for the soul, most good."

Inside, Knute was shoving tables and chairs back into place. Sage's mother and Ida were at the kitchen sink, busy washing up beneath the building's only electric light globes. Catching sight of him, his mother nodded toward the open back door.

Outside, Matthew sat on the steps. Sage settled down beside him. Tears glinted on the young man's face. Matthew reached up to wipe them away with the back of his hand before he looked at Sage.

Sage spoke softly. "You know, Matthew, you're welcome to stay here with your aunt and uncle. I think I can find some work for you, and maybe you'd like to return to school."

"Thank you, Mr. Adair. That's a kind offer. I guess I'm just not sure what I want to do. Nothing turned out the way it was supposed to. I've been thinking that maybe I should just go back home. I wish me and Billy would have stayed there, then none of this would have happened."

"I understand, Matthew. Take your time deciding. Just remember that you'd be welcome here. Whatever you decide, you'll always be welcome here."

Matthew was silent, his head hanging down, his clenched hands turning his knuckles bone white, as if each were stopping the other from breaking something. Then his words came in an angry rush. "I understand about Steele, and that prostitute girl, and Gilcrease, but why Billy? He never harmed anyone. He was nothing but a real good person. Why Billy?"

Matthew's voice rose with the question, catching in a sob that he swallowed before continuing. "How am I supposed to go on wanting to live, knowing that the world is like that? Knowing that someone good like Billy is killed for no reason, for no damn reason at all? How does a person go on, Mr. Adair? How do you go on?" Pain made his voice ragged.

Sage cleared his throat to speak, his voice low. "Things do happen for reasons, Matthew. There were reasons why Billy died. One thing led to another, until Clancy Steele did what he did. It wasn't just Steele that killed Billy, it was other things, things that happened to Steele, things that made him mean and hateful. That's not an excuse. I'm just saying that bad things happening in one person's life affects other people, sometimes for a long time into the future."

Matthew wasn't comforted. "I don't know how I can go on in a world like that, where there's so much ugliness. A person can't know what's going to happen next or why. How can a person live like that?"

Sage parsed out the answer for himself even as he spoke the words, "I can't say what decides a person to go on. Some folks just quit. Most of us decide to go on for one reason or another. Every person has to find his own way to answer that question." For a long, silent moment Sage gazed into the dark patch of sky above the buildings where stars glittered like ice crystals.

When Sage spoke again, his voice was nearly inaudible, "As for me, Matthew, well, I . . . I guess my reason is that it's just in me to keep on climbing toward the light."

THE END

Historical Notes

Timber Beasts is a work of fiction that relies on certain historical facts, some of which are the following:

1. Railroad bulls killed hobos with the bouncing rod. William O. Douglas, decades before he became a U.S. Supreme Court justice, saved one hobo's life by advising him to lay upon a stout wooden plank for protection against the rod.

2. Chinese men immigrated to the United States to work on the construction of the transcontinental railroads. Once the railroads reached from sea to sea, these men were forced into urban areas where they usually worked in a servant status. In Portland, they were restricted to living within an area covering the few city blocks that comprised Chinatown. Very few of them were allowed to bring their wives to the States.

3. Southern Afro-Americans were recruited to work in the new Portland Hotel. Besides working in the hotel, many of them ran other businesses on the side, eventually becoming leading members of Portland's Afro-American middle class community. The New Golden West was one hotel that served black railroad porters and its original building exists to this day.

4. Despite an outward appearance of staid propriety, Portland had over 400 houses of ill repute operating during the early 1900s. Many of these establishments were

owned by the "respectable" men of the city. Some historians also report that male children were removed from a Christian helping agency to work in brothels.

5. The conditions in the logging camps were worse than those described. When an influenza epidemic hit the Pacific Northwest in the early 1900s, thousands of loggers died, their bodies having been weakened by the arduous work and unhealthy living conditions.

6. The longshoremen working West Coast docks came from different ethnic backgrounds. Many of them, however, were large in stature given the brutal stevedoring workload which is accurately depicted in this novel as it is taken directly from a union report.

7. Flying Squadrons of itinerant worker-defenders did exist although they came into existence a few years after the setting of this book. These loosely organized groups of men traveled the rails protecting hobos and teaching railroad bulls and other predators a lesson – usually by throwing them off slow moving trains.

8. The Forest Reserve Act, enacted in 1898, was exploited by timber barons in the manner detailed. The land fraud at the heart of this tale did occur. It was prosecuted by the U.S. District Attorney from San Francisco because Portland's federal District Attorney was, in fact, implicated in the scheme. One of those convicted was a U.S. Senator.

9. There was a labor leader known as "The Saint." This was the name hobos, and those fighting for economic justice, gave to Vincent St. John. He subsequently helped found the Industrial Workers of the World (IWW or "Wobblies") in 1905. Working people across the country loved St. John for his courage and his kindness. Alas, there is no evidence that he used agents like Sage Adair to advance the interests of the working class.

About the Author

S. L. Stoner is a native of the Pacific Northwest who has worked as a citizen change agent and as a labor union and civil rights attorney for many years.

Acknowledgments

Like every other human being on the planet I am mostly the sum of all those I have known, loved or hated. This work and the others to follow are also influenced by the same. My family and friends are what makes life worthwhile. Their support is first and, foremost, my greatest treasure. I am also grateful to union leader Ron Heintzman for giving me the opportunity to serve union men and women who daily demonstrate the courage, intelligence and perseverance of America's workers. Despite its problems, I believe that the U.S. labor movement, and other populist groups, offer the best chance we have to achieve economic morality and balance in our nation.

For the Sage Adair series in particular, I want to thank Dr. Charles Tracy, who set my feet on the engrossing path of historical research. For their encouragement and advice that seemed to come at precisely the right moments, I want to thank professional writers Rosellen Brown, who also started me down the writing path, Meg Jensen, Merridawn Duckler and Ursula Le Guin.

Lastly, and most immediately, I acknowledge the assistance and intelligent contributions made by this novel's initial readers: Denise L. Collins, George Slanina, Sally Stoner, Rich Layton, Bob Fuller, Hekate, Sally Frese, Helen Nickum, Mary Joan O'Connell, and Sarah Smith each of whom lent invaluable skills, insights and support to this endeavor. All mistakes, however, are solely my own.

Sage Adair Mysteries coming soon ..

Land Sharks

Two union organizers have disappeared and so Sage Adair begins
a desperate search that takes him into the stygian blackness of
Portland's underground to confront mercenary shanghaiers, the
pain of a lost friendship and his own fears.

Dry Rot

A losing labor strike, a dead construction boss, a union leader
framed for murder, a ragpicker poet, and collapsing city bridges,
all compete for Sage Adair's attention as he sloughs through the
Pacific Northwest's rain and mud to find answers before someone
else dies.

Two New Pacific Northwest Mysteries Based
on Historical Facts

Request for Pre-Publication Notice

If you would like to receive notice of the publication dates of the second and third Sage Adair historical mystery novels, *Land Sharks* and *Dry Rot*, please complete and return the form below or contact Yamhill Press at www.yamhillpress.com.

Your Name: _____

Street Address: _____

City: _____ State: _____ Zip: _____

E-mail Address: _____

Website: www.yamhillpress.com

Postal: Yamhill Press, P.O. Box 42348, Portland, OR 97242